Joseph Conrad

ALMAYER'S FOLLY

A STORY OF AN EASTERN RIVER

Edited by
OWEN KNOWLES
University of Hull
Consultant Editor for this Volume
CEDRIC WATTS
University of Sussex

EVERYMAN
J. M. DENT • LONDON
CHARLES E. TUTTLE
VERMONT

Almayer's Folly first published with *Tales of Unrest*
in Everyman in 1973
This edition first published in Everyman in 1995

J. M. Dent
Orion Publishing Group
Orion House
5 Upper St Martin's Lane
London WC2H 9EA
and
Charles E. Tuttle Co. Inc.
28 South Main Street
Rutland, Vermont 05701, USA

Typeset by CentraCet Limited, Cambridge
Printed in Great Britain by
The Guernsey Press Co. Ltd, Guernsey, C. I.

British Library Cataloguing-in-Publication Data is
available upon request

ISBN 0 460 87634 1

CONTENTS

NOTE ON THE AUTHOR AND EDITOR

JOSEPH CONRAD (originally Józef Teodor Konrad Nałęcz Korzeniowski) was born in 1857 in a part of Poland long annexed by Russia. His parents, ardent Polish patriots, were exiled to Russia for their underground political activities and both died when Conrad was still a child. In 1874 he left Poland for France and began a sea career that, spanning the next twenty years, took him to then remote parts of the world. In 1878, he joined the British Merchant Navy and slowly came to regard Britain as his second 'home'. He obtained British naturalisation in 1886; began in 1889 to write his first novel, *Almayer's Folly*, in English, his third language; and settled permanently in England in the mid-1890s, when he also married Jessie George.

With the publication of *Almayer's Folly* in 1895, Conrad began a punishingly arduous career as a full-time writer. During the next fifteen years he produced such 'Modernist' classics as *Heart of Darkness* (1899), *Lord Jim* (1900), *Nostromo* (1904), *The Secret Agent* (1907) and *Under Western Eyes* (1911). In these works a restless experimentation with narrative structure and symbolic method accompanies a searchingly pessimistic view of man's personal and social destiny. Though Conrad's major novels received immediate critical acclaim, their sales were disappointing until the commercial success of *Chance* (1913) brought him financial security and a wide public. In 1923 he enjoyed an enormously successful promotional visit to the United States and was offered (but declined) a knighthood shortly before his death in 1924. Conrad's works have had a powerful influence on later writers, artists and film-makers such as T. S. Eliot, F. Scott Fitzgerald, Graham Greene, Orson Welles and V. S. Naipaul. He also enjoys an international reputation as 'our contemporary', a writer who continues to challenge present-day readers and whose works figure centrally (and often controversially) in the cultural debate about language, gender and race.

OWEN KNOWLES is Senior Lecturer in English at the University of Hull. The author of *A Conrad Chronology* (1989) and *An Annotated Critical Bibliography of Joseph Conrad* (1992), he is a Vice-Chairman of the Joseph Conrad Society (UK) and a former editor of its journal, *The Conradian*.

CHRONOLOGY OF CONRAD'S LIFE

Year	*Age*	*Life*
1857		Józef Teodor Konrad Nałęcz Korzeniowski (Joseph Conrad) born in the Ukraine on 3 December
1861	3	Conrad's father, Apollo Korzeniowski, arrested in Warsaw for patriotic conspiracy
1862	4	Conrad's parents exiled to Vologda, Russia; he goes with them
1863	5	Family moves to Chernikhov
1865	7	Death of Conrad's mother, Ewelina Korzeniowska
1869	11	Death of his father. Tadeusz Bobrowski becomes his guardian
1870	12	Taught by Adam Pulman in Kraków
1871	13	Also taught by Izydor Kopernicki
1872	14	Resolves to go to sea
1873	15	Tour of Switzerland with Adam Pulman
1874	16	Leaves Poland for Marseille
1875	17	Sails Atlantic in *Mont-Blanc*
1876	18	Serves as steward in *Saint-Antoine*
1878	20	Shoots himself, recovers, and joins British ship *Mavis*
1879	21	Serves in clipper *Duke of Sutherland*
1880	22	Sails to Australia in *Loch Etive*
1881	23	Second mate of *Palestine*

CHRONOLOGY OF HIS TIMES

Year	*Literary Context*	*Historical Events*
1857	Flaubert, *Madame Bovary* Baudelaire, *Les Fleurs du mal*	Indian Mutiny begins
1859	Dickens, *A Tale of Two Cities*	Darwin, *Origin of Species*
1861	Dickens, *Great Expectations* George Eliot, *Silas Marner*	American Civil War begins Nansen born
1862	Turgenev, *Fathers and Sons* Hugo, *Les Misérables*	Bismarck gains power in Prussia
1863	Thackeray dies	American slaves freed Polish uprising
1865	Kipling and Yeats born	American Civil War ends
1869	Tolstoy, *War and Peace* Gide born	Gandhi born Suez Canal opens
1870	Dickens dies	Franco-Prussian War
1871	Dostoyevsky, *The Devils*	Paris Commune
1872	George Eliot, *Middlemarch* Butler, *Erewhon*	Mazzini dies Bertrand Russell born
1873	Ford Madox Hueffer born	Livingstone dies
1874	Hardy, *Far From the Madding Crowd*	Churchill born
1875	Mann born	Schweitzer born
1876	George Sand dies James, *Roderick Hudson*	Queen Victoria declared Empress of India
1878	Hardy, *The Return of the Native*	Second Afghan War Congress of Berlin
1879	Ibsen, *A Doll's House* Meredith, *The Egoist*	Zulu War Einstein and Stalin born
1880	Dostoyevsky, *The Brothers Karamazov*	Boer uprising in Transvaal
1881	Dostoyevsky and Carlyle die	Tsar Alexander II assassinated

Year	*Age*	*Life*
1882	24	Storm-damaged *Palestine* repaired
1883	25	Shipwrecked when *Palestine* sinks
1885	26	Sails to Calcutta in *Tilkhurst*
1886	28	Becomes a British subject; qualifies as captain
1887	29	Sails to Java in *Highland Forest*
1888	30	Master of the *Otago*, his sole command
1889	31	Resigns from *Otago*; begins to write *Almayer's Folly*
1890	32	Works in Congo Free State
1891	33	Mate of *Torrens* (until 1893)
1892	34	Voyages to Australia
1893	35–6	Visits Bobrowski in Ukraine. Joins steamship *Adowa*
1894	36	*Almayer's Folly* accepted by Unwin. Meets Edward Garnett and Jessie George
1895	37	*Almayer's Folly* published. Completes *An Outcast of the Islands*
1896	38	*An Outcast of the Islands* published. Marries Jessie George
1897	39	Befriended by Cunninghame Graham. *The Nigger of the 'Narcissus'*
1898	40	First son (Borys) born. *Tales of Unrest*. Collaborates with Ford Madox Hueffer (later surnamed Ford). Friendship with Stephen Crane
1899	41	'The Heart of Darkness' serialised. Serialisation of *Lord Jim* begins
1900	42	*Lord Jim* (book). J. B. Pinker becomes Conrad's agent
1901	43	*The Inheritors* (co-author Hueffer)
1902	44	*Youth* volume (including 'Heart of Darkness')
1903	45	*Typhoon* volume. *Romance* (co-author Hueffer)
1904	46	*Nostromo*
1905	47	*One Day More* (play) fails

Year	*Literary Context*	*Historical Events*
1882	Virginia Woolf and Joyce born	Darwin and Garibaldi die
1883	Nietzsche, *Thus Spake Zarathustra*	Marx dies Mussolini born
1885	D. H. Lawrence born	'Congo Free State' recognised
1886	Stevenson, *Dr Jekyll and Mr Hyde*	Salisbury becomes premier Graham becomes MP
1887	Marianne Moore born	'Bloody Sunday' riot in London
1888	T. S. Eliot born	Wilhelm II becomes Kaiser
1889	Browning dies	Hitler born
1890	Ibsen, *Hedda Gabler*	Bismarck resigns
1891	Hardy, *Tess of the d'Urbervilles*	Parnell dies
1892	Tennyson dies	Gladstone's fourth ministry
1893	Maupassant dies	Independent Labour Party formed
1894	Stevenson dies Huxley born	Nicholas II becomes Tsar Greenwich explosion
1895	Crane, *The Red Badge of Courage*	Marconi invents 'wireless' telegraphy
1896	Morris and Verlaine die Chekhov, *The Seagull*	Nobel Prizes established
1897	Kipling, *Captains Courageous* James, *What Maisie Knew*	Queen Victoria's Diamond Jubilee
1898	Wilde, 'The Ballad of Reading Gaol' Wells, *The War of the Worlds*	War between Spain and USA Bismarck and Gladstone die Fashoda incident
1899	Hemingway born	Dreyfus freed Boer War begins
1900	Ruskin, Wilde and Crane die	Russia occupies Manchuria
1901	Kipling, *Kim*	Queen Victoria dies
1902	Zola dies	Boer War ends
1903	James, *The Ambassadors*	First powered aircraft flight
1904	Chekhov, *The Cherry Orchard*	Russo-Japanese War begins
1905	Wells, *Kipps*	Russia defeated by Japan

Year	*Age*	*Life*
1906	48	Second son (John) born. *The Mirror of the Sea* (aided by Hueffer)
1907	49	*The Secret Agent*
1908	50	*A Set of Six* (tales). Heavily indebted to Pinker. Involved in *English Review*
1909	51	Quarrels with Hueffer
1910	52	Nervous breakdown on completion of *Under Western Eyes*. Awarded a Civil List pension of £100 per year
1911	53	*Under Western Eyes* published
1912	54	*Some Reminiscences* (later known by the title of the USA edition, *A Personal Record*). *'Twixt Land and Sea* (tales). *Chance* serialised in *New York Herald*
1913	55	Meets Bertrand Russell
1914	56	Book of *Chance* has large sales. Conrad prospers
1915	57	*Within the Tides* (tales). *Victory*. Borys Conrad enlists in Army
1916	58	Conrad flies in a naval aircraft and goes to sea in H.M.S. *Ready*
1917	59	*The Shadow-Line*. Conrad in poor health. Relinquishes Civil List pension
1918	60	Borys Conrad wounded in war. *Typhon* (Gide's translation of *Typhoon*)
1919	61	*The Arrow of Gold*. Macdonald Hastings' version of *Victory* staged. Film of *Victory*
1920	62	*The Rescue* (published 24 years after commencement). Conrad and Pinker adapt 'Gaspar Ruiz'
1920–8		Collected editions by Doubleday (N.Y.), Heinemann (London), Gresham (London) and Grant (Edinburgh)
1921	63	*Notes on Life and Letters*
1922	64	Death of Pinker. Conrad meets Ravel. Borys marries. *The Secret Agent* (play) fails

Year	Literary Context	Historical Events
1906	Beckett born Ibsen dies	Liberals win British election
1907	Auden born	Lord Kelvin dies
1908	Bennett, *The Old Wives' Tale* Forster, *A Room with a View*	Feminist agitation; Mrs Pankhurst jailed
1909	Swinburne dies	Blériot flies across Channel
1910	Forster, *Howards End* Yeats, *The Green Helmet*	King Edward VII dies; accession of George V
1911	Golding born	Industrial unrest in UK
1912	Patrick White born Pound, *Ripostes*	First Balkan War Sinking of *Titanic* Wilson elected President
1913	Lawrence, *Sons and Lovers*	Second Balkan War
1914	Joyce, *Dubliners*	World War I begins
1915	Lawrence's *The Rainbow* banned	Italy enters war Gallipoli disaster
1916	James dies Joyce, *A Portrait*	Battle of Jutland Battle of the Somme
1917	T. S. Eliot, *Prufrock* Anthony Burgess born	USA enters war Russian Revolution
1918	Rosenberg and Owen die Wyndham Lewis, *Tarr*	Armistice Polish Republic restored Women enfranchised in UK
1919	Virginia Woolf, *Night and Day* Hardy, *Poetical Works*	UK's first woman MP Versailles Treaty
1920	Lawrence, *Women in Love* Katherine Mansfield, *Bliss*	Poles rout Russian invaders League of Nations created
1921	Huxley, *Crome Yellow*	Irish Free State founded
1922	T. S. Eliot, *The Waste Land* Joyce, *Ulysses*	Mussolini gains power in Italy

Year	*Age*	*Life*
1923	65	Declines honorary degree from Cambridge. Acclaimed on visit to USA. *The Rover*
1923–7		Collected ('Uniform') edition by Dent (London)
1924	66	Declines knighthood. Dies of heart attack; buried at Canterbury
1925		*Tales of Hearsay* and the incomplete *Suspense*
1926		*Last Essays*
1927		*Joseph Conrad: Life & Letters*, written and edited by G. Jean-Aubry

Year	*Literary Context*	*Historical Events*
1923	Yeats wins Nobel Prize Wells, *Men Like Gods*	Moscow becomes capital of USSR
1924	Forster, *A Passage to India* Shaw, *St Joan* Anatole France dies	Lenin dies MacDonald heads first Labour Government in UK
1925	T. S. Eliot, *Poems 1909–25*	Hitler publishes *Mein Kampf*
1926	Kafka, *The Castle*	General Strike in UK
1927	Virginia Woolf, *To the Lighthouse*	Lindbergh flies Atlantic

INTRODUCTION

Almayer's Folly, published in 1895 under the author's pen-name of Joseph Conrad, marks the beginning of a wonderfully rich and productive career that spanned almost three decades. The thirty-one-year-old individual who in September 1889 began to compose what would be his first novel was in his fifteenth year as a seaman, and still retained his Polish name – Józef Teodor Konrad Nałęcz Korzeniowski – and was writing a story in his third language. Looking back on that period in his autobiographical *A Personal Record* (1912), Conrad asserted that the coming into existence of his first book was an 'inexplicable event'. It was begun, he explains, during an extended period of shore-leave in his Pimlico lodgings as a light holiday task with no thought of a published book. The impulse to write may have been obscure, but the story's subsequent evolution, as described in the same memoir, soon draws upon the language of compulsion and 'haunting': the beginning writer enjoyed 'the idleness of a haunted man', was spell-bound by the 'hallucination of the Eastern Archipelago' and felt 'as if already the story-teller were being born into the body of a seaman' (Ch. 1). Korzeniowski remained a seaman for another five years, intermittently at work on the manuscript of *Almayer's Folly*, until 1894 when, with his novel accepted for publication by T. Fisher Unwin, he began the full-time transition from ship's deck to writing-desk.

Korzeniowski had suffered a bleak childhood in a province of Poland that had long been under autocratic Russian rule, was orphaned at the age of twelve and, five years later, left his homeland to become a seaman in France. In several ways he developed into a man characteristically at home with shifting borderlines and dual allegiances. By temperament, he seems to have combined elements of the Don Quixote as well as the Sancho Panza, and, unusually, his careers straddled a life of action and the sedentary life of the desk-bound writer. Though

Conrad as a seaman found sustaining social ideals in the British Merchant service, he would later define himself as *homo duplex* by virtue of his 'standing jumps' between cultures.[1] As a writer, he also delighted in the marginal position open to him by virtue of his émigré status – a position that set him apart from native British literary traditions, but allowed him access to a richer and wider European inheritance. By writing *Almayer's Folly* in the English language, Conrad was undoubtedly engaged in negotiating with the complex weave of a tri-cultural and tri-linguistic inheritance – Polish, French and English. By 1889, moreover, Conrad the seaman had acquired a prodigiously wide experience of then-remote parts of the world, and at a time when he could observe the shifting contact-points between European and non-European within the wider context of European colonialist expansion abroad. No wonder that Henry James would later write to Conrad admiring 'the prodigy of your past experiences': 'No one has *known* – for intellectual use – the things that you know.'[2] One other set of contact-points seems especially significant. A great reader from an early age, the young Conrad had spent his childhood in close proximity to the literary life. His father Apollo, a revolutionary patriot, was a writer and translator of some note, who was chiefly responsible for his young son's exposure to literatures, languages and the practice of writing. These early contacts must surely have had a distinct bearing upon that 'inexplicable' literary event of 1889.

Almayer's Folly, as with most of Conrad's fiction, rests upon an act of retrospective memory, in this case his memories of four trips he had made to eastern Borneo in 1887, when he had come into contact with Charles Olmeijer, a Dutch Eurasian living and working on the remote Berau river, the basis of the fictional 'Sambir'. In *A Personal Record* Conrad typically stresses the 'actual' meeting with Olmeijer as the inspiring force behind his first work, but it seems equally clear that the novel draws indirectly upon the history of his own youthful experience. In particular, Nina's dilemma as an individual with roots in two cultures but who belongs to neither provides a resonant echo of Conrad's own quest to forge an Anglo-Polish identity out of conflicting national claims. The possibility of any strong umbilical link between Almayer and his creator seems less likely, though even Almayer may function as a mockingly distorted mirror-image, reflecting both upon the quixotic strains of the youthful Korzeniowski and the obsessive 'hallucination' to which the beginning writer was devoting himself.

Ian Watt's admirable survey in *Conrad in the Nineteenth Century* of the formative influences upon *Almayer's Folly* tends to enforce the picture of a writer richly poised on the borderlines between varying national literary traditions as well as genres.[3] Two major French novelists, Gustave Flaubert and Guy de Maupassant, figure centrally in Watt's account of early influences, leading him to speak of Almayer as 'a Borneo Bovary' and of Conrad as subject to the powerful technical influence of Maupassant. But along with these, other important models and inheritances can be detected in Conrad's re-working of the conventions of French exotic literature (as found in the fiction of Pierre Loti) and the tradition of Stevensonian romance. In addition, Watt's analogies between Conrad and Thomas Hardy suggest a literary kinship that has not yet been sufficiently explored. More mundanely, *Almayer's Folly* resonates with the kind of detail that Conrad was in the habit of picking up from bed-side books – travel journals, popular magazine stories and semi-scientific accounts of natural life and customs in the Malay Archipelago. With his astonishingly retentive memory, he was already in 1889 becoming a writer upon whom no experience was lost.

On its publication in 1895 the first reviewers of *Almayer's Folly* categorised it as a 'romance' or novel of 'local colour' by virtue of its remote Eastern location, exotic atmosphere, and love-interest. Bornean settings had already provided material for the late-Victorian romance industry, exploited by writers to satisfy the tastes of growing metropolitan audiences for fresh sensation, heightened incident and pleasing escapism.[4] As advertised by its publisher, Conrad's first novel was clearly intended to excite these popular expectations, with a story 'as picturesque as the world offers' and 'vivid incidents attaching to the life of pirates and smugglers'.[5] But many reviewers also rightly realised that this was a 'romance' with marked differences from its kind: it had no happy ending, was not over-coloured, exhibited a first-hand knowledge of things Malay and had 'no place in the prevalent fiction of the hour'.[6] However impressionistic in manner, these early reviewers offer a basis upon which to build a more systematic account of the novel's teasingly oblique relation to the semi-popular fictional traditions of its time. In its partial emulation of the conventions of exotic and adventure fiction, *Almayer's Folly* can be seen to stand at the end of a tradition of writing, whose passing it sometimes elegiacally and sometimes mockingly salutes. But it is also more excitingly disobedient in using the jaded popular conventions of the time as a means of producing what Jefferson Hunter calls 'a fiction of reversals': 'That fiction would be about the failure of action to relieve mental anguish, the devastating isolation of the hero, the corruption of heroism for political purposes, and the puniness of human action when set against the mindless immensity of nature.'[7] And finally, in modifying and complicating the materials of exotic romance, *Almayer's Folly* marks a significant stage in the passage towards a more grown-up type of colonial novel as well as a modernist novel of predicament. Published in the same year as Hardy's last major work, *Jude the Obscure*, Conrad's first novel seems an equally significant landmark.

I

In one of the most representative debates of the 1880s, Robert Louis Stevenson, in 'A Gossip on Romance' (1882) and 'A Humble Remonstrance' (1884), had argued against Henry James's view that the seriousness of the novel as a form was intimately associated with its capacity to produce an intense illusion of reality. Stevenson offers a direct counter-argument, aligning romance fiction with the power to allow readers a way of escape and transcendence beyond the real and, through heightened action, to restore them to the colour and vitality of youthful primary emotions. The essence of such romance lies in the typical nature of its situations, its stress upon 'action' rather than 'character' and upon incidents enabling the reader to play at being the hero and through that hero to transform anxiety into meaningful action: 'we forget the characters, then we push the hero aside; then we plunge into the tale in our own person and bathe in fresh experience, and then, and only then, do we say we have been reading a romance.'[8] Another central function of romance is, in Stevenson's view, its power to foster dreams and the habit of wish-fulfilment, so allowing the writer and reader to *forget* the pressing realities of late-Victorian life: 'When I suffer in mind, stories are my refuge; I take them like opium ..... what we want now is a drug.'[9] Popular late-Victorian adventure literature had much in common with exotic romance which, as an identifiable form, flourished simultaneously in France. Through its evocations of the picturesque Orient or mysterious East, French exotic literature shared many of the ultimate aims of Stevenson's heirs: to restore to metropolitan readers a colour, innocence and simplicity that had been lost through drab social uniformity, to allow a transcendence beyond the real by recourse to the sensations evoked by the exotic, and to allay anxieties by offering a 'new idealism'. As Michael G. Lerner points out, French exotic literature came to provide a haven for numerous different kinds of writer – from the social rebel to the aesthetic voyeur – with the result that the 'means of expressing the exotic became more and more refined after 1870 as the rift between writer and society became wider, culminating in the nervous impressionism of the Goncourts, the decadent dandyism of Huysmans' *A Rebours*, and the hermeticism of the Symbolists'.[10]

Almayer's Folly most conforms to the formulas of exotic romance in its inclusion of the love relationship between Nina and the Balinese prince Dain. They represent the world of youthful passion and vitality, love-at-first-sight and commitment to an ideal that finally yields an escape to dream-like independence in Bali. In their presentation Conrad combines the 'poetry of circumstance' with the near-idyllic reverie characteristic of the exotic genre. Ian Watt has argued, however, that there is a total contradiction in *Almayer's Folly* between two kinds of fictional allegiance: 'The worlds of adventure and romance in general ask us for an uncritical acceptance of fantasy; but in *Almayer's Folly*, the fantasies which are mocked in Almayer are used uncritically in the case of Nina; Conrad's presentation of his heroine asks us to luxuriate in that very immunity from reality which is the defining essence of her father's folly.'[11] Watt here misreads what, I think, is the first appearance of a structural feature that will become central in some of Conrad's later novels: that of counterpointing two very different value-based worlds which implicitly enter into sustained debate with each other. The epigraph chosen from Amiel for *Almayer's Folly*

('Which of us has not his promised land, his day of ecstasy and his death in exile?') surely points to a twin apprehension of life: on the one hand the paradise available to a youthfully hopeful sense of the world, and on the other the consciousness of sombre exile and lost paradise inevitably present in late adulthood. Throughout the novel, this double focus seems more deliberately devised than Watt allows, with the logic of the youthful day-dream uncomfortably framed and complicated by a pattern of inevitable decline and fall. Even at its end, the twin stories are juxtaposed with an ambiguity reminiscent of Keats's 'The Eve of St Agnes', where two youthful lovers escape to a fairy-tale realm, leaving the world to the aged and wrinkled. There is surely in this no simple 'uncritical acceptance of fantasy'.

Nevertheless, Watt seems right to stress the element of anti-romantic mockery that pervades the presentation of Almayer and his world and makes the novel predominantly a fiction of reversals. The traditional equation of romance with youth and the fulfilment of youthful dream is, in *Almayer's Folly*, severely complicated by Conrad's inclusion of what the traditional form can rarely accommodate – a foolish, middle-aged dreamer who is about to experience the utter ruination of a lifetime's wishful hopes. Indeed, in Almayer's dream at the very beginning of the narrative one of the main motivating urges of the exotic novel – the flight from metropolitan Europe to the liberating freshness of the mysterious East – is immediately reversed. His is an exhausted yearning for the opposite, a release from the prison-like Bornean jungle to Amsterdam. Moreover, the spectacle of the middle-aged Almayer's absorption in his 'dream' raises questions rarely asked in late-Victorian romances: notably, questions about the neurotic origins of the fantasy-habit and the persistent use of 'dreams' as a compensatory drug-like fiction by which to obliterate the unwelcome present. Deeply rooted in the country-born colonial's feelings of being an outcast from Europe, Almayer's yearning presents itself in the form of a sublimating wish-fulfilment that combines conventional *petit bourgeois* fantasies and hackneyed rags-to-riches myths. The status of Almayer's 'dream' is further questioned by the way in which, in middle age itself, it becomes a needed soporific fiction to stave off the facts of disappointment and, later, a retrogressive obsession that, fed by a lifetime's failure, culminates in a type of madness. In pursuing the progress of an atrophying fantasy to an extreme point of breakdown, Conrad may be seen to reflect upon the progressive enfeeblement of the wider Romantic dream in the later nineteenth century:

> 'What? What?' he [Almayer] murmured sleepily, without moving or opening his eyes. His head still felt heavy, and he had not the courage to raise his eyelids. In his ears there still lingered the sound of entreating whisper. – 'Am I awake? – Why do I hear the voices?' he argued to himself, hazily. – 'I cannot get rid of the horrible nightmare yet. – I have been very drunk. – What is that shaking me? I am dreaming yet. – I must open my eyes and be done with it. I am only half awake, it is evident.' (Ch. 10)

Certain allusions here suggest a backward parodic connection with Keats's 'Ode to a Nightingale' ('Fled is that music: – Do I wake or sleep?'), while at the same time evoking the more hallucinatory moods of Decadent literature of the 1890s. But its predominant note is a forward-looking one, vividly anticipating the neurotic apathy of the middle-aged dreamer in T. S. Eliot's 'The Love Song of J. Alfred Prufrock'.

The novel's handling of the mainspring of the Stevensonian kind of romance – physical action conceived as movement into an open future and the necessary field for heroic endeavour – is similarly deflationary. While its plot includes potentially 'exciting' romance material, in the form of Lingard's battle with Sulu pirates or Dain's escape from the Dutch authorities, virtually all of these actions have an off-stage presence. They are mainly important for their delayed effect upon the major characters, who must live with the disastrous aftermath of unthinking and misplaced impulsiveness. This, together with the fact that many of the novel's events are engineered to deceive, renders the status and meaning of action suspect. In Almayer's story, moreover, adventure- or quest-movement is replaced by a frustratingly static and motionless condition of waiting for a future endlessly deferred. The very manner in which his story is told – beginning *in medias res* with the middle-aged fantasist, then backtracking retrospectively for four chapters, before returning to the 'present' to focus upon Almayer's crucial collapse – has the effect of dismantling some of the most cherished principles of adventure fiction. While Almayer harbours the traditional dreamer's conviction that his ego is at the centre of the universe, the narrative in which he figures speaks otherwise. It decelerates and reverses the linear, headlong movement of the novel of action, throwing emphasis on Almayer as a passive victim of an atrophying dream and his life as an inevitable cycle of abject failure. Teasingly, Conrad also thereby frustrates the traditional rhetorical end of romance – the release of the reader's anxiety through meaningful action. As in T. S. Eliot's 'Prufrock' poem, the reader is lured by the promise of action (the equivalent of Prufrock's 'Let us go then .....') only to be embroiled in all the anxieties that obstruct purposeful action.

Stevenson had, moreover, insisted that romance should remove the reader from 'the world of mud and of old iron, cheap desires and cheap fears'.[12] However, as a fiction of reversals and adjustments, *Almayer's Folly* has as its larger setting a recognisably contemporary spectacle, an emergent colonial world that turns upon the conjunction of adventure, mercantilism and 'cheap desires':

> At that time Macassar was teming with life and commerce. It was the point in the islands where tended all those bold spirits who, fitting out schooners on the Australian coast, invaded the Malay Archipelago in search of money and adventure. Bold, reckless, keen in business ..... making money fast, they used to have a general 'rendezvous' in the bay for purposes of trade and dissipation. (Ch. 1)

The term 'adventure' keeps strange company in this description, linked as it is with the bold and reckless 'invasion' of trading interests following upon European settlement. In making Lingard the presiding 'king' at the centre of the Archipelago's mercantile life, Conrad moves well beyond the myth of 'pure' adventure that had sustained a whole tradition of popular heroic fiction. Rather, his emphasis falls upon the way in which the impulsive Englishman, as the representative product of a phase of exploitative colonialism, unthinkingly participates in the prevailing scramble for trade monopoly. In the process, the hero of adventure fiction conceived as a model of right conduct is, through Lingard, transformed into a new type of 'hero' whose exploits derive from a dangerously ambiguous marriage of adventurous impulse, mercantilism and empire-building.

'Ragged, dishevelled, enthusiastic' (Ch. 2), Lingard is only distinguishable from the average colonial buccaneer by the fame he acquires in discovering a river. Otherwise, he is a here-today-and-gone-tomorrow visitor, who impulsively risks other lives as well as his own, and whose reckless adventurism seems a manifestation of 'cheap desires' generally at work in the Malay Archipelago. As Lingard's inheritor and adoptive 'son', Almayer lives by an even more cheaply representative fantasy which leads him to risk an enforced marriage and a life in Sambir in the hope that it will yield him his ultimate conquest. A country-born colonial who feels himself an outcast from Europe, Almayer is partly driven by the *petit bourgeois* class ideals of his expatriate Dutch parents. But his fantasy of enormous wealth is chiefly fired by the myth of the colony-as-Eldorado fostered by Lingard and Macassar trading houses. *Almayer's Folly* could never be regarded as an adventure novel, but it is a novel *about* adventure that brings a severely sceptical eye to the motives, origins and ends of commercial adventurism in what would now be called a developing third-world country. By its probing of the conjunction between adventure, trade and the larger 'invasion' of the East, *Almayer's Folly* clearly refuses to indulge the games of make-believe played by the heirs of Stevenson.

Late-Victorian romances, it has been observed, invariably prefer an empty or imaginatively evacuated landscape that can be modelled into the contour of the youthful dream, and where disturbing thoughts of mortality remain hidden. None of these conditions prevails in the world available to Almayer. In the first place, Conrad creates in fictional Sambir a tightly woven web of obstructive intrigue and deception that enmeshes the passive hero and renders him increasingly helpless. Landscape too is similarly alien to the yearning imagination, embodying a Darwinian conception of the tenacious struggle for existence and the inevitable extinction of less competitive forms. Against this background, the features of the man-made world surrounding Almayer – the ruined offices of the Lingard trading company, piles of empty bottles, squalid domestic neglect – suggest the inevitable exhaustion attending the battle to survive and the extinction awaiting the ill-adapted. In characterising the world as a prison in which Almayer must endure a life-sentence, Conrad transforms the motif of the temporary 'castaway' common in adventure fiction into an image of Almayer as a permanent metaphysical castaway, for whom the only escape lies in the release into oblivion and death. The death-haunted quality of the later parts of *Almayer's Folly* inevitably has the effect of transforming the features of exotic romance itself into an unreal and possibly extinct form, whose overall quality in *Almayer's Folly* may be summarised by a landscape description in *Romance* (1903), a novel written by Conrad in collaboration with Ford Madox Ford:

> The general effect of the place was of vitality exhausted, of a body calcined, of romance turned into stone. The still air, the hot sunshine, the white beach curving around the deserted sheet of water, the sombre green of the hills, had the motionlessness of things petrified, the vividness of things painted, the sadness of things abandoned, desecrated. (Ch. 2)

Conrad's scepticism may also be felt to extend beyond the types and myths of exotic romance to embrace its traditional ends as daydream and intoxicant. As noted previously, Stevenson suggests that one of its functions is to allow us to forget: it acts like an opium-drug in banishing disagreeables and offers a reading process at once 'absorbing and voluptuous', in which 'we should gloat over a book, be rapt clean out of ourselves'.[13] In confronting in Almayer the inveterate dreamer whose entire life is a history of greedily feeding off fictions in an effort to stave off the reality of his position and who finally seeks 'forgetfulness' through, first of all, gin and then opium, Conrad seems indirectly to follow to their extreme some of the motives that prompted readers of the 1890s to 'forget' their world and devour romantic fictions. Almayer's dream enables him to indulge vicariously in the distant past (through his sentimental recall of the infant Nina) and in the distant future (through his yearning for a life in Amsterdam), but it unfits him for living in the present. The kind of mindless oblivion sought by Almayer, a virtual sleepwalker towards the end of the novel, can only be found in his infantile baby-talk with an imaginary Nina or in the dreamer's final passage into an 'easeful death'. Conrad's interest in how Almayer 'reads' his world leads to a tellingly oblique metacomment upon how a generation of late-Victorian readers – a large number of them middle-aged males – had been invited to sublimate their fears and anxieties through the pleasing illusion of eternal youth. As a study of atrophying dream and disappointed dreamer, *Almayer's Folly* implicitly reverses a tradition of easy, self-gratifying reading and prepares for new ways of making the reader *see*.

2

However insular in its assumptions, Victorian exotic and adventure fiction had served to introduce metropolitan British readers to remote countries and different races. During the period's last two decades, however, these popular kinds inevitably became involved with the wider Imperial adventure and yielded a thriving body of 'naïve' colonial literature (as represented by the works of G. A. Henty, H. Rider Haggard and Captain Mayne Reid), in which the mission of Empire itself furnished patriotic adventure, heroic possibilities and recurring tests upon manhood. By contrast, Conrad's major colonial fictions from *Heart of Darkness* to *Nostromo* (1898–1905) belong to a period when the entire Imperial mission fell increasingly under suspicion and when the very term 'imperialism' was to acquire its present pejorative meanings. From a position of hindsight, we can now see that Conrad's early Malay fiction, written at a time when he was probably not so nervously sensitive to the susceptibilities of his English readers, seems crucial in forging a passage from the 'naïve' tradition of Empire fiction to a new kind of sceptical and interrogative colonial novel. Significantly, too, *Almayer's Folly* would in 1895 find a newly inaugurated publishing vehicle suited to its more serious aims, T. Fisher Unwin's 'Colonial Library' (later the Overseas Library). Devised by Edward Garnett in 1895, the series was planned to challenge, even while exploiting, the readership created by 'naïve' colonial adventure. Its prospectus envisaged a series with 'no pretence at Imperial drum-beating' and promised a more sceptical measuring of the debits and credits of European colonialism through a depiction of 'the actual life of the English immigrants, travellers, traders, officers, overseas, away among foreign and native races, black or white'.[14]

The preface Conrad wrote immediately after finishing the novel (but which remained unpublished until 1921) is an important indicator of the beginning writer's sense of high mission. In it, he begins by tilting ironically at the popular conventions shaping both 'naïve' colonial literature and the exotic romance. But Conrad's more positive purpose is to position his own attitudes in the novel well apart from prevailing Eurocentric responses to the supposed 'inferiority' of non-European peoples. The immediate object of Conrad's attack is Alice Meynell, a well-known poet and critic of the 1890s who, in an essay called 'Decivilised' (1893),[15] had scornfully dismissed colonial literature and other forms of 'decivilised' art for their connection with degraded and outlandish subjects that depart from a civilised English norm. Echoing Matthew Arnold's concern for cultural continuity and giving voice to topical fears of degeneration, Meynell represents herself as speaking for the 'well-born' assailed by the vulgar, the metropolitan endangered by the provincial and for the ethnocentric view that regards all non-Europeans as permanently trapped at a lower stage in the history of human development. Conrad's basic response is first of all to attack the stereotypical views of those who believe that in non-European 'distant lands all joy is a yell and a war dance, all pathos is a howl and a ghastly grin of filed teeth, and that the solution of all problems is found in the barrel of a revolver or on the point of an assegai'. Teasingly paralleling life in London and Borneo, he goes on to assert that there are no basic differences between Europeans and 'that humanity so far away': 'I am content to sympathise with common mortals, no matter where they live; in houses or in huts, in the streets under a fog, or in the forests behind the dark line of dismal mangroves that fringe the vast solitude of the sea' (Author's Note).

Though such an egalitarian sympathy might have shocked Mrs Meynell, it is, in fact, recognisable as an extension of cherished Romantic beliefs, specifically the Wordsworthian view that 'In spite of difference of soil and climate, of language, and manners, of laws and customs ..... the Poet binds together by passion and knowledge the vast empire of human society as it is spread over the whole earth, and over all time.'[16] As Hugh Ridley further points out, this 'idealist' understanding of the human family characteristically 'prefers to concentrate on the ideal unity rather than the actual diversity of the world's population' and could often be easily purchased in later European colonial literature and even used to underpin the Imperial endeavour itself. Nevertheless, as Ridley adds, the cross-cultural habits of mind that initially prompted such egalitarianism also came to foster a more consciously sceptical and probing type of colonial literature, one that increasingly acknowledged the world's problematic variety and diversity.[17]

In practice, *Almayer's Folly* is more mobile, wavering and self-challenging in its attitudes to non-European peoples than its 'idealist' preface might imply. The attempt to sustain a sympathetic egalitarianism in the novel often co-exists, disconcertingly, with judgements based upon conventional late-Victorian perceptions of the difference between 'civilisation' and 'savagery', while elsewhere the very flintiness of the racial dilemma embracing the Almayer family questions the basis of the narrator's attempt to find unity in diversity. These conflicting 'voices' should not simply be seen as awkward vestiges of unconscious or 'naïve' colonial literature. In *Almayer's Folly*, they belong to a wider field of conflicting cultural, religious and linguistic codes that vie with each other as alternative ways of seeing and feeling. The relationship between Conrad's preface and his actual novel might be glossed by Adorno's proposition that 'One cannot "correct" stereotypy by experience; one has to reconstitute the capacity for *having* experience'.[18] The 'idealist' position of Conrad's preface is not abandoned in the novel, but it too is reconstituted as only one of many ways 'for *having* experience', taking its place among other possibilities for achieving that end. For example, the novel admits a wider range of non-European voices and codes than most other colonial novels of the time and attempts an imaginative entry into the inner life of such different individuals as Nina, Taminah and Mrs Almayer. In addition, from the habit of making similitudes between East and West comes the further challenge of what Cedric Watts has seen as a persistent feature of Conrad's major fiction, that of analogical mobility.[19] The novel delights in recurring triangular situations (Lingard/Almayer/Mrs Almayer, Almayer/Mrs Almayer/Nina, Nina/Dain/Taminah, Nina/Dain/Almayer) and so allows an 'idealist' position to be questioned by extreme cultural relativity. Finally, the basis for cross-cultural similitude in the novel is rarely a fixed one. If, in his preface, Conrad draws a number of contrasts between 'here' (Europe) and 'there' (non-

European countries and peoples), the novel itself often reverses the pattern and offers Malay characters the opportunity to speak of 'here' (Borneo) in contrast to 'there' (Europe). On one memorable occasion, it allows Nina to stand apart from both cultures and express her sense of detached alienation from an East and a West that, through her eyes, are essentially alike in their quest to gratify selfish desires:

> It seemed to Nina that there was no change and no difference; . . . . . whether they plotted for their own ends under the protection of laws and according to the rules of Christian conduct, or whether they sought the gratification of their desires with the savage cunning and the unrestrained fierceness of natures as innocent of culture as their own immense and gloomy forests, Nina saw only the same manifestations of love and hate and of sordid greed chasing the uncertain dollar in all its multifarious and vanishing shapes. To her resolute nature, however, after all these years, the savage and uncompromising sincerity of purpose shown by her Malay kinsmen seemed at last preferable to the sleek hypocrisy, to the polite disguises, to the virtuous pretences of such white people as she had had the misfortune to come in contact with. (Ch. 3)

Nina's view here – that no one race is essentially better than any other – presents an uncomfortable challenge both to popular racial mythologies of Conrad's own time and to more recent post-colonial orthodoxies. Such a challenge derives, significantly, from the author's capacity to stand apart, exploit a marginal viewpoint and share the vision of a young woman who is the product of two societies but does not feel herself to belong to either.

Cross-cultural mobility is not merely an incidental feature of the novel, but an essential outcome of the Conradian attempt to confront and explore colliding racial myths at the point where individuals experience their disturbances – Almayer's racial shame, Mrs Almayer's cultural revenge, Nina's felt sense of rootlessness, the inter-tribal rivalry in Sambir between Malay and Arabs. Signs of the ambitious challenge Conrad set himself are evident in the way that he modified and altered the racial history of the original Olmeijer family. The fictional Almayer is a white man born of Dutch parents, a country-born colonial, and not a Eurasian like the original Olmeijer; Mrs Almayer is a Malay of Sulu origin, and not – like her original – the Eurasian daughter of a Dutch soldier; where the Almayers have a single daughter, a Eurasian girl, the Olmeijers parented a total of eleven children (although many of them did not survive adolescence). Such changes have the obvious effect of heightening racial differences between the Almayers and making the family unit itself a microcosm and representative test-case.

Crucial to that test-case is, of course, the fact that the Almayer marriage is a racially mixed one, from which there arise a complex of issues relating to miscegenation. As Gail Fraser has suggested, the treatment of miscegenation in Conrad's Malay fiction generally is original and provocative, having an important representative function in revealing 'the logic if racial myths and phobias – the imaginative and emotional constructs that inform imperialist ideology'.[20] The other related problem in the novel, that of the Eurasian Nina's early enforced acculturation to European norms and her subsequent quest for authentic racial and cultural traditions, is again a provocative one. The sensitive Nina's dilemma in relation to prevailing European norms goes some way to making *Almayer's Folly* an intractable social-problem novel with a distinctively colonial character. A careful reading of the novel reveals how insidiously she is betrayed. The early chapters show Nina as a hapless victim of her father's racial phobias and driven by his needs. As a character naïvely acting out the rituals of his own presumed superiority as the only white man in Sambir, Almayer himself reveals much of the stony egotism underlying European caste assumptions. As an individual who has himself violated that rigid caste system by entering into a mixed marriage and who knows how inflexible it can be, he nevertheless naïvely and selfishly believes that he can expiate his own racial shame by giving Nina a 'white' education in preparation for their re-entry into European life. But Nina's position as a Eurasian – part Dutch and part Malay – serves to make the more telling point that these inherently rigid caste systems are subject to even more insidious manipulation. Official European racial policy in the Dutch East Indies from 1856 onwards made no legal distinction between whites and Eurasians, all being classified as Europeans. Hence the native Sambir community invariably regard the Eurasian Nina as a 'white' woman. The bitter irony (which Almayer blithely ignores in his attempt to give Nina a 'white' education) is that European colonial society, in the shape of Mrs Vinck, is even more cruelly exclusive than official law promises. It is Captain Ford who acts as mouthpiece for the blunt reality: 'You can't make her [Nina] white' (Ch. 2). The direct challenge to European racial needs and phobias that takes place in Chapter 11 (with the triangular confrontation between Nina, Dain and Almayer) provides a good example of how in Conrad's first novel, colonial fiction is already developing a grown-up maturity. In response to Almayer's claim that there is an insurmountable racial barrier between Nina and Dain, Nina responds: 'Between your people and me there is also a barrier that nothing can remove', and she poses the challenge to Almayer: 'You call him [Dain] a savage! What do you call my mother, your wife?' Acute critic that she is, Nina tells Dain, 'You do not know the mind of a white man. He would rather see me dead than standing where I am.' Through Nina's rejection of her father's traditions as 'exhausted' in favour of a living Malay inheritance, Conrad implicitly reverses Meynell's view in a more challenging way than his preface might imply. In fact, the preface's notion of the single unified family of man is interestingly qualified at the end of the novel with the break-up of the Almayer family and its replacement by a new one made up of Nina, Dain and child in 'independent' Bali.

3

Almayer's Folly is not, however, a novel whose sense of the problematic is shaped by racial determinants alone, important though these are. Indeed, its strenuous global sense of breakdown and predicament is the very thing that most characterises it as a novel of the 1890s. We can speak of the novel's general 'landscape' as a characteristically epochal one: it registers a sense of the Bornean natural world as remorselessly Darwinian and therefore essentially impersonal and alien to merely human hopes; on the other hand, the nearer scene as associated with Almayer appears to resemble a shrinking prison-house or a wasteland characterised by squalid neglect, premature ageing and impotence. Its pervading mood is, in other words, that of the *fin du globe*, a mood prompted by the late-Victorian sense of itself as 'Between two worlds / One dead, the other powerless to be born' (Matthew Arnold). In these respects *Almayer's Folly* and its central spectacle of the impotent dreamer shares much with a novel of predicament like Hardy's *The Return of the Native* (1878), where Eustacia Vye is, like Almayer, 'imprisoned' on Egdon Heath and spends a lifetime futilely dreaming of physical escape to a Paris which she has never seen, but romantically associates with power, poetry and romantic fulfilment. Again like Almayer, her gathering predicament brings intolerable consciousness and with it the increasing perception that death will be her only way of escape.

As a novel that seems to share Hardy's abiding interest in 'the ache of modernism' and its sources, *Almayer's Folly* is centrally concerned with the individual's disempowerment in a world apparently indifferent to human hopes and dreams. This interest is pursued through the evidence offered by individuals who, in a variety of ways, are subject to the conditions of slavery. That condition is manifested in literal form in Taminah who, as a slave, is legally owned by a person who controls her life and liberty. Another application links with the phenomenon of self-enslavement, as in the case of individuals such as Lingard and Almayer who, while apparently free agents, increasingly fall under the domination of powerful fixed ideas. A related interest in empowerment and its opposite runs through the novel's treatment of man–woman relations, as when Nina recognises that her mother (who regards herself as Almayer's 'slave') is right to predict that Nina can make Dain *her* slave. It is, however, in his treatment of slavery as a fundamental condition of being in the world that Conrad approaches his most sombre paradoxes.

Several of Conrad's letters from the 1890s provide a revealing context for the novel's wider preoccupation with disempowered 'slaves'. For example, he writes to R. B. Cunninghame Graham:

> What makes mankind tragic is not that they are the victims of nature, it is that they are conscious of it. To be part of the animal kingdom under the conditions of this earth is very well – but as soon as you know of your slavery the pain, the anger, the strife – the tragedy begins . . . . . There is no morality, no knowledge, and

> no hope; there is only the consciousness of ourselves which drives us about a world that whether seen in a convex or a concave mirror is always but a vain and floating appearance.[21]

The very terms of this letter echo in the description the slave-girl Taminah, for whom 'the full consciousness of life came ..... through pain and anger' and who, as we shall see, acts as a focus for Conrad's interest in the sources of servitude. Another letter pursues this same preoccupation:

> Man must drag the ball and chain of his individuality to the very end. It is the [price] one pays for the infernal and divine privilege of thought; consequently, it is only the elect who are convicts in this life – the glorious company of those who understand and who lament, but who tread the earth amid a multitude of ghosts with maniacal gestures, with idiotic grimaces. Which do you prefer – idiot or convict?[22]

Much of the power of *Almayer's Folly* as a novel of predicament seems to derive from its involvement with the terms of Conrad's final question – 'idiot or convict?' Behind this question lie two interrelated assumptions. Firstly, there is the bleak assumption that the world available to advanced 'modern' cultures has, through the attenuation of faith, the growth of scientific knowledge and the spread of philosophic doubt, increasingly presented itself as coldly amoral and purposeless – a mere mechanical knitting machine, as Conrad elsewhere describes it.[23] And a second inescapable emphasis falls upon the peril awaiting individuals who, having become conscious of themselves as suffering victims in a purposeless world, are then forced to persist in life with the full burden of that dark knowledge: 'as soon as you know of your slavery ..... the tragedy begins'.

These dark assumptions are most boldly developed through a minor character in the novel who can easily be overlooked, the figure of Taminah. A physical slave throughout, this largely silent girl enters the novel as one who paradoxically enjoys the freedom of a precious 'unconscious resignation' and who lives 'like the tall palms ..... seeking the light, desiring the sunshine, fearing the storm, unconscious of either'. Significantly, Taminah is defined by negatives that ultimately take on a positive force in suggesting that her well-being rests upon her *not* knowing and *not* hoping: 'She had no wish, no hope, no love, no fear except of a blow, and no vivid feeling but that of occasional hunger.' In the course of the novel, however, Taminah is born into tortured complexity with the birth of her desire for Dain and consequent burning jealousy of Nina. From this point onwards, she is a victim not simply of disappointed love, but of the deep-seated anguish that comes with being newly conscious of herself as a victim in a world that merely mocks her desires. She becomes, therefore, a slave in several senses: 'Her half-formed, savage mind, the slave of her body, was the slave of another's will .....', and she is further enslaved by 'the crushing weight that the mysterious hand of Fate had laid so suddenly upon her slender shoulders' (Ch. 8). To be conscious is, according to the bleak logic of Conrad's first novel, to be conscious of oneself as permanently trapped and betrayed in a world of perpetual duality. Unlike other characters in the novel, Taminah is given no voice by which to protest; but, like the minor figure of Little Father Time in Hardy's *Jude the Obscure*, her life and death carry the force of a protest against the ill-formed scheme of things. Simply but movingly, Conrad explores in Taminah's passage from the 'enchanted circle' of her physical slavery to her final death the terms of a tragic predicament that will haunt his major fiction: idiot or convict?

It is, however, through the novel's central figure that Conrad registers the shock of such disillusion upon a more fragile, unstable and recognisably 'modern' sensibility. The dramatisation of Almayer's later state of mind constitutes the first of Conrad's portraits of a kind of hysteria that results when shocking knowledge is forced upon a short-sighted pilgrim of the world. From the moment when Almayer's longed-for purposes collapse and he is brought to realise the fundamental hollowness of his life's dream, he becomes a character writhing on the razor's edge separating the 'idiot' from the 'convict'. At a crucial point in the narrative, events thrust upon him the horrifying knowledge that he is superfluous to the whole scheme of creation, after which initiation follows an 'infernal' cycle of hysterical panic – narcissistic indulgence in his victim-position, morbid imaginings of coming collapse, feeble attempts to revive past fictions, a Sisyphean sense of absurdity and, finally, the self-destructive urge not to live. The final stages of this vicious cycle involve the fruitless quest to *forget* what experience has painfully made known to him, and it can only be achieved by Almayer's embrace of a zombie-like mindlessness that represents his abdication of the right to exist in the world at all. At his death, the broken Almayer is linked with a despoiled wooden Mr Punch figure, a 'man-doll broken and flung there out of the way' (Ch. 12).[24]

The figure of Nina, it should be added, stands in more ambiguous relation to the bleak assumptions prevailing in the novel as a whole. She enters the action 'unconscious of herself' (Ch. 1) but, unlike Taminah, is unhappy, unmoored and imprisoned by virtue of her unthinking resignation. She can only develop and acquire a sense of identity, it is implied, on condition that she grows into self-awareness. Hence, in the early part of the novel she is the only character to achieve an alliance between open-eyed consciousness and trust in life: 'In the cold ashes of that hateful and miserable past she would find the sign of love, the fitting expression of the boundless felicity of the present, the pledge of a bright and splendid future' (Ch. 5). Through the link made between self-consciousness and empowerment in Nina's growth into maturity, Conrad would appear to challenge his own darkest intimations. Yet, ambiguously, the description in Chapter 11 of Nina's final commitment to Dain returns to metaphors of slavery ('The man was her slave') and reverts to the large perspectives and imagery of the novel's Amielian epigraph: 'Men that had felt in their breasts the awful exultation such a look awakens become mere things of today – which is paradise; forget yesterday – which was suffering; care not for tomorrow – which may be perdition.' The ironic qualification here makes us pause. Is the final culmination of Nina and Dain's relationship an example of hope and desire fulfilled – or disillusion deferred? As in many of his later works, Conrad's ambiguous answer comes in the form of a bifurcated ending to the novel: while the lovers escape to *their* world in Bali, we follow in Almayer's footsteps to participate in the final ruinous stages of what, it is implied, is *our* predicament.

4

With the first paragraph of *Almayer's Folly* the curtain opens upon a first novel and a precocious literary talent:

> 'Kaspar! Makan!'
>
> The well-known shrill voice startled Almayer from his dream of splendid future into the unpleasant realities of the present hour. An unpleasant voice too. He had heard it for many years, and with every year he liked it less. No matter; there would be an end to all this soon.
>
> He shuffled uneasily, but took no further notice of the call. Leaning with both his elbows on the balustrade of the verandah, he went on looking fixedly at the great river that flowed – indifferent and hurried – before his eyes. He liked to look at it about the time of sunset; perhaps because at that time the sinking sun would spread a glowing gold tinge on the waters of the Pantai, and Almayer's thoughts were often busy with gold; gold he had failed to secure; gold the others had secured – dishonestly, of course – or gold he meant to secure yet, through his own honest exertions, for himself and Nina. He absorbed himself in his dream of wealth and power away from this coast where he had dwelt for so many years, forgetting the bitterness of toil and strife in the vision of a great and splendid reward. They would live in Europe, he and his daughter. They would be rich and respected. Nobody would think of her mixed blood in the presence of her great beauty and of his immense wealth.

Already, here, there is a striking foretaste of the elusive 'mobilities' at work in the novel as a whole.[25] These mobilities are of (a) a temporal kind – in the form of a beginning *in medias res*, accompanied by a type of 'delayed decoding' or deferred explanation (here involving the agent of the opening command, itself conveyed in a puzzling foreign language) and leading to a reverie that veers dizzily between past, present and future; (b) a narrational kind, particularly through a method of 'free indirect speech' that both renders and reports on the contents of Almayer's reverie; and (c) a visual kind, notably in the 'stream' of vivid snapshots of the river and sunset that suggestively image the basis of Almayer's present reality and future dreams.

It is not my intention here to offer a detailed account of Conrad's technical practices in the novel as a whole. But it is important to indicate some large connections between these mobilities and their characteristic rhetorical ends in

Conrad's first work: their link, for example, with new and surprising ways of seeing; their place in fashioning a more active reader; and their role in persuading us into difficult responses.

Many of the temporal mobilities in the novel derive from the extension into narrative presentation of what Ian Watt has termed 'delayed decoding', a form of delayed information that 'combines the forward temporal progression of the mind as it receives impressions with the backward process of understanding them'.[26] The most obvious example of such a technique is the crucial episode involving Dain's supposed death, a simulation devised by Mrs Almayer and Nina, but unknown to Almayer. This event we register through the unknowing Almayer's eyes until such time as we are given a 'backward' understanding of the reality, largely through the slave-girl Taminah. In some ways, the device is not unlike the false clue or red herring laid for the reader in detective fiction, a form that exploits simple varieties of 'delayed understanding'. While Conrad partially emulates the detective writer's habit of teasing the reader, however, he does so in a way that is more elusive, unsettling and disconcerting. It is elusive because, unlike the detective writer, Conrad, from an early point in the narrative, leaves us in no doubt about its outcome (Almayer's ultimate failure) but embroils us in the complicated process of finding out how it came about. It is unsettling because we are ambiguously poised between omniscient understanding and relative insight – that is, sometimes wise before events, but often only wise after they have happened. And it is disconcerting because the process of delayed understanding can suddenly recoil upon *us*, highlighting the need for simple judgements to be replaced by more complex ones. As a largely retrospective novel, *Almayer's Folly* involves a continuous exercise in 'backward' reading. One effect of such a technique is that the portrait of the yearning dreamer given on the first page has to be continually modified as we meet facts about Almayer's present that he has chosen to push to one side. But the temporal order is even more involved, since during the first four chapters Almayer's retrospective survey itself is a limited one, selective in its contents and partial in understanding. Again, a fuller knowledge only emerges piecemeal and cumulatively as we read forward into the second half of the novel and arrive at a fuller 'backward' comprehension than Almayer's reveries allow. The unfolding narrative in *Almayer's Folly* leaves us in no doubt about Almayer's past or his imagined future: what remains to be 'decoded' by the reader is the present reality that Almayer either ignores or refuses to acknowledge.

In Conrad's devising of this erratic process of reading forwards to gain backward understanding one can detect a simpler version of the much more experimental rhetorical embroilments that characterise the later *Lord Jim* (1900) and *Nostromo* (1904). This backward perspective on *Almayer's Folly* can be useful to the critic too. It throws into bolder relief the ways in which Conrad's first narrative works to frustrate easy and conventional reading habits by meeting some of our expectations while playfully defeating others. In the process, the kind of vicarious reading demanded by the conventional romance is disallowed. Far from providing a simple release for the reader's needs, Conrad can be found to capitalise upon our anxieties and insecurities in fruitfully disruptive ways. Many of these insecurities in the reader's position become clear if we consider our relationship to the novel's pervasive ironies. On many occasions, Conrad's narrative offers a recognisable form of dramatic irony, allowing the reader a large foreknowledge of events that Almayer does not have. But this is not always true, and on several occasions we discover shocking ironies thrown up by the present action only at the point where Almayer himself meets and experiences them. Hence, in certain respects, we may feel ourselves to be co-sufferers with Almayer in a dangerously ungovernable world, sharing his horror at what a present reality has suddenly thrown up. Furthermore, given Conrad's delaying of vital information, the reader can in the early part of the novel *miss* the presence of certain ironies altogether. When for example, in Chapter 1 we learn that Almayer and Nina are 'all in all to each other' and hear Almayer say to Nina (in relation to his vision of their life in Amsterdam) 'you cannot imagine what is before you', we do not have enough knowledge about events to recognise the underlying irony. The fact that Nina is, in reality, 'all in all' to Dain and *can* imagine a future for herself without Almayer is only made known to the reader much later on in the novel. In an example like this, Almayer is the object of irony, but the real joke is played upon readers by a text that dallies with our relative ignorance and prepares for later ambushes.

The reader's shifting position in relation to ironies actual and potential in *Almayer's Folly* is interestingly glossed in a general way by Robert Kiely's observation that 'the most significant characteristic of the late Victorian quest for paradise is that it shifts uneasily and awkwardly between the ideal and the real'.[27] But a more particular question relates to how these awkward shifts determine our responses to Almayer himself. On the face of it, he is not an obvious candidate for sympathy. The novel's description of him as 'a grey-headed and foolish dreamer' (Ch. 3) and its early mockery of his extravagant dreams may easily tempt the reader into believing that he or she can remain securely dissociated from both the dreams and the dreamer. The large surprise awaiting us lies in the degree to which we will be pressed into partial identification with a figure who can be so stupidly short-sighted. How is this achieved? I have suggested that the process of 'backward' reading can often create an unusual partnership between Almayer and the reader. But in addition, as the opening paragraph of the novel indicates, Conrad's use of the device of free indirect speech invariably creates a careful balance of involved participation and detached assessment in the presentation of Almayer's wishful hopes. Yet another kind of narrative management is crucial to the appeal for sympathy implicitly made on Almayer's behalf. While the early chapters of the novel employ a good deal of detached mockery at the expense of Almayer's dream, that mockery tends to dissolve at the point where, with the final and irrevocable collapse of his fantasy, the hopeless victim emerges to face the consequences of his failure. From this point onwards, we are pressed into identification with the solitary Almayer's inner ordeal in a much more sustained way, sharing intimately in the stream-of-consciousness of a mind unhinged. With its emphasis upon Almayer's inward suffering, the final chapter fittingly allows Almayer centre-stage in a way described by Conrad in a letter: it 'begins with a *trio* . . . . . and it ends with a long *solo* for Almayer which is almost as long as the solo in Wagner's *Tristan*'.[28]

In their own way, the final paragraphs of the novel outlining the scene of Almayer's death are as memorable as the first in establishing the scrupulously impersonal sympathy for 'common mortals' anticipated in Conrad's Author's Note. An element of mockery (in the final recall of Almayer as the 'only white man on the east coast') accompanies a last crowning irony (since Almayer's elegy is delivered by his greatest enemy, Abdulla) in a longer description that re-emphasises the incongruity between Almayer and his world (the 'serene look' of the dead man is returned by heaven's 'indifferent eyes'). While conceding little to sentimentality, Conrad nevertheless rescues a form of steely pathos from the novel's final spectacle: that is, from the ironic spectacle of the dead Almayer, once a man absorbed by a dream of westward escape, now a figure transformed into the object of Islamic prayer.

OWEN KNOWLES

References

1. Conrad's description of himself as '*homo duplex*' appears in a letter to Kazimierz Waliszewski of 1903 and can be found in *The Collected Letters of Joseph Conrad, Volume 3: 1903–1907*, ed. Frederick R. Karl and Laurence Davies (Cambridge: Cambridge University Press, 1988), p. 89. Hereafter this multi-volume collection is abbreviated as *Letters*. The phrase 'standing jump' is used by Conrad himself when describing his departure from Poland in *A Personal Record* (Ch. 6).
2. *Twenty Letters to Joseph Conrad*, ed. G. Jean-Aubry (London: Curwen Press, 1926).
3. Ian Watt, *Conrad in the Nineteenth Century* (London: Chatto & Windus, 1980), pp. 41–55.
4. See, for example, James Greenwood's *The Adventures of Reuben Davidger: Seventeen Years and Four Months Captive Among the Dyaks of Borneo* (London: Ward, Lock, 1869), described by its author as 'a yarn pitched by a grown-up boy for the amusement of his more youthful brethren' (p. v), and Captain Mayne Reid's *The Castaways: A Story of Adventure in the Wilds of Borneo* (London: Nelson, 1892).
5. Norman Sherry, *Conrad: The Critical Heritage* (London: Routledge & Kegan Paul, 1973), p. 48.

6. *Ibid.*, p. 60.
7. Jefferson Hunter, *Edwardian Fiction* (Cambridge, Mass.: Harvard University Press, 1983), p. 128.
8. Robert Louis Stevenson, *Works*, Thistle Edition (New York: Scribner's, 1902), XIII, 349.
9. *Letters of Robert Louis Stevenson to his Family and Friends*, ed. Sidney Colvin (London: Methuen, 1911), I, 322.
10. *Pierre Loti* (New York: Twayne, 1974), p. 146.
11. Watt, p. 47.
12. Stevenson, *Works*, XV, 244.
13. Stevenson, *Works*, XIII, 327.
14. Quoted by Douglas Jefferson, *Edward Garnett: A Life in Literature* (London: Jonathan Cape, 1982), p. 46.
15. For the full text of Alice Meynell's essay, see the concluding 'Appendix', p. 190–192.
16. Quoted by David Leon Higdon, 'The Text and Context of Conrad's First Essay', *Polish Review*, 20 (1975), 105. Higdon's entire article provides valuable contextual material on the 'Author's Note' and its relationship to the novel.
17. See Hugh Ridley, *Images of Empire* (London: Croom Helm, 1983), pp. 53–4.
18. Theodor W. Adorno, *The Authoritarian Personality* (New York: Harper, 1950), p. 617.
19. Cedric Watts, *A Preface to Conrad* (London: Longman, second edn., 1993), p. 151.
20. Gail Fraser, 'Empire of the Senses: Miscegenation in *An Outcast of the Islands*', in *Contexts for Conrad*, ed. Keith Carabine, Owen Knowles and Wiesław Krajka (Boulder: East European Monographs, 1993), Vol. 2, p. 127.
21. *Letters*, 2, 30.
22. *Letters*, 1, 162–3.
23. *Letters*, 1, 425.
24. For the basis of this link between Almayer and Mr Punch, see note to p. 159 in the Notes.
25. Watts, pp. 150–51. I am also indebted to Watts for the categories that follow in this paragraph.
26. Watt, 'Pink Toads and Yellow Curs: An Impressionistic Device in *Lord Jim*', *Joseph Conrad Colloquy in Poland: Contributions, First Series*, ed. Roza Jabłkowska (Wrocław: Polish Academy of Sciences, 1972), 274. In *Conrad in the Nineteenth Century*, Watt

later revised the wording of his 1972 definition of 'delayed decoding' in a way that dilutes its original vividness.

27. Robert Kiely, *Robert Louis Stevenson and the Fiction of Adventure* (Cambridge, Mass.: Harvard University Press, 1964), p. 153.

28. *Letters*, 1, 156.

NOTE ON THE TEXT

Conrad wrote *Almayer's Folly* over a period spanning the autumn of 1889 and April 1894. The manuscript of the novel is held at the Rosenbach Museum and Library, Philadelphia, and its final corrected typescript at the Humanities Research Center, University of Texas at Austin. The novel was not serialised before book publication. It was first published in Britain by T. Fisher Unwin on 29 April 1895 (2,000 copies), and in the United States by Macmillan on 3 May 1895 (650 copies). There are some substantive variants between the two editions. Conrad revised the text of *Almayer's Folly* in 1916 in preparation for planned collected editions of his works – the first American Limited Collected Edition (the 'Sun-Dial' Edition by Doubleday, Page) and the First English Limited Edition (by Heinemann) – both of which appeared in 1921. While Conrad's marked copy provided a common printer's text for both editions, each has its own substantive variants. Further differences are created by the two contrasting 'house styles', with the Heinemann edition being punctuated more heavily and prescriptively than the 'Sun-Dial'.

For this edition, I have chosen as copy-text the British first edition published by Unwin on the grounds that such an edition brings the reader close to Conrad's early creative intentions and reflects more authentically his handling of literary English at the very beginning of his career as a writer. It also recovers the more idiosyncratic punctuation of the first edition as well as the writer's occasional problems with correct English usage. This choice of text, moreover, acknowledges the historical importance of the Unwin first edition: that is, as the one that the first British readers and reviewers would have seen, and the one whose reception most preoccupied Conrad. David Leon Higdon and Floyd Eugene Eddleman have suggested that the 440 variants between the 1895 Unwin text and the collected edition texts raise the further question of 'whether they reflect a mature artist confidently sophisticating his first novel or an artist exhausted by the years and corrupting his text' ('Collected Edition Variants in Conrad's *Almayer's Folly*', *Conradiana*, 9 [1977], 77). If the answer cannot be a simple one, it may nevertheless be argued that many of the cuts to the first edition later made by Conrad (most of which are from the first four chapters) represent a dilution and, in some cases, a marked defusion of its energy. This edition both restores material excised from the 1921 and many subsequent editions of *Almayer's Folly* and identifies the most important of these substantive variants in the explanatory notes. Hence, a selected body of evidence is signposted for readers who wish to make an independent approach to the question raised by Higdon and Eddleman. My only emendations to the text of the first edition correct misspellings and faulty accentuation of foreign words, amend evident typographical and printing errors, and include the few small repairs to punctuation incorporated in subsequent printings of the first edition. These emendations are listed below. Page numbers refer to this Everyman edition; the 1895 reading is enclosed in square brackets.

8 Rajah Laut [Rajah-Laut]
13 after, the [after the]
19 Rajah Laut [Rajah-Laut]
22 Sambir [Sambira]
22 Orang Blanda [Orang Blando]
27 as he called it [as she called it]
30 salt-water [salt water]
38 was [as]
38 *cortège* [cortege]
45 *cortège* [*cortége*]
46 know, Tuan [know Tuan]
47 birds' nests [bird's nests]
66 generosity [g nerosity]
66 prestige of his [prestige his]
78 pig's [pigs]
80 drank, his [drank his]
114 obtrusive [obstrusive]
117 speak, her [speak her]
123 had she [she had]

127 disappointment, happiness [disappointment happiness]
140 this, Dain [this Dain]
145 land, white [land white]
156 This done, [This done]

The publishers have made the following conventional changes to the original Unwin 'house style': the full stop is omitted after certain common abbreviations (*e.g.* 'Mr' and 'Mrs'); a punctuation mark that follows an italicised word is not italicised; where the original text uses double quotation marks, this text uses single ones, and *vice versa*; some punctuation marks that were originally placed within quotations are now placed after them (so that, for example, 'Almayer's Folly.' becomes 'Almayer's Folly'.); and hyphens have been removed from some words now spelt without them (thus 'to-day' becomes 'today').

The Author's Note which prefaces the text is, with slight emendation, that which appeared in the 1921 Doubleday, Page 'Sun-Dial' edition.

In quotations appearing in the editorial material, a row of five points (. . . . .) represents an omission made by the editor; a row of three or four points represents an ellipsis already present in the quoted material.

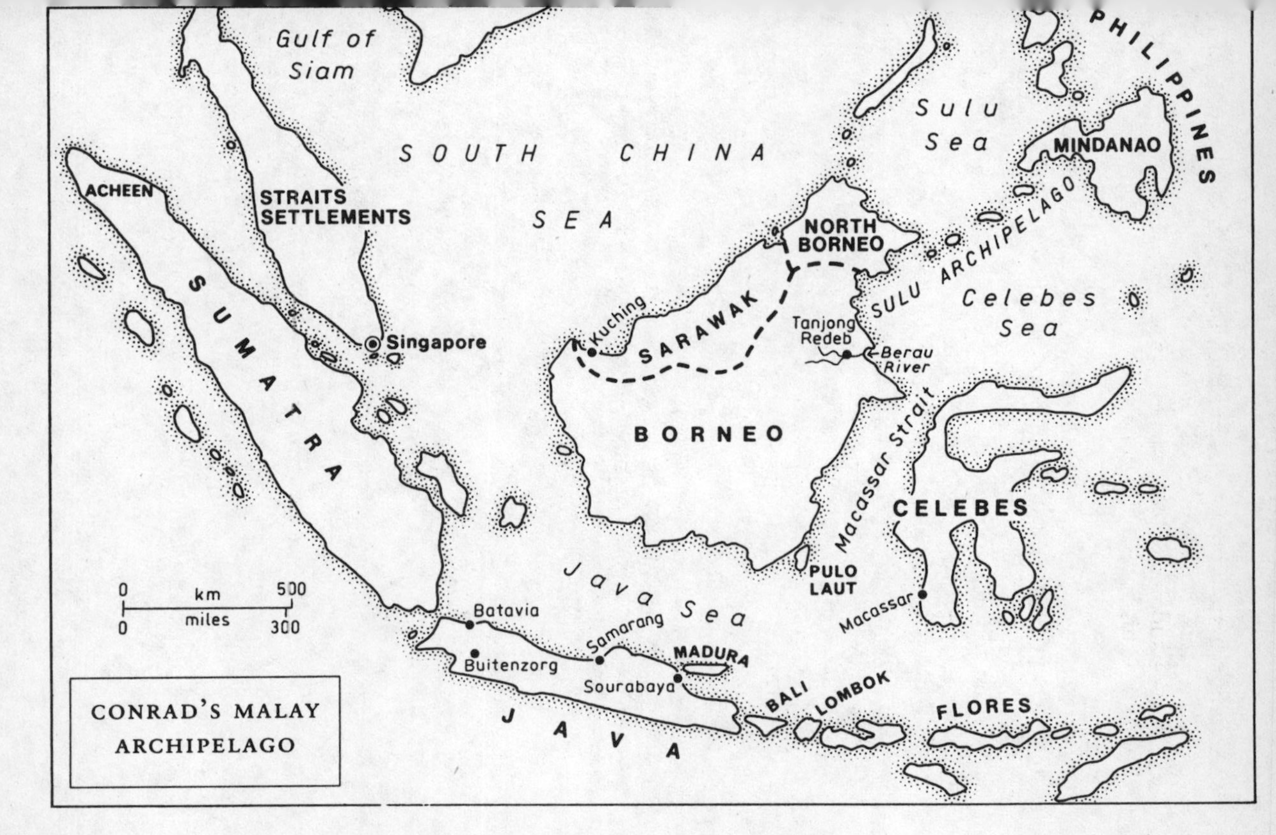

CONRAD'S MALAY ARCHIPELAGO

ALMAYER'S FOLLY*

A STORY OF AN EASTERN RIVER

Qui de nous n'a eu sa terre promise, son jour d'extase et sa fin en exile?

AMIEL*

To the memory of T. B.*

AUTHOR'S NOTE*

I am informed that in criticising that literature which preys on strange people and prowls in far-off countries, under the shade of palms, in the unsheltered glare of sunbeaten beaches, amongst honest cannibals and the more sophisticated pioneers of our glorious virtues, a lady* – distinguished in the world of letters – summed up her disapproval of it by saying that the tales it produced were 'decivilised'.* And in that sentence not only the tales but, I apprehend, the strange people and the far-off countries also, are finally condemned in a verdict of contemptuous dislike.

A woman's judgment: intuitive, clever, expressed with felicitous charm – infallible. A judgment that has nothing to do with justice. The critic and the judge seems to think that in those distant lands all joy is a yell and a war dance, all pathos is a howl and a ghastly grin of filed teeth, and that the solution of all problems is found in the barrel of a revolver or on the point of an assegai.* And yet it is not so. But the erring magistrate may plead in excuse the misleading nature of the evidence.

The picture of life, there as here, is drawn with the same elaboration of detail, coloured with the same tints. Only in the cruel serenity of the sky, under the merciless brilliance of the sun, the dazzled eye misses the delicate detail, sees only the strong outlines, while the colours, in the steady light, seem crude and without shadows. Nevertheless it is the same picture.

And there is a bond between us and that humanity so far away. I am speaking here of men and women – not of the charming and graceful phantoms that move about in our mud and smoke and are softly luminous with the radiance of all our virtues; that are possessed of all refinements, of all sensibilities, of all wisdom – but, being only phantoms, possess no heart.

The sympathies of those are (probably) with the immortals: with the angels above or the devils below. I am content to sympathise with common mortals, no matter where they live; in houses or in huts, in the streets under a fog, or in the forests behind the dark line of dismal mangroves that fringe the vast solitude of the sea. For, their land – like ours – lies under the inscrutable eyes of the Most High. Their hearts – like ours – must endure the load of the gifts from Heaven: the curse of facts and the blessing of illusions, the bitterness of our wisdom and the deceptive consolation of our folly.

J. C.
1895

CHAPTER I

'Kaspar! Makan!'*

The well-known shrill voice startled Almayer* from his dream of splendid future into the unpleasant realities of the present hour. An unpleasant voice too. He had heard it for many years, and with every year he liked it less. No matter; there would be an end to all this soon.

He shuffled uneasily, but took no further notice of the call. Leaning with both his elbows on the balustrade of the verandah, he went on looking fixedly at the great river that flowed – indifferent and hurried – before his eyes. He liked to look at it about the time of sunset; perhaps because at that time the sinking sun would spread a glowing gold tinge on the waters of the Pantai,* and Almayer's thoughts were often busy with gold;* gold he had failed to secure; gold the others had secured – dishonestly, of course – or gold he meant to secure yet, through his own honest exertions, for himself and Nina. He absorbed himself in his dream of wealth and power away from this coast where he had dwelt for so many years, forgetting the bitterness of toil and strife in the vision of a great and splendid reward. They would live in Europe, he and his daughter. They would be rich and respected. Nobody would think of her mixed blood in the presence of her great beauty and of his immense wealth. Witnessing her triumphs he would grow young again, he would forget the twenty-five years of heart-breaking struggle on this coast where he felt like a prisoner. All this was nearly within his reach. Let only Dain* return! And return soon he must – in his own interest, for his own share. He was now more than a week late! Perhaps he would return tonight.

Such were Almayer's thoughts as, standing on the verandah of his new but already decaying house – that last failure of his life – he looked on the broad river. There was no tinge of gold on it this evening, for it had been swollen by the rains,* and rolled an angry and muddy flood under his inattentive eyes, carrying small drift-wood and big dead logs, and whole uprooted trees with branches and foliage, amongst which the water swirled and roared angrily.

One of those drifting trees grounded on the shelving shore, just by the house, and Almayer, neglecting his dream, watched it with languid interest. The tree swung slowly round, amid the hiss and foam of the water, and soon getting free of the obstruction began to move down stream again, rolling slowly over, raising upwards a long, denuded branch, like a hand lifted in mute appeal to heaven against the river's brutal and unnecessary violence. Almayer's interest in the fate of that tree increased rapidly. He leaned over to see if it would clear the low point below. It did; then he drew back, thinking that now its course was free down to the sea, and he envied the lot of that inanimate thing now growing small and indistinct in the deepening darkness. As he lost sight of it altogether he began to wonder how far out to sea it would drift. Would the current carry it north or south? South, probably, till it drifted in sight of Celebes, as far as Macassar,* perhaps!

Macassar! Almayer's quickened fancy distanced the tree on its imaginary voyage, but his memory lagging behind some twenty years or more in point of time saw a young and slim Almayer, clad all in white and modest-looking, landing from the Dutch mail-boat on the dusty jetty of Macassar, coming to woo fortune in the godowns* of old Hudig.* It was an important epoch in his life, the beginning of a new existence for him. His father, a subordinate official employed in the Botanical Gardens of Buitenzorg,* was no doubt delighted to place his son in such a firm. The young man himself too was nothing loth to leave the poisonous shores of Java, and the meagre comforts of the parental bungalow, where the father grumbled all day at the stupidity of native gardeners, and the mother from the depths of her long easy-chair* bewailed the lost glories of Amsterdam, where she had been brought up, and of her position as the daughter of a cigar dealer there.

Almayer had left his home with a light heart and a lighter pocket, speaking English well, and strong in arithmetic; ready to conquer the world, never doubting that he would.

After those twenty years, standing in the close and stifling heat of a Bornean evening, he recalled with pleasurable regret the image of Hudig's lofty and cool warehouses with their long and straight avenues of gin cases and bales of Manchester goods; the big door swinging noiselessly; the dim light of the place, so delightful after the glare of the streets; the little railed-off spaces amongst piles of merchandise where the Chinese clerks, neat, cool, and sad-eyed, wrote rapidly and in silence amidst the din of the working gangs rolling casks or shifting cases to a muttered song, ending with a desperate yell. At the upper end, facing the great door, there was a larger space railed off, well lighted; there the noise was subdued by distance, and above it rose the soft and continuous clink of silver guilders* which other discreet Chinamen were counting and piling up under the supervision of Mr Vinck, the cashier, the genius presiding in the place – the right hand of the Master.

In that clear space Almayer worked at his table not far from a little green painted door, by which always stood a Malay in a red sash and turban, and whose hand, holding a small string dangling from above, moved up and down with the regularity of a machine. The string worked a punkah* on the other side of the green door, where the so-called private office was, and where old Hudig – the Master – sat enthroned, holding noisy receptions. Sometimes the little door would fly open disclosing to the outer world, through the bluish haze of tobacco smoke, a long table loaded with bottles of various shapes and tall water-pitchers, rattan* easy-chairs occupied by noisy men in sprawling attitudes, while the Master would put his head through and, holding by the handle, would grunt confidentially to Vinck; perhaps send an order thundering down the warehouse, or spy a hesitating stranger and greet him with a friendly roar, 'Wel-gome, Gapitan! ver' you gome vrom? Bali,* eh? Got bonies?* I vant bonies! Vant all you got; ha! ha! ha! Gome in!' Then the stranger was dragged in, in a tempest of yells, the door was shut, and the usual noises refilled the place; the song of the workmen, the rumble of barrels, the scratch of rapid pens; while above all rose the musical chink of broad silver pieces streaming ceaselessly through the yellow fingers of the attentive Chinamen.

At that time Macassar was teeming with life and commerce. It was the point in the islands where tended all those bold spirits who, fitting out schooners* on the Australian coast, invaded the

Malay Archipelago* in search of money and adventure. Bold, reckless, keen in business, not disinclined for a brush with the pirates that were to be found on many a coast as yet, making money fast, they used to have a general 'rendezvous' in the bay for purposes of trade and dissipation. The Dutch merchants called those men English pedlars; some of them were undoubtedly gentlemen for whom that kind of life had a charm; most were seamen; the acknowledged king of them all was Tom Lingard,* he whom the Malays, honest or dishonest, quiet fishermen or desperate cut-throats, recognised as 'the Rajah Laut'* – the King of the Sea.

Almayer had heard of him before he had been three days in Macassar, had heard the stories of his smart business transactions, his loves, and also of his desperate fights with the Sulu pirates,* together with the romantic tale of some child – a girl – found in a piratical prau* by the victorious Lingard, when, after a long contest, he boarded the craft, driving the crew overboard. This girl, it was generally known, Lingard had adopted, was having her educated in some convent in Java, and spoke of her as 'my daughter'. He had sworn a mighty oath to marry her to a white man before he went home and to leave her all his money. 'And Captain Lingard has lots of money,' would say Mr Vinck solemnly, with his head on one side, 'lots of money; more than Hudig!' And after a pause – just to let his hearers recover from their astonishment at such an incredible assertion – he would add in an explanatory whisper, 'You know, he has discovered a river.'*

That was it! He had discovered a river! That was the fact placing old Lingard so much above the common crowd of seagoing adventurers who traded with Hudig in the daytime and drank champagne, gambled, sang noisy songs, and made love to half-caste girls under the broad verandah of the Sunda Hotel* at night. Into that river, whose entrances himself only knew, Lingard used to take his assorted cargo of Manchester goods, brass gongs, rifles and gunpowder. His brig* *Flash*, which he commanded himself, would on those occasions disappear quietly during the night from the roadstead* while his companions were sleeping off the effects of the midnight carouse, Lingard seeing them drunk under the table before going on board, himself unaffected by any amount of liquor. Many tried to follow him and find that land of plenty for gutta-percha and rattans, pearl shells and birds' nests, wax and gum-dammar,* but the little *Flash* could outsail every craft in those seas. A few of them came to grief on hidden sandbanks and coral reefs, losing their all and barely escaping with life from the cruel grip of this sunny and smiling sea; others got discouraged; and for many years the green and peaceful-looking islands guarding the entrances to the promised land kept their secret with all the merciless serenity of tropical nature. And so Lingard came and went on his secret or open expeditions, becoming a hero in Almayer's eyes by the boldness and enormous profits of his ventures, seeming to Almayer a very great man indeed as he saw him marching up the warehouse, grunting a 'how are you?' to Vinck, or greeting Hudig, the Master, with a boisterous 'Hallo, old pirate! Alive yet?' as a preliminary to transacting business behind the little green door. Often of an evening, in the silence of the then deserted warehouse, Almayer putting away his papers before driving home with Mr Vinck, in whose household he lived, would pause listening to the noise of a hot discussion in the private office, would hear the deep and monotonous growl of the Master, and the roared-out interruptions of Lingard – two mastiffs fighting over a marrowy bone. But to Almayer's ears it sounded like a quarrel of Titans – a battle of the gods.*

After a year or so Lingard, having been brought often in contact with Almayer in the course of business, took a sudden and, to the onlookers, a rather inexplicable fancy to the young man. He sang his praises, late at night, over a convivial glass to his cronies in the Sunda Hotel, and one fine morning electrified Vinck by declaring that he must have 'that young fellow for a supercargo.* Kind of captain's clerk. Do all my quill-driving* for me.' Hudig consented. Almayer, with youth's natural craving for change, was nothing loth, and packing his few belongings, started in the *Flash* on one of those long cruises when the old seaman was wont to visit almost every island in the archipelago. Months slipped by, and Lingard's friendship seemed to increase. Often pacing the deck with Almayer, when the faint night breeze, heavy with aromatic exhalations of the islands, shoved the brig gently along under the peaceful and sparkling sky, did the old seaman open his heart to his entranced listener. He spoke of his past life, of escaped dangers, of big profits in his trade, of new combinations that were in the future to bring profits bigger still. Often he had mentioned his daughter, the girl found in the pirate prau, speaking of her with a strange assumption of fatherly tenderness. 'She must be a big girl now,' he used to say. 'It's nigh unto four years since I have seen her! Damme, Almayer, if I don't think we will run into Sourabaya* this trip.' And after such a declaration he always dived into his cabin muttering to himself, 'Something must be done – must be done.' More than once he would astonish Almayer by walking up to him rapidly, clearing his throat with a powerful 'Hem!' as if he was going to say something, and then turning abruptly away to lean over the bulwarks* in silence, and watch, motionless, for hours, the gleam and sparkle of the phosphorescent sea along the ship's side. It was the night before arriving in Sourabaya when one of those attempts at confidential communication succeeded. After clearing his throat he spoke. He spoke to some purpose. He wanted Almayer to marry his adopted daughter. 'And don't you kick because you're white!' he shouted, suddenly, not giving the surprised young man the time to say a word. 'None of that with me! Nobody will see the colour of your wife's skin. The dollars are too thick for that, I tell you! And mind you, they will be thicker yet before I die. There will be millions, Kaspar! Millions I say! And all for her – and for you, if you do what you are told.'

Startled by the unexpected proposal, Almayer hesitated, and remained silent for a minute. He was gifted with a strong and active imagination, and in that short space of time he saw, as in a flash of dazzling light, great piles of shining guilders, and realised all the possibilities of an opulent existence. The consideration, the indolent ease of life – for which he felt himself so well fitted – his ships, his warehouses, his merchandise (old Lingard would not live for ever), and, crowning all, in the far future gleamed like a fairy palace the big mansion in Amsterdam, that earthly paradise of his dreams, where, made king amongst men by old Lingard's money, he would pass the evening of his days in inexpressible splendour. As to the other side of the picture – the companionship for life of a Malay girl, that legacy of a boatful of pirates – there was only within him a confused consciousness of shame that he a white man— Still, a convent education of four years! – and then she may mercifully die. He was always lucky, and money is powerful! Go through it. Why not? He had a vague idea of shutting her up somewhere, anywhere, out of his gorgeous future. Easy enough to dispose of a Malay woman, a slave, after all, to his Eastern mind, convent or no convent, ceremony or no ceremony.

He lifted his head and confronted the anxious yet irate seaman.

'I – of course – anything you wish, Captain Lingard.'

'Call me father, my boy. She does,' said the mollified old adventurer. 'Damme, though, if I didn't think you were going to refuse. Mind you, Kaspar, I always get my way, so it would have been no use. But you are no fool.'

He remembered well that time – the look, the accent, the words, the effect they produced on him, his very surroundings. He remembered the narrow slanting deck of the brig, the silent sleeping coast, the smooth black surface of the sea with a great bar of gold laid on it by the rising moon. He remembered it all, and he remembered his feelings of mad exultation at the thought of that fortune thrown into his hands. He was no fool then, and he was no fool now. Circumstances had been against him; the fortune was gone, but hope remained.

He shivered in the night air, and suddenly became aware of the intense darkness which, on the sun's departure, had closed in upon the river, blotting out the outlines of the opposite shore. Only the fire of dry branches lit outside the stockade of the Rajah's compound called fitfully into view the ragged trunks of the surrounding trees, putting a stain of glowing red half-way across the river where the drifting logs were hurrying towards the sea through the impenetrable gloom. He had a hazy recollection of having been called some time during the evening by his wife. To his dinner probably. But a man busy contemplating the wreckage of his past in the dawn of new hopes cannot be hungry whenever his rice is ready. Time he went home, though; it was getting late.

He stepped cautiously on the loose planks towards the ladder. A lizard, disturbed by the noise, emitted a plaintive note and scurried through the long grass growing on the bank. Almayer descended the ladder carefully, now thoroughly recalled to the realities of life by the care necessary to prevent a fall on the uneven ground where the stones, decaying planks, and half-sawn beams were piled up in inextricable confusion. As he turned towards the house where he lived – 'my old house' he called it – his ear detected the splash of paddles away in the darkness of the river. He stood still in the path, attentive and surprised at anybody being on the river at this late hour during such a heavy freshet.* Now he could hear the paddles distinctly, and even a rapidly exchanged word in low tones, the heavy breathing of men fighting with the current, and hugging the bank on which he stood. Quite close, too, but it was too dark to distinguish anything under the overhanging bushes.

'Arabs, no doubt,' muttered Almayer to himself, peering into the solid blackness. 'What are they up to now? Some of Abdulla's* business; curse him!'

The boat was very close now.

'Oh, ya!* Man!' hailed Almayer.

The sound of voices ceased, but the paddles worked as furiously as before. Then the bush in front of Almayer shook, and the sharp sound of the paddles falling into the canoe rang in the quiet night. They were holding on to the bush now; but Almayer could hardly make out an indistinct dark shape of a man's head and shoulders above the bank.

'You Abdulla?' said Almayer, doubtfully.

A grave voice answered –

'Tuan* Almayer is speaking to a friend. There is no Arab here.'

Almayer's heart gave a great leap.

'Dain!' he exclaimed. 'At last! at last! I have been waiting for you every day and every night. I had nearly given you up.'

'Nothing could have stopped me from coming back here,' said the other, almost violently. 'Not even death,' he whispered to himself.

'This is a friend's talk, and is very good,' said Almayer, heartily. 'But you are too far here. Drop down to the jetty and let your men cook their rice in my campong* while we talk in the house.'

There was no answer to that invitation.

'What is it?' asked Almayer, uneasily. 'There is nothing wrong with the brig, I hope?'

'The brig is where no Orang Blanda* can lay his hands on

her,' said Dain, with a gloomy tone in his voice, which Almayer, in his elation, failed to notice.

'Right,' he said. 'But where are all your men? There are only two with you.'

'Listen, Tuan Almayer,' said Dain. 'Tomorrow's sun shall see me in your house, and then we will talk. Now I must go to the Rajah.'

'To the Rajah! Why? What do you want with Lakamba?'

'Tuan, tomorrow we talk like friends. I must see Lakamba tonight.'

'Dain, you are not going to abandon me now, when all is ready?' asked Almayer, in a pleading voice.

'Have I not returned? But I must see Lakamba first for your good and mine.'

The shadowy head disappeared abruptly. The bush, released from the grasp of the bowman,* sprung back with a swish, scattering a shower of muddy water over Almayer, as he bent forward, trying to see.

In a little while the canoe shot into the streak of light that streamed on the river from the big fire on the opposite shore, disclosing the outline of two men bending to their work, and a third figure in the stern flourishing the steering paddle, his head covered with an enormous round hat, like a fantastically exaggerated mushroom.

Almayer watched the canoe till it passed out of the line of light. Shortly after, the murmur of many voices reached him across the water. He could see the torches being snatched out of the burning pile, and rendering visible for a moment the gate in the stockade round which they crowded. Then they went in apparently. The torches disappeared, and the scattered fire sent out only a dim and fitful glare.

Almayer stepped homewards with long strides and mind uneasy. Surely Dain was not thinking of playing him false. It was absurd. Dain and Lakamba were both too much interested in the success of his scheme. Trusting to Malays was poor work; but then even Malays have some sense and understand their own interest. All would be well – must be well. At this point in his meditation he found himself at the foot of the steps leading to the verandah of his home. From the low point of land where he stood he could see both branches of the river. The main branch of the Pantai was lost in complete darkness, for the fire at the Rajah's had gone out altogether; but up the Sambir reach* his eye could follow the long line of Malay houses crowding the bank, with here and there a dim light twinkling through bamboo walls, or a smoky torch burning on the platforms built out over the river. Further away, where the island ended in a low cliff, rose a dark mass of buildings towering above the Malay structures. Founded solidly on a firm ground with plenty of space, starred by many lights burning strong and white, with a suggestion of paraffin and lamp-glasses, stood the house and the godowns of Abdulla bin Selim, the great trader of Sambir. To Almayer the sight was very distasteful, and he shook his fist towards the buildings that in their evident prosperity looked to him cold and insolent, and contemptuous of his own fallen fortunes.

He mounted the steps of his house slowly.

In the middle of the verandah there was a round table. On it a paraffin lamp without a globe shed a hard glare on the three inner sides. The fourth side was open, and faced the river. Between the rough supports of the high-pitched roof hung torn rattan screens. There was no ceiling, and the harsh brilliance of the lamp was toned above into a soft half-light that lost itself in the obscurity amongst the rafters. The front wall was cut in two by the doorway of a central passage closed by a red curtain. The women's room opened into that passage, which led to the back courtyard and to the cooking shed. In one of the side walls there was a doorway. Half obliterated words – 'Office: Lingard and Co.' – were still legible on the dusty door, which looked as if it had not been opened for a very long time. Close to the other side wall stood a bent-wood* rocking-chair, and by the table and about the verandah four wooden armchairs straggled forlornly, as if ashamed of their shabby surroundings. A heap of common mats lay in one corner, with an old hammock slung diagonally above. In the other corner, his head wrapped in a piece of red calico, huddled into a shapeless heap, slept a Malay, one of Almayer's domestic slaves – 'my own people', he used to call them. A numerous and representative assembly of moths were holding high revels round the lamp to the spirited music of swarming mosquitoes. Under the palm-leaf thatch lizards raced on the beams calling softly. A monkey, chained to one of the verandah supports – retired for the night under the eaves – peered and grinned at Almayer, as it swung to one of the bamboo roof sticks and caused a shower of dust and bits of dried leaves to settle on the shabby table. The floor was uneven, with many withered plants and dried earth scattered about. A general air of squalid neglect pervaded the place. Great red stains on the floor and walls testified to frequent and indiscriminate betel-nut chewing.* The light breeze from the river swayed gently the tattered blinds, sending from the woods opposite a faint and sickly perfume as of decaying flowers.

Under Almayer's heavy tread the boards of the verandah creaked loudly. The sleeper in the corner moved uneasily, muttering indistinct words. There was a slight rustle behind the curtained doorway, and a soft voice asked in Malay, 'Is it you, father?'

'Yes, Nina. I am hungry. Is everybody asleep in this house?'

Almayer spoke jovially and dropped with a contented sigh into the armchair nearest to the table. Nina Almayer came through the curtained doorway followed by an old Malay woman, who busied herself in setting upon the table a plateful of rice and fish, a jar of water, and a bottle half full of genever.* After carefully placing before her master a cracked glass tumbler and a tin spoon she went away noiselessly. Nina stood by the table, one hand lightly resting on its edge, the other hanging listlessly by her side. Her face turned towards the outer darkness, through which her dreamy eyes seemed to see some entrancing picture, wore a look of impatient expectancy. She was tall for a half-caste, with the correct profile of the father, modified and strengthened by the squareness of the lower part of the face inherited from her maternal ancestors – the Sulu pirates. Her firm mouth, with the lips slightly parted and disclosing a gleam of white teeth, put a vague suggestion of ferocity into the impatient expression of her features. And yet her dark and perfect eyes had all the tender softness of expression common to Malay women, but with a gleam of superior intelligence; they looked gravely, wide open and steady, as if facing something invisible to all other eyes, while she stood there all in white, straight, flexible, graceful, unconscious of herself, her low but broad forehead crowned with a shining mass of long black hair that fell in heavy tresses over her shoulders, and made her pale olive complexion look paler still by the contrast of its coal-black hue.

Almayer attacked his rice greedily, but after a few mouthfuls he paused, spoon in hand, and looked at his daughter curiously.

'Did you hear a boat pass about half an hour ago Nina?' he asked.

The girl gave him a quick glance, and moving away from the light stood with her back to the table.

'No,' she said, slowly.

'There was a boat. At last! Dain himself; and he went on to Lakamba. I know it, for he told me so. I spoke to him, but he would not come here tonight. Will come tomorrow, he said.'

He swallowed another spoonful, then said –

'I am almost happy tonight, Nina. I can see the end of a long road, and it leads us away from this miserable swamp. We shall soon get away from here, I and you, my dear little girl, and then –'

He rose from the table and stood looking fixedly before him as if contemplating some enchanting vision.

'And then,' he went on, 'we shall be happy, you and I. Live rich and respected far from here, and forget this life, and all this struggle, and all this misery!'

He approached his daughter and passed his hand caressingly over her hair.

'It is bad to have to trust a Malay,' he said, 'but I must own that this Dain is a perfect gentleman – a perfect gentleman,' he repeated.

'Did you ask him to come here, father?' inquired Nina, not looking at him.

'Well, of course. We shall start on the day after tomorrow,' said Almayer, joyously. 'We must not lose any time. Are you glad, little girl?'

She was nearly as tall as himself, but he liked to recall the time when she was little and they were all in all to each other.

'I am glad,' she said, very low.

'Of course,' said Almayer, vivaciously, 'you cannot imagine what is before you.* I myself have not been to Europe, but I have heard my mother talk so often that I seem to know all about it. We shall live a – a glorious life. You shall see.'

Again he stood silent by his daughter's side looking at that enchanting vision. After a while he shook his clenched hand towards the sleeping settlement.

'Ah! my friend Abdulla,' he cried, 'we shall see who will have the best of it after all these years!'

He looked up the river and remarked calmly:

'Another thunderstorm. Well! No thunder will keep me awake tonight, I know! Goodnight, little girl,' he whispered, tenderly kissing her cheek. 'You do not seem to be very happy tonight, but tomorrow you will show a brighter face. Eh?'

Nina had listened to her father with her face unmoved, with her half-closed eyes still gazing into the night now made more intense by a heavy thunder-cloud that had crept down from the hills blotting out the stars, merging sky, forest, and river into one mass of almost palpable blackness. The faint breeze had died out, but the distant rumble of thunder and pale flashes of lightning gave warning of the approaching storm. With a sigh the girl turned towards the table.

Almayer was in his hammock now, already half asleep.

'Take the lamp, Nina,' he muttered, drowsily. 'This place is full of mosquitoes. Go to sleep, daughter.'

But Nina put the lamp out and turned back again towards the balustrade of the verandah, standing with her arm round the wooden support and looking eagerly towards the Pantai reach. And motionless there in the oppressive calm of the tropical night she could see at each flash of lightning the forest lining both banks up the river, bending before the furious blast of the coming tempest, the upper reach of the river whipped into white foam by the wind, and the black clouds torn into fantastic shapes trailing low over the swaying trees. Round her all was as yet stillness and peace, but she could hear afar off the roar of the wind, the hiss of heavy rain, the wash of the waves on the tormented river. It came nearer and nearer, with loud thunder-claps and long flashes of vivid lightning, followed by short periods of appalling blackness. When the storm reached the low point dividing the river, the house shook in the wind, and the rain pattered loudly on the palm-leaf roof, the thunder spoke in one prolonged roll, and the incessant lightning disclosed a turmoil of leaping waters, driving logs, and the big trees bending before a brutal and merciless force.*

Undisturbed by the nightly event of the rainy monsoon, the

father slept quietly, oblivious alike of his hopes, his misfortunes, his friends, and his enemies; and the daughter stood motionless, at each flash of lightning eagerly scanning the broad river with a steady and anxious gaze.

CHAPTER 2

When, in compliance with Lingard's abrupt demand, Almayer consented to wed the Malay girl, no one knew that on the day when the interesting young convert had lost all her natural relations and found a white father, she had been fighting desperately like the rest of them on board the prau, and was only prevented from leaping overboard, like the few other survivors, by a severe wound in the leg. There, on the fore-deck* of the prau, old Lingard found her under a heap of dead and dying pirates, and had her carried on the poop* of the *Flash* before the Malay craft was set on fire and sent adrift. She was conscious, and in the great peace and stillness of the tropical evening succeeding the turmoil of the battle, she watched all she held dear on earth after her own savage manner, drift away into the gloom in a great roar of flame and smoke. She lay there unheeding the careful hands attending to her wound, silent and absorbed in gazing at the funeral pile of those brave men she had so much admired and so well helped in their contest with the redoubtable 'Rajah Laut'.

The light night breeze fanned the brig gently to the southward, and the great blaze of light got smaller and smaller till it twinkled only on the horizon like a setting star. It set: the heavy canopy of smoke reflected the glare of hidden flames for a short time and then disappeared also.

She realised that with this vanishing gleam her old life departed too. Thenceforth there was slavery in the far countries, amongst strangers, in unknown and perhaps terrible surroundings. Being fourteen years old, she realised her position and came to that conclusion, the only one possible to a Malay girl, soon ripened under a tropical sun, and not unaware of her personal charms, of which she heard many a young brave warrior of her father's crew express an appreciative admiration.* There was in her the dread of the unknown; otherwise she accepted her position calmly, after the manner of her people, and even considered it quite natural; for was she not a daughter of warriors, conquered in battle, and did she not belong rightfully to the victorious Rajah? Even the evident kindness of the terrible old man must spring, she thought, from admiration for his captive, and the flattered vanity eased for her the pangs of sorrow after such an awful calamity. Perhaps had she known of the high walls, the quiet gardens, and the silent nuns of the Samarang* convent, where her destiny was leading her, she would have sought death in her dread and hate of such a restraint. But in imagination she pictured to herself the usual life of a Malay girl – the usual succession of heavy work and fierce love, of intrigues, gold ornaments, of domestic drudgery, and of that great but occult influence which is one of the few rights of half-savage womankind. But her destiny in the rough hands of the old sea-dog, acting under unreasoning impulses of the heart, took a strange and to her a terrible shape. She bore it all – the restraint and the teaching and the new faith – with calm submission, concealing her hate and contempt for all that new life. She learned the language very easily, yet understood but little of the new faith the good sisters taught her, assimilating quickly only the superstitious elements of the religion. She called Lingard father, gently and caressingly, at each of his short and noisy visits, under the clear impression that he was a great and dangerous power it was good to propitiate. Was he not now her master? And during those long four years she nourished a hope of finding favour in his eyes and ultimately becoming his wife, counsellor, and guide.

Those dreams of the future were dispelled by the Rajah Laut's 'fiat',* which made Almayer's fortune, as that young man fondly hoped. And dressed in the hateful finery of Europe, the centre of an interested circle of Batavian society,* the young convert stood before the altar with an unknown and sulky-looking white man. For Almayer was uneasy, a little disgusted, and greatly inclined to run away. A judicious fear of the adopted father-in-law and a just regard for his own material welfare prevented him from making a scandal; yet, while swearing fidelity, he was concocting plans for getting rid of the pretty Malay girl in a more or less distant future. She, however, had retained enough of conventual teaching to understand well that according to white men's laws she was going to be Almayer's companion and not his slave, and promised to herself to act accordingly.

So when the *Flash* freighted with materials for building a new house left the harbour of Batavia, taking away the young couple into the unknown Borneo, she did not carry on her deck so much love and happiness as old Lingard was wont to boast of before his casual friends in the verandahs of various hotels. The old seaman himself was perfectly happy. Now he had done his duty by the girl. 'You know I made her an orphan,' he often concluded solemnly, when talking about his own affairs to a scratch audience of shore loafers – as it was his habit to do. And the approbative shouts of his half-intoxicated auditors filled his simple soul with delight and pride. 'I carry everything right through,' was another of his sayings, and in pursuance of that principle he pushed the building of house and godowns on the Pantai River with feverish haste. The house for the young couple; the godowns for the big trade Almayer was going to develop while he (Lingard) would be able to give himself up to some mysterious work which was only spoken of in hints, but was understood to relate to gold and diamonds in the interior of the island. Almayer was impatient too. Had he known what was before him he might not have been so eager and full of hope as he stood watching the last canoe of the Lingard expedition disappear in the bend up the river. When, turning round, he beheld the pretty little house, the big godowns built neatly by an army of Chinese carpenters, the new jetty round which were clustered the trading canoes, he felt a sudden elation in the thought that the world was his.

But the world had to be conquered first, and its conquest was not so easy as he thought. He was very soon made to understand that he was not wanted in that corner of it where old Lingard and his own weak will placed him, in the midst of unscrupulous intrigues and of a fierce trade competition. The Arabs had found out the river,* had established a trading post in Sambir, and where they traded they would be masters and suffer no rival. Lingard returned unsuccessful from his first expedition, and departed again spending all the profits of the legitimate trade on his mysterious journeys. Almayer struggled with the difficulties of his position, friendless and unaided, save for the protection given to him for Lingard's sake by the old Rajah, the predecessor of Lakamba. Lakamba himself, then living as a private individual on a rice clearing, seven miles* down the river, exercised all his influence towards the help of the white man's enemies, plotting against the old Rajah and Almayer with a certainty of combination, pointing clearly to a profound knowledge of their most secret affairs. Outwardly friendly, his portly form was often to be seen on Almayer's verandah; his green turban and gold-embroidered jacket shone in the front rank of the decorous throng of Malays coming to greet Lingard on his returns from the interior; his salaams* were of the lowest, and his handshakings of the heartiest, when welcoming the old trader. But his small eyes took in the signs of the times, and he departed from those interviews with a satisfied and furtive smile to hold long consultations with his friend and ally, Syed* Abdulla, the chief of the Arab trading post, a man of great wealth and of great influence in the islands.

It was currently believed at that time in the settlement that Lakamba's visits to Almayer's house were not limited to those official interviews. Often on moonlight nights the belated fishermen of Sambir saw a small canoe shooting out from the narrow creek at the back of the white man's house, and the solitary occupant* paddle cautiously down the river in the deep shadows of the bank; and those events, duly reported, were discussed round the evening fires far into the night with the cynicism of expression common to aristocratic Malays, and with a malicious pleasure in the domestic misfortunes of the Orang Blanda – the hated Dutchman.* Almayer went on struggling desperately, but with a feebleness of purpose depriving him of all chance of success against men so unscrupulous and resolute as his rivals the Arabs. The trade fell away from the large godowns, and the godowns themselves rotted piecemeal. The old man's banker, Hudig of Macassar, failed,* and with this went the whole available capital. The profits of past years had been swallowed up in Lingard's exploring craze. Lingard was in the interior – perhaps dead – at all events giving no sign of life. Almayer stood alone in the midst of those adverse circumstances, deriving only a little comfort from the companionship of his little daughter, born two years after the marriage, and at the time some six years old. His wife had soon commenced to treat him with a savage contempt expressed by sulky silence, only occasionally varied by a flood of savage invective. He felt she hated him, and saw her jealous eyes watching himself and the child with almost an expression of hate. She was jealous of the little girl's evident preference for the father, and Almayer felt he was not safe with that woman in the house. While she was burning the furniture, and tearing down the pretty curtains in her unreasoning hate of those signs of civilisation, Almayer, cowed by these outbursts of savage nature, meditated in silence on the best way of getting rid of her. He thought of everything; even planned murder in an undecided and feeble sort of way, but dared do nothing – expecting every day the return of Lingard with news of some immense good fortune. He returned indeed, but aged, ill, a ghost of his former self, with the fire of fever burning in his sunken eyes, almost the only survivor of the numerous expedition. But he was successful at last! Untold riches were in his grasp; he wanted more money – only a little more to realise a dream of fabulous fortune. And Hudig had failed! Almayer scraped all he could together, but the old man wanted more. If Almayer could not get it he would go to Singapore – to Europe even, but before all to Singapore; and he would take the little Nina with him. The child must be brought up decently. He had good friends in Singapore who would take care of her and have her taught properly. All would be well, and that girl, upon whom the old seaman seemed to have transferred all his former affection for the mother, would be the richest woman in the East – in the world even. So old Lingard shouted, pacing the verandah with his heavy quarter-deck* step, gesticulating with a smouldering cheroot; ragged, dishevelled, enthusiastic; and Almayer, sitting huddled up on a pile of mats, thought with dread of the separation with the only human being he loved – with greater dread still, perhaps, of the scene with his wife, the savage tigress deprived of her young. She will poison me, thought the poor wretch, well aware of that easy and final manner of solving the social, political, or family problems in Malay life.

To his great surprise she took the news very quietly, giving only him and Lingard a furtive glance, and saying not a word. This, however, did not prevent her the next day from jumping into the river and swimming after the boat in which Lingard was carrying away the nurse with the screaming child. Almayer had to give chase with his whale-boat* and drag her in by the hair in the midst of cries and curses enough to make heaven fall. Yet after two days spent in wailing, she returned to her former mode of life, chewing betel-nut, and sitting all day amongst her women in stupefied idleness. She aged very rapidly after that, and only roused herself from her apathy to acknowledge by a scathing remark or an insulting exclamation the accidental presence of her husband. He had built for her a riverside hut in the compound where she dwelt in perfect seclusion. Lakamba's visits had ceased when, by a convenient decree of Providence and the help of a little scientific manipulation, the old ruler of Sambir departed this life. Lakamba reigned in his stead now, having been well served by his Arab friends with the Dutch authorities. Syed Abdulla was the great man and trader of the Pantai. Almayer lay ruined and helpless under the close-meshed net of their intrigues, owing his life only to his supposed knowledge of Lingard's valuable secret. Lingard had disappeared. He wrote once from Singapore saying the child was well, and under the care of a Mrs Vinck,* and that he himself was going to Europe to raise money for the great enterprise. 'He was coming back soon. There would be no difficulties,' he wrote; 'people would rush in with their money.' Evidently they did not, for there was only one letter more from him saying he was ill, had found no relation living, but little else besides. Then came a complete silence. Europe had swallowed up the Rajah Laut* apparently, and Almayer looked vainly westward for a ray of light out of the gloom of his shattered hopes. Years passed, and the rare letters from Mrs Vinck, later on from the girl herself, were the only thing to be looked to to make life bearable amongst the triumphant savagery of the river. Almayer lived now alone, having even ceased to visit his debtors who would not pay, sure of Lakamba's protection. The faithful Sumatrese* Ali cooked his rice and made his coffee, for he dared not trust any one else, and least of all his wife. He killed time wandering sadly in the overgrown paths round the house, visiting the ruined godowns where a few brass guns covered with verdigris* and only a few broken cases of mouldering Manchester goods reminded him of the good early times when all this was full of life and merchandise, and he overlooked a busy scene on the river bank, his little daughter by his side. Now the up-country canoes glided past the little rotten wharf of Lingard and Co., to paddle up the Pantai branch, and cluster round the new jetty belonging to Abdulla. Not that they loved Abdulla, but they dared not trade with the man whose star had set. Had they done so they knew there was no mercy to be expected from Arab or Rajah; no rice to be got on credit in the times of scarcity from either; and Almayer could not help them, having at times hardly enough for himself. Almayer, in his isolation and despair, often envied his near neighbour the Chinaman, Jim-Eng, whom he could see stretched on a pile of cool mats, a wooden pillow under his head, an opium pipe in his nerveless fingers. He did not seek, however, consolation in opium – perhaps it was too expensive – perhaps his white man's pride saved him from that degradation; but most likely it was the thought of his little daughter in the far-off Straits Settlements.* He heard from her oftener since Abdulla bought a steamer, which ran now between Singapore and the Pantai settlement every three months or so. Almayer felt himself nearer his daughter. He longed to see her, and planned a voyage to Singapore, but put off his departure from year to year, always expecting some favourable turn of fortune. He did not want to meet her with empty hands and with no words of hope on his lips. He could not take her back into that savage life to which he was condemned himself. He was also a little afraid of her. What would she think of him? He reckoned the years. A grown woman. A civilised woman, young and hopeful; while he felt old and hopeless, and very much like those savages round him. He asked himself what was going to be her future. He could not answer that question yet, and he dared not face her. And yet he longed after her. He hesitated for years.

His hesitation was put an end to by Nina's unexpected appearance in Sambir. She arrived in the steamer under the captain's care. Almayer beheld her with surprise not unmixed with wonder. During those ten years the child had changed into a woman, black-haired, olive-skinned, tall, and beautiful, with great sad eyes, where the startled expression common to Malay womankind was modified by a thoughtful tinge inherited from her European ancestry. Almayer thought with dismay of the meeting of his wife and daughter, of what this grave girl in

European clothes would think of her betel-nut chewing mother, squatting in a dark hut, disorderly, half naked, and sulky. He also feared an outbreak of temper on the part of that pest of a woman he had hitherto managed to keep tolerably quiet, thereby saving the remnants of his dilapidated furniture. And he stood there before the closed door of the hut in the blazing sunshine listening to the murmur of voices, wondering what went on inside, wherefrom all the servant-maids had been expelled at the beginning of the interview, and now stood clustered by the palings with half-covered faces in a chatter of curious speculation. He forgot himself there trying to catch a stray word through the bamboo walls, till the captain of the steamer, who had walked up with the girl, fearing a sunstroke, took him under the arm and led him into the shade of his own verandah where Nina's trunk stood already, having been landed by the steamer's men. As soon as Captain Ford* had his glass before him and his cheroot lighted, Almayer asked for the explanation of his daughter's unexpected arrival. Ford said little beyond generalising in vague but violent terms upon the foolishness of women in general, and of Mrs Vinck in particular.

'You know, Kaspar,' said he, in conclusion, to the excited Almayer, 'it is deucedly awkward to have a half-caste girl in the house. There's such a lot of fools about. There was that young fellow from the bank who used to ride to the Vinck bungalow early and late. That old woman thought it was for that Emma of hers. When she found out what he wanted exactly, there was a row, I can tell you. She would not have Nina – not an hour longer – in the house. Fact is, I heard of this affair and took the girl to my wife. My wife is a pretty good woman – as women go – and upon my word we would have kept the girl for you, only she would not stay. Now, then! Don't flare up, Kaspar. Sit still. What can you do? It is better so. Let her stay with you. She was never happy over there. Those two Vinck girls are no better than dressed-up monkeys. They slighted her. You can't make her white. It's no use you swearing at me. You can't. She is a good girl for all that, but she would not tell my wife anything. If you want to know, ask her yourself; but if I was you I would leave her alone. You are welcome to her passage money, old fellow, if you are short now.' And the skipper, throwing away his cigar, walked off to 'wake them up on board', as he expressed it.

Almayer vainly expected to hear of the cause of his daughter's return from his daughter's lips. Not that day, not on any other day did she ever allude to her Singapore life. He did not care to ask, awed by the calm impassiveness of her face, by those solemn eyes looking past him on the great, still forests sleeping in majestic repose to the murmur of the broad river. He accepted the situation, happy in the gentle and protecting affection the girl showed him, fitfully enough, for she had, as he called it, her bad days when she used to visit her mother and remain long hours in the riverside hut, coming out as inscrutable as ever, but with a contemptuous look and a short word ready to answer any of his speeches. He got used even to that, and on those days kept quiet, although greatly alarmed by his wife's influence upon the girl. Otherwise Nina adapted herself wonderfully to the circumstances of a half-savage and miserable life. She accepted without question or apparent disgust the neglect, the decay, the poverty of the household, the absence of furniture, and the preponderance of rice diet on the family table. She lived with Almayer in the little house (now sadly decaying) built originally by Lingard for the young couple. The Malays eagerly discussed her arrival. There were at the beginning crowded levées* of Malay women with their children, seeking eagerly after 'Ubat'* for all the ills of the flesh from the young Mem Putih.* In the cool of the evening grave Arabs in long white shirts and yellow sleeveless jackets walked slowly on the dusty path by the riverside towards Almayer's gate, and made solemn calls upon that Unbeliever* under shallow pretences of business, only to get a glimpse of the young girl in a highly decorous manner. Even Lakamba came out of his stockade in a great pomp of war canoes and red umbrellas, and landed on the rotten little jetty of Lingard and Co. He came, he said, to buy a couple of brass guns as a present to his friend the chief of Sambir Dyaks;* and while Almayer, suspicious but polite, busied himself in unearthing the old popguns in the godowns, the Rajah sat on an armchair in the verandah, surrounded by his respectful retinue waiting in vain for Nina's appearance. She was in one of her bad days, and remained in her mother's hut watching with her the ceremonious proceedings on the verandah. The Rajah departed, baffled but courteous, and soon Almayer began to reap the benefit of improved relations with the ruler in the shape of the recovery of some debts, paid to him with many apologies and many a low salaam by debtors till then considered hopelessly insolvent. Under these improving circumstances Almayer brightened up a little. All was not lost perhaps. Those Arabs and Malays saw at last that he was a man of some ability, he thought. And he began, after his manner, to plan great things, to dream of great fortunes for himself and Nina. Especially for Nina! Under these vivifying impulses he asked Captain Ford to write to his friends in England making inquiries after Lingard. Was he alive or dead? If dead, had he left any papers, documents; any indications or hints as to his great enterprise? Meantime he had found amongst the rubbish in one of the empty rooms a notebook belonging to the old adventurer. He studied the crabbed handwriting of its pages and often grew meditative over it. Other things also woke him up from his apathy. The stir made in the whole of the island by the establishment of the British Borneo Company* affected even the sluggish flow of the Pantai life. Great changes were expected; annexation was talked of; the Arabs grew civil. Almayer began building his new house for the use of the future engineers, agents, or settlers of the new Company. He spent every available guilder on it with a confiding heart. One thing only disturbed his happiness: his wife came out of her seclusion, importing her green jacket, scant sarongs,* shrill voice, and witch-like appearance, into his quiet life in the small bungalow. And his daughter seemed to accept that savage intrusion into their daily existence with wonderful equanimity. He did not like it, but dared say nothing.

CHAPTER 3

The deliberations conducted in London have a far-reaching importance, and so the decision issued from the fog-veiled offices of the Borneo Company darkened for Almayer the brilliant sunshine of the Tropics, and added another drop of bitterness to the cup of his disenchantments. The claim to that part of the East Coast was abandoned, leaving the Pantai river under the nominal power of Holland.* In Sambir there was joy and excitement. The slaves were hurried out of sight* into the forest and jungle, and the flags were run up to tall poles in the Rajah's compound in expectation of a visit from Dutch man-of-war boats.

The frigate* remained anchored outside the mouth of the river, and the boats came up in tow of the steam launch, threading their way cautiously amongst a crowd of canoes filled with gaily dressed Malays. The officer in command listened gravely to the loyal speeches of Lakamba, returned the salaams of Abdulla, and assured those gentlemen in choice Malay of the great Rajah's* – down in Batavia – friendship and goodwill towards the ruler and inhabitants of this model state of Sambir.

Almayer from his verandah watched across the river the festive proceedings, heard the report of brass guns saluting the new flag presented to Lakamba, and the deep murmur of the crowd of spectators surging round the stockade. The smoke of the firing rose in white clouds on the green background of the forests, and he could not help comparing his own fleeting hopes to the rapidly disappearing vapour. He was by no means patriotically elated by the event, yet he had to force himself into a gracious behaviour when, the official reception being over, the naval officers of the Commission crossed the river to pay a visit to the solitary white man of whom they had heard, no doubt wishing also to catch a glimpse of his daughter. In that they were disappointed, Nina refusing to show herself; but they seemed easily consoled by the gin and cheroots set before them by the hospitable Almayer; and sprawling comfortably on the lame armchairs* under the shade of the verandah, while the blazing sunshine outside seemed to set the great river simmering in the heat, they filled the little bungalow with the unusual sounds of European languages, with noise and laughter produced by naval witticisms at the expense of the fat Lakamba whom they had been complimenting so much that very morning. The younger men in an access of good fellowship made their host talk, and Almayer, excited by the sight of European faces, by the sound of European voices, opened his heart before the sympathising strangers, unaware of the amusement the recital of his many misfortunes caused to those future admirals. They drank his health, wished him many big diamonds and a mountain of gold, expressed even an envy of the high destinies awaiting him yet. Encouraged by so much friendliness, the grey-headed and foolish dreamer invited his guests to visit his new house. They went there through the long grass in a straggling procession while their boats were got ready for the return down the river in the cool of the evening. And in the great empty rooms where the tepid wind entering through the sashless windows whirled gently the dried leaves and the dust of many days of neglect, Almayer in his white jacket and flowered sarong, surrounded by a circle of glittering uniforms, stamped his foot to show the solidity of the neatly-fitting floors and expatiated upon the beauties and convenience of the building. They listened and assented, amazed by the wonderful simplicity and the foolish hopefulness of the man, till Almayer, carried away by his excitement, disclosed his regret at the non-arrival of the English, 'who knew how to develop a rich country', as he expressed it. There was a general laugh amongst the Dutch officers at that unsophisticated statement, and a move was made towards the boats; but when Almayer, stepping cautiously on the rotten boards of the Lingard jetty, tried to approach the chief of the Commission with some timid hints anent* the protection required by the Dutch subject against the wily Arabs, that salt-water diplomat told him significantly that the Arabs were better subjects than Hollanders who dealt illegally in gunpowder with the Malays. The innocent Almayer recognised there at once the oily tongue of Abdulla and the solemn persuasiveness of Lakamba, but ere he had time to frame an indignant protest the steam launch and the string of boats moved rapidly down the river leaving him on the jetty, standing open-mouthed in his surprise and anger. There are thirty miles of river from Sambir to the gem-like islands of the estuary where the frigate was awaiting the return of the boats. The moon rose long before the boats had traversed half that distance, and the black forest sleeping peacefully under her cold rays woke up that night to the ringing laughter in the small flotilla* provoked by some reminiscence of Almayer's lamentable narrative. Salt-water jests at the poor man's expense were passed from boat to boat, the non-appearance of his daughter was commented upon with severe displeasure, and the half-finished house built for the reception of Englishmen received on that joyous night the name of 'Almayer's Folly' by the unanimous vote of the lighthearted seamen.

For many weeks after this visit life in Sambir resumed its even and uneventful flow. Each day's sun shooting its morning rays above the tree-tops lit up the usual scene of daily activity. Nina walking on the path that formed the only street in the settlement saw the accustomed sight of men lolling on the shady side of the houses, on the high platforms; of women busily engaged in husking the daily rice; of naked brown children racing along the shady and narrow paths leading to the clearings. Jim-Eng, strolling before his house, greeted her with a friendly nod before climbing up indoors to seek his beloved opium pipe. The elder children clustered round her, daring from long acquaintance, pulling the skirts of her white robe with their dark fingers, and showing their brilliant teeth in expectation of a shower of glass beads. She greeted them with a quiet smile, but always had a few friendly words for a Siamese girl, a slave owned by Bulangi, whose numerous wives were said to be of a violent temper. Well-founded rumour said also that the domestic squabbles of that industrious cultivator ended generally in a combined assault of all his wives upon the Siamese slave. The girl herself never complained – perhaps from dictates of prudence, but more likely through the strange, resigned apathy of half-savage womankind. From early morning she was to be seen on the paths amongst the houses – by the riverside or on the jetties, the tray of pastry, it was her mission to sell, skilfully balanced on her head. During the great heat of the day she usually sought refuge in Almayer's campong, often finding shelter in a shady corner of the verandah, where she squatted with her tray before her, when invited by Nina. For 'Mem Putih' she had always a smile, but the presence of Mrs Almayer, the very sound of her shrill voice, was the signal for a hurried departure.

To this girl Nina often spoke; the other inhabitants of Sambir seldom or never heard the sound of her voice. They got used to the silent figure moving in their midst calm and white-robed, a being from another world and incomprehensible to them. Yet Nina's life for all her outward composure, for all the seeming detachment from the things and people surrounding her, was far from quiet, in consequence of Mrs Almayer being much too active for the happiness and even safety of the household. She had resumed some intercourse with Lakamba, not personally, it is true (for the dignity of that potentate* kept him inside his stockade), but through the agency of that potentate's prime minister, harbour master, financial adviser, and general factotum.* That gentleman – of Sulu origin – was certainly endowed with statesmanlike qualities, although he was totally devoid of personal charms. In truth he was perfectly repulsive, possessing only one eye and a pock-marked face, with nose and lips horribly disfigured by the small-pox. This unengaging individual often strolled into Almayer's garden in unofficial costume, composed of a piece of pink calico round his waist. There at the back of the house, squatting on his heels on scattered embers, in close proximity to the great iron boiler, where the family daily rice was being cooked by the women under Mrs Almayer's superintendence, did that astute negotiator carry on long conversations in Sulu language with Almayer's wife. What the subject of their discourses was might have been guessed from the subsequent domestic scenes by Almayer's hearthstone.

Of late Almayer had taken to excursions up the river. In a small canoe with two paddlers and the faithful Ali for a steersman he would disappear for a few days at a time. All his movements were no doubt closely watched by Lakamba and Abdulla, for the man once in the confidence of Rajah Laut was supposed to be in possession of valuable secrets. The coast population of Borneo believes implicitly in diamonds of fabulous value, in gold mines of enormous richness in the interior. And all those imaginings are heightened by the difficulty of penetrating far inland, especially on the north-east coast, where the Malays and the river tribes of Dyaks or Head-hunters* are eternally quarrelling. It is true enough that some gold reaches the coast in the hands of those Dyaks when, during short periods of truce in the desultory warfare, they visit the coast settlements of Malays. And so the wildest exaggerations are built up and added to on the slight basis of that fact.

Almayer in his quality of* white man – as Lingard before him – had somewhat better relations with the up-river tribes. Yet even his excursions were not without danger, and his returns were eagerly looked for by the impatient Lakamba. But every time the Rajah was disappointed. Vain were the conferences by the rice-pot of his factotum Babalatchi* with the white man's wife. The white man himself was impenetrable – impenetrable to persuasion, coaxing, abuse; to soft words and shrill revilings; to desperate beseechings or murderous threats; for Mrs Almayer, in her extreme desire to persuade her husband into an alliance with Lakamba, played upon the whole gamut of passion. With her soiled robe wound tightly under the armpits across her lean bosom, her scant grayish hair tumbled in disorder over her projecting cheek-bones, in suppliant attitude, she depicted with shrill volubility the advantages of close union with a man so good and so fair dealing.

'Why don't you go to the Rajah?' she screamed. 'Why do you go back to those Dyaks in the great forest? They should be killed. You cannot kill them, you cannot; but our Rajah's men are brave! You tell the Rajah where the old white man's treasure is. Our Rajah is good! He is our very grandfather, Datu Besar!* He will kill those wretched Dyaks, and you shall have half the treasure. Oh, Kaspar, tell where the treasure is! Tell me! Tell me out of the old man's surat* where you read so often at night.'

On those occasions Almayer sat with rounded shoulders bending to the blast of this domestic tempest, accentuating only each pause in the torrent of his wife's eloquence by an angry growl, 'There is no treasure! Go away, woman!' Exasperated by the sight of his patiently bent back, she would at last walk round so as to face him across the table, and clasping her robe with one hand she stretched the other lean arm and claw-like hand to emphasise, in a passion of anger and contempt, the rapid rush of scathing remarks and bitter cursings heaped on the head of the man unworthy to associate with brave Malay chiefs. It ended generally by Almayer rising slowly, his long pipe in hand, his face set into a look of inward pain, and walking away in silence. He descended the steps and plunged into the long grass on his way to the solitude of his new house, dragging his feet in a state of physical collapse from disgust and fear before that fury. She followed to the head of the steps, and sent the shafts of indiscriminate abuse after the retreating form. And each of those scenes was concluded by a piercing shriek, reaching him far away. 'You know, Kaspar, I am your wife! your own Christian wife after your own Blanda law!' For she knew that this was the bitterest thing of all; the greatest regret of that man's life.

All these scenes Nina witnessed unmoved. She might have been deaf, dumb, without any feeling as far as any expression of opinion went. Yet oft when her father had sought the refuge of the great dusty rooms of 'Almayer's Folly', and her mother, exhausted by rhetorical efforts, squatted wearily on her heels with her back against the leg of the table, Nina would approach her curiously, guarding her skirts from betel juice besprinkling the floor, and gaze down upon her as one might look into the quiescent crater of a volcano after a destructive eruption. Mrs Almayer's thoughts, after these scenes, were usually turned into a channel of childhood reminiscences, and she gave them utterance in a kind of monotonous recitative – slightly disconnected, but generally describing the glories of the Sultan of Sulu, his great splendour, his power, his great prowess; the fear which benumbed the hearts of white men at the sight of his swift piratical praus. And these muttered statements of her grandfather's might were mixed up with bits of later recollections, where the great fight with the 'White Devil's' brig and the convent life in Samarang occupied the principal place. At that point she usually dropped the thread of her narrative, and pulling out the little brass cross, always suspended round her neck, she contemplated it with superstitious awe. That superstitious feeling connected with some vague talismanic properties of the little bit of metal, and the still more hazy but terrible notion of some bad Djinns* and horrible torments invented, as she thought, for her especial punishment by the good Mother Superior in case of the loss of the above charm, were Mrs

Almayer's only theological luggage for the stormy road of life. Mrs Almayer had at least something tangible to cling to, but Nina, brought up under the Protestant wing of the proper Mrs Vinck, had not even a little piece of brass to remind her of past teaching. And listening to the recital of those savage glories, those barbarous fights and savage feasting, to the story of deeds valorous, albeit somewhat bloodthirsty, where men of her mother's race shone far above the Orang Blanda, she felt herself irresistibly fascinated, and saw with vague surprise the narrow mantle of civilised morality, in which good-meaning people had wrapped her young soul, fall away and leave her shivering and helpless as if on the edge of some deep and unknown abyss. Strangest of all, this abyss did not frighten her when she was under the influence of the witch-like being she called her mother. She seemed to have forgotten in civilised surroundings her life before the time when Lingard had, so to speak, kidnapped her from Brow.* Since then she had had Christian teaching, social education, and a good glimpse of civilised life. Unfortunately her teachers did not understand her nature, and the education ended in a scene of humiliation, in an outburst of contempt from white people for her mixed blood. She had tasted the whole bitterness of it and remembered distinctly that the virtuous Mrs Vinck's indignation was not so much directed against the young man from the bank as against the innocent cause of that young man's infatuation. And there was also no doubt in her mind that the principal cause of Mrs Vinck's indignation was the thought that such a thing should happen in a white nest, where her snow-white doves, the two Misses Vinck, had just returned from Europe, to find shelter under the maternal wing, and there await the coming of irreproachable men of their destiny. Not even the thought of the money so painfully scraped together by Almayer, and so punctually sent for Nina's expenses, could dissuade Mrs Vinck from her virtuous resolve. Nina was sent away, and in truth the girl herself wanted to go, although a little frightened by the impending change.* And now she had lived on the river for three years with a savage mother and a father walking about amongst pitfalls, with his head in the clouds, weak, irresolute, and unhappy. She had lived a life devoid of all the decencies of civilisation, in miserable domestic conditions; she had breathed in the atmosphere of sordid plottings for gain, of the no less disgusting intrigues and crimes for lust or money; and those things, together with the domestic quarrels, were the only events of her three years' existence. She did not die from despair and disgust the first month, as she expected and almost hoped for. On the contrary, at the end of half a year it had seemed to her that she had known no other life. Her young mind having been unskilfully permitted to glance at better things, and then thrown back again into the hopeless quagmire of barbarism, full of strong and uncontrolled passions, had lost the power to discriminate. It seemed to Nina that there was no change and no difference. Whether they traded in brick godowns or on the muddy river bank; whether they reached after much or little; whether they made love under the shadows of the great trees or in the shadow of the cathedral on the Singapore promenade;* whether they plotted for their own ends under the protection of laws and according to the rules of Christian conduct, or whether they sought the gratification of their desires with the savage cunning and the unrestrained fierceness of natures as innocent of culture as their own immense and gloomy forests, Nina saw only the same manifestations of love and hate and of sordid greed chasing the uncertain dollar in all its multifarious and vanishing shapes. To her resolute nature, however, after all these years, the savage and uncompromising sincerity of purpose shown by her Malay kinsmen seemed at last preferable to the sleek hypocrisy, to the polite disguises, to the virtuous pretences of such white people as she had had the misfortune to come in contact with. After all it was her life; it was going to be her life, and so thinking she fell more and more under the influence of her mother. Seeking, in her ignorance, a better side to that life, she listened with avidity to the old woman's tales of the departed glories of the Rajahs, from whose race she had sprung, and she became gradually more indifferent, more contemptuous of the white side of her descent represented by a feeble and traditionless father.

Almayer's difficulties were by no means diminished by the girl's presence in Sambir. The stir caused by her arrival had died out, it is true, and Lakamba had not renewed his visits; but about a year after the departure of the man-of-war boats the nephew of Abdulla, Syed Reshid, returned from his pilgrimage to Mecca, rejoicing in a green jacket and the proud title of

Hadji.* There was a great letting off of rockets on board the steamer which brought him in, and a great beating of drums all night in Abdulla's compound, while the feast of welcome was prolonged far into the small hours of the morning. Reshid was the favourite nephew and heir of Abdulla, and that loving uncle, meeting Almayer one day by the riverside, stopped politely to exchange civilities and to ask solemnly for an interview. Almayer suspected some attempt at a swindle, or at any rate something unpleasant, but of course consented with a great show of rejoicing. Accordingly the next evening, after sunset, Abdulla came, accompanied by several other greybeards* and by his nephew. That young man – of a very rakish and dissipated appearance – affected the greatest indifference as to the whole of the proceedings. When the torch-bearers had grouped themselves below the steps, and the visitors had seated themselves on various lame chairs, Reshid stood apart in the shadow, examining his aristocratically small hands with great attention. Almayer, surprised by the great solemnity of his visitors, perched himself on the corner of the table with a characteristic want of dignity quickly noted by the Arabs with grave disapproval. But Abdulla spoke now, looking straight past Almayer at the red curtain hanging in the doorway, where a slight tremor disclosed the presence of women on the other side. He began by neatly complimenting Almayer upon the long years they had dwelt together in cordial neighbourhood, and called upon Allah to give him many more years to gladden the eyes of his friends by his welcome presence. He made a polite allusion to the great consideration shown him (Almayer) by the Dutch 'Commissie',* and drew thence the flattering inference of Almayer's great importance amongst his own people. He – Abdulla – was also important amongst all the Arabs, and his nephew Reshid would be heir of that social position and of great riches. Now Reshid was a Hadji. He was possessor of several Malay women, went on Abdulla, but it was time he had a favourite wife, the first of the four allowed by the Prophet. And, speaking with well-bred politeness, he explained further to the dumbfounded Almayer that, if he would consent to the alliance of his offspring with that true believer and virtuous man Reshid, she would be the mistress of all the splendours of Reshid's house, and first wife of the first Arab in the Islands, when he – Abdulla – was called to the joys of Paradise by Allah the All-merciful.* 'You know, Tuan,' he said, in conclusion, 'the other women would be her slaves, and Reshid's house is great. From Bombay* he has brought great divans, and costly carpets, and European furniture. There is also a great looking-glass in a frame shining like gold. What could a girl want more?' And while Almayer looked upon him in silent dismay Abdulla spoke in a more confidential tone, waving his attendants away, and finished his speech by pointing out the material advantages of such an alliance, and offering to settle upon Almayer three thousand dollars as a sign of his sincere friendship and the price of the girl.

Poor Almayer was nearly having a fit. Burning with the desire of taking Abdulla by the throat, he had but to think of his helpless position in the midst of lawless men to comprehend the necessity of diplomatic conciliation. He mastered his impulses, and spoke politely and coldly, saying the girl was young and was the apple of his eye. Tuan Reshid, a Faithful and a Hadji, would not want an infidel woman in his harem; and, seeing Abdulla smile sceptically at that last objection, he remained silent, not trusting himself to speak more, not daring to refuse point-blank, nor yet to say anything compromising. Abdulla understood the meaning of that silence, and rose to take leave with a grave salaam. He wished his friend Almayer 'a thousand years', and moved down the steps, helped dutifully by Reshid. The torchbearers shook their torches, scattering a shower of sparks into the river, and the *cortège* moved off, leaving Almayer agitated but greatly relieved by their departure. He dropped into a chair and watched the glimmer of the lights amongst the tree trunks till they disappeared and complete silence succeeded the tramp of feet and the murmur of voices. He did not move till the curtain rustled and Nina came out on the verandah and sat in the rocking-chair, where she used to spend many hours every day. She gave a slight rocking motion to her seat, leaning back with half-closed eyes, her long hair shading her face from the smoky light of the lamp on the table. Almayer looked at her furtively, but the face was as impassible* as ever. She turned her head slightly towards her father, and, speaking, to his great surprise, in English, asked –

'Was that Abdulla here?'

'Yes,' said Almayer – 'just gone.'

'And what did he want, father?'

'He wanted to buy you for Reshid,' answered Almayer, brutally, his anger getting the better of him, and looking at the girl as if in expectation of some outbreak of feeling. But Nina remained apparently unmoved, gazing dreamily into the black night outside.

'Be careful, Nina,' said Almayer, after a short silence and rising from his chair, 'when you go paddling alone into the creeks in your canoe. That Reshid is a violent scoundrel, and there is no saying what he may do. Do you hear me?'

She was standing now, ready to go in, one hand grasping the curtain in the doorway. She turned round, throwing her heavy tresses back by a sudden gesture.

'Do you think he would dare?' she asked, quickly, and then turned again to go in, adding in a lower tone, 'He would not dare. Arabs are all cowards.'

Almayer looked after her, astonished. He did not seek the repose of his hammock. He walked the floor absently, sometimes stopping by the balustrade to think. The lamp went out. The first streak of dawn broke over the forest; Almayer shivered in the damp air. 'I give it up,' he muttered to himself, lying down wearily. 'Damn those women! Well! If the girl did not look as if she wanted to be kidnapped!'*

And he felt a nameless fear creep into his heart, making him shiver again.

CHAPTER 4

That year, towards the breaking up of the south-west monsoon,* disquieting rumours reached Sambir. Captain Ford, coming up to Almayer's house for an evening's chat, brought late numbers of the *Straits Times** giving the news of Acheen war* and of the unsuccessful Dutch expedition. The Nakhodas* of the rare trading praus ascending the river paid visits to Lakamba, discussing with that potentate the unsettled state of affairs, and wagged their heads gravely over the recital of Orang Blanda exaction, severity, and general tyranny, as exemplified in the total stoppage of gunpowder trade and the rigorous visiting of all suspicious craft trading in the straits of Macassar. Even the loyal soul of Lakamba was stirred into a state of inward discontent by the withdrawal of his license for powder and by the abrupt confiscation of one hundred and fifty barrels of that commodity by the gunboat *Princess Amelia*, when, after a hazardous voyage, it had almost reached the mouth of the river. The unpleasant news was given him by Reshid, who, after the unsuccessful issue of his matrimonial projects, had made a long voyage amongst the islands for trading purposes; had bought the powder for his friend, and was overhauled and deprived of it on his return when actually congratulating himself on his acuteness in avoiding detection. Reshid's wrath was principally directed against Almayer, whom he suspected of having notified the Dutch authorities of the desultory warfare carried on by the Arabs and the Rajah with the up-river Dyak tribes.

To Reshid's great surprise the Rajah received his complaints very coldly, and showed no signs of vengeful disposition towards the white man. In truth, Lakamba knew very well that Almayer was perfectly innocent of any meddling in state affairs; and besides, his attitude towards that much persecuted individual was wholly changed in consequence of a reconciliation effected between him and his old enemy by Almayer's newly-found friend, Dain Maroola.

Almayer had now a friend. Shortly after Reshid's departure on his commercial journey, Nina, drifting slowly with the tide in the canoe on her return home after one of her solitary excursions, heard in one of the small creeks a splashing, as if of heavy ropes dropping in the water, and the prolonged song of Malay seamen when some heavy pulling is to be done. Through the thick fringe of bushes hiding the mouth of the creek she saw the tall spars of some European-rigged sailing vessel overtopping the summits of the Nipa palms.* A brig was being hauled out of the small creek into the main stream. The sun had set, and during the short moments of twilight Nina saw the brig, aided by the evening breeze and the flowing tide, head towards Sambir under her set foresail.* The girl turned her canoe out of the main river into one of the many narrow channels amongst the wooded islets, and paddled vigorously over the black and sleepy backwaters towards Sambir. Her canoe brushed the water-palms, skirted the short spaces of muddy bank where sedate alligators looked at her with lazy unconcern, and, just as darkness was setting in, shot out into the broad junction of the two main branches of the river, where the brig was already at anchor with sails furled, yards squared,* and decks seemingly untenanted by any human being. Nina had to cross the river and pass pretty close to the brig in order to reach home on the low promontory between the two branches of the Pantai. Up both branches, in the houses built on the banks and over the water, the lights twinkled already, reflected in the still waters below. The hum of voices, the occasional cry of a child, the rapid and abruptly interrupted roll of a wooden drum, together with some distant hailing in the darkness by the returning fishermen, reached her over the broad expanse of the river. She hesitated a little before crossing, the sight of such an unusual object as an European-rigged vessel causing her some uneasiness, but the river in its wide expansion was dark enough to render a small canoe invisible. She urged her small craft with swift strokes of her paddle, kneeling in the bottom and bending forward to catch any suspicious sound while she steered towards the little jetty of Lingard and Co., to which the strong light of the paraffin lamp shining on the whitewashed verandah of Almayer's bungalow served as a convenient guide. The jetty itself, under the shadow of the bank overgrown by drooping bushes, was hidden in darkness. Before even she could see it she heard the hollow bumping of a large boat against its rotten posts, and heard also the murmur of whispered conversation in that boat whose white paint and great dimensions, faintly visible on nearer approach, made her rightly guess that it belonged to the brig just anchored. Stopping her course by a rapid motion of her paddle, with another swift stroke she sent it whirling away from the wharf and steered for a little rivulet which gave access to the back courtyard of the house. She landed at the muddy head of the creek and made her way towards the house over the trodden grass of the courtyard. To the left, from the cooking shed, shone a red glare through the banana plantation she skirted, and the noise of feminine laughter reached her from there in the silent evening. She rightly judged her mother was not near, laughter and Mrs Almayer not being close neighbours. She must be in the house, thought Nina, as she ran lightly up the inclined plane of shaky planks leading to the back door of the narrow passage dividing the house in two. Outside the doorway, in the black shadow, stood the faithful Ali.

'Who is there?' asked Nina.

'A great Malay man has come,' answered Ali, in a tone of suppressed excitement. 'He is a rich man. There are six men with lances. Real Soldat,* you understand. And his dress is very brave. I have seen his dress. It shines! What jewels! Don't go there, Mem Nina. Tuan said not; but the old Mem is gone. Tuan will be angry. Merciful Allah! what jewels that man has got!'

Nina slipped past the outstretched hand of the slave into the dark passage where, in the crimson glow of the hanging curtain, close by its other end, she could see a small dark form crouching near the wall. Her mother was feasting her eyes and ears with what was taking place on the front verandah, and Nina approached to take her share in the rare pleasure of some novelty. She was met by her mother's extended arm and by a low murmured warning not to make a noise.

'Have you seen them, mother?' asked Nina, in a breathless whisper.

Mrs Almayer turned her face towards the girl, and her sunken eyes shone strangely in the red half-light of the passage.

'I saw him,' she said, in an almost inaudible tone, pressing her daughter's hand with her bony fingers. 'A great Rajah has come to Sambir – a Son of Heaven,'* muttered the old woman to herself. 'Go away, girl!'

The two women stood close to the curtain, Nina wishing to approach the rent in the stuff, and her mother defending the position with angry obstinacy. On the other side there was a lull in the conversation, but the breathing of several men, the occasional light tinkling of some ornaments, the clink of metal scabbards, or of brass siri-vessels* passed from hand to hand, was audible during the short pause. The women struggled silently, when there was a shuffling noise and the shadow of Almayer's burly form fell on the curtain.

The women ceased struggling and remained motionless. Almayer had stood up to answer his guest, turning his back to the doorway, unaware of what was going on on the other side. He spoke in a tone of regretful irritation.

'You have come to the wrong house, Tuan Maroola, if you want to trade as you say. I was a trader once, not now, whatever you may have heard about me in Macassar. And if you want anything, you will not find it here; I have nothing to give, and want nothing myself. You should go to the Rajah here; you can see in the daytime his houses across the river, there, where those fires are burning on the shore. He will help you and trade with you. Or, better still, go to the Arabs over there,' he went on bitterly, pointing with his hand towards the houses of Sambir. 'Abdulla is the man you want. There is nothing he would not buy, and there is nothing he would not sell; believe me, I know him well.'

He waited for an answer a short time, then added –

'All that I have said is true, and there is nothing more.'

Nina, held back by her mother, heard a soft voice reply with a calm evenness of intonation peculiar to the better class Malays –

'Who would doubt a white Tuan's words? A man seeks his friends where his heart tells him. Is this not true also? I have come, although so late, for I have something to say which you may be glad to hear. Tomorrow I will go to the Sultan; a trader wants the friendship of great men. Then I shall return here to speak serious words, if Tuan permits. I shall not go to the Arabs; their lies are very great! What are they? Chelakka!'*

Almayer's voice sounded a little more pleasantly in reply.

'Well, as you like. I can hear you tomorrow at any time if you have anything to say. Bah! After you have seen the Sultan Lakamba you will not want to return here, Inchi* Dain. You will see. Only mind, I will have nothing to do with Lakamba. You may tell him so. What is your business with me, after all?'

'Tomorrow we talk, Tuan, now I know you,' answered the Malay. 'I speak English a little, so we can talk and nobody will understand, and then—'

He interrupted himself suddenly, asking surprised, 'What's that noise, Tuan?'

Almayer had also heard the increasing noise of the scuffle recommenced on the women's side of the curtain. Evidently Nina's strong curiosity was on the point of overcoming Mrs Almayer's exalted sense of social proprieties. Hard breathing was distinctly audible, and the curtain shook during the contest, which was mainly physical, although Mrs Almayer's voice was heard in angry remonstrance with its usual want of strictly logical reasoning, but with the well-known richness of invective.

'You shameless woman! Are you a slave?' shouted shrilly the irate matron. 'Veil your face, abandoned wretch! You white snake, I will not let you!'

Almayer's face expressed annoyance and also doubt as to the advisability of interfering between mother and daughter. He glanced at his Malay visitor, who was waiting silently for the end of the uproar in an attitude of amused expectation, and waving his hand contemptuously he murmured –

'It is nothing. Some women.'

The Malay nodded his head gravely, and his face assumed an expression of serene indifference, as etiquette demanded after such an explanation. The contest was ended behind the curtain, and evidently the younger will had its way, for the rapid shuffle and click of Mrs Almayer's high-heeled sandals died away in the distance. The tranquillised master of the house was going to resume the conversation when, struck by an unexpected change in the expression of his guest's countenance, he turned his head and saw Nina standing in the doorway.

After Mrs Almayer's retreat from the field of battle, Nina, with a contemptuous exclamation, 'It's only a trader,' had lifted the conquered curtain and now stood in full light, framed in the dark background on the passage, her lips slightly parted, her hair in disorder* after the exertion, the angry gleam not yet faded out of her glorious and sparkling eyes. She took in at a glance the group of white-clad lancemen standing motionless in the shadow of the far-off end of the verandah, and her gaze rested curiously on the chief of that imposing *cortège*. He stood, almost facing her, a little on one side, and struck by the beauty of the unexpected apparition had bent low, elevating his joint hands above his head in a sign of respect accorded by Malays only to the great of this earth. The crude light of the lamp shone on the gold embroidery of his black silk jacket, broke in a thousand sparkling rays on the jewelled hilt of his kriss* protruding from under the many folds of the red sarong gathered into a sash round his waist, and played on the precious stones of the many rings on his dark fingers. He straightened himself up quickly after the low bow, putting his hand with a graceful ease on the hilt of his heavy short sword ornamented with brilliantly dyed fringes of horsehair. Nina, hesitating on the threshold, saw an erect lithe figure of medium height with a breadth of shoulder suggesting great power. Under the folds of a blue turban, whose fringed ends hung gracefully over the left shoulder, was a face full of determination and expressing a reckless good-humour, not devoid, however, of some dignity. The squareness of lower jaw, the full red lips, the mobile nostrils, and the proud carriage of the head gave the impression of a being half-savage, untamed, perhaps cruel, and corrected the liquid softness of the almost feminine eye, that general characteristic of the race. Now, the first surprise over, Nina saw those eyes fixed upon her with such an uncontrolled expression of admiration and desire that she felt a hitherto unknown feeling of shyness, mixed with alarm and some delight, enter and penetrate her whole being. Confused by those unusual sensations she stopped in the doorway and instinctively drew the lower part of the curtain across her face, leaving only half a rounded cheek, a stray tress, and one eye exposed, wherewith to contemplate the gorgeous and bold being so unlike in appearance to the rare specimens of traders she had seen before on that same verandah.

Dain Maroola, dazzled by the unexpected vision, forgot the confused Almayer, forgot his brig, his escort staring in open-mouthed admiration,* the object of his visit and all things else, in his overpowering desire to prolong the contemplation of so much loveliness met so suddenly in such an unlikely place – as he thought.

'It is my daughter,' said Almayer, in an embarrassed manner. 'It is of no consequence. White women have their customs, as you know Tuan, having travelled much, as you say. However, it is late; we will finish our talk tomorrow.'

Dain bent low trying to convey in a last glance towards the girl the bold expression of his overwhelming admiration. The next minute he was shaking Almayer's hand with grave courtesy, his face wearing a look of stolid unconcern as to any feminine presence. His men filed off, and he followed them quickly, closely attended by a thick-set, savage-looking Sumatrese he had introduced before as the commander of his brig. Nina walked to the balustrade of the verandah and saw the sheen of moonlight on the steel spear-heads and heard the rhythmic jingle of brass anklets as the men moved in single file towards the jetty. The boat shoved off after a little while, looming large in the full light of the moon, a black shapeless mass in the slight haze hanging over the water. Nina fancied she could distinguish the graceful figure of the trader standing erect in the stern sheets,* but in a little while all the outlines got blurred, confused, and soon disappeared in the folds of white vapour shrouding the middle of the river.

Almayer had approached his daughter, and leaning with both arms over the rail, was looking moodily down on the heap of rubbish and broken bottles at the foot of the verandah.

'What was all that noise just now?' he growled peevishly, without looking up. 'Confound you and your mother! What did she want? What did you come out for?'

'She did not want to let me come out,' said Nina. 'She is angry. She says the man just gone is some Rajah. I think she is right now.'

'I believe all you women are crazy,' snarled Almayer. 'What's that to you, to her, to anybody? The man wants to collect trepang* and birds' nests* on the islands. He told me so, that Rajah of yours. He will come tomorrow. I want you both to keep away from the house, and let me attend to my business in peace.'

Dain Maroola came the next day and had a long conversation

with Almayer. This was the beginning of a close and friendly intercourse which, at first, was much remarked in Sambir, till the population got used to the frequent sight of many fires burning in Almayer's campong, where Maroola's men were warming themselves during the cold nights of the north-east monsoon, while their master had long conferences with the Tuan Putih – as they styled Almayer amongst themselves. Great was the curiosity in Sambir on the subject of the new trader. Had he seen the Sultan? What did the Sultan say? Had he given any presents? What would he sell? What would he buy? Those were the questions broached eagerly by the inhabitants of bamboo houses built over the river. Even in more substantial buildings, in Abdulla's house, in the residences of principal traders, Arab, Chinese, and Bugis,* the excitement ran high, and lasted many days. With inborn suspicion they would not believe the simple account of himself the young trader was always ready to give. Yet it had all the appearance of truth. He said he was a trader, and sold rice. He did not want to buy gutta-percha or beeswax, because he intended to employ his numerous crew in collecting trepang on the coral reefs outside the river, and also in seeking for birds' nests on the mainland. Those two articles he professed himself ready to buy if there were any to be obtained in that way. He said he was from Bali, and a Brahmin, which last statement he made good by refusing all food* during his often repeated visits to Lakamba's and Almayer's houses. To Lakamba he went generally at night and had long audiences. Babalatchi, who was always a third party at those meetings of potentate and trader, knew how to resist all attempts on the part of the curious to ascertain the subject of so many long talks. When questioned with languid courtesy by the grave Abdulla he sought refuge in a vacant stare of his one eye, and in the affectation of extreme simplicity.

'I am only my master's slave,' murmured Babalatchi, in a hesitating manner. Then as if making up his mind suddenly for a reckless confidence he would inform Abdulla of some transaction in rice, repeating the words, 'A hundred big bags the Sultan bought; a hundred, Tuan!' in a tone of mysterious solemnity. Abdulla, firmly persuaded of the existence of some more important dealings, received, however, the information with all the signs of respectful astonishment. And the two would separate, the Arab cursing inwardly the wily dog, while Babalatchi went on his way walking on the dusty path, his body swaying, his chin with its few grey hairs pushed forward, resembling an inquisitive goat bent on some unlawful expedition. Attentive eyes watched his movements. Jim-Eng, descrying Babalatchi far away, would shake off the stupor of an habitual opium smoker and, tottering on to the middle of the road, would await the approach of that important person, ready with hospitable invitation. But Babalatchi's discretion was proof even against the combined assaults of good fellowship and of strong gin generously administered by the open-hearted Chinaman. Jim-Eng, owning himself beaten, was left uninformed with the empty bottle, and gazed sadly after the departing form of the statesman of Sambir pursuing his devious and unsteady way, which, as usual, led him to Almayer's compound. Ever since a reconciliation had been effected by Dain Maroola between his white friend and the Rajah, the one-eyed diplomatist had again become a frequent guest in the Dutchman's house. To Almayer's great disgust he was to be seen there at all times, strolling about in an abstracted kind of way on the verandah, skulking in the passages, or else popping round unexpected corners, always willing to engage Mrs Almayer in confidential conversation. He was very shy of the master himself, as if suspicious that the pent-up feelings of the white man towards his person might find vent in a sudden kick. But the cooking shed was his favourite place, and he became an habitual guest there, squatting for hours amongst the busy women, with his chin resting on his knees, his lean arms clasped round his legs, and his one eye roving uneasily – the very picture of watchful ugliness. Almayer wanted more than once to complain to Lakamba of his Prime Minister's intrusion, but Dain dissuaded him. 'We cannot say a word here that he does not hear,' growled Almayer.

'Then come and talk on board the brig,' retorted Dain, with a quiet smile. 'It is good to let the man come here. Lakamba thinks he knows much. Perhaps the Sultan thinks I want to run away. Better let the one-eyed crocodile sun himself in your campong, Tuan.'

And Almayer assented unwillingly muttering vague threats of personal violence, while he eyed malevolently the aged statesman sitting with quiet obstinacy by his domestic rice-pot.

CHAPTER 5

At last the excitement had died out in Sambir. The inhabitants got used to the sight of comings and goings between Almayer's house and the vessel, now moored to the opposite bank, and speculation as to the feverish activity displayed by Almayer's boatmen in repairing old canoes ceased to interfere with the due discharge of domestic duties by the women of the Settlement. Even the baffled Jim-Eng left off troubling his muddled brain with secrets of trade, and relapsed by the aid of his opium pipe into a state of stupefied bliss, letting Babalatchi pursue his way past his house uninvited and seemingly unnoticed.

So on that warm afternoon, when the deserted river sparkled under the vertical sun, the statesman of Sambir could, without any hindrance from friendly inquirers, shove off his little canoe from under the bushes, where it was usually hidden during his visits to Almayer's compound. Slowly and languidly Babalatchi paddled, crouching low in the boat, making himself small under his enormous sun hat to escape the scorching heat reflected from the water. He was not in a hurry; his master, Lakamba, was surely reposing at this time of the day. He would have ample time to cross over and greet him on his waking with important news. Will he be displeased? Will he strike his ebony wood staff angrily on the floor, frightening him by the incoherent violence of his exclamations; or will he squat down with a good-humoured smile, and, rubbing his hands gently over his stomach with a familiar gesture, expectorate* copiously into the brass siri-vessel, giving vent to a low, approbative murmur? Such were Babalatchi's thoughts as he skilfully handled his paddle, crossing the river on his way to the Rajah's campong, whose stockades showed from behind the dense foliage of the bank just opposite to Almayer's bungalow.

Indeed, he had a report to make. Something certain at last to confirm the daily tale of suspicions, the daily hints of familiarity, of stolen glances he had seen, of short and burning words he had overheard exchanged between Dain Maroola and Almayer's daughter. Lakamba had, till then, listened to it all, calmly and with evident distrust; now he was going to be convinced, for Babalatchi had the proof; had it this very morning, when fishing at break of day in the creek over which stood Bulangi's house. There from his skiff* he saw Nina's long canoe drift past, the girl sitting in the stern bending over Dain, who was stretched in the bottom with his head resting on the girl's knees. He saw it. He followed them, but in a short time they took to the paddles and got away from under his observant eye. A few minutes afterwards he saw Bulangi's slave-girl paddling in a small dug-out to the town with her cakes for sale. She also had seen them in the grey dawn. And Babalatchi grinned confidentially to himself at the recollection of the slave-girl's discomposed face, of the hard look in her eyes, of the tremble in her voice, when answering his questions. That little Taminah evidently admired Dain Maroola. That was good! And Babalatchi laughed aloud at the notion; then becoming suddenly serious, he began by some strange association of ideas to speculate upon the price for which Bulangi would, possibly, sell the girl. He shook his head sadly at the thought that Bulangi was a hard man, and had refused one hundred dollars for that same Taminah only a few weeks ago; then he became suddenly aware that the canoe had drifted too far down during his meditation. He shook off the despondency caused by the certitude of Bulangi's mercenary disposition, and, taking up his paddle, in a few strokes sheered* alongside the water-gate of the Rajah's house.

That afternoon Almayer, as was his wont lately, moved about on the water-side, overlooking the repairs to his boats. He had decided at last. Guided by the scraps of information contained in old Lingard's pocket-book, he was going to seek for the rich gold-mine, for that place where he had only to stoop to gather up an immense fortune and realise the dream of his young days. To obtain the necessary help he had shared his knowledge with Dain Maroola, he had consented to be reconciled with Lakamba, who gave his support to the enterprise on condition of sharing the profits; he had sacrificed his pride, his honour, and his loyalty in the face of the enormous risk of his undertaking, dazzled by the greatness of the results to be achieved by this alliance so distasteful yet so necessary The dangers were great, but Maroola was brave; his men seemed as reckless as their chief, and with Lakamba's aid success seemed assured.

For the last fortnight Almayer was absorbed in the preparations, walking amongst his workmen and slaves in a kind of waking trance, where practical details as to the fitting out of the boats were mixed up with vivid dreams of untold wealth, where the present misery of burning sun, of the muddy and malodorous river bank disappeared in a gorgeous vision of a splendid future existence for himself and Nina. He hardly saw Nina during these last days, although the beloved daughter was ever present in his thoughts. He hardly took notice of Dain, whose constant presence in his house had become a matter of course to him now they were connected by a community of interests. When meeting the young chief he gave him an absent greeting and passed on, seemingly wishing to avoid him, bent upon forgetting the hated reality of the present by absorbing himself in his work, or else by letting his imagination soar far above the tree-tops into the great white clouds away to the westward, where the paradise of Europe was awaiting the future Eastern millionaire. And Maroola, now the bargain was struck and there was no more business to be talked over, evidently did not care for the white man's company. Yet Dain was always about the house, but he seldom stayed long by the riverside. On his daily visits to the white man the Malay chief preferred to make his way quietly through the central passage of the house, and would come out into the garden at the back, where the fire was burning in the cooking shed, with the rice kettle swinging over it, under the watchful supervision of Mrs Almayer. Avoiding that shed, with its black smoke and the warbling of soft, feminine voices, Dain would turn to the left. There, on the edge of a banana plantation, a clump of palms and mango trees formed a shady spot, a few scattered bushes giving it a certain seclusion into which only the serving women's chatter or an occasional burst of laughter could penetrate. Once in, he was invisible; and hidden there, leaning against the smooth trunk of a tall palm, he waited with gleaming eyes and an assured smile to hear the faint rustle of dried grass under the light footsteps of Nina.

From the very first moment when his eyes beheld this – to him – perfection of loveliness he felt in his inmost heart the conviction that she would be his; he felt the subtle breath of mutual understanding passing between their two savage natures, and he did not want Mrs Almayer's encouraging smiles to take every opportunity of approaching the girl; and every time he spoke to her, every time he looked into her eyes, Nina, although averting her face, felt as if this bold-looking being who spoke burning words into her willing ear was the embodiment of her fate, the creature of her dreams – reckless, ferocious, ready with flashing kriss for his enemies, and with passionate embrace for his beloved – the ideal Malay chief of her mother's tradition.

She recognised with a thrill of delicious fear the mysterious consciousness of her identity with that being. Listening to his words, it seemed to her she was born only then to a knowledge of a new existence, that her life was complete only when near him, and she abandoned herself to a feeling of dreamy happiness, while with half-veiled face and in silence – as became a Malay girl – she listened to Dain's words giving up to her the whole treasure of love and passion his nature was capable of with all the unrestrained enthusiasm of a man totally untrammelled by any influence of civilised self-discipline.

And they used to pass many a delicious and fast fleeting hour under the mango trees behind the friendly curtain of bushes till Mrs Almayer's shrill voice gave the signal of unwilling separation. Mrs Almayer had undertaken the easy task of watching her husband lest he should interrupt the smooth course of her daughter's love affair, in which she took a great and benignant interest. She was happy and proud to see Dain's infatuation, believing him to be a great and powerful chief, and she found also a gratification of her mercenary instincts in Dain's openhanded generosity.

On the eve of the day when Babalatchi's suspicions were confirmed by ocular demonstration, Dain and Nina had remained longer than usual in their shady retreat. Only Almayer's heavy step on the verandah and his querulous clamour for food decided Mrs Almayer to lift a warning cry. Maroola leaped lightly over the low bamboo fence, and made his way stealthily through the banana plantation down to the muddy shore of the back creek, while Nina walked slowly towards the house to minister to her father's wants, as was her wont every evening. Almayer felt happy enough that evening; the preparations were nearly completed; tomorrow he would launch his boats. In his mind's eye he saw the rich prize in his grasp; and, with tin spoon in his hand, he was forgetting the plateful of rice before him in the fanciful arrangement of some splendid banquet to take place on his arrival in Amsterdam. Nina, reclining in the long chair, listened absently to the few disconnected words escaping from her father's lips. Expedition! Gold! What did she care for all that? But at the name of Maroola mentioned by her father she was all attention. Dain was going down the river with his brig tomorrow to remain away for a few days, said Almayer. It was very annoying, this delay. As soon as Dain returned they would have to start without loss of time, for the river was rising. He would not be surprised if a great flood was coming. And he pushed away his plate with an impatient gesture on rising from the table. But now Nina heard him not. Dain going away! That's why he had ordered her, with that quiet masterfulness it was her delight to obey, to meet him at break of day in Bulangi's creek. Was there a paddle in her canoe? she thought. Was it ready? She would have to start early – at four in the morning, in a very few hours.

She rose from her chair, thinking she would require rest before the long pull in the early morning. The lamp was burning dimly, and her father, tired with the day's labour, was already in his hammock. Nina put the lamp out and passed into a large room she shared with her mother on the left of the central passage. Entering, she saw that Mrs Almayer had deserted the pile of mats serving her as bed in one corner of the room, and was now bending over the opened lid of her large wooden chest. Half a shell of cocoanut filled with oil, where a cotton rag floated for a wick, stood on the floor, surrounding her with a ruddy halo of light shining through the black and odorous smoke. Mrs Almayer's back was bent, and her head and shoulders hidden in the deep box. Her hands rummaged in the interior, where a soft clink as of silver money could be heard. She did not notice at first her daughter's approach, and Nina, standing silently by her, looked down on many little canvas bags ranged in the bottom of the chest, wherefrom her mother extracted handfuls of shining guilders and Mexican dollars,* letting them stream slowly back again through her claw-like fingers. The music of tinkling silver seemed to delight her, and her eyes sparkled with the reflected gleam of freshly-minted coins. She was muttering to herself: 'And this, and this, and yet this! Soon he will give more – as much more as I ask. He is a great Rajah – a Son of Heaven!* And she will be a Ranee* – he gave all this for her! Who ever gave anything for me? I am a slave! Am I? I am the mother of a great Ranee!' She became aware suddenly of her daughter's presence, and ceased her droning, shutting the lid down violently; then, without rising from her crouching position, she looked up at the girl standing by with a vague smile on her dreamy face.

'You have seen. Have you?' she shouted, shrilly. 'That is all mine, and for you. It is not enough! He will have to give more before he takes you away to the southern island where his father is king. You hear me? You are worth more, granddaughter of Rajahs! More! More!'

The sleepy voice of Almayer was heard on the verandah recommending silence. Mrs Almayer extinguished the light and crept into her corner of the room. Nina laid down on her back on a pile of soft mats, her hands entwined under her head, gazing through the shutterless hole, serving as a window, at the stars twinkling on the black sky; she was awaiting the time of start* for her appointed meeting-place. With quiet happiness she thought of that meeting in the great forest, far from all human eyes and sounds. Her soul, lapsing again into the savage mood, which the genius of civilisation working by the hand of Mrs Vinck could never destroy, experienced a feeling of pride and of some slight trouble at the high value her worldly-wise mother had put upon her person; but she remembered the expressive glances and words of Dain, and, tranquillised, she closed her eyes in a shiver of pleasant anticipation.

There are some situations where the barbarian and the, so-called, civilised man meet upon the same ground. It may be supposed that Dain Maroola was not exceptionally delighted with his prospective mother-in-law, nor that he actually approved of that worthy woman's appetite for shining dollars. Yet on that foggy morning when Babalatchi, laying aside the cares of state, went to visit his fish-baskets in the Bulangi creek, Maroola had no misgivings, experienced no feelings but those of impatience and longing, when paddling to the east side of the island forming the backwater in question. He hid his canoe in the bushes and strode rapidly across the islet, pushing with impatience through the twigs of heavy undergrowth intercrossed over his path. From motives of prudence he would not take his canoe to the meeting-place, as Nina had done. He had left it in the main stream till his return from the other side of the island. The heavy warm fog was closing rapidly round him, but he managed to catch a fleeting glimpse of a light away to the left, proceeding from Bulangi's house. Then he could see nothing in the thickening vapour, and kept to the path only by a sort of instinct, which also led him to the very point on the opposite shore he wished to reach. A great log had stranded there, at right angles to the bank, forming a kind of jetty against which the swiftly flowing stream broke with a loud ripple. He stepped on it with a quick but steady motion, and in two strides found himself at the outer end, with the rush and swirl of the foaming water at his feet.

Standing there alone, as if separated from the world; the heavens, earth; the very water roaring under him swallowed up in the thick veil of the morning fog, he breathed out the name of Nina before him into the apparently limitless space, sure of being heard, instinctively sure of the nearness of the delightful creature; certain of her being aware of his near presence as he was aware of hers.

The bow of Nina's canoe loomed up close to the log, canted* high out of the water by the weight of the sitter in the stern. Maroola laid his hand on the stem and leaped lightly in, giving it a vigorous shove off. The light craft, obeying the new impulse, cleared the log by a hair's breadth, and the river, with obedient complicity, swung it broadside to* the current, and bore it off silently and rapidly between the invisible banks. And once more Dain, at the feet of Nina, forgot the world, felt himself carried away helpless by a great wave of supreme emotion, by a rush of joy, pride, and desire; understood once more with overpowering certitude that there was no life possible without that being he held clasped in his arms with passionate strength in a prolonged embrace.

Nina disengaged herself gently with a low laugh.

'You will overturn the boat, Dain,' she whispered.

He looked into her eyes eagerly for a minute and let her go with a sigh, then lying down in the canoe he put his head on her knees, gazing upwards and stretching his arms backwards till his hands met round the girl's waist. She bent over him, and, shaking her head, framed both their faces in the falling locks of her long black hair.

And so they drifted on, he speaking with all the rude eloquence of a savage nature giving itself up without restraint to an overmastering passion, she bending low to catch the murmur of words sweeter to her than life itself. To those two nothing existed then outside the gunwales* of the narrow and fragile craft. It was their world, filled with their intense and all-absorbing love. They took no heed of thickening mist, or of the breeze dying away before sunrise; they forgot the existence of the great forests surrounding them, of all the tropical nature awaiting the advent of the sun in a solemn and impressive silence.

Over the low river-mist hiding the boat with its freight of young passionate life and all-forgetful happiness, the stars paled, and a silvery-grey tint crept over the sky from the eastward. There was not a breath of wind, not a rustle of stirring leaf, not a splash of leaping fish to disturb the serene repose of all living things on the banks of the great river. Earth, river, and sky were wrapped up in a deep sleep, from which it seemed there would be no waking. All the seething life and movement of tropical nature seemed concentrated in the ardent eyes, in the tumultuously beating hearts of the two beings drifting in the canoe, under the white canopy of mist, over the smooth surface of the river.

Suddenly a great sheaf of yellow rays shot upwards from behind the black curtain of trees lining the banks of the Pantai. The stars went out; the little black clouds at the zenith glowed for a moment with crimson tints, and the thick mist, stirred by the gentle breeze, the sigh of waking nature, whirled round and broke into fantastically torn pieces, disclosing the wrinkled surface of the river sparkling in the broad light of day. Great flocks of white birds wheeled screaming above the swaying tree-tops. The sun had risen on the east coast.

Dain was the first to return to the cares of everyday life. He rose and glanced rapidly up and down the river. His eye detected Babalatchi's boat astern, and another small black speck on the glittering water, which was Taminah's canoe. He moved cautiously forward, and, kneeling, took up a paddle; Nina at the stern took hers. They bent their bodies to the work, throwing up the water at every stroke, and the small craft went swiftly ahead, leaving a narrow wake fringed with a lace-like border of white and gleaming foam. Without turning his head, Dain spoke.

'Somebody behind us, Nina. We must not let him gain. I think he is too far to recognise us.'

'Somebody before us also,' panted out Nina, without ceasing to paddle.

'I think I know,' rejoined Dain. 'The sun shines over there, but I fancy it is the girl Taminah. She comes down every morning to my brig to sell cakes – stays often all day. It does not matter; steer more into the bank; we must get under the bushes. My canoe is hidden not far from here.'

As he spoke his eyes watched the broad-leaved nipas* which they were brushing in their swift and silent course.

'Look out, Nina,' he said at last; 'there, where the water palms end and the twigs hang down under the leaning tree. Steer for the big green branch.'

He stood up attentive, and the boat drifted slowly in shore, Nina guiding it by a gentle and skilful movement of her paddle. When near enough Dain laid hold of the big branch, and leaning back shot the canoe under a low green archway of thickly matted creepers giving access to a miniature bay formed by the caving in of the bank during the last great flood. His own boat was there anchored by a stone, and he stepped into it, keeping his hand on the gunwale of Nina's canoe. In a moment the two little nutshells with their occupants floated quietly side by side, reflected by the black water in the dim light struggling through a high canopy of dense foliage; while above, away up in the broad day, flamed immense red blossoms sending down on their heads a shower of great dew-sparkling petals that descended rotating slowly in a continuous and perfumed stream; and over them, under them, in the sleeping water;* all around them in a ring of luxuriant vegetation bathed in the warm air charged with strong and harsh perfumes, the intense work of tropical nature went on: plants shooting upward, entwined, interlaced in inextricable confusion, climbing madly and brutally over each other in the terrible silence of a desperate struggle towards the life-giving sunshine above – as if struck with sudden horror at the seething mass of corruption below, at the death and decay from which they sprang.

'We must part now,' said Dain, after a long silence. 'You must return at once, Nina. I will wait till the brig drifts down here, and shall get on board then.'

'And will you be long away, Dain?' asked Nina, in a low voice.

'Long!' exclaimed Dain. 'Would a man willingly remain long in a dark place? When I am not near you, Nina, I am like a man that is blind. What is life to me without light?'

Nina leaned over, and with a proud and happy smile took Dain's face between her hands, looking into his eyes with a fond yet questioning gaze. Apparently she found there the confirmation of the words just said, for a feeling of grateful security lightened for her the weight of sorrow at the hour of parting. She believed that he, the descendant of many great Rajahs, the son of a great chief, the master of life and death, knew the sunshine of life only in her presence. An immense wave of gratitude and love welled forth out of her heart towards him. How could she make an outward and visible sign of all she felt for the man who had filled her heart with so much joy and so much pride? And in the great tumult of passion, like a flash of lightning came to her the reminiscence of that despised and almost forgotten civilisation she had only glanced at in her days of restraint, of sorrow, and of anger. In the cold ashes of that hateful and miserable past she would find the sign of love, the fitting expression of the boundless felicity of the present, the pledge of a bright and splendid future. She threw her arms around Dain's neck and pressed her lips to his in a long and burning kiss.* He closed his eyes, surprised and frightened at the storm raised in his breast by the strange and to him hitherto unknown contact, and long after Nina had pushed her canoe into the river he remained motionless, without daring to open his eyes, afraid to lose the sensation of intoxicating delight he had tasted for the first time.

Now he wanted but immortality, he thought, to be the equal of gods, and the creature that could open so the gates of paradise must be his – soon would be his for ever!

He opened his eyes in time to see through the archway of

creepers the bows of his brig come slowly into view, as the vessel drifted past on its way down the river. He must go on board now, he thought; yet he was loth to leave the place where he had learned to know what happiness meant. 'Time yet. Let them go,' he muttered to himself; and he closed his eyes again under the red shower of scented petals, trying to recall the scene with all its delight and all its fear.

He must have been able to join his brig in time, after all, and found much occupation outside, for it was in vain that Almayer looked for his friend's speedy return. The lower reach of the river where he so often and so impatiently directed his eyes remained deserted, save for the rapid flitting of some fishing canoe; but down the upper reaches came black clouds and heavy showers heralding the final setting in of the rainy season with its thunderstorms and great floods making the river almost impossible of ascent for native canoes.

Almayer, strolling along the muddy beach between his houses, watched uneasily the river rising inch by inch, creeping slowly nearer to the boats, now ready and hauled up in a row under the cover of dripping Kajang-mats.* Fortune seemed to elude his grasp, and in his weary tramp backwards and forwards under the steady rain falling from the lowering sky, a sort of despairing indifference took possession of him. What did it matter? It was just his luck! Those two infernal savages, Lakamba and Dain, induced him, with their promises of help, to spend his last dollar in the fitting out of boats, and now one of them was gone somewhere, and the other shut up in his stockade would give no sign of life. No, not even the scoundrelly Babalatchi, thought Almayer, would show his face near him, now they had sold him all the rice, brass gongs, and cloth necessary for his expedition. They had his very last coin, and did not care whether he went or stayed. And with a gesture of abandoned discouragement Almayer would climb up slowly to the verandah of his new house to get out of the rain, and leaning on the front rail with his head sunk between his shoulders he would abandon himself to the current of bitter thoughts, oblivious of the flight of time and the pangs of hunger, deaf to the shrill cries of his wife calling him to the evening meal. When, roused from his sad meditations by the first roll of the evening thunderstorm, he stumbled slowly towards the glimmering light of his old house, his half-dead hope made his ears preternaturally acute to any sound on the river. Several nights in succession he had heard the splash of paddles and had seen the indistinct form of a boat, but when hailing the shadowy apparition, his heart bounding with sudden hope of hearing Dain's voice, he was disappointed each time by the sulky answer conveying to him the intelligence that the Arabs were on the river, bound on a visit to the home-staying Lakamba. This caused him many sleepless nights, spent in speculating upon the kind of villainy those estimable personages were hatching now. At last, when all hope seemed dead, he was overjoyed on hearing Dain's voice; but Dain also appeared very anxious to see Lakamba, and Almayer felt uneasy owing to a deep and ineradicable distrust as to that ruler's disposition towards himself. Still, Dain had returned at last. Evidently he meant to keep to his bargain. Hope revived, and that night Almayer slept soundly, while Nina watched the angry river* under the lash of the thunderstorm sweeping onward towards the sea.

CHAPTER 6

Dain was not long in crossing the river after leaving Almayer. He landed at the water-gate of the stockade enclosing the group of houses which composed the residence of the Rajah of Sambir. Evidently somebody was expected there, for the gate was open, and men with torches were ready to precede the visitor up the inclined plane of planks leading to the largest house where Lakamba actually resided, and where all the business of state was invariably transacted. The other buildings within the enclosure served only to accommodate the numerous household and the wives of the ruler.

Lakamba's own house was a strong structure of solid planks, raised on high piles, with a verandah of split bamboos surrounding it on all sides; the whole was covered in by an immensely high-pitched roof of palm-leaves, resting on beams blackened by the smoke of many torches.

The building stood parallel to the river, one of its long sides facing the water-gate of the stockade. There was a door in the short side looking up the river, and the inclined plank-way led straight from the gate to that door. By the uncertain light of smoky torches, Dain noticed the vague outlines of a group of armed men in the dark shadows to his right. From that group Babalatchi stepped forward to open the door, and Dain entered the audience chamber of the Rajah's residence. About one-third of the house was curtained off, by heavy stuff of European manufacture, for that purpose; close to the curtain there was a big arm-chair of some black wood, much carved, and before it a rough deal table. Otherwise the room was only furnished with mats in great profusion. To the left of the entrance stood a rude arm-rack,* with three rifles with fixed bayonets in it. By the wall, in the shadow, the body-guard of Lakamba – all friends or relations – slept in a confused heap of brown arms, legs, and multi-coloured garments, from whence issued an occasional snore or a subdued groan of some uneasy sleeper. An European lamp with a green shade standing on the table made all this indistinctly visible to Dain.

'You are welcome to your rest here,' said Babalatchi, looking at Dain interrogatively.

'I must speak to the Rajah at once,' answered Dain.

Babalatchi made a gesture of assent, and, turning to the brass gong suspended under the arm-rack, struck two sharp blows.

The ear-splitting din woke up the guard. The snores ceased; outstretched legs were drawn in; the whole heap moved, and slowly resolved itself into individual forms, with much yawning and rubbing of sleepy eyes; behind the curtains there was a burst of feminine chatter; then the bass voice of Lakamba was heard.

'Is that the Arab trader?'

'No, Tuan,' answered Babalatchi; 'Dain has returned at last. He is here for an important talk, bitcharra* – if you mercifully consent.'

Evidently Lakamba's mercy went so far – for in a short while he came out from behind the curtain – but it did not go to the length of inducing him to make an extensive toilet. A short red sarong tightened hastily round his hips was his only garment. The merciful ruler of Sambir looked sleepy and rather sulky. He sat in the arm-chair, his knees well apart, his elbows on the arm-rests, his chin on his breast, breathing heavily and waiting malevolently for Dain to open the important talk.

But Dain did not seem anxious to begin. He directed his gaze towards Babalatchi, squatting comfortably at the feet of his master, and remained silent with a slightly bent head as if in attentive expectation of coming words of wisdom.

Babalatchi coughed discreetly, and, leaning forward, pushed over a few mats for Dain to sit upon, then lifting up his squeaky voice he assured him with eager volubility of everybody's delight at this long-looked-for-return. His heart had hungered for the sight of Dain's face, and his ears were withering for the want of the refreshing sound of his voice. Everybody's hearts and ears were in the same sad predicament, according to Babalatchi, as he indicated with a sweeping gesture the other bank of the river where the settlement slumbered peacefully, unconscious of the great joy awaiting it on the morrow when Dain's presence amongst them would be disclosed. 'For' – went on Babalatchi –

'what is the joy of a poor man if not the open hand of a generous trader or of a great—'

Here he checked himself abruptly with a calculated embarrassment of manner, and his roving eye sought the floor, while an apologetic smile dwelt for a moment on his misshapen lips. Once or twice during this opening speech an amused expression flitted across Dain's face, soon to give way, however, to an appearance of grave concern. On Lakamba's brow a heavy frown had settled, and his lips moved angrily as he listened to his Prime Minister's oratory. In the silence that fell upon the room when Babalatchi ceased speaking arose a chorus of varied snores from the corner where the body-guard had resumed their interrupted slumbers, but the distant rumble of thunder filling then Nina's heart with apprehension for the safety of her lover passed unheeded by those three men intent each on their own purposes, for life or death.

After a short silence, Babalatchi, discarding now the flowers of polite eloquence, spoke again, but in short and hurried sentences and in a low voice. They had been very uneasy. Why did Dain remain so long absent? The men dwelling on the lower reaches of the river heard the reports of big guns and saw a fire-ship* of the Dutch amongst the islands of the estuary. So they were anxious. Rumours of a disaster had reached Abdulla a few days ago, and since then they had been waiting for Dain's return under the apprehension of some misfortune. For days they had closed their eyes in fear, and woke up alarmed, and walked abroad trembling, like men before an enemy. And all on account of Dain. Would he not allay their fears for his safety, not for themselves? They were quiet and faithful, and devoted to the great Rajah in Batavia* – may his fate lead him ever to victory for the joy and profit of his servants! 'And here,' went on Babalatchi, 'Lakamba my master was getting thin in his anxiety for the trader he had taken under his protection; and so was Abdulla, for what would wicked men not say if perchance—'

'Be silent, fool!' growled Lakamba, angrily.

Babalatchi subsided into silence with a satisfied smile, while Dain, who had been watching him as if fascinated, turned with a sigh of relief towards the ruler of Sambir. Lakamba did not move, and, without raising his head, looked at Dain from under his eyebrows, breathing audibly, with pouted lips, in an air of general discontent.

'Speak! O Dain!' he said at last. 'We have heard many rumours. Many nights in succession has my friend Reshid come here with bad tidings. News travels fast along the coast. But they may be untrue; there are more lies in men's mouths in these days than when I was young, but I am not easier to deceive now.'

'All my words are true,' said Dain, carelessly. 'If you want to know what befell my brig, then learn that it is in the hands of the Dutch. Believe me, Rajah,' he went on, with sudden energy, 'the Orang Blanda have good friends in Sambir, or else how did they know I was coming thence?'

Lakamba gave Dain a short and hostile glance. Babalatchi rose quietly, and, going to the arm-rack, struck the gong violently.

Outside the door there was a shuffle of bare feet; inside, the guard woke up and sat staring in sleepy surprise.

'Yes, you faithful friend of the white Rajah,' went on Dain, scornfully, turning to Babalatchi, who had returned to his place, 'I have escaped, and I am here to gladden your heart. When I saw the Dutch ship I ran the brig inside the reefs and put her ashore. They did not dare to follow with the ship, so they sent the boats. We took to ours and tried to get away, but the ship dropped fireballs at us, and killed many of my men. But I am left, O Babalatchi! The Dutch are coming here. They are seeking for me. They are coming to ask their faithful friend Lakamba and his slave Babalatchi. Rejoice!'

But neither of his hearers appeared to be in a joyful mood. Lakamba had put one leg over his knee, and went on gently scratching it with a meditative air, while Babalatchi, sitting cross-legged, seemed suddenly to become smaller and very limp, staring straight before him vacantly. The guard evinced some interest in the proceedings, stretching themselves full length on the mats to be nearer the speaker. One of them got up and now stood leaning against the arm-rack, playing absently with the fringes of his sword-hilt.

Dain waited till the crash of thunder had died away in distant mutterings before he spoke again.

'Are you dumb, O ruler of Sambir, or is the son of a great

Rajah unworthy of your notice? I am come here to seek refuge and to warn you, and want to know what you intend doing.'

'You came here because of the white man's daughter,' retorted Lakamba, quickly. 'Your refuge was with your father, the Rajah of Bali, the Son of Heaven, the "Anak Agong"* himself. What am I to protect great princes? Only yesterday I planted rice in a burnt clearing; today you say I hold your life in my hand.'

Babalatchi glanced at his master. 'No man can escape his fate,' he murmured piously. 'When love enters a man's heart he is like a child – without any understanding. Be merciful, Lakamba,' he added, twitching the corner of the Rajah's sarong warningly.

Lakamba snatched away the skirt of the sarong angrily. Under the dawning comprehension of intolerable embarrassments caused by Dain's return to Sambir he began to lose such composure as he had been, till then, able to maintain; and now he raised his voice loudly above the whistling of the wind and the patter of rain on the roof in the hard squall passing over the house.

'You came here first as a trader with sweet words and great promises, asking me to look the other way while you worked your will on the white man there. And I did. What do you want now? When I was young I fought. Now I am old, and want peace. It is easier for me to have you killed than to fight the Dutch. It is better for me.'

The squall had now passed, and, in the short stillness of the lull in the storm, Lakamba repeated softly, as if to himself, 'Much easier. Much better.'

Dain did not seem greatly discomposed by the Rajah's threatening words. While Lakamba was speaking he had glanced once rapidly over his shoulder, just to make sure that there was nobody behind him, and, tranquillised* in that respect, he had extracted a siri-box* out of the folds of his waist-cloth, and was wrapping carefully the little bit of betel-nut and a small pinch of lime in the green leaf tendered him politely by the watchful Babalatchi. He accepted this as a peace-offering from the silent statesman – a kind of mute protest against his master's undiplomatic violence, and as an omen of a possible understanding to be arrived at yet. Otherwise Dain was not uneasy. Although recognising the justice of Lakamba's surmise that he had come back to Sambir only for the sake of the white man's daughter, yet he was not conscious of any childish lack of understanding, as suggested by Babalatchi. In fact, Dain knew very well that Lakamba was too deeply implicated in the gunpowder smuggling to care for an investigation by the Dutch authorities into that matter. When sent off by his father, the independent Rajah of Bali,* at the time when the hostilities between Dutch and Malays threatened to spread from Sumatra over the whole archipelago, Dain had found all the big traders deaf to his guarded proposals, and above the temptation of the great prices he was ready to give for gunpowder. He went to Sambir as a last and almost hopeless resort, having heard in Macassar of the white man there, and of the regular steamer trading from Singapore – allured also by the fact that there was no Dutch resident* on the river, which would make things easier, no doubt. His hopes got nearly wrecked against the stubborn loyalty of Lakamba arising from well-understood self-interest; but at last the young man's generosity, his persuasive enthusiasm, the prestige of his father's great name, overpowered the prudent hesitation of the ruler of Sambir. Lakamba would have nothing to do himself with any illegal traffic. He also objected to the Arabs being made use of in that matter; but he suggested Almayer, saying that he was a weak man easily persuaded, and that his friend, the English captain of the steamer, could be made very useful – very likely even would join in the business, smuggling the powder in the steamer without Abdulla's knowledge. There again Dain met in Almayer with unexpected resistance; Lakamba had to send Babalatchi over with the solemn promise that his eyes would be shut in friendship for the white man, Dain paying for the promise and the friendship in good silver guilders of the hated Orang Blanda. Almayer, at last consenting, said the powder would be obtained, but Dain must trust him with dollars to send to Singapore in payment for it. He would induce Ford to buy and smuggle it in the steamer on board the brig. He did not want any money for himself out of the transaction, but Dain must help him in his great enterprise after sending off the brig. Almayer had explained to Dain that he could not trust Lakamba alone in that matter; he would be afraid of losing his treasure and his life through the cupidity of the Rajah; yet the Rajah had to be told, and insisted on taking a share in that operation, or else his eyes would remain shut no longer. To this Almayer had to submit. Had Dain not seen Nina he would have probably refused to engage himself and his men in the projected expedition to Gunong Mas* – the mountain of gold. As it was he intended to return with half of his men as soon as the brig was clear of the reefs, but the persistent chase given him by the Dutch frigate had forced him to run south and ultimately to wreck and destroy his vessel in order to preserve his liberty or perhaps even his life. Yes, he had come back to Sambir for Nina, although aware that the Dutch would look for him there, but he had also calculated his chances of safety in Lakamba's hands. For all his ferocious talk, the merciful ruler would not kill him, for he had long ago been impressed with the notion that Dain possessed the secret of the white man's treasure; neither would he give him up to the Dutch, for fear of some fatal disclosure of complicity in the treasonable trade. So Dain felt tolerably secure as he sat meditating quietly his answer to the Rajah's bloodthirsty speech. Yes, he would point out to him the aspect of his position should he – Dain – fall into the hands of the Dutch and should he speak the truth. He would have nothing more to lose then, and he would speak the truth. And if he did return to Sambir, disturbing thereby Lakamba's peace of mind, what then? He came to look after his property. Did he not pour a stream of silver into Mrs Almayer's greedy lap? He had paid, for the girl, a price worthy of a great prince, although unworthy of that delightfully maddening creature for whom his untamed soul longed in an intensity of desire far more tormenting than the sharpest pain. He wanted his happiness. He had the right to be in Sambir.

He rose, and, approaching the table, leaned both his elbows on it; Lakamba responsively edged his seat a little closer, while Babalatchi scrambled to his feet and thrust his inquisitive head between his master's and Dain's. They interchanged their ideas rapidly, speaking in whispers into each other's faces, very close now, Dain suggesting, Lakamba contradicting, Babalatchi conciliating and anxious in his vivid apprehension of coming difficulties. He spoke most, whispering earnestly, turning his head slowly from side to side so as to bring his solitary eye to bear upon each of his interlocutors in turn. Why should there be strife? said he. Let Tuan Dain, whom he loved only less than his master, go trustfully into hiding. There were many places for that. Bulangi's house away in the clearing was best. Bulangi was a safe man. In the network of crooked channels no white man could find his way. White men were strong, but very foolish. It was undesirable to fight them, but deception was easy. They were like silly women – they did not know the use of reason, and he was a match for any of them – went on Babalatchi, with all the confidence of deficient experience. Probably the Dutch would seek Almayer. Maybe they would take away their countryman if they were suspicious of him. That would be good. After the Dutch went away Lakamba and Dain would get the treasure without any trouble, and there would be one person less to share it. Did he not speak wisdom? Will Tuan Dain go to Bulangi's house till the danger is over, go at once?

Dain accepted this suggestion of going into hiding with a certain sense of conferring a favour upon Lakamba and the anxious statesman, but he met the proposal of going at once with a decided no, looking Babalatchi meaningly in the eye. The statesman sighed as a man accepting the inevitable would do, and pointed silently towards the other bank of the river. Dain bent his head slowly.

'Yes, I am going there,' he said.

'Before the day comes?' asked Babalatchi.

'I am going there now,' answered Dain, decisively. 'The Orang Blanda will not be here before tomorrow night, perhaps, and I must tell Almayer of our arrangements.'

'No, Tuan. No; say nothing,' protested Babalatchi. 'I will go over myself at sunrise and let him know.'

'I will see,' said Dain, preparing to go.

The thunderstorm was recommencing outside, the heavy clouds hanging low overhead now. There was a constant rumble of distant thunder punctuated by the nearer sharp crashes, and in the continuous play of blue lightning the woods and the river showed fitfully, with all the elusive distinctness of detail characteristic of such a scene. Outside the door of the Rajah's house Dain and Babalatchi stood on the shaking verandah as if dazed and stunned by the violence of the storm. They stood there amongst the cowering forms of the Rajah's slaves and retainers seeking shelter from the rain, and Dain called aloud to his boatmen, who responded with an unanimous 'Ada!* Tuan!' while they looked uneasily at the river.

'This is a great flood!' shouted Babalatchi into Dain's ear. 'The river is very angry. Look! Look at the drifting logs! Can you go?'

Dain glanced doubtfully on the livid expanse of seething water bounded far away on the other side by the narrow black line of the forests. Suddenly, in a vivid white flash, the low point of land with the bending trees on it and Almayer's house, leaped into view, flickered and disappeared. Dain pushed Babalatchi aside and ran down to the water-gate followed by his shivering boatmen.

Babalatchi backed slowly in and closed the door, then turned round and looked silently upon Lakamba. The Rajah sat still, glaring stonily upon the table, and Babalatchi gazed curiously at the perplexed mood of the man he had served so many years through good and evil fortune. No doubt the one-eyed statesman felt within his savage and much sophisticated breast the unwonted feelings of sympathy with, and perhaps even pity for, the man he called his master. From the safe position of a confidential adviser, he could, in the dim vista of past years, see himself – a casual cut-throat – finding shelter under that man's roof in the modest rice-clearing of early beginnings. Then came a long period of unbroken success, of wise counsels, and deep plottings resolutely carried out by the fearless Lakamba, till the whole east coast from Poulo Laut to Tanjong Batu* listened to Babalatchi's wisdom speaking through the mouth of the ruler of Sambir. In those long years how many dangers escaped, how many enemies bravely faced, how many white men successfully circumvented! And now he looked upon the result of so many years of patient toil: the fearless Lakamba cowed by the shadow of an impending trouble. The ruler was growing old, and Babalatchi, aware of an uneasy feeling at the pit of his stomach,* put both his hands there with a suddenly vivid and sad perception of the fact that he himself was growing old too; that the time of reckless daring was past for both of them, and that they had to seek refuge in prudent cunning. They wanted peace; they were disposed to reform; they were ready even to retrench, so as to have the wherewithal to bribe the evil days away, if bribed away they could be. Babalatchi sighed for the second time that night as he squatted again at his master's feet and tendered him his betel-nut box in mute sympathy. And they sat there in close yet silent communion of betel-nut chewers, moving their jaws slowly, expectorating decorously into the wide-mouthed brass vessel they passed to one another, and listening to the awful din of the battling elements outside.

'There is a very great flood,' remarked Babalatchi, sadly.

'Yes,' said Lakamba. 'Did Dain go?'

'He went, Tuan. He ran down to the river like a man possessed of the Sheitan* himself.'

There was another long pause.

'He may get drowned,' suggested Lakamba at last, with some show of interest.

'The floating logs are many,' answered Babalatchi, 'but he is a good swimmer,' he added languidly.

'He ought to live,' said Lakamba; 'he knows where the treasure is.'

Babalatchi assented with an ill-humoured grunt. His want of success in penetrating the white man's secret as to the locality where the gold was to be found was a sore point with the statesman of Sambir, as the only conspicuous failure in an otherwise brilliant career.

A great peace had now succeeded the turmoil of the storm. Only the little belated clouds, which hurried past overhead to catch up the main body flashing silently in the distance, sent down short showers that pattered softly with a soothing hiss over the palm-leaf roof.

Lakamba roused himself from his apathy with an appearance of having grasped the situation at last.

'Babalatchi,' he called briskly, giving him a slight kick.

'Ada Tuan! I am listening.'

'If the Orang Blanda come here, Babalatchi, and take Almayer to Batavia to punish him for smuggling gunpowder, what will he do, you think?'

'I do not know, Tuan.'

'You are a fool,' commented Lakamba, exultingly. 'He will tell them where the treasure is, so as to find mercy. He will.'

Babalatchi looked up at his master and nodded his head with by no means a joyful surprise. He had not thought of this; there was a new complication.

'Almayer must die,' said Lakamba, decisively, 'to make our secret safe. He must die quietly, Babalatchi. You must do it.'

Babalatchi assented, and rose wearily to his feet. 'Tomorrow?' he asked.

'Yes; before the Dutch come. He drinks much coffee,' answered Lakamba, with seeming irrelevancy.

Babalatchi stretched himself yawning, but Lakamba, in the flattering consciousness of a knotty problem solved by his own unaided intellectual efforts, grew suddenly very wakeful.

'Babalatchi,' he said to the exhausted statesman, 'fetch the box of music the white captain gave me. I cannot sleep.'

At this order a deep shade of melancholy settled upon Babalatchi's features. He went reluctantly behind the curtain and soon reappeared carrying in his arms a small hand-organ,* which he put down on the table with an air of deep dejection. Lakamba settled himself comfortably in his arm-chair.

'Turn, Babalatchi, turn,' he murmured, with closed eyes.

Babalatchi's hand grasped the handle with the energy of despair, and as he turned, the deep gloom on his countenance changed into an expression of hopeless resignation. Through the open shutter the notes of Verdi's music* floated out on the great silence over the river and forest. Lakamba listened with closed eyes and a delighted smile; Babalatchi turned, at times dozing off and swaying over, then catching himself up in a great fright with a few quick turns of the handle. Nature slept in an exhausted repose after the fierce turmoil, while under the unsteady hand of the statesman of Sambir the Trovatore fitfully wept, wailed, and bade goodbye to his Leonore again and again in a mournful round of tearful and endless iteration.

CHAPTER 7

The bright sunshine of the clear mistless morning, after the stormy night, flooded the main path of the settlement leading from the low shore of the Pantai branch of the river to the gate of Abdulla's compound. The path was deserted this morning; it stretched its dark yellow surface, hard beaten by the tramp of many bare feet, between the clusters of palm trees, whose tall trunks barred it with strong black lines at irregular intervals, while the newly risen sun threw the shadows of their leafy heads far away over the roofs of the buildings lining the river, even over the river itself as it flowed swiftly and silently past the deserted houses. For the houses were deserted too. On the narrow strip of trodden grass intervening between their open doors and the road, the morning fires smouldered untended, sending thin fluted columns of smoke into the cool air, and spreading the thinnest veil of mysterious blue haze over the sunlit solitude of the settlement. Almayer, just out of his hammock, gazed sleepily at the unwonted appearance of Sambir, wondering vaguely at the absence of life. His own house was very quiet; he could not hear his wife's voice, nor the sound of Nina's footsteps in the big room, opening on the verandah, which he called his sitting-room, whenever, in the company of white men, he wished to assert his claims to the commonplace decencies of civilisation. Nobody ever sat there; there was nothing there to sit upon, for Mrs Almayer in her savage moods, when excited by the reminiscences of the piratical period of her life, had torn off the curtains to make sarongs for the slave-girls, and had burnt the showy furniture piecemeal to cook the family rice. But Almayer was not thinking of his furniture now. He was thinking of Dain's return, of Dain's nocturnal interview with Lakamba, of its possible influence on his long-matured plans, now nearing the period of their execution. He was also uneasy at the non-appearance of Dain who had promised him an early visit. 'The fellow had plenty of time to cross the river,' he mused, 'and there was so much to be done today. The settling of details for the early start on the morrow; the launching of the boats; the thousand and one finishing touches. For the expedition must start complete, nothing should be forgotten, nothing should—'

The sense of the unwonted solitude grew upon him suddenly, and in the unusual silence he caught himself longing even for the usually unwelcome sound of his wife's voice to break the oppressive stillness which seemed, to his frightened fancy, to portend the advent of some new misfortune. 'What has happened?' he muttered half aloud, as he shuffled in his imperfectly adjusted slippers towards the balustrade of the verandah. 'Is everybody asleep or dead?'

The settlement was alive and very much awake. It was awake ever since the early break of day, when Mahmat Banjer, in a fit of unheard-of energy, arose and, taking up his hatchet, stepped over the sleeping forms of his two wives and walked shivering to the water's edge to make sure that the new house he was building had not floated away during the night.

The house was being built by the enterprising Mahmat on a large raft, and he had securely moored it just inside the muddy point of land at the junction of the two branches of the Pantai so as to be out of the way of drifting logs that would no doubt strand on the point during the freshet. Mahmat walked through the wet grass saying bourrouh,* and cursing softly to himself the hard necessities of active life that drove him from his warm couch into the cold of the morning. A glance showed him that his house was still there, and he congratulated himself on his foresight in hauling it out of harm's way, for the increasing light showed him a confused wrack of drift-logs, half-stranded on the muddy flat, interlocked into a shapeless raft by their branches, tossing to and fro and grinding together in the eddy caused by the meeting currents of the two branches of the river. Mahmat walked down to the water's edge to examine the rattan moorings of his house just as the sun cleared the trees of the forest on the opposite shore. As he bent over the fastenings he glanced again carelessly at the unquiet jumble of logs and saw there something that caused him to drop his hatchet and stand up, shading his eyes with his hand from the rays of the rising sun. It was something red, and the logs rolled over it, at times closing round it, sometimes hiding it. It looked to him at first like a strip of red cloth. The next moment Mahmat had made it out and raised a great shout.

'Ah ya! There!' yelled Mahmat. 'There's a man amongst the logs.' He put the palms of his hand to his lips and shouted, enunciating distinctly, his face turned towards the settlement: 'There's a body of a man in the river! Come and see! A dead – stranger!'

The women of the nearest house were already outside kindling the fires and husking the morning rice. They took up the cry shrilly, and it travelled so from house to house, dying away in the distance. The men rushed out excited but silent, and ran towards the muddy point where the unconscious logs tossed and ground and bumped and rolled over the dead stranger with the stupid persistency of inanimate things. The women followed, neglecting their domestic duties and disregarding the possibilities of domestic discontent, while groups of children brought up the rear, warbling joyously, in the delight of unexpected excitement.

Almayer called aloud for his wife and daughter, but receiving no response, stood listening intently. The murmur of the crowd reached him faintly, bringing with it the assurance of some unusual event. He glanced at the river just as he was going to leave the verandah and checked himself at the sight of a small canoe crossing over from the Rajah's landing-place. The solitary occupant (in whom Almayer soon recognised Babalatchi) effected the crossing a little below the house and paddled up to the Lingard jetty in the dead water under the bank. Babalatchi clambered out slowly and went on fastening his canoe with fastidious care, as if not in a hurry to meet Almayer, whom he saw looking at him from the verandah. This delay gave Almayer time to notice and greatly wonder at Babalatchi's official get-up. The statesman of Sambir was clad in a costume befitting his high rank. A loudly checkered sarong encircled his waist, and from its many folds peeped out the silver hilt of the kriss that saw the light only on great festivals or during official receptions. Over the left shoulder and across the otherwise unclad breast of the aged diplomatist glistened a patent leather belt bearing a brass plate with the arms of Netherlands under the inscription, 'Sultan of Sambir'. Babalatchi's head was covered by a red turban, whose fringed ends falling over the left cheek and shoulder gave to his aged face a ludicrous expression of joyous recklessness. When the canoe was at last fastened to his satisfaction he straightened himself up, shaking down the folds of his sarong, and moved with long strides towards Almayer's house, swinging regularly his long ebony staff, whose gold head ornamented with precious stones flashed in the morning sun. Almayer waved his hand to the right towards the point of land, to him invisible, but in full view from the jetty.

'Oh, Babalatchi! oh!' he called out; 'what is the matter there? can you see?'

Babalatchi stopped and gazed intently at the crowd on the river bank, and after a little while the astonished Almayer saw him leave the path, gather up his sarong in one hand, and break into a trot through the grass towards the muddy point. Almayer, now greatly interested, ran down the steps of the verandah. The murmur of men's voices and the shrill cries of women reached him quite distinctly now, and as soon as he turned the corner of his house he could see the crowd on the low promontory swaying and pushing round some object of interest. He could indistinctly hear Babalatchi's voice, then the crowd opened before the aged statesman and closed after him with an excited hum, ending in a loud shout.

As Almayer approached the throng a man ran out and rushed past him towards the settlement, unheeding his call to stop and explain the cause of this excitement. On the very outskirts of the crowd Almayer found himself arrested by an unyielding mass of humanity, regardless of his entreaties for a passage, insensible to his gentle pushes as he tried to work his way through it towards the riverside.

In the midst of his gentle and slow progress he fancied suddenly he had heard his wife's voice in the thickest of the throng. He could not mistake very well Mrs Almayer's high-pitched tones, yet the words were too indistinct for him to understand their purport. He paused in his endeavours to make a passage for himself, intending to get some intelligence from those around him, when a long and piercing shriek rent the air, silencing the murmurs of the crowd and the voices of his informants. For a moment Almayer remained as if turned into stone with astonishment and horror, for he was certain now that he had heard his wife wailing for the dead. He remembered

Nina's unusual absence, and maddened by his apprehensions as to her safety, he pushed blindly and violently forward, the crowd falling back with cries of surprise and pain before his frantic advance.

On the point of land in a little clear space lay the body of the stranger just hauled out from amongst the logs. On one side stood Babalatchi, his chin resting on the head of his staff and his one eye gazing steadily at the shapeless mass of broken limbs, torn flesh, and bloodstained rags. As Almayer burst through the ring of horrified spectators, Mrs Almayer threw her own head-veil over the upturned face of the drowned man, and, squatting by it, with another mournful howl, sent a shiver through the now silent crowd. Mahmat, dripping wet, turned to Almayer, eager to tell his tale.

In the first moment of reaction from the anguish of his fear the sunshine seemed to waver before Almayer's eyes, and he listened to words spoken around him without comprehending their meaning. When, by a strong effort of will, he regained the possession of his senses, Mahmat was saying –

'That is the way, Tuan. His sarong was caught in the broken branch, and he hung with his head under water. When I saw what it was I did not want it here. I wanted it to get clear and drift away. Why should we bury a stranger in the midst of our houses for his ghost to frighten our women and children? Have we not enough ghosts about this place?'

A murmur of approval interrupted him here. Mahmat looked reproachfully at Babalatchi.

'But the Tuan Babalatchi ordered me to drag the body ashore' – he went on looking round at his audience, but addressing himself only to Almayer – 'and I dragged him by the feet; in through the mud I have dragged him, although my heart longed to see him float down the river to strand perchance on Bulangi's clearing – may his father's grave be defiled!'

There was subdued laughter at this, for the enmity of Mahmat and Bulangi was a matter of common notoriety and of undying interest to the inhabitants of Sambir. In the midst of that mirth Mrs Almayer wailed suddenly again.

'Allah! What ails the woman!' exclaimed Mahmat, angrily. 'Here, I have touched this carcass which came from nobody knows where, and have most likely defiled myself before eating rice. By orders of Tuan Babalatchi I did this thing to please the white man. Are you pleased, O Tuan Almayer? And what will be my recompense? Tuan Babalatchi said a recompense there will be, and from you. Now consider. I have been defiled, and if not defiled I may be under the spell. Look at his anklets! Who ever heard of a corpse appearing during the night amongst the logs with gold anklets on its legs? There is witchcraft there. However,' added Mahmat, after a reflective pause, 'I will have the anklet if there is permission, for I have a charm against the ghosts and am not afraid. God is great!'

A fresh outburst of noisy grief from Mrs Almayer checked the flow of Mahmat's eloquence. Almayer, bewildered, looked in turn at his wife, at Mahmat, at Babalatchi, and at last arrested his fascinated gaze on the body lying on the mud with covered face in a grotesquely unnatural contortion of mangled and broken limbs, one twisted and lacerated arm, with white bones protruding in many places through the torn flesh, stretched out; the hand with outspread fingers nearly touching his foot.

'Do you know who this is?' he asked of Babalatchi, in a low voice.

Babalatchi, staring straight before him, hardly moved his lips, while Mrs Almayer's persistent lamentations drowned the whisper of his murmured reply intended only for Almayer's ear.

'It was fate. Look at your feet, white man. I can see a ring on those torn fingers which I know well.'

Saying this, Babalatchi stepped carelessly forward, putting his foot as if accidentally on the hand of the corpse and pressing it into the soft mud. He swung his staff menacingly towards the crowd, which fell back a little.

'Go away,' he said sternly, 'and send your women to their cooking fires, which they ought not to have left to run after a dead stranger. This is men's work here. I take him now in the name of the Rajah. Let no man remain here but Tuan Almayer's slaves. Now go!'

The crowd reluctantly began to disperse. The women went first, dragging away the children that hung back with all their weight on the maternal hand. The men strolled slowly after them in ever forming and changing groups that gradually dissolved as they neared the settlement and every man regained his own house with steps quickened by the hungry anticipation of the morning rice. Only on the slight elevation where the land sloped down towards the muddy point a few men, either friends or enemies of Mahmat, remained gazing curiously for some time longer at the small group standing around the body on the river bank.

'I do not understand what you mean, Babalatchi,' said Almayer. 'What is the ring you are talking about? Whoever he is, you have trodden the poor fellow's hand right into the mud. Uncover his face,' he went on, addressing Mrs Almayer, who, squatting by the head of the corpse, rocked herself to and fro, shaking from time to time her dishevelled grey locks, and muttering mournfully.

'Hai!'* exclaimed Mahmat, who had lingered close by. 'Look, Tuan; the logs came together so,' and here he pressed the palms of his hands together, 'and his head must have been between them, and now there is no face for you to look at. There are his flesh and his bones, the nose, and the lips, and maybe his eyes, but nobody could tell the one from the other. It was written the day he was born that no man could look at him in death and be able to say, "This is my friend's face." '

'Silence, Mahmat; enough!' said Babalatchi, 'and take thy eyes off his anklet, thou eater of pig's flesh.* Tuan Almayer,' he went on, lowering his voice, 'have you seen Dain this morning?'

Almayer opened his eyes wide and looked alarmed. 'No,' he said quickly; 'haven't you seen him? Is he not with the Rajah? I am waiting; why does he not come?'

Babalatchi nodded his head sadly.

'He is come, Tuan. He left last night when the storm was great and the river spoke angrily. The night was very black, but he had within him a light that showed the way to your house as smooth as a narrow backwater, and the many logs no bigger than wisps of dried grass. Therefore he went; and now he lies here.' And Babalatchi nodded his head towards the body.

'How can you tell?' said Almayer, excitedly, pushing his wife aside. He snatched the cover off and looked at the formless mass of flesh, hair, and drying mud, where the face of the drowned man should have been. 'Nobody can tell,' he added, turning away with a shudder.

Babalatchi was on his knees wiping the mud from the stiffened fingers of the outstretched hand. He rose to his feet and flashed before Almayer's eyes a gold ring set with a large green stone.

'You know this well,' he said. 'This never left Dain's hand. I had to tear the flesh now to get it off. Do you believe now?'

Almayer raised his hands to his head and let them fall listlessly by his side in the utter abandonment of despair. Babalatchi, looking at him curiously, was astonished to see him smile. A strange fancy had taken possession of Almayer's brain, distracted by this new misfortune. It seemed to him that for many years he had been falling into a deep precipice. Day after day, month after month, year after year, he had been falling, falling, falling; it was a smooth, round, black thing, and the black walls had been rushing upwards with wearisome rapidity. A great rush, the noise of which he fancied he could hear yet; and now, with an awful shock, he had reached the bottom, and behold! he was alive and whole, and Dain was dead with all his bones broken. It struck him as funny. A dead Malay; he had seen many dead Malays without any emotion; and now he felt inclined to weep, but it was over the fate of a white man he knew; a man that fell over a deep precipice and did not die. He seemed somehow to himself to be standing on one side, a little way off, looking at a certain Almayer who was in great trouble. Poor, poor fellow! Why doesn't he cut his throat? He wished to encourage him; he was very anxious to see him lying dead over that other corpse. Why does he not die and end this suffering? He groaned aloud unconsciously and started with affright at the sound of his own voice. Was he going mad? Terrified by the thought he turned away and ran towards his house repeating to himself, 'I am not going mad; of course not, no, no, no!' He tried to keep a firm hold of the idea.* Not mad, not mad. He stumbled as he ran blindly up the steps repeating fast and ever faster those words wherein seemed to lie his salvation. He saw Nina standing there, and wished to say something to her, but could not remember what, in his extreme anxiety not to forget that he was not going mad, which he still kept repeating mentally as he ran round the table, till he stumbled against one of the arm-chairs and dropped into it exhausted. He sat staring wildly at Nina, still assuring himself mentally of his own sanity and wondering why the girl shrank from him in open-eyed alarm. What was the matter with her? This was foolish. He struck the table violently with his clenched fist and shouted hoarsely, 'Give me some gin! Run!' Then, while Nina ran off, he remained in the chair, very still and quiet, astonished at the noise he had made.

Nina returned with a tumbler half filled with gin, and found her father staring absently before him. Almayer felt very tired now, as if he had come from a long journey. He felt as if he had walked miles and miles that morning and now wanted to rest very much. He took the tumbler with a shaking hand, and as he drank, his teeth chattered against the glass which he drained and set down heavily on the table. He turned his eyes slowly towards Nina standing beside him, and said steadily –

'Now all is over, Nina. He is dead, and I may as well burn all my boats.'

He felt very proud of being able to speak so calmly. Decidedly he was not going mad. This certitude was very comforting, and he went on talking about the finding of the body, listening to his own voice complacently. Nina stood quietly, her hand resting lightly on her father's shoulder, her face unmoved, but every line of her features, the attitude of her whole body expressing the most keen and anxious attention.

'And so Dain is dead,' she said coldly, when her father ceased speaking.

Almayer's elaborately calm demeanour gave way in a moment to an outburst of violent indignation.

'You stand there as if you were only half alive, and talk to me,' he exclaimed angrily, 'as if it was a matter of no importance. Yes, he is dead! Do you understand? Dead! What do you care? You never cared; you saw me struggle, and work, and strive, unmoved; and my suffering you could never see. No, never. You have no heart, and you have no mind, or you would have understood that it was for you, for your happiness I was working. I wanted to be rich; I wanted to get away from here. I wanted to see white men bowing low before the power of your beauty and your wealth. Old as I am I wished to seek a strange land, a civilisation to which I am a stranger, so as to find a new life in the contemplation of your high fortunes, of your triumphs, of your happiness. For that I bore patiently the burden of work, of disappointment, of humiliation amongst these savages here, and I had it all nearly in my grasp.'

He looked at his daughter's attentive face and jumped to his feet upsetting the chair.

'Do you hear? I had it all there; so; within reach of my hand.'

He paused, trying to keep down his rising anger, and failed.

'Have you no feeling?' he went on. 'Have you lived without hope?' Nina's silence exasperated him; his voice rose, although he tried to master his feelings.

'Are you content to live in this misery and die in this wretched hole? Say something, Nina; have you no sympathy? Have you no word of comfort for me? I that loved you so.'

He waited for a while for an answer, and receiving none shook his fist in his daughter's face.

'I believe you are an idiot!' he yelled.

He looked round for the chair, picked it up and sat down stiffly. His anger was dead within him, and he felt ashamed of his outburst, yet relieved to think that now he had laid clear before his daughter the inner meaning of his life. He thought so in perfect good faith, deceived by the emotional estimate of his motives, unable to see the crookedness of his ways, the unreality of his aims, the futility of his regrets. And now his heart was filled only with a great tenderness and love for his daughter. He wanted to see her miserable, and to share with her his despair; but he wanted it only as all weak natures long for a companionship in misfortune with beings innocent of its cause. If she suffered herself she would understand and pity him; but now she would not, or could not, find one word of comfort or love for him in his dire extremity. The sense of his absolute loneliness came home to his heart with a force that made him shudder.* He swayed and fell forward with his face on the table, his arms stretched straight out, extended and rigid. Nina made a quick movement towards her father and stood looking at the grey head, on the broad shoulders shaken convulsively by the violence of feelings that found relief at last in sobs and tears.

Nina sighed deeply and moved away from the table. Her features lost the appearance of stony indifference that had exasperated her father into his outburst of anger and sorrow. The expression of her face, now unseen by her father, underwent a rapid change. She had listened to Almayer's appeal for sympathy, for one word of comfort, apparently indifferent, yet with her breast torn by conflicting impulses raised unexpectedly by events she had not foreseen, or at least did not expect to happen so soon. With her heart deeply moved by the sight of Almayer's misery, knowing it in her power to end it with a word, longing to bring peace to that troubled heart, she heard with terror the voice of her overpowering love commanding her to be silent. And she submitted after a short and fierce struggle of her old self against the new principle of her life. She wrapped herself up in absolute silence, the only safeguard against some fatal admission. She could not trust herself to make a sign, to murmur a word for fear of saying too much; and the very violence of the feelings that stirred the innermost recesses of her soul seemed to turn her person into a stone. The dilated nostrils and the flashing eyes were the only signs of the storm raging within, and those signs of his daughter's emotion Almayer did not see, for his sight was dimmed by self-pity, by anger, and by despair.

Had Almayer looked at his daughter as she leant over the front rail of the verandah he could have seen the expression of indifference give way to a look of pain, and that again pass away, leaving the glorious beauty of her face marred by deep-drawn lines of watchful anxiety. The long grass in the neglected courtyard stood very straight before her eyes in the noonday heat. From the river-bank there were voices and a shuffle of bare feet approaching the house; Babalatchi could be heard giving directions to Almayer's men, and Mrs Almayer's subdued wailing became audible as the small procession bearing the body of the drowned man and headed by that sorrowful matron turned the corner of the house. Babalatchi had taken the broken anklet off the man's leg, and now held it in his hand as he moved by the side of the bearers, while Mahmat lingered behind timidly, in the hopes of the promised reward.

'Lay him there,' said Babalatchi to Almayer's men, pointing to a pile of drying planks in front of the verandah. 'Lay him there. He was a Kaffir* and the son of a dog, and he was the white man's friend. He drank the white man's strong water,'* he added, with affected horror. 'That I have seen myself.'

The men stretched out the broken limbs on two planks they had laid level, while Mrs Almayer covered the body with a piece of white cotton cloth, and after whispering for some time with Babalatchi departed to her domestic duties. Almayer's men, after laying down their burden, dispersed themselves in quest of shady spots wherein to idle the day away. Babalatchi was left alone by the corpse that laid rigid under the white cloth in the bright sunshine.

Nina came down the steps and joined Babalatchi, who put his hand to his forehead, and squatted down with great deference.

'You have a bangle there,' said Nina, looking down on Babalatchi's upturned face and into his solitary eye.

'I have, Mem Putih,' returned the polite statesman. Then turning towards Mahmat he beckoned him closer, calling out, 'Come here!'

Mahmat approached with some hesitation. He avoided looking at Nina, but fixed his eyes on Babalatchi.

'Now, listen,' said Babalatchi, sharply. 'The ring and the anklet you have seen, and you know they belonged to Dain the trader, and to no other. Dain returned last night in a canoe. He spoke with the Rajah, and in the middle of the night left to cross over to the white man's house. There was a great flood, and this morning you found him in the river.'

'By his feet I dragged him out,' muttered Mahmat under his breath. 'Tuan Babalatchi, there will be a recompense!' he exclaimed aloud.

Babalatchi held up the gold bangle before Mahmat's eyes. 'What I have told you, Mahmat, is for all ears. What I give you now is for your eyes only. Take.'

Mahmat took the bangle eagerly and hid it in the folds of his waist-cloth. 'Am I a fool to show this thing in a house with three women in it?' he growled. 'But I shall tell them about Dain the trader, and there will be talk enough.'

He turned and went away, increasing his pace as soon as he was outside Almayer's compound.

Babalatchi looked after him till he disappeared behind the bushes. 'Have I done well, Mem Putih?' he asked, humbly addressing Nina.

'You have,' answered Nina. 'The ring you may keep yourself.'

Babalatchi touched his lips and forehead,* and scrambled to his feet. He looked at Nina, as if expecting her to say something more, but Nina turned towards the house and went up the steps, motioning him away with her hand.

Babalatchi picked up his staff and prepared to go. It was very warm, and he did not care for the long pull to the Rajah's house.

Yet he must go and tell the Rajah – tell of the event; of the change in his plans; of all his suspicions. He walked to the jetty and began casting off the rattan painter* of his canoe.

The broad expanse of the lower reach, with its shimmering surface dotted by the black specks of the fishing canoes, lay before his eyes. The fishermen seemed to be racing. Babalatchi paused in his work, and looked on with sudden interest. The man in the foremost canoe, now within hail of the first houses of Sambir, laid in his paddle and stood up shouting –

'The boats! the boats! The man-of-war's boats are coming! They are here!'

In a moment the settlement was again alive with people rushing to the riverside. The men began to unfasten their boats, the women stood in groups looking towards the bend down the river. Above the trees lining the reach a slight puff of smoke appeared like a black stain on the brilliant blue of the cloudless sky.

Babalatchi stood perplexed, the painter in his hand. He looked down the reach, then up towards Almayer's house, and back again at the river as if undecided what to do. At last he made the canoe fast again hastily, and ran towards the house and up the steps of the verandah.

'Tuan! Tuan!' he called, eagerly. 'The boats are coming. The man-of-war's boats. You had better get ready. The officers will come here, I know.'

Almayer lifted his head slowly from the table, and looked at him stupidly.

'Mem Putih!' exclaimed Babalatchi to Nina, 'look at him. He does not hear. You must take care,' he added meaningly.

Nina nodded to him with an uncertain smile, and was going to speak, when a sharp report from the gun* mounted in the bow of the steam launch that was just then coming into view arrested the words on her parted lips. The smile died out, and was replaced by the old look of anxious attention. From the hills far away the echo came back like a long-drawn and mournful sigh, as if the land had sent it in answer to the voice of its masters.

CHAPTER 8

The news as to the identity of the body lying now in Almayer's compound spread rapidly over the settlement. During the forenoon most of the inhabitants remained in the long street discussing the mysterious return and the unexpected death of the man who had become known to them as the trader. His arrival during the north-east monsoon, his long sojourn in their midst, his sudden departure with his brig, and, above all, the mysterious appearance of the body, said to be his, amongst the logs, were subjects to wonder at and to talk over and over again with undiminished interest. Mahmat moved from house to house and from group to group, always ready to repeat his tale: how he saw the body caught by the sarong in a forked log; how Mrs Almayer coming, one of the first, at his cries, recognised it, even before he had it hauled on shore; how Babalatchi ordered him to bring it out of the water. 'By the feet I dragged him in, and there was no head,' exclaimed Mahmat, 'and how could the white man's wife know who it was? She was a witch, it was well known. And did you see how the white man himself ran away at the sight of the body? Like a deer he ran!' And here Mahmat imitated Almayer's long strides, to the great joy of the beholders. And for all his trouble he had nothing. The ring with the green stone Tuan Babalatchi kept. 'Nothing! Nothing!' He spat down at his feet in sign of disgust, and left that group to seek further on a fresh audience.

The news spreading to the furthermost parts of the settlement found out Abdulla in the cool recess of his godown, where he sat overlooking his Arab clerks and the men loading and unloading the up-country canoes. Reshid, who was busy on the jetty, was summoned into his uncle's presence and found him, as usual, very calm and even cheerful, but very much surprised. The rumour of the capture or destruction of Dain's brig had reached the Arab's ears three days before from the sea-fishermen and through the dwellers on the lower reaches of the river. It had been passed upstream from neighbour to neighbour till Bulangi, whose clearing was nearest to the settlement, had brought that news himself to Abdulla whose favour he courted. But rumour also spoke of a fight and of Dain's death on board his own vessel. And now all the settlement talked of Dain's visit to the Rajah and of his death when crossing the river in the dark to see Almayer. They could not understand this. Reshid thought that it was very strange. He felt uneasy and doubtful. But Abdulla, after the first shock of surprise, with the old age's dislike for solving riddles, showed a becoming resignation. He remarked that the man was dead now at all events, and consequently no more dangerous. Where was the use to wonder at the decrees of Fate, especially if they were propitious to the True Believers? And with a pious ejaculation to Allah the Merciful, the Compassionate,* Abdulla seemed to regard the incident as closed for the present.

Not so Reshid. He lingered by his uncle, pulling thoughtfully his neatly trimmed beard.

'There are many lies,' he murmured. 'He has been dead once before, and came to life to die again now. The Dutch will be here before many days and clamour for the man. Shall I not believe my eyes sooner than the tongues of women and idle men?'

'They say that the body is being taken to Almayer's compound,' said Abdulla. 'If you want to go there you must go before the Dutch arrive here. Go late. It should not be said that we have been seen inside that man's enclosure lately.'

Reshid assented to the truth of this last remark and left his uncle's side. He leaned against the lintel* of the big doorway and looked idly across the courtyard through the open gate on to the main road of the settlement. It lay empty, straight, and yellow under the flood of light. In the hot noontide the smooth trunks of palm trees, the outlines of the houses, and away there at the other end of the road the roof of Almayer's house visible over the bushes on the dark background of forest, seemed to quiver in the heat radiating from the steaming earth. Swarms of yellow butterflies rose, and settled to rise again in short flights before Reshid's half-closed eyes. From under his feet arose the dull hum of insects in the long grass of the courtyard. He looked on sleepily.

From one of the side paths amongst the houses a woman stepped out on the road, a slight girlish figure walking under the shade of a large tray balanced on its head. The consciousness of something moving stirred Reshid's half-sleeping senses into a comparative wakefulness. He recognised Taminah, Bulangi's slave-girl, with her tray of cakes for sale – an apparition of daily recurrence and of no importance whatever. She was going towards Almayer's house. She could be made useful. He roused himself up and ran towards the gate calling out, 'Taminah O!' The girl stopped, hesitated, and came back slowly. Reshid waited, signing to her impatiently to come nearer.

When near Reshid Taminah stood with downcast eyes. Reshid looked at her a while before he asked –

'Are you going to Almayer's house? They say in the settlement that Dain the trader, he that was found drowned this morning, is lying in the white man's campong.'

'I have heard this talk,' whispered Taminah; 'and this morning by the riverside I saw the body. Where it is now I do not know.'

'So you have seen it?' asked Reshid, eagerly. 'Is it Dain? You have seen him many times. You would know him.'

The girl's lips quivered and she remained silent for a while, breathing quickly.

'I have seen him, not a long time ago,' she said at last. 'The talk is true; he is dead. What do you want from me, Tuan? I must go.'

Just then the report of the gun fired on board the steam launch was heard, interrupting Reshid's reply. Leaving the girl he ran to the house, and met in the courtyard Abdulla coming towards the gate.

'The Orang Blanda are come,' said Reshid, 'and now we shall have our reward.'

Abdulla shook his head doubtfully. 'The white men's rewards are long in coming,' he said. 'White men are quick in anger and slow in gratitude. We shall see.'

He stood at the gate stroking his grey beard and listening to the distant cries of greeting at the other end of the settlement. As Taminah was turning to go he called her back.

'Listen, girl,' he said: 'there will be many white men in

Almayer's house. You shall be there selling your cakes to the men of the sea. What you see and what you hear you may tell me. Come here before the sun sets and I will give you a blue handkerchief with red spots. Now go, and forget not to return.'

He gave her a push with the end of his long staff as she was going away and made her stumble.

'This slave is very slow,' he remarked to his nephew, looking after the girl with great disfavour.

Taminah walked on, her tray on the head, her eyes fixed on the ground. From the open doors of the houses were heard, as she passed, friendly calls inviting her within for business purposes, but she never heeded them, neglecting her sales in the preoccupation of intense thinking. Since the very early morning she had heard much, she had also seen much that filled her heart with a joy mingled with great suffering and fear. Before the dawn, before she left Bulangi's house to paddle up to Sambir she had heard voices outside the house when all in it but herself were asleep. And now, with her knowledge of the words spoken in the darkness, she held in her hand a life and carried in her breast a great sorrow. Yet from her springy step, erect figure, and face veiled over by the everyday look of apathetic indifference, nobody could have guessed of the double load she carried under the visible burden of the tray piled up high with cakes manufactured by the thrifty hands of Bulangi's wives. In that supple figure straight as an arrow, so graceful and free in its walk, behind those soft eyes that spoke of nothing but of unconscious resignation, there slept all feelings and all passions, all hopes and all fears, the curse of life and the consolation of death. And she knew nothing of it all. She lived like the tall palms amongst whom she was passing now, seeking the light, desiring the sunshine, fearing the storm, unconscious of either. The slave had no hope, and knew of no change. She knew of no other sky, no other water, no other forest, no other world, no other life. She had no wish, no hope, no love, no fear except of a blow, and no vivid feeling but that of occasional hunger, which was seldom, for Bulangi was rich and rice was plentiful in the solitary house in his clearing. The absence of pain and hunger was her happiness, and when she felt unhappy she was simply tired, more than usual, after the day's labour. Then in the hot nights of the south-west monsoon she slept dreamlessly under the bright stars on the platform built outside the house and over the river. Inside they slept too: Bulangi by the door; his wives further in; the children with their mothers. She could hear their breathing; Bulangi's sleepy voice; the sharp cry of a child soon hushed with tender words. And she closed her eyes to the murmur of the water below her, to the whisper of the warm wind above, ignorant of the never-ceasing life of that tropical nature that spoke to her in vain with the thousand faint voices of the near forest, with the breath of tepid wind; in the heavy scents that lingered around her head; in the white wraiths of morning mist that hung over her in the solemn hush of all creation before the dawn.

Such had been her existence before the coming of the brig with the strangers. She remembered well that time; the uproar in the settlement, the never-ending wonder, the days and nights of talk and excitement. She remembered her own timidity with the strange men, till the brig moored to the bank became in a manner part of the settlement, and the fear wore off in the familiarity of constant intercourse. The call on board then became part of her daily round. She walked hesitatingly up the slanting planks of the gangway amidst the encouraging shouts and more or less decent jokes of the men idling over the bulwarks. There she sold her wares to those men that spoke so loud and carried themselves so free. There was a throng, a constant coming and going; calls interchanged, orders given and executed with shouts; the rattle of blocks,* the flinging about of coils of rope. She sat out of the way under the shade of the awning, with her tray before her, the veil drawn well over her face, feeling shy amongst so many men. She smiled at all buyers, but spoke to none, letting their jests pass with stolid unconcern. She heard many tales told around her of far-off countries, of strange customs, of events stranger still. Those men were brave; but the most fearless of them spoke of their chief with fear. Often the man they called their master passed before her, walking erect and indifferent, in the pride of youth, in the flash of rich dress, with a tinkle of gold ornaments, while everybody stood aside watching anxiously for a movement of his lips, ready to do his bidding. Then all her life seemed to rush into her eyes, and from under her veil she gazed at him, charmed, yet fearful to attract attention. One day he noticed her and asked,

'Who is that girl?' 'A slave, Tuan! A girl that sells cakes,' a dozen voices replied together. She rose in terror to run on shore, when he called her back; and as she stood trembling with head hung down before him, he spoke kind words, lifting her chin with his hand and looking into her eyes with a smile. 'Do not be afraid,' he said. He never spoke to her any more. Somebody called out from the river bank; he turned away and forgot her existence. Taminah saw Almayer standing on the shore with Nina on his arm. She heard Nina's voice calling out gaily, and saw Dain's face brighten with joy as he leaped on shore. She hated the sound of that voice ever since.

After that day she left off visiting Almayer's compound, and passed the noon hours under the shade of the brig awning. She watched for his coming with heart beating quicker and quicker, as he approached, into a wild tumult of newly-aroused feelings of joy and hope and fear that died away with Dain's retreating figure, leaving her tired out, as if after a struggle, sitting still for a long time in dreamy languor. Then she paddled home slowly in the afternoon, often letting her canoe float with the lazy stream in the quiet backwater of the river. The paddle hung idle in the water as she sat in the stern, one hand supporting her chin, her eyes wide open, listening intently to the whispering of her heart that seemed to swell at last into a song of extreme sweetness. Listening to that song she husked the rice at home; it dulled her ears to the shrill bickerings of Bulangi's wives, to the sound of angry reproaches addressed to herself. And when the sun was near its setting she walked to the bathing-place and heard it as she stood on the tender grass of the low bank, her robe at her feet, and looked at the reflection of her figure on the glass-like surface of the creek. Listening to it she walked slowly back, her wet hair hanging over her shoulders; laying down to rest under the bright stars, she closed her eyes to the murmur of the water below, of the warm wind above; to the voice of nature speaking through the faint noises of the great forest, and to the song of her own heart.

She heard, but did not understand, and drank in the dreamy joy of her new existence without troubling about its meaning or its end, till the full consciousness of life came to her through pain and anger. And she suffered horribly the first time she saw Nina's long canoe drift silently past the sleeping house of

Bulangi, bearing the two lovers into the white mist of the great river. Her jealousy and rage culminated into a paroxysm of physical pain that left her lying panting on the river bank, in the dumb agony of a wounded animal. But she went on moving patiently in the enchanted circle of slavery, going through her task day after day with all the pathos of the grief she could not express, even to herself, locked within her breast. She shrank from Nina as she would have shrunk from the sharp blade of a knife cutting into her flesh, but she kept on visiting the brig to feed her dumb, ignorant soul on her own despair. She saw Dain many times. He never spoke, he never looked. Could his eyes see only one woman's image? Could his ears hear only one woman's voice? He never noticed her; not once.

And then he went away. She saw him and Nina for the last time on that morning when Babalatchi, while visiting his fish baskets, had his suspicions of the white man's daughter's love affair with Dain confirmed beyond the shadow of doubt. Dain disappeared, and Taminah's heart, where lay useless and barren the seeds of all love and of all hate, the possibilities of all passions and of all sacrifices, forgot its joys and its sufferings when deprived of the help of the senses. Her half-formed, savage mind, the slave of her body – as her body was the slave of another's will – forgot the faint and vague image of the ideal that had found its beginning in the physical promptings of her savage nature. She dropped back into the torpor of her former life and found consolation – even a certain kind of happiness – in the thought that now Nina and Dain were separated, probably for ever. He would forget. This thought soothed the last pangs of dying jealousy that had nothing now to feed upon, and Taminah found peace. It was like the dreary tranquillity of a desert, where there is peace only because there is no life.

And now he had returned. She had recognised his voice calling aloud in the night for Bulangi. She had crept out after her master to listen closer to the intoxicating sound. Dain was there, in a boat, talking to Bulangi. Taminah, listening with arrested breath, heard another voice. The maddening joy, that only a second before she thought herself incapable of containing within her fast-beating heart, died out, and left her shivering in the old anguish of physical pain that she had suffered once before at the sight of Dain and Nina. Nina spoke now, ordering and entreating in turns, and Bulangi was refusing, expostulating, at last consenting. He went in to take a paddle from the heap lying behind the door. Outside the murmur of two voices went on, and she caught a word here and there. She understood that he was fleeing from white men, that he was seeking a hiding-place, that he was in some danger. But she heard also words which woke the rage of jealousy that had been asleep for so many days in her bosom. Crouching low on the mud in the black darkness amongst the piles, she heard the whisper in the boat that made light of toil, of privation, of danger, of life itself, if in exchange there could be but a short moment of close embrace, a look from the eyes, the feel of light breath, the touch of soft lips. So spoke Dain as he sat in the canoe holding Nina's hands while waiting for Bulangi's return; and Taminah, supporting herself by the slimy pile, felt as if a heavy weight was crushing her down, down into the black oily water at her feet. She wanted to cry out; to rush at them and tear their vague shadows apart; to throw Nina into the smooth water, cling to her close, hold her to the bottom where that man could not find her. She could not cry, she could not move. Then footsteps were heard on the bamboo platform above her head; she saw Bulangi get into his smallest canoe and take the lead, the other boat following, paddled by Dain and Nina. With a slight splash of the paddles dipped stealthily into the water, their indistinct forms passed before her aching eyes and vanished in the darkness of the creek.

She remained there in the cold and wet, powerless to move, breathing painfully under the crushing weight that the mysterious hand of Fate had laid so suddenly upon her slender shoulders, and shivering, she felt within a burning fire, that seemed to feed upon her very life. When the breaking day had spread a pale golden ribbon over the black outline of the forests, she took up her tray and departed towards the settlement, going about her task purely from the force of habit. As she approached Sambir she could see the excitement and she heard with momentary surprise of the finding of Dain's body. It was not true, of course. She knew it well. She regretted that he was not dead. She should have liked Dain to be dead, so as to be parted from that woman – from all women. She felt a strong desire to see Nina, but without any clear object. She hated her, and feared her, and she felt an irresistible impulse pushing her towards

Almayer's house to see the white woman's face, to look close at those eyes, to hear again that voice, for the sound of which Dain was ready to risk his liberty, his life even. She had seen her many times; she had heard her voice daily for many months past. What was there in her? What was there in that being to make a man speak as Dain had spoken, to make him blind to all other faces, deaf to all other voices?

She left the crowd by the riverside, and wandered aimlessly among the empty houses, resisting the impulse that pushed her towards Almayer's campong to seek there in Nina's eyes the secret of her own misery. The sun mounting higher, shortened the shadows and poured down upon her a flood of light and of stifling heat as she passed on from shadow to light, from light to shadow, amongst the houses, the bushes, the tall trees, in her unconscious flight from the pain in her own heart. In the extremity of her distress she could find no words to pray for relief, she knew of no heaven to send her prayer to, and she wandered on with tired feet in the dumb surprise and terror at the injustice of the suffering inflicted upon her without cause and without redress.

The short talk with Reshid, the proposal of Abdulla steadied her a little and turned her thoughts into another channel. Dain was in some danger. He was hiding from white men. So much she had overheard last night. They all thought him dead. She knew he was alive, and she knew of his hiding-place. What did the Arabs want to know about the white men? The white men want with Dain? Did they wish to kill him? She could tell them all – no, she would say nothing, and in the night she would go to him and sell him his life for a word, for a smile, for a gesture even, and be his slave in far-off countries, away from Nina. But there were dangers. The one-eyed Babalatchi who knew everything; the white man's wife – she was a witch. Perhaps they would tell. And then there was Nina. She must hurry on and see.

In her impatience she left the path and ran towards Almayer's dwelling through the undergrowth between the palm trees. She came out at the back of the house, where a narrow ditch, full of stagnant water that overflowed from the river, separated Almayer's campong from the rest of the settlement. The thick bushes growing on the bank were hiding from her sight the large courtyard with its cooking shed. Above them rose several thin columns of smoke, and from behind the sound of strange voices informed Taminah that the Men of the Sea belonging to the warship had already landed and were camped between the ditch and the house. To the left one of Almayer's slave-girls came down to the ditch and bent over the shiny water, washing a kettle. To the right the tops of the banana plantation, visible above the bushes, swayed and shook under the touch of invisible hands gathering the fruit. On the calm water several canoes moored to a heavy stake were crowded together, nearly bridging the ditch just at the place where Taminah stood. The voices in the courtyard rose at times into an outburst of calls, replies, and laughter, and then died away into a silence that soon was broken again by a fresh clamour. Now and again the thin blue smoke rushed out thicker and blacker, and drove in odorous masses over the creek, wrapping her for a moment in a suffocating veil; then, as the fresh wood caught well alight, the smoke vanished in the bright sunlight, and only the scent of aromatic wood drifted afar, to leeward* of the crackling fires.

Taminah rested her tray on a stump of a tree, and remained standing with her eyes turned towards Almayer's house, whose roof and part of a whitewashed wall were visible over the bushes. The slave-girl finished her work, and after looking for a while curiously at Taminah, pushed her way through the dense thicket back to the courtyard. Round Taminah there was now a complete solitude. She threw herself down on the ground, and hid her face in her hands. Now when so close she had no courage to see Nina. At every burst of louder voices from the courtyard she shivered in the fear of hearing Nina's voice. She came to the resolution of waiting where she was till dark, and then going straight to Dain's hiding-place. From where she was she could watch the movements of white men, of Nina, of all Dain's friends, and of all his enemies. Both were hateful alike to her, for both would take him away beyond her reach. She hid herself in the long grass to wait anxiously for the sunset that seemed so slow to come.

On the other side of the ditch, behind the bush, by the clear fires, the seamen of the frigate had encamped on the hospitable invitation of Almayer. Almayer, roused out of his apathy by the prayers and importunity of Nina, had managed to get down in time to the jetty so as to receive the officers at their landing. The lieutenant in command accepted his invitation to his house with the remark that in any case their business was with Almayer – and perhaps not very pleasant, he added. Almayer hardly heard him. He shook hands with them absently and led the way towards the house. He was scarcely conscious of the polite words of welcome he greeted the strangers with, and afterwards repeated several times over again in his efforts to appear at ease. The agitation of their host did not escape the officer's eyes, and the chief confided to his subordinate, in a low voice, his doubts as to Almayer's sobriety. The young sub-lieutenant laughed and expressed in a whisper the hope that the white man was not intoxicated enough to neglect the offer of some refreshments. 'He does not seem very dangerous,' he added, as they followed Almayer up the steps of the verandah.

'No, he seems more of a fool than a knave; I have heard of him,' returned the senior.

They sat around the table. Almayer with shaking hands made gin cocktails, offered them all round, and drank himself, with every gulp feeling stronger, steadier, and better able to face all the difficulties of his position. Ignorant of the fate of the brig he did not suspect the real object of the officer's visit. He had a general notion that something must have leaked out about the gunpowder trade, but apprehended nothing beyond some temporary inconvenience. After emptying his glass he began to chat easily, lying back in his chair with one of his legs thrown negligently over the arm. The lieutenant astride on his chair, a glowing cheroot in the corner of his mouth, listened with a sly smile from behind the thick volumes of smoke that escaped from his compressed lips. The young sub-lieutenant, leaning with both elbows on the table, his head between his hands, looked on sleepily in the torpor induced by fatigue and the gin. Almayer talked on –

'It is a great pleasure to see white faces here. I have lived here many years in great solitude. The Malays, you understand, are not company for a white man; moreover they are not friendly; they do not understand our ways. Great rascals they are. I believe I am the only white man on the east coast* that is a settled resident. We get visitors from Macassar or Singapore sometimes – traders, agents, or explorers, but they are rare. There was a scientific explorer* here a year or more ago. He lived in my house: drank from morning to night. He lived joyously for a few months, and when the liquor he brought with him was gone he returned to Batavia with a report on the mineral wealth of the interior. Ha, ha, ha! Good, is it not?'

He ceased abruptly and looked at his guests with a meaningless stare. While they laughed he was reciting to himself the old story: 'Dain dead, all my plans destroyed. This is the end of all hope and of all things.' His heart sank within him. He felt a kind of deadly sickness.

'Very good. Capital!' exclaimed both officers.

Almayer came out of his despondency with another burst of talk.

'Eh! what about the dinner? You have got a cook with you. That's all right. There is a cooking shed in the other courtyard. I can give you a goose. Look at my geese – the only geese on the east coast* – perhaps on the whole island. Is that your cook? Very good. Here, Ali, show this Chinaman the cooking place and tell Mem Almayer to let him have room there. My wife, gentlemen, does not come out; my daughter may. Meantime have some more drink. It is a hot day.'

The lieutenant took the cigar out of his mouth, looked at the ash critically, shook it off and turned towards Almayer.

'We have a rather unpleasant business with you,' he said.

'I am sorry,' returned Almayer. 'It can be nothing very serious, surely.'

'If you think an attempt to blow up forty men at least, not a serious matter you will not find many people of your opinion,' retorted the officer sharply.

'Blow up! What? I know nothing about it,' exclaimed Almayer. 'Who did that, or tried to do it?'

'A man with whom you had some dealings,' answered the lieutenant. 'He passed here under the name of Dain Maroola. You sold him the gunpowder he had in that brig we captured.'

'How did you hear about the brig?' asked Almayer. 'I know nothing about the powder he may have had.'

'An Arab trader of this place has sent the information* about your goings on here to Batavia, a couple of months ago,' said the officer. 'We were waiting for the brig outside, but he slipped past us at the mouth of the river, and we had to chase the fellow to the southward. When he sighted us he ran inside the reefs and put the brig ashore. The crew escaped in boats before we could take possession. As our boats neared the craft it blew up with a tremendous explosion; one of the boats being too near got swamped. Two men drowned – that is the result of your speculation, Mr Almayer. Now we want this Dain. We have good grounds to suppose he is hiding in Sambir. Do you know where he is? You had better put yourself right with the authorities as much as possible by being perfectly frank with me. Where is this Dain?'

Almayer got up and walked towards the balustrade of the verandah. He seemed not to be thinking of the officer's question. He looked at the body laying straight and rigid under its white cover on which the sun, declining amongst the clouds to the westward, threw a pale tinge of red. The lieutenant waited for the answer, taking quick pulls at his half-extinguished cigar. Behind them Ali moved noiselessly laying the table, ranging solemnly the ill-assorted and shabby crockery, the tin spoons, the forks with broken prongs, and the knives with saw-like blades and loose handles. He had almost forgotten how to prepare the table for white men. He felt aggrieved; Mem Nina would not help him. He stepped back to look at his work admiringly, feeling very proud. This must be right; and if the master afterwards is angry and swears, then so much the worse for Mem Nina. Why did she not help? He left the verandah to fetch the dinner.

'Well, Mr Almayer, will you answer my question as frankly as it is put to you?' asked the lieutenant, after a long silence.

Almayer turned round and looked at his interlocutor steadily. 'If you catch this Dain what will you do with him?' he asked.

The officer's face flushed. 'This is not an answer,' he said, annoyed.

'And what will you do with me?' went on Almayer, not heeding the interruption.

'Are you inclined to bargain?' growled the other. 'It would be bad policy, I assure you. At present I have no orders about your person, but we expected your assistance in catching this Malay.'

'Ah!' interrupted Almayer, 'just so: you can do nothing

without me, and I, knowing the man well, am to help you in finding him.'

'This is exactly what we expect,' assented the officer. 'You have broken the law, Mr Almayer, and you ought to make amends.'

'And save myself?'

'Well, in a sense yes. Your head is not in any danger,' said the lieutenant, with a short laugh.

'Very well,' said Almayer, with decision, 'I shall deliver the man up to you.'

Both officers rose to their feet quickly, and looked for their side-arms which they had unbuckled. Almayer laughed harshly.

'Steady, gentlemen!' he exclaimed. 'In my own time and in my own way. After dinner, gentlemen, you shall have him.'

'This is preposterous,' urged the lieutenant. 'Mr Almayer, this is no joking matter. The man is a criminal. He deserves to hang. While we dine he may escape; the rumour of our arrival—'

Almayer walked towards the table. 'I give you my word of honour, gentlemen, that he shall not escape; I have him safe enough.'

'The arrest should be effected before dark,' remarked the young sub.*

'I shall hold you responsible for any failure. We are ready, but can do nothing just now without you,' added the senior, with evident annoyance.

Almayer made a gesture of assent. 'On my word of honour,' he repeated vaguely. 'And now let us dine,' he added briskly.

Nina came through the doorway and stood for a moment holding the curtain aside for Ali and the old Malay woman bearing the dishes; then she moved towards the three men by the table.

'Allow me,' said Almayer, pompously. 'This is my daughter. Nina, these gentlemen, officers of the frigate outside, have done me the honour to accept my hospitality.'

Nina answered the low bows of the two officers by a slow inclination of the head and took her place at the table opposite her father. All sat down. The coxswain* of the steam launch came up carrying some bottles of wine.

'You will allow me to have this put upon the table?' said the lieutenant to Almayer.

'What! Wine! You are very kind. Certainly. I have none myself. Times are very hard.'

The last words of his reply were spoken by Almayer in a faltering voice. The thought that Dain was dead recurred to him vividly again, and he felt as if an invisible hand was gripping his throat. He reached for the gin bottle while they were uncorking the wine and swallowed a big gulp. The lieutenant, who was speaking to Nina, gave him a quick glance. The young sub began to recover from the astonishment and confusion caused by Nina's unexpected appearance and great beauty. 'She was very beautiful and imposing,' he reflected, 'but after all a half-caste girl.' This thought caused him to pluck up heart and look at Nina sideways. Nina, with composed face, was answering in a low, even voice the elder officer's polite questions as to the country and her mode of life. Almayer pushed his plate away and drank his guest's wine in gloomy silence.

CHAPTER 9

'Can I believe what you tell me? It is like a tale for men that listen only half awake by the camp fire, and it seems to have run off a woman's tongue.'

'Who is there here for me to deceive, O Rajah?' answered Babalatchi. 'Without you I am nothing. All I have told you I believe to be true. I have been safe for many years in the hollow of your hand. This is no time to harbour suspicions. The danger is very great. We should advise* and act at once, before the sun sets.'

'Right. Right,' muttered Lakamba, pensively.

They had been sitting for the last hour together in the audience chamber of the Rajah's house, for Babalatchi, as soon as he had witnessed the landing of the Dutch officers, had crossed the river to report to his master the events of the morning, and to confer with him upon the line of conduct to pursue in the face of altered circumstances. They were both puzzled and frightened by the unexpected turn the events had taken. The Rajah, sitting crosslegged on his chair, looked fixedly at the floor; Babalatchi was squatting close by in an attitude of deep dejection.

'And where did you say he is hiding now?' asked Lakamba, breaking at last the silence full of gloomy forebodings in which they both had been lost for a long while.

'In Bulangi's clearing – the furthest one, away from the house. They went there that very night. The white man's daughter took him there. She told me so herself, speaking to me openly, for she is half white and has no decency. She said she was waiting for him while he was here; then, after a long time, he came out of the darkness and fell at her feet exhausted. He lay like one dead, but she brought him back to life in her arms, and made him breathe again with her own breath. That is what she said, speaking to my face, as I am speaking now to you, Rajah. She is like a white woman and knows no shame.'

He paused, deeply shocked. Lakamba nodded his head. 'Well, and then?' he asked.

'They called the old woman,' went on Babalatchi, 'and he told them all – about the brig, and how he tried to kill many men. He knew the Orang Blanda were very near, although he had said nothing to us about that; he knew his great danger. He thought he had killed many, but there were only two dead, as I have heard from the men of the sea that came in the warship's boats.'

'And the other man, he that was found in the river?' interrupted Lakamba.

'That was one of his boatmen. When his canoe was overturned by the logs those two swam together, but the other man must have been hurt. Dain swam, holding him up. He left him in the bushes when he went up to the house. When they all came down his heart had ceased to beat; then the old woman spoke; Dain thought it was good. He took off his anklet and broke it, twisting it round the man's foot. His ring he put on that slave's hand. He took off his sarong and clothed that thing that wanted no clothes, the two women holding it up meanwhile, their intent being to deceive all eyes and to mislead the minds in the settlement, so that they could swear to the thing that was not, and that there could be no treachery when the white men came. Then Dain and the white woman departed to call up Bulangi and find a hiding-place. The old woman remained by the body.'

'Hai!' exclaimed Lakamba. 'She has wisdom.'

'Yes, she has a Devil of her own to whisper counsel in her ear,' assented Babalatchi. 'She dragged the body with great toil to the point where many logs were stranded. All these things were done in the darkness after the storm had passed away. Then she waited. At the first sign of daylight she battered the face of the dead with a heavy stone, and she pushed him amongst the logs. She remained near, watching. At sunrise Mahmat Banjer came and found him. They all believed; I myself was deceived, but not for long. The white man believed, and, grieving, fled to his house. When we were alone I, having doubts, spoke to the woman, and she, fearing my anger and your might, told me all, asking for help in saving Dain.'

'He must not fall into the hands of the Orang Blanda,' said Lakamba; 'but let him die, if the thing can be done quietly.'

'It cannot, Tuan! Remember there is that woman who, being half white, is ungovernable, and would raise a great outcry. Also the officers are here. They are angry enough already. Dain must escape; he must go. We must help him now for our own safety.'

'Are the officers very angry?' inquired Lakamba, with interest.

'They are. The principal chief used strong words when speaking to me – to me when I salaamed in your name. I do not think,' added Babalatchi, after a short pause and looking very worried – 'I do not think I saw a white chief so angry before. He said we were careless or even worse. He told me he would speak to the Rajah, and that I was of no account.'

'Speak to the Rajah!' repeated Lakamba, thoughtfully. 'Listen, Babalatchi: I am sick, and shall withdraw; you cross over and tell the white men.'

'Yes,' said Babalatchi, 'I am going over at once; and as to Dain?'

'You get him away as you can best. This is a great trouble in my heart,' sighed Lakamba.

Babalatchi got up, and, going close to his master, spoke earnestly.

'There is one of our praus at the southern mouth of the river. The Dutch warship is to the northward watching the main entrance. I shall send Dain off tonight in a canoe, by the hidden channels, on board the prau. His father is a great prince, and shall hear of our generosity. Let the prau take him to Ampanam.* Your glory shall be great, and your reward in powerful friendship. Almayer will no doubt deliver the dead body as Dain's to the officers, and the foolish white men shall say, "This is very good; let there be peace." And the trouble shall be removed from your heart, Rajah.'

'True! true!' said Lakamba.

'And, this being accomplished by me who am your slave, you shall reward with a generous hand. That I know! The white man is grieving for the lost treasure, in the manner of white men who thirst after dollars. Now, when all other things are in order, we shall perhaps obtain the treasure from the white man. Dain must escape, and Almayer must live.'

'Now go, Babalatchi, go!' said Lakamba, getting off his chair. 'I am very sick, and want medicine. Tell the white chief so.'

But Babalatchi was not to be got rid of in this summary

manner. He knew that his master, after the manner of the great, liked to shift the burden of toil and danger on to his servants' shoulders, but in the difficult straits in which they were now the Rajah must play his part. He may be very sick for the white men, for all the world if he liked, as long as he would take upon himself the execution of part at least of Babalatchi's carefully thought-of plan. Babalatchi wanted a big canoe manned by twelve men to be sent out after dark towards Bulangi's clearing. Dain may have to be overpowered. A man in love cannot be expected to see clearly the path of safety if it leads him away from the object of his affections, argued Babalatchi, and in that case they would have to use force in order to make him go. Would the Rajah see that trusty men manned the canoe? The thing must be done secretly. Perhaps the Rajah would come himself, so as to bring all the weight of his authority to bear upon Dain if he should prove obstinate and refuse to leave his hiding-place. The Rajah would not commit himself to a definite promise, and anxiously pressed Babalatchi to go, being afraid of the white men paying him an unexpected visit. The aged statesman reluctantly took his leave and went into the courtyard.

Before going down to his boat Babalatchi stopped for a while in the big open space where the thick-leaved trees put black patches of shadow which seemed to float on a flood of smooth, intense light that rolled up to the houses and down to the stockade and over the river, where it broke and sparkled in thousands of glittering wavelets, like a band woven of azure and gold edged with the brilliant green of the forests guarding both banks of the Pantai. In the perfect calm before the coming of the afternoon breeze the irregularly jagged line of tree-tops stood unchanging, as if traced by an unsteady hand on the clear blue of the hot sky. In the space sheltered by the high palisades there lingered the smell of decaying blossoms from the surrounding forest, a taint of drying fish; with now and then a whiff of acrid smoke from the cooking fires when it eddied down from under the leafy boughs and clung lazily about the burnt-up grass.

As Babalatchi looked up at the flagstaff overtopping a group of low trees in the middle of the courtyard, the tricolour flag of the Netherlands stirred slightly for the first time since it had been hoisted that morning on the arrival of the man-of-war boats. With a faint rustle of trees the breeze came down in light puffs, playing capriciously for a time with this emblem of Lakamba's power, that was also the mark of his servitude; then the breeze freshened in a sharp gust of wind, and the flag flew out straight and steady above the trees. A dark shadow ran along the river, rolling over and covering up the sparkle of declining sunlight. A big white cloud sailed slowly across the darkening sky, and hung to the westward as if waiting for the sun to join it there. Men and things shook off the torpor of the hot afternoon and stirred into life under the first breath of the sea breeze.

Babalatchi hurried down to the water-gate; yet before he passed through it he paused to look round the courtyard, with its light and shade, with its cheery fires, with the groups of Lakamba's soldiers and retainers scattered about. His own house stood amongst the other buildings in that enclosure, and the statesman of Sambir asked himself with a sinking heart when and how would it be given him to return to that house. He had to deal with a man more dangerous than any wild beast of his experience: a proud man, a man wilful after the manner of princes, a man in love. And he was going forth to speak to that man words of cold and worldly wisdom. Could anything be more appalling? What if that man should take umbrage at some fancied slight to his honour or disregard of his affections and suddenly 'amok'?* The wise adviser would be the first victim, no doubt, and death would be his reward. And underlying the horror of this situation there was the danger of those meddlesome fools, the white men. A vision of comfortless exile in far-off Madura* rose up before Babalatchi. Wouldn't that be worse than death itself? And there was that half-white woman with threatening eyes. How could he tell what an incomprehensible creature of that sort would or would not do? She knew so much that she made the killing of Dain an impossibility. That much was certain. And yet the sharp, rough-edged kriss is a good and discreet friend, thought Babalatchi, as he examined his own lovingly, and put it back in the sheath, with a sigh of regret, before unfastening his canoe. As he cast off the painter, pushed out into the stream, and took up his paddle, he realised vividly how unsatisfactory it was to have women mixed up in state affairs. Young women, of course. For Mrs Almayer's mature wisdom, and for the easy aptitude in intrigue that comes with years to the feminine mind, he felt the most sincere respect.

He paddled leisurely, letting the canoe drift down as he crossed towards the point. The sun was high yet, and nothing pressed.* His work would commence only with the coming of darkness. Avoiding the Lingard jetty, he rounded the point, and paddled up the creek at the back of Almayer's house. There were many canoes lying there, their noses all drawn together, fastened all to the same stake. Babalatchi pushed his little craft in amongst them and stepped on shore. On the other side of the ditch something moved in the grass.

'Who's that hiding?' hailed Babalatchi. 'Come out and speak to me.'

Nobody answered. Babalatchi crossed over, passing from boat to boat, and poked his staff viciously in the suspicious place. Taminah jumped up with a cry.

'What are you doing here?' he asked, surprised. 'I have nearly stepped on your tray. Am I a Dyak that you should hide at my sight?'

'I was weary, and – I slept,' whispered Taminah, confusedly.

'You slept! You have not sold anything today, and you will be beaten when you return home,' said Babalatchi.

Taminah stood before him abashed and silent. Babalatchi looked her over carefully with great satisfaction. Decidedly he would offer fifty dollars more to that thief Bulangi. The girl pleased him.

'Now you go home. It is late,' he said sharply. 'Tell Bulangi that I shall be near his house before the night is half over, and that I want him to make all things ready for a long journey. You understand? A long journey to the southward. Tell him that before sunset, and do not forget my words.'

Taminah made a gesture of assent, and watched Babalatchi recross the ditch and disappear through the bushes bordering Almayer's compound. She moved a little further off the creek and sank in the grass again, lying down on her face, shivering in dry-eyed misery.

Babalatchi walked straight towards the cooking-shed looking for Mrs Almayer. The courtyard was in a great uproar. A strange Chinaman had possession of the kitchen fire and was noisily demanding another saucepan. He hurled objurgations,* in the Canton dialect* and bad Malay, against the group of slave-girls standing a little way off, half frightened, half amused, at his violence. From the camping fires round which the seamen of the frigate were sitting came words of encouragement, mingled with laughter and jeering. In the midst of this noise and confusion Babalatchi met Ali, an empty dish in his hand.

'Where are the white men?' asked Babalatchi.

'They are eating in the front verandah,' answered Ali. 'Do not stop me, Tuan. I am giving the white men their food and am busy.'

'Where's Mem Almayer?'

'Inside in the passage. She is listening to the talk.'

Ali grinned and passed on; Babalatchi ascended the plankway to the rear verandah, and beckoning out Mrs Almayer, engaged her in earnest conversation. Through the long passage, closed at the further end by the red curtain, they could hear from time to time Almayer's voice mingling in conversation with an abrupt loudness that made Mrs Almayer look significantly at Babalatchi.

'Listen,' she said. 'He has drunk much.'

'He has,' whispered Babalatchi. 'He will sleep heavily tonight.'

Mrs Almayer looked doubtful.

'Sometimes the devil of strong gin makes him keep awake, and he walks up and down the verandah all night, cursing; then we stand afar off,' explained Mrs Almayer, with the fuller knowledge born of twenty odd years of married life.

'But then he does not hear, nor understand, and his hand, of course, has no strength. We do not want him to hear tonight.'

'No,' assented Mrs Almayer, energetically, but in a cautiously subdued voice. 'If he hears he will kill.'

Babalatchi looked incredulous.

'Hai Tuan, you may believe me. Have I not lived many years with that man? Have I not seen death in that man's eyes more than once when I was younger and he guessed at many things. Had he been a man of my own people I would not have seen such a look twice; but he—'

With a contemptuous gesture she seemed to fling unutterable scorn on Almayer's weak-minded aversion to sudden bloodshed.

'If he has the wish but not the strength, then what do we

fear?' asked Babalatchi, after a short silence during which they both listened to Almayer's loud talk till it subsided into the murmur of general conversation. 'What do we fear?' repeated Babalatchi again.

'To keep the daughter whom he loves he would strike into your heart and mine without hesitation,' said Mrs Almayer. 'When the girl is gone he will be like the devil unchained. Then you and I had better beware.'

'I am an old man and fear not death,' answered Babalatchi, with a mendacious assumption of indifference. 'But what will you do?'

'I am an old woman, and wish to live,' retorted Mrs Almayer. 'She is my daughter also. I shall seek safety at the feet of our Rajah, speaking in the name of the past when we both were young, and he—'

Babalatchi raised his hand.

'Enough. You shall be protected,' he said soothingly.

Again the sound of Almayer's voice was heard, and again interrupting their talk, they listened to the confused but loud utterance coming in bursts of unequal strength, with unexpected pauses and noisy repetitions that made some words and sentences fall clear and distinct on their ears out of the meaningless jumble of excited shoutings emphasised by the thumping of Almayer's fist upon the table. On the short intervals of silence, the high complaining note of tumblers, standing close together and vibrating to the shock, lingered, growing fainter, till it leapt up again into tumultuous ringing, when a new idea started a new rush of words and brought down the heavy hand again. At last the quarrelsome shouting ceased, and the thin plaint of disturbed glass died away into reluctant quietude.

Babalatchi and Mrs Almayer had listened curiously, their bodies bent and their ears turned towards the passage. At every louder shout they nodded at each other with a ridiculous affectation of scandalised propriety, and they remained in the same attitude for some time after the noise had ceased.

'This is the devil of gin,' whispered Mrs Almayer. 'Yes; he talks like that sometimes when there is nobody to hear him.'

'What does he say?' inquired Babalatchi, eagerly. 'You ought to understand.'

'I have forgotten their talk. A little I understood. He spoke without any respect of the white ruler in Batavia,* and of protection, and said he had been wronged; he said that several times. More I did not understand. Listen! Again he speaks!'

'Tse! tse! tse!'* clicked Babalatchi, trying to appear shocked, but with a joyous twinkle of his solitary eye. 'There will be great trouble between those white men. I will go round now and see. You tell your daughter that there is a sudden and a long journey before her, with much glory and splendour at the end. And tell her that Dain must go, or he must die, and that he will not go alone.'

'No, he will not go alone,' slowly repeated Mrs Almayer, with a thoughtful air, as she crept into the passage after seeing Babalatchi disappear round the corner of the house.

The statesman of Sambir, under the impulse of vivid curiosity, made his way quickly to the front of the house, but once there he moved slowly and cautiously as he crept step by step up the stairs of the verandah. On the highest step he sat down quietly, his feet on the steps below, ready for flight should his presence prove unwelcome. He felt pretty safe so. The table stood nearly endways to him, and he saw Almayer's back; at Nina he looked full face, and had a side view of both officers; but of the four persons sitting at the table only Nina and the younger officer noticed his noiseless arrival. The momentary dropping of Nina's eyelids acknowledged Babalatchi's presence; she then spoke at once to the young sub, who turned towards her with attentive alacrity, but her gaze was fastened steadily on her father's face while Almayer was speaking uproariously.

'. . . disloyalty and unscrupulousness! What have you ever done to make me loyal? You have no grip on this country. I had to take care of myself, and when I asked for protection I was met with threats and contempt, and had Arab slander thrown in my face. I! a white man!'

'Don't be violent, Almayer,' remonstrated the lieutenant; 'I have heard all this already.'

'Then why do you talk to me about scruples? I wanted money, and I gave powder in exchange. How could I know that some of your wretched men were going to be blown up? Scruples! Pah!'

He groped unsteadily amongst the bottles, trying one after

another, grumbling to himself the while. 'No more wine,' he muttered discontentedly.

'You have had enough, Almayer,' said the lieutenant, as he lighted a cigar. 'Is it not time to deliver to us your prisoner? I take it you have that Dain Maroola stowed away safely somewhere. Still we had better get that business over, and then we shall have more drink. Come! don't look at me like this.'

Almayer was staring with stony eyes, his trembling fingers fumbling about his throat.

'Gold,' he said with difficulty. 'Hem! A hand on the windpipe,* you know. Sure you will excuse. I wanted to say – a little gold for a little powder. What's that?'

'I know, I know,' said the lieutenant soothingly.

'No! You don't know. Not one of you knows!' shouted Almayer. 'The government is a fool, I tell you. Heaps of gold. I am the man that knows; I and another one. But he won't speak. He is—'

He checked himself with a feeble smile, and, making an unsuccessful attempt to pat the officer on the shoulder, knocked over a couple of empty bottles.

'Personally you are a fine fellow,' he said very distinctly, in a patronising manner. His head nodded drowsily as he sat muttering to himself.

The two officers looked at each other helplessly.

'This won't do,' said the lieutenant, addressing his junior. 'Have the men mustered in the compound here. I must get some sense out of him. Hi! Almayer! Wake up, man. Redeem your word. You gave your word. You gave your word of honour, you know.'

Almayer shook off the officer's hand with impatience, but his ill-humour vanished at once, and he looked up, putting his forefinger to the side of his nose.

'You are very young; there is time for all things,' he said, with an air of great sagacity.

The lieutenant turned towards Nina, who, leaning back in her chair, watched her father steadily.

'Really I am very much distressed by all this for your sake,' he exclaimed. 'I do not know,' he went on, speaking with some embarrassment, 'whether I have any right to ask you anything, unless, perhaps, to withdraw from this painful scene, but I feel that I must – for your father's good – suggest that you should—I mean if you have any influence over him you ought to exert it now to make him keep the promise he gave me before he – before he got into this state.'

He observed with discouragement that she seemed not to take any notice of what he said sitting still with half-closed eyes.

'I trust—' he began again.

'What is the promise you speak of?' abruptly asked Nina, leaving her seat and moving towards her father.

'Nothing that is not just and proper. He promised to deliver to us a man who in time of profound peace took the lives of innocent men to escape the punishment he deserved for breaking the law. He planned his mischief on a large scale. It is not his fault if it failed, partially. Of course you have heard of Dain Maroola. Your father secured him, I understand. We know he escaped up this river. Perhaps you—'

'And he killed white men!' interrupted Nina.

'I regret to say they were white. Yes, two white men lost their lives through that scoundrel's freak.'*

'Two only!' exclaimed Nina.

The officer looked at her in amazement.

'Why! why! You—' he stammered, confused.

'There might have been more,' interrupted Nina. 'And when you get this – this scoundrel will you go?'

The lieutenant, still speechless, bowed his assent.

'Then I would get him for you if I had to seek him in a burning fire,' she burst out with intense energy. 'I hate the sight of your white faces. I hate the sound of your gentle voices. That is the way you speak to women, dropping sweet words before any pretty face. I have heard your voices before. I hoped to live here without seeing any other white face but this,' she added in a gentler tone, touching lightly her father's cheek.

Almayer ceased his mumbling and opened his eyes. He caught hold of his daughter's hand and pressed it to his face, while Nina with the other hand smoothed his rumpled grey hair, looking defiantly over her father's head at the officer, who had now regained his composure and returned her look with a cool, steady stare. Below, in front of the verandah, they could hear the tramp of seamen mustering there according to orders. The sub-lieutenant came up the steps, while Babalatchi stood up uneasily and, with finger on lip, tried to catch Nina's eye.

'You are a good girl,' whispered Almayer, absently, dropping his daughter's hand.

'Father! father!' she cried, bending over him with passionate entreaty. 'See those two men looking at us. Send them away. I cannot bear it any more. Send them away. Do what they want and let them go.'

She caught sight of Babalatchi and ceased speaking suddenly, but her foot tapped the floor with rapid beats in a paroxysm of nervous restlessness. The two officers stood close together looking on curiously.

'What has happened? What is the matter?' whispered the younger man.

'Don't know,' answered the other, under his breath. 'One is furious, and the other is drunk. Not so drunk, either. Queer, this. Look!'

Almayer had risen, holding on to his daughter's arm. He hesitated a moment, then he let go his hold and lurched halfway across the verandah. There he pulled himself together, and stood very straight, breathing hard and glaring round angrily.

'Are the men ready?' asked the lieutenant.

'All ready, sir.'

'Now, Mr Almayer, lead the way,' said the lieutenant.

Almayer rested his eyes on him as if he saw him for the first time.

'Two men,' he said thickly. The effort of speaking seemed to interfere with his equilibrium. He took a quick step to save himself from a fall, and remained swaying backwards and forwards. 'Two men,' he began again, speaking with difficulty. 'Two white men – men in uniform – honourable men. I want to say – men of honour. Are you?'

'Come! None of that,' said the officer impatiently. 'Let us have that friend of yours.'

'What do you think I am?' asked Almayer, fiercely.

'You are drunk, but not so drunk as not to know what you are doing. Enough of this tomfoolery,' said the officer sternly, 'or I will have you put under arrest in your own house.'

'Arrest!' laughed Almayer, discordantly. 'Ha! ha! ha! Arrest! Why, I have been trying to get out of this infernal place for twenty years, and I can't. You hear, man! I can't, and never shall! Never!'

He ended his words with a sob, and walked unsteadily down the stairs. When in the courtyard the lieutenant approached him, and took him by the arm. The sub-lieutenant and Babalatchi followed close.

'That's better, Almayer,' said the officer encouragingly. 'Where are you going to? There are only planks there. Here,' he went on, shaking him slightly, 'do we want the boats?'

'No,' answered Almayer, viciously. 'You want a grave.'

'What? Wild again! Try to talk sense.'

'Grave!' roared Almayer, struggling to get himself free. 'A hole in the ground. Don't you understand? You must be drunk. Let me go! Let go, I tell you!'

He tore away from the officer's grasp, and reeled towards the planks where the body lay under its white cover; then he turned round quickly, and faced the semicircle of interested faces. The sun was sinking rapidly, throwing long shadows of house and trees over the courtyard, but the light lingered yet on the river, where the logs went drifting past in midstream, looking very distinct and black in the pale red glow. The trunks of the trees in the forest on the east bank were lost in gloom while their highest branches swayed gently in the departing sunlight. The air felt heavy and cold in the breeze, expiring in slight puffs that came over the water.

Almayer shivered as he made an effort to speak, and again with an uncertain gesture he seemed to free his throat from the grip of an invisible hand. His bloodshot eyes wandered aimlessly from face to face.

'There!' he said at last. 'Are you all there? He is a dangerous man.'

He dragged at the cover with hasty violence, and the body rolled stiffly off the planks and fell at his feet in rigid helplessness.

'Cold, perfectly cold,' said Almayer, looking round with a mirthless smile. 'Sorry can do no better. And you can't hang him, either. As you observe, gentlemen,' he added gravely, 'there is no head, and hardly any neck.'

The last ray of light was snatched away from the tree-tops, the river grew suddenly dark, and in the great stillness the murmur of the flowing water seemed to fill the vast expanse of grey shadow that descended upon the land.

'This is Dain,' went on Almayer to the silent group that surrounded him. 'And I have kept my word. First one hope, then another, and this is my last. Nothing is left now. You think there is one dead man here? Mistake, I 'sure you. I am much more dead. Why don't you hang me?' he suggested suddenly, in a friendly tone, addressing the lieutenant. 'I assure, assure you it would be a mat – matter of form altog – altogether.'

These last words he muttered to himself, and walked zigzaging towards his house. 'Get out!' he thundered at Ali, who was approaching timidly with offers of assistance. From afar, scared groups of men and women watched his devious progress. He dragged himself up the stairs by the banister, and managed to reach a chair into which he fell heavily. He sat for awhile panting with exertion and anger, and looking round vaguely for Nina; then making a threatening gesture towards the compound, where he had heard Babalatchi's voice, he overturned the table with his foot in a great crash of smashed crockery. He muttered yet menacingly to himself, then his head fell on his breast, his eyes closed, and with a deep sigh he fell asleep.

That night – for the first time in its history – the peaceful and flourishing settlement of Sambir saw the lights shining about 'Almayer's Folly'. These were the lanterns of the boats hung up by the seamen under the verandah where the two officers were holding a court of inquiry into the truth of the story related to them by Babalatchi. Babalatchi had regained all his importance. He was eloquent and persuasive, calling Heaven and Earth to witness the truth of his statements. There were also other witnesses. Mahmat Banjer and a good many others underwent a close examination that dragged its weary length far into the evening. A messenger was sent for Abdulla, who excused himself from coming on the score of his venerable age, but sent Reshid. Mahmat had to produce the bangle, and saw with rage and mortification the lieutenant put it in his pocket, as one of the proofs of Dain's death, to be sent in with the official report of the mission. Babalatchi's ring was also impounded for the same purpose, but the experienced statesman was resigned to that loss from the very beginning. He did not mind as long as he was sure, that the white men believed. He put that question to himself earnestly as he left, one of the last, when the proceedings came to a close. He was not certain. Still, if they believed only for a night, he would put Dain beyond their reach and feel safe himself. He walked away fast, looking from time to time over his shoulder in the fear of being followed, but he saw and heard nothing.

'Ten o'clock,' said the lieutenant, looking at his watch and yawning. 'I shall hear some of the captain's complimentary remarks when we get back. Miserable business, this.'

'Do you think all this is true?' asked the younger man.

'True! It is just possible. But if it isn't true what can we do? If we had a dozen boats we could patrol the creeks; and that wouldn't be much good. That drunken madman was right; we haven't enough hold on this coast. They do what they like. Are our hammocks slung?'

'Yes, I told the coxswain. Strange couple over there,' said the sub, with a wave of his hand towards Almayer's house.

'Hem! Queer, certainly. What have you been telling her? I was attending to the father most of the time.'

'I assure you I have been perfectly civil,' protested the other warmly.

'All right. Don't get excited. She objects to civility, then, from what I understand. I thought you might have been tender. You know we are on service.'

'Well, of course. Never forget that. Coldly civil. That's all.'

They both laughed a little, and not feeling sleepy began to pace the verandah side by side. The moon rose stealthily above the trees, and suddenly changed the river into a stream of scintillating silver. The forest came out of the black void and stood sombre and pensive over the sparkling water. The breeze died away into a breathless calm.

Seamanlike, the two officers tramped measuredly up and down without exchanging a word. The loose planks rattled rhythmically under their steps with obtrusive dry sound in the perfect silence of the night. As they were wheeling round again the younger man stood attentive.

'Did you hear that?' he asked.

'No!' said the other. 'Hear what?'

'I thought I heard a cry. Ever so faint. Seemed a woman's voice.* In that other house. Ah! Again! Hear it?'

'No,' said the lieutenant, after listening awhile. 'You young fellows always hear women's voices. If you are going to dream you had better get into your hammock. Goodnight.'

The moon mounted higher, and the warm shadows grew smaller and crept away as if hiding before the cold and cruel light.

CHAPTER 10

'It has set at last,' said Nina to her mother, pointing towards the hills behind which the sun had sunk.* 'Listen, mother, I am going now to Bulangi's creek, and if I should never return—'

She interrupted herself, and something like doubt dimmed for a moment the fire of suppressed exaltation that had glowed in her eyes and had illuminated the serene impassiveness of her features with a ray of eager life during all that long day of excitement – the day of joy and anxiety, of hope and terror, of vague grief and indistinct delight. While the sun shone with that dazzling light in which her love was born and grew till it possessed her whole being, she was kept firm in her unwavering resolve by the mysterious whisperings of desire which filled her heart with impatient longing for the darkness that would mean the end of danger and strife, the beginning of happiness, the fulfilling of love, the completeness of life. It had set at last! The short tropical twilight went out before she could draw the long breath of relief; and now the sudden darkness seemed to be full of menacing voices calling upon her to rush headlong into the unknown; to be true to her own impulses, to give herself up to the passion she had evoked and shared. He was waiting! In the solitude of the secluded clearing, in the vast silence of the forest he was waiting alone, a fugitive in fear of his life. Indifferent to his danger he was waiting for her. It was for her only that he had come; and now as the time approached when he should have his reward, she asked herself with dismay what meant that chilling doubt of her own will and of her own desire? With an effort she shook off the fear of the passing weakness. He should have his reward. Her woman's love and her woman's honour overcame the faltering distrust of that unknown future waiting for her in the darkness of the river.

'No, you will not return,' muttered Mrs Almayer, prophetically. 'Without you he will not go, and if he remains here—' She waved her hand towards the lights of 'Almayer's Folly', and the unfinished sentence died out in a threatening murmur.

The two women had met behind the house, and now were walking slowly together towards the creek where all the canoes were moored. Arrived at the fringe of bushes they stopped by a common impulse, and Mrs Almayer, laying her hand on her daughter's arm, tried in vain to look close into the girl's averted face. When she attempted to speak, her first words were lost in a stifled sob that sounded strangely coming from that woman who, of all human passions, seemed to know only those of anger and hate.

'You are going away to be a great Ranee,' she said at last, in a voice that was steady enough now, 'and if you be wise you shall have much power that will endure many days, and even last into your old age. What have I been? A slave all my life, and I have cooked rice for a man who had no courage and no wisdom. Hai! I! even I, was given in gift by a chief and a warrior to a man that was neither. Hai! Hai!'

She wailed to herself softly, lamenting the lost possibilities of murder and mischief that could have fallen to her lot had she been mated with a congenial spirit. Nina bent down over Mrs Almayer's slight form and scanned attentively, under the stars that had rushed out on the black sky and now hung breathless over that strange parting, her mother's shrivelled features, and looked close into the sunken eyes that could see into her own dark future by the light of a long and a painful experience. Again she felt herself fascinated, as of old, by her mother's exalted mood and by the oracular certainty of expression which, together with her fits of violence, had contributed not a little to the reputation for witchcraft she enjoyed in the settlement.

'I was a slave, and you shall be a queen,' went on Mrs Almayer, looking straight before her; 'but remember men's strength and their weakness. Tremble before his anger, so that he may see your fear in the light of day; but in your heart you may laugh, for after sunset he is your slave.'

'A slave! He! The master of life! You do not know him, mother.'

Mrs Almayer condescended to laugh contemptuously.

'You speak like a fool of a white woman,' she exclaimed.

'What do you know of men's anger and of men's love? Have you watched the sleep of men weary of dealing death? Have you felt about you the strong arm that could drive a kriss deep into a beating heart? Yah! you are a white woman, and ought to pray to a woman-god!'

'Why do you say this? I have listened to your words so long that I have forgotten my old life. If I was white would I stand here, ready to go? Mother, I shall return to the house and look once more at my father's face.'

'No!' said Mrs Almayer, violently. 'No, he sleeps now the sleep of gin; and if you went back he might awake and see you. No, he shall never see you. When the terrible old man took you away from me when you were little, you remember—'

'It was such a long time ago,' murmured Nina.

'I remember,' went on Mrs Almayer, fiercely. 'I wanted to look at your face again. He said no! I heard you cry and jumped into the river. You were his daughter then; you are my daughter now. Never shall you go back to that house; you shall never cross this courtyard again. No! no!'

Her voice rose almost to a shout. On the other side of the creek there was a rustle in the long grass. The two women heard it, and listened for a while in startled silence.

'I shall go,' said Nina, in a cautious but intense whisper. 'What is your hate or your revenge to me?'

She moved towards the house, Mrs Almayer clinging to her and trying to pull her back.

'Stop, you shall not go!' she gasped.

Nina pushed away her mother impatiently and gathered up her skirts for a quick run, but Mrs Almayer ran forward and turned round, facing her daughter with outstretched arms.

'If you move another step,' she exclaimed, breathing quickly, 'I shall cry out. Do you see those lights in the big house? There sit two white men, angry because they cannot have the blood of the man you love. And in those dark houses,' she continued, more calmly as she pointed towards the settlement, 'my voice could wake up men that would lead the Orang Blanda soldiers to him who is waiting – for you.'

She could not see her daughter's face, but the white figure before her stood silent and irresolute in the darkness. Mrs Almayer pursued her advantage.

'Give up your old life! Forget!' she said in entreating tones. 'Forget that you ever looked at a white face; forget their words; forget their thoughts. They speak lies. And they think lies because they despise us that are better than they are, but not so strong. Forget their friendship and their contempt; forget their many gods. Girl, why do you want to remember the past when there is a warrior and a chief ready to give many lives – his own life – for one of your smiles?'

While she spoke she pushed gently her daughter towards the canoes, hiding her own fear, anxiety, and doubt under the flood of passionate words that left Nina no time to think and no opportunity to protest, even if she had wished it. But she did not wish it now. At the bottom of that passing desire to look again at her father's face there was no strong affection. She felt no scruples and no remorse at leaving suddenly that man whose sentiment towards herself she could not understand, she could not even see. There was only an instinctive clinging to old life, to old habits, to old faces; that fear of finality which lurks in every human breast and prevents so many heroisms and so many crimes. For years she had stood between her mother and her father, the one so strong in her weakness, the other so weak where he could have been strong. Between those two beings so dissimilar, so antagonistic, she stood with mute heart wondering and angry at the fact of her own existence. It seemed so unreasonable, so humiliating to be flung there in that settlement and to see the days rush by into the past, without a hope, a desire, or an aim that would justify the life she had to endure in ever-growing weariness. She had little belief and no sympathy for her father's dreams; but the savage ravings of her mother chanced to strike a responsive chord, deep down somewhere in her despairing heart; and she dreamed dreams of her own with the persistent absorption of a captive thinking of liberty within the walls of his prison cell. With the coming of Dain she found the road to freedom by obeying the voice of the new-born impulses, and with surprised joy she thought she could read in his eyes the answer to all the questionings of her heart. She understood now the reason and the aim of life; and in the triumphant unveiling of that mystery she threw away disdainfully her past with its sad thoughts, its bitter feelings, and its faint affections, now withered and dead in contact with her fierce passion.

Mrs Almayer unmoored Nina's own canoe and, straightening herself painfully, stood, painter in hand, looking at her daughter.

'Quick,' she said; 'get away before the moon rises, while the river is dark. I am afraid of Abdulla's slaves. The wretches prowl in the night often, and might see and follow you. There are two paddles in the canoe.'

Nina approached her mother and hesitatingly touched lightly with her lips the wrinkled forehead. Mrs Almayer snorted contemptuously in protest against that tenderness which she, nevertheless, feared could be contagious.

'Shall I ever see you again, mother?' murmured Nina.

'No,' said Mrs Almayer, after a short silence. 'Why should you return here where it is my fate to die? You will live far away in splendour and might. When I hear of white men driven from the islands, then I shall know that you are alive, and that you remember my words.'

'I shall always remember,' returned Nina, earnestly; 'but where is my power, and what can I do?'

'Do not let him look too long in your eyes, nor lay his head on your knees without reminding him that men should fight before they rest. And if he lingers, give him his kriss yourself and bid him go, as the wife of a mighty prince should do when the enemies are near. Let him slay the white men that come to us to trade, with prayers on their lips and loaded guns in their hands. Ah' – she ended with a sigh – 'they are on every sea, and on every shore; and they are very many!'

She swung the bow of the canoe towards the river, but did not let go the gunwale, keeping her hand on it in irresolute thoughtfulness. Nina put the point of the paddle against the bank, ready to shove off into the stream.

'What is it, mother?' she asked, in a low voice. 'Do you hear anything?'

'No,' said Mrs Almayer, absently. 'Listen, Nina,' she continued, abruptly, after a slight pause, 'in after years there will be other women—'

A stifled cry in the boat interrupted her, and the paddle rattled in the canoe as it slipped from Nina's hands, which she put out in a protesting gesture. Mrs Almayer fell on her knees on the bank and leaned over the gunwale so as to bring her own face close to her daughter's.

'There will be other women,' she repeated firmly; 'I tell you that, because you are half white, and may forget that he is a great chief, and that such things must be. Hide your anger, and do not let him see on your face the pain that will eat your heart. Meet him with joy in your eyes and wisdom on your lips, for to you he will turn in sadness or in doubt. As long as he looks upon many women your power will last, but should there be one, one only with whom he seems to forget you, then—'

'I could not live,' exclaimed Nina, covering her face with both her hands. 'Do not speak so, mother; it could not be.'

'Then,' went on Mrs Almayer, steadily, 'to that woman, Nina, show no mercy.'

She moved the canoe down towards the stream by the gunwale, and gripped it with both her hands, the bow pointing into the river.

'Are you crying?' she asked sternly of her daughter, who sat still with covered face. 'Arise, and take your paddle, for he has waited long enough. And remember, Nina, no mercy; and if you must strike, strike with a steady hand.'

She put out all her strength, and swinging her body over the water, shot the light craft far into the stream. When she recovered herself from the effort she tried vainly to catch a glimpse of the canoe that seemed to have dissolved suddenly into the white mist trailing over the heated waters of the Pantai. After listening for a while intently on her knees, Mrs Almayer rose with a deep sigh, while two tears wandered slowly down her withered cheeks. She wiped them off quickly with a wisp of her grey hair as if ashamed of herself, but could not stifle another loud sigh, for her heart was heavy and she suffered much, being unused to tender emotions. This time she fancied she had heard a faint noise, like the echo of her own sigh, and she stopped, straining her ears to catch the slightest sound, and peering apprehensively towards the bushes near her.

'Who is there?' she asked, in an unsteady voice, while her imagination peopled the solitude of the riverside with ghost-like forms. 'Who is there?' she repeated faintly.

There was no answer: only the voice of the river murmuring in sad monotone behind the white veil seemed to swell louder for a moment, to die away again in a soft whisper of eddies washing against the bank.

Mrs Almayer shook her head as if in answer to her own thoughts, and walked quickly away from the bushes, looking to the right and left watchfully. She went straight towards the cooking-shed, observing that the embers of the fire there glowed more brightly than usual, as if somebody had been adding fresh fuel to the fires during the evening. As she approached, Babalatchi, who had been squatting in the warm glow, rose and met her in the shadow outside.

'Is she gone?' asked the anxious statesman, hastily.

'Yes,' answered Mrs Almayer. 'What are the white men doing? When did you leave them?'

'They are sleeping now, I think. May they never wake!' exclaimed Babalatchi, fervently. 'Oh! but they are devils, and made much talk and trouble over that carcase. The chief threatened me twice with his hand, and said he would have me tied up to a tree. Tie me up to a tree! Me!' he repeated, striking his breast violently.

Mrs Almayer laughed tauntingly.

'And you salaamed and asked for mercy. Men with arms by their side acted otherwise when I was young.'

'And where are they, the men of your youth? You mad woman!' retorted Babalatchi, angrily. 'Killed by the Dutch. Aha! But I shall live to deceive them. A man knows when to fight and when to tell peaceful lies. You would know that if you were not a woman.'

But Mrs Almayer did not seem to hear him. With bent body and outstretched arm she appeared to be listening to some noise behind the shed.

'There are strange sounds,'* she whispered, with evident alarm. 'I have heard in the air the sounds of grief, as of a sigh and weeping. That was by the riverside. And now again I heard—'

'Where?' asked Babalatchi, in an altered voice. 'What did you hear?'

'Close here. It was like a breath long drawn. I wish I had burnt the paper over the body before it was buried.'*

'Yes,' assented Babalatchi. 'But the white men had him thrown into a hole at once. You know he found his death on the river,' he added cheerfully, 'and his ghost may hail the canoes, but would leave the land alone.'

Mrs Almayer, who had been craning her neck to look round the corner of the shed, drew back her head.

'There is nobody there,' she said, reassured. 'Is it not time for the Rajah war-canoe to go to the clearing?'

'I have been waiting for it here, for I myself must go,' explained Babalatchi. 'I think I will go over and see what makes them late. When will you come? The Rajah gives you refuge.'

'I shall paddle over before the break of day. I cannot leave my dollars behind,' muttered Mrs Almayer.

They separated. Babalatchi crossed the courtyard towards the creek to get his canoe, and Mrs Almayer walked slowly to the house, ascended the plankway, and passing through the back verandah entered the passage leading to the front of the house; but before going in she turned in the doorway and looked back at the empty and silent courtyard, now lit up by the rays of the rising moon. No sooner had she disappeared, however, than a vague shape flitted out from amongst the stalks of the banana plantation, darted over the moonlit space, and fell in the darkness at the foot of the verandah. It might have been the shadow of a driving cloud, so noiseless and rapid was its passage, but for the trail of disturbed grass, whose feathery heads trembled and swayed for a long time in the moonlight before they rested motionless and gleaming, like a design of silver sprays embroidered on a sombre background.

Mrs Almayer lighted the cocoanut lamp,* and lifting cautiously the red curtain, gazed upon her husband, shading the light with her hand. Almayer, huddled up in the chair, one of his arms hanging down, the other thrown across the lower part of his face as if to ward off an invisible enemy, his legs stretched straight out, slept heavily, unconscious of the unfriendly eyes that looked upon him in disparaging criticism. At his feet lay the overturned table, amongst a wreck of crockery and broken bottles. The appearance as of traces left by a desperate struggle was accentuated by the chairs, which seemed to have been scattered violently all over the place, and now lay about the verandah with a lamentable aspect of inebriety in their helpless attitudes. Only Nina's big rocking-chair, standing black and motionless on its high runners, towered above the chaos of demoralised furniture, unflinchingly dignified and patient, waiting for its burden.

With a last scornful look towards the sleeper, Mrs Almayer passed behind the curtain into her own room. A couple of bats, encouraged by the darkness and the peaceful state of affairs, resumed their silent and oblique gambols above Almayer's head, and for a long time the profound quiet of the house was unbroken, save for the deep breathing of the sleeping man and the faint tinkle of silver in the hands of the woman preparing for flight. In the increasing light of the moon that had risen now above the night mist, the objects on the verandah came out strongly outlined in black splashes of shadow with all the uncompromising ugliness of their disorder, and a caricature of the sleeping Almayer appeared on the dirty whitewash of the wall behind him in a grotesquely exaggerated detail of attitude and feature enlarged to a heroic size. The discontented bats departed in quest of darker places, and a lizard came out in short, nervous rushes, and, pleased with the white table-cloth, stopped on it in breathless immobility that would have suggested sudden death had it not been for the melodious call he exchanged with a less adventurous friend hiding amongst the lumber in the courtyard. Then the boards in the passage creaked, the lizard vanished, and Almayer stirred uneasily with a sigh: slowly, out of the senseless annihilation of drunken sleep, he was returning, through the land of dreams, to waking consciousness. Almayer's head rolled from shoulder to shoulder in the oppression of his dream; the heavens had descended upon him like a heavy mantle, and trailed in starred folds far under him. Stars above, stars all round him; and from the stars under his feet rose a whisper full of entreaties and tears, and sorrowful faces flitted amongst the clusters of light filling the infinite space below. How escape from the importunity of lamentable cries and from the look of staring, sad eyes in the faces which pressed round him till he gasped for breath under the crushing weight of worlds that hung over his aching shoulders? Get away! But how? If he attempted to move he would step off into nothing, and perish in the crashing fall of that universe of which he was the only support. And what were the voices saying? Urging him to move! Why? Move to destruction! Not likely! The absurdity of the thing filled him with indignation. He got a firmer foothold and stiffened his muscles in heroic resolve to carry his burden to all eternity. And ages passed in the superhuman labour, amidst the rush of circling worlds; in the plaintive murmur of sorrowful voices urging him to desist before it was too late – till the mysterious power that had laid upon him the giant task seemed at last to seek his destruction. With terror he felt an irresistible hand shaking him by the shoulder, while the chorus of voices swelled louder into an agonised prayer to go, go before it is too late. He felt himself slipping, losing his balance, as something dragged at his legs, and he fell. With a faint cry he glided out of the anguish of perishing creation into an imperfect waking that seemed to be still under the spell of his dream.*

'What? What?' he murmured sleepily, without moving or opening his eyes. His head still felt heavy, and he had not the courage to raise his eyelids. In his ears there still lingered the sound of entreating whisper. – 'Am I awake? – Why do I hear the voices?' he argued to himself, hazily. – 'I cannot get rid of the horrible nightmare yet. – I have been very drunk. – What is that shaking me? I am dreaming yet. – I must open my eyes and be done with it. I am only half awake, it is evident.'

He made an effort to shake off his stupor and saw a face close to his, glaring at him with staring eyeballs. He closed his eyes again in amazed horror and sat up straight in the chair, trembling in every limb. What was this apparition? – His own fancy, no doubt. – His nerves had been much tried the day before – and then the drink! He would not see it again if he had the courage to look. – He would look directly. – Get a little steadier first. – So. – Now.

He looked. The figure of a woman standing in the steely light, her hands stretched forth in a suppliant gesture, confronted him from the far-off end of the verandah; and in the space between him and the obstinate phantom floated the murmur of words that fell on his ears in a jumble of torturing sentences, the meaning of which escaped the utmost efforts of his brain. Who spoke the Malay words? Who ran away? Why too late – and too late for what? What meant those words of hate and love mixed so strangely together, the ever-recurring names falling on his ears again and again – Nina, Dain; Dain, Nina? Dain was dead, and Nina was sleeping, unaware of the terrible experience through which he was now passing. Was he going to be tormented for ever, sleeping or waking, and have no peace either night or day? What was the meaning of this?

He shouted the last words aloud. The shadowy woman seemed to shrink and recede a little from him towards the doorway, and there was a shriek. Exasperated by the incomprehensible nature of his torment, Almayer made a rush upon the apparition, which eluded his grasp, and he brought up heavily against the wall. Quick as lightning he turned round and pursued fiercely the mysterious figure fleeing from him with piercing shrieks that were like fuel to the flames of his anger. Over the furniture, round the overturned table, and now he had it cornered behind Nina's chair. To the left, to the right they dodged, the chair rocking madly between them, she sending out shriek after shriek at every feint, and he growling meaningless curses through his hard set teeth. 'Oh! the fiendish noise that split his head and seemed to choke his breath. – It would kill him. – It must be stopped!' An insane desire to crush that yelling thing induced him to cast himself recklessly over the chair with a desperate grab, and they came down together in a cloud of dust amongst the splintered wood. The last shriek died out under him in a faint gurgle, and he had secured the relief of absolute silence.

He looked at the woman's face under him. A real woman! He knew her. By all that is wonderful! Taminah! He jumped up ashamed of his fury and stood perplexed, wiping his forehead. The girl struggled to a kneeling posture and embraced his legs in a frenzied prayer for mercy.

'Don't be afraid,' he said, raising her. 'I shall not hurt you. Why do you come to my house in the night? And if you had to come, why not go behind the curtain where the women sleep?'

'The place behind the curtain is empty,' gasped Taminah, catching her breath between the words. 'There are no women in your house any more, Tuan. I saw the old Mem go away before I tried to wake you. I did not want your women, I wanted you.'

'Old Mem!' repeated Almayer. 'Do you mean my wife?'

She nodded her head.

'But of my daughter you are not afraid?' said Almayer.

'Have you not heard me?' she exclaimed. 'Have I not spoken for a long time when you lay there with eyes half open? She is gone too.'

'I was asleep. Can you not tell when a man is sleeping and when awake?'

'Sometimes,' answered Taminah in a low voice; 'sometimes the spirit lingers close to a sleeping body and may hear. I spoke a long time before I touched you, and I spoke softly for fear it would depart at a sudden noise and leave you sleeping for ever. I took you by the shoulder only when you began to mutter words I could not understand. Have you not heard, then, and do you know nothing?'

'Nothing of what you said. What is it? Tell again if you want me to know.'

He took her by the shoulder and led her unresisting to the front of the verandah into a stronger light. She wrung her hands with such an appearance of grief that he began to be alarmed.

'Speak,' he said. 'You made noise enough to wake even dead men. And yet nobody living came,' he added to himself in an uneasy whisper. 'Are you mute? Speak!' he repeated.

In a rush of words which broke out after a short struggle from her trembling lips she told him the tale of Nina's love and her own jealousy. Several times he looked angrily into her face and told her to be silent; but he could not stop the sounds that seemed to him to run out in a hot stream, swirl about his feet, and rise in scalding waves about him, higher, higher, drowning his heart, touching his lips with a feel of molten lead, blotting out his sight in scorching vapour, closing over his head, merciless and deadly. When she spoke of the deception as to Dain's death of which he had been the victim only that day, he glanced again at her with terrible eyes, and made her falter for a second, but he turned away directly, and his face suddenly lost all expression in a stony stare far away over the river. Ah! the river! His old friend and his old enemy, speaking always with the same voice as he runs from year to year bringing fortune or disappointment, happiness or pain, upon the same varying but unchanged surface of glancing currents and swirling eddies. For many years he had listened to the passionless and soothing murmur that sometimes was the song of hope, at times the song of triumph, of encouragement; more often the whisper of consolation that spoke of better days to come. For so many years! So many years! And now to the accompaniment of that murmur he listened to the slow and painful beating of his heart. He listened attentively, wondering at the regularity of its beats. He began to count mechanically. One, two. Why count? At the next beat it must stop. No heart could suffer so and beat so steadily for long. Those regular strokes as of a muffled hammer that rang in his ears must stop soon. Still beating unceasing and cruel. No man can bear this; and is this the last, or will the next one be the last? – How much longer? O God! how much longer?* His hand weighed heavier unconsciously on the girl's shoulder, and she spoke the last words of her story crouching at his feet with tears of pain and shame and anger. Was her revenge to fail her? This white man was like a senseless stone. Too late! Too late!

'And you saw her go?' Almayer's voice sounded harshly above her head.

'Did I not tell you?' she sobbed, trying to wriggle gently out from under his grip. 'Did I not tell you that I saw the witch-woman push the canoe? I lay hidden in the grass and heard all the words. She that we used to call the white Mem wanted to return to look at your face, but the witchwoman forbade her, and—'

She sank lower yet on her elbow, turning half round under the downward push of the heavy hand, her face lifted up to him with spiteful eyes.

'And she obeyed,' she shouted out in a half-laugh, half-cry of pain. 'Let me go, Tuan. Why are you angry with me? Hasten, or you shall be too late to show your anger to the deceitful woman.'

Almayer dragged her up to her feet and looked close into her face while she struggled, turning her head away from his wild stare.

'Who sent you here to torment me?' he asked, violently. 'I do not believe you. You lie.'

He straightened his arm suddenly and flung her across the verandah towards the doorway, where she lay immobile and silent, as if she had left her life in his grasp, a dark heap, without a sound or a stir.

'Oh! Nina!' whispered Almayer, in a voice in which reproach and love spoke together in pained tenderness. 'Oh! Nina! I do not believe.'

A light draught from the river ran over the courtyard in a wave of bowing grass and, entering the verandah, touched Almayer's forehead with its cool breath, in a caress of infinite pity. The curtain in the women's doorway blew out and instantly collapsed with startling helplessness. He stared at the fluttering stuff.

'Nina!' cried Almayer. 'Where are you, Nina?'

The wind passed out of the empty house in a tremulous sigh, and all was still.

Almayer hid his face in his hands as if to shut out a loathsome sight. When, hearing a slight rustle, he uncovered his eyes, the dark heap by the door was gone.

CHAPTER II

In the middle of a shadowless square of moonlight, shining on a smooth and level expanse of young rice-shoots, a little shelter-hut perched on high posts, the pile of brushwood near by and the glowing embers of a fire with a man stretched before it, seemed very small and as if lost in the pale green iridescence reflected from the ground. On three sides of the clearing, appearing very far away in the deceptive light, the big trees of the forest, lashed together with manifold bonds by a mass of tangled creepers, looked down at the growing young life at their feet with the sombre resignation of giants that had lost faith in their strength. And in the midst of them the merciless creepers clung to the big trunks in cable-like coils, leaped from tree to tree, hung in thorny festoons from the lower boughs, and, sending slender tendrils on high to seek out the smallest branches, carried death to their victims in an exulting riot of silent destruction.

On the fourth side, following the curve of the bank of that branch of the Pantai that formed the only access to the clearing, ran a black line of young trees, bushes, and thick second growth, unbroken save for a small gap chopped out in one place. At that gap began the narrow footpath leading from the water's edge to the grass-built shelter used by the night watchers when the ripening crop had to be protected from the wild pigs. The pathway ended at the foot of the piles on which the hut was built, in a circular space covered with ashes and bits of burnt wood. In the middle of that space, by the dim fire, lay Dain.

He turned over on his side with an impatient sigh, and, pillowing his head on his bent arm, lay quietly with his face to the dying fire. The glowing embers shone redly in a small circle, throwing a gleam into his wide-open eyes, and at every deep breath the fine white ash of bygone fires rose in a light cloud before his parted lips, and danced away from the warm glow into the moonbeams pouring down upon Bulangi's clearing.* His body was weary with the exertion of the past few days, his mind more weary still with the strain of solitary waiting for his fate. Never before had he felt so helpless. He had heard the report of the gun fired on board the launch, and he knew that his life was in untrustworthy hands, and that his enemies were very near. During the slow hours of the afternoon he roamed about on the edge of the forest, or, hiding in the bushes, watched the creek with unquiet eyes for some sign of danger. He feared not death, yet he desired ardently to live, for life to him was Nina. She had promised to come, to follow him, to share his danger and his splendour. But with her by his side he cared not for danger, and without her there could be no splendour and no joy in existence. Crouching in his shady hiding-place, he closed his eyes, trying to evoke the gracious and charming image of the white figure that for him was the beginning and the end of life. With eyes shut tight, his teeth hard set, he tried in a great effort of passionate will to keep his hold on that vision of supreme delight. In vain! His heart grew heavy as the figure of Nina faded away to be replaced by another vision this time – a vision of armed men, of angry faces, of glittering arms – and he seemed to hear the hum of excited and triumphant voices as they discovered him in his hiding-place. Startled by the vividness of his fancy, he would open his eyes, and, leaping out into the sunlight, resume his aimless wanderings around the clearing. As he skirted in his weary march the edge of the forest he glanced now and then into its dark shade, so enticing in its deceptive appearance of coolness, so repellent with its unrelieved gloom, where lay, entombed and rotting, countless generations of trees, and where their successors stood as if mourning, in dark green foliage, immense and helpless, awaiting their turn. Only the parasites seemed to live there in a sinuous rush upwards into the air and sunshine, feeding on the dead and the dying alike, and crowning their victims with pink and blue flowers that gleamed amongst the boughs, incongruous and cruel, like a strident and mocking note in the solemn harmony of the doomed trees.

A man could hide there, thought Dain, as he approached a place where the creepers had been torn and hacked into an archway that might have been the beginning of a path. As he bent down to look through he heard angry grunting, and a sounder* of wild pig crashed away in the undergrowth. An acrid smell of damp earth and of decaying leaves took him by the throat, and he drew back with a scared face, as if he had been touched by the breath of Death itself. The very air seemed dead in there – heavy and stagnating, poisoned with the corruption of countless ages. He went on, staggering on his way, urged by the nervous restlessness that made him feel tired yet caused him to loathe the very idea of immobility and repose. Was he a wild man to hide in the woods and perhaps be killed there – in the darkness – where there was no room to breathe? He would wait for his enemies in the sunlight, where he could see the sky and feel the breeze. He knew how a Malay chief should die. The sombre and desperate fury, that peculiar inheritance of his race, took possession of him, and he glared savagely across the clearing towards the gap in the bushes by the riverside. They would come from there. In imagination he saw them now. He saw the bearded faces and the white jackets of the officers, the light on the levelled barrels of the rifles. What is the bravery of the greatest warrior before the firearms in the hand of a slave? He would walk toward them with a smiling face, with his hands held out in a sign of submission till he was very near them. He would speak friendly words – come nearer yet – yet nearer – so near that they could touch him with their hands and stretch them out to make him a captive. That would be the time: with a shout and a leap he would be in the midst of them, kriss in hand, killing, killing, killing, and would die with the shouts of his enemies in his ears, their warm blood spurting before his eyes.

Carried away by his excitement, he snatched the kriss hidden in his sarong, and, drawing a long breath, rushed forward, struck at the empty air, and fell on his face. He lay as if stunned in the sudden reaction from his exaltation, thinking that, even if he died thus gloriously, it would have to be before he saw Nina. Better so. If he saw her again he felt that death would be too terrible. With horror he, the descendant of Rajahs and of conquerors, had to face the doubt of his own bravery. His desire of life tormented him in a paroxysm of agonising remorse. He had not the courage to stir a limb. He had lost faith in himself, and there was nothing else in him of what makes a man. The suffering remained, for it is ordered that it should abide in the human body even to the last breath, and fear remained. Dimly he could look into the depths of his passionate love, see its strength and its weakness, and felt afraid.

The sun went down slowly. The shadow of the western forest marched over the clearing, covered the man's scorched shoulders with its cool mantle, and went on hurriedly to mingle with the shadows of other forests on the eastern side. The sun lingered for a while amongst the light tracery of the higher branches, as if in friendly reluctance to abandon the body stretched in the green paddy-field.* Then Dain, revived by the cool of the evening breeze, sat up and stared round him. As he did so the sun dipped sharply, as if ashamed of being detected in a sympathising attitude, and the clearing, which during the day was all light, became suddenly all darkness, where the fire gleamed like an eye. Dain walked slowly towards the creek, and, divesting himself of his torn sarong, his only garment, entered the water cautiously. He had had nothing to eat that day, and had not dared show himself in daylight by the water-side to drink. Now, as he swam silently, he swallowed a few mouthfuls of water that lapped about his lips. This did him good, and he walked with greater confidence in himself and others as he returned towards the fire. Had he been betrayed by Lakamba all would have been over by this. He made up a big blaze, and while it lasted dried himself, and then lay down by the embers. He could not sleep, but he felt a great numbness in all his limbs. His restlessness was gone, and he was content to lay still, measuring the time by watching the stars that rose in endless succession above the forests, while the slight puffs of wind under the cloudless sky seemed to fan their twinkle into a greater brightness. Dreamily he assured himself over and over again that she would come, till the certitude crept into his heart and filled him with a great peace. Yes, when the next day broke, they would be together on the great blue sea that was like life – away from the forests that were like death. He murmured the name of Nina into the silent space with a tender smile: this seemed to break the spell of stillness, and far away by the creek a frog croaked loudly as if in answer. A chorus of loud roars and plaintive calls rose from the mud along the line of bushes. He laughed heartily; doubtless it was their love-song. He felt affectionate towards the frogs and listened, pleased with the noisy life near him.

When the moon peeped above the trees he felt the old impatience and the old restlessness steal over him. Why was she so late? True, it was a long way to come with a single paddle. With what skill and what endurance could those small hands manage a heavy paddle! It was very wonderful – such small hands, such soft little palms that knew how to touch his cheek with a feel lighter than the fanning of a butterfly's wing. Wonderful! He lost himself lovingly in the contemplation of this tremendous mystery, and when he looked at the moon again it had risen a hand's breadth above the trees. Would she come? He forced himself to lay still, overcoming the impulse to rise and rush round the clearing again. He turned this way and that; at last, quivering with the effort, he lay on his back, and saw her face among the stars looking down on him.

The croaking of frogs suddenly ceased. With the watchfulness of a hunted man Dain sat up, listening anxiously, and heard several splashes in the water as the frogs took rapid headers into the creek. He knew that they had been alarmed by something, and stood up suspicious and attentive. A slight grating noise, then the dry sound as of two pieces of wood struck against each other. Somebody was about to land! He took up an armful of brushwood, and, without taking his eyes from the path, held it over the embers of his fire. He waited, undecided, and saw something gleam amongst the bushes; then a white figure came out of the shadows and seemed to float towards him in the pale light. His heart gave a great leap and stood still, then went on shaking his frame in furious beats. He dropped the brushwood upon the glowing coals, and had an impression of shouting her name – of rushing to meet her; yet he emitted no sound, he stirred not an inch, but he stood silent and motionless like chiselled bronze under the moonlight that streamed over his naked shoulders. As he stood still, fighting with his breath, as if bereft of his senses by the intensity of his delight, she walked up to him with quick, resolute steps, and, with the appearance of one about to leap from a dangerous height, threw both her arms round his neck with a sudden gesture. A small blue gleam crept amongst the dry branches, and the crackling of reviving fire was the only sound as they faced each other in the speechless emotion of that meeting; then the dry fuel caught at once, and a bright hot flame shot upwards in a blaze as high as their heads, and in its light they saw each other's eyes.

Neither of them spoke. He was regaining his senses in a slight tremor that ran upwards along his rigid body and hung about his trembling lips. She drew back her head and fastened her eyes on his in one of those long looks that are a woman's most terrible weapon; a look that is more stirring than the closest touch, and more dangerous than the thrust of a dagger, because it also whips the soul out of the body, but leaves the body alive and helpless, to be swayed here and there by the capricious tempests of passion and desire; a look that enwraps the whole body, and that penetrates into the innermost recesses of the being,* bringing terrible defeat in the delirious uplifting of accomplished conquest. It has the same meaning for the man of the forests and the sea as for the man threading the paths of the more dangerous wilderness of houses and streets. Men that had felt in their breasts the awful exultation such a look awakens become mere things of today – which is paradise; forget yesterday – which was suffering; care not for tomorrow – which may be perdition. They wish to live under that look for ever. It is the look of woman's surrender.

He understood, and, as if suddenly released from his invisible bonds, fell at her feet with a shout of joy, and, embracing her knees, hid his head in the folds of her dress, murmuring disjointed words of gratitude and love. Never before had he felt so proud as now, when at the feet of that woman that half belonged to his enemies. Her fingers played with his hair in an absent-minded caress as she stood absorbed in thought. The thing was done. Her mother was right. The man was her slave. As she glanced down at his kneeling form she felt a great pitying tenderness for that man she was used to call – even in her thoughts – the master of life. She lifted her eyes and looked sadly at the southern heavens under which lay the path of their lives – her own, and that man's at her feet. Did he not say himself that she was the light of his life? She would be his light and his wisdom; she would be his greatness and his strength; yet hidden from the eyes of all men she would be, above all, his only and lasting weakness. A very woman! In the sublime vanity of her kind she was thinking already of moulding a god from the clay at her feet. A god for others to worship. She was content to see him as he was now, and to feel him quiver at the slightest touch of her light fingers. And while her eyes looked sadly at the southern stars a faint smile seemed to be playing about her firm lips. Who can tell in the fitful light of a camp fire? It might have been a smile of triumph, or of conscious power, or of tender pity, or, perhaps, of love.

She spoke softly to him, and he rose to his feet, putting his arm round her in quiet consciousness of his ownership; she laid her head on his shoulder with a sense of defiance to all the world in the encircling protection of that arm. He was hers with all his qualities and all his faults. His strength and his courage, his recklessness and his daring, his simple wisdom and his savage cunning – all were hers. As they passed together out of the red light of the fire into the silver shower of rays that fell upon the clearing he bent his head over her face, and she saw in his eyes the dreamy intoxication of boundless felicity from the close touch of her slight figure clasped to his side. With a rhythmical swing of their bodies they walked through the light towards the outlying shadows of the forests that seemed to guard their happiness in solemn immobility. Their forms melted in the play of light and shadow at the foot of the big trees, but the murmur of tender words lingered over the empty clearing, grew faint, and died out. A sigh as of immense sorrow passed over the land in the last effort of the dying breeze, and in the deep silence which succeeded, the earth and the heavens were suddenly hushed up in the mournful contemplation of human love and human blindness.

They walked slowly back to the fire. He made for her a seat out of the dry branches, and, throwing himself down at her feet, lay his head in her lap and gave himself up to the dreamy delight of the passing hour. Their voices rose and fell, tender or animated as they spoke of their love and of their future. She, with a few skilful words spoken from time to time, guided his thoughts, and he let his happiness flow in a stream of talk passionate and tender, grave or menacing, according to the mood which she evoked. He spoke to her of his own island, where the gloomy forests and the muddy rivers were unknown. He spoke of its terraced fields, of the murmuring clear rills of sparkling water that flowed down the sides of great mountains, bringing life to the land and joy to its tillers. And he spoke also of the mountain peak* that rising lonely above the belt of trees knew the secrets of the passing clouds, and was the dwelling-place of the mysterious spirit of his race, of the guardian genius of his house. He spoke of vast horizons swept by fierce winds that whistled high above the summits of burning mountains. He spoke of his forefathers that conquered ages ago the island of which he was to be the future ruler. And then as, in her interest, she brought her face nearer to his, he, touching lightly the thick tresses of her long hair, felt a sudden impulse to speak to her of the sea he loved so well; and he told her of its never-ceasing voice, to which he had listened as a child, wondering at its hidden meaning that no living man has penetrated yet; of its enchanting glitter; of its senseless and capricious fury; how its surface was for ever changing, and yet always enticing, while its depths were for ever the same, cold and cruel, and full of the wisdom of destroyed life. He told her how it held men slaves of its charm for a lifetime, and then, regardless of their devotion, swallowed them up, angry at their fear of its mystery, which it would never disclose, not even to those that loved it most. While he talked, Nina's head had been gradually sinking lower, and her face almost touched his now. Her hair was over his eyes, her breath was on his forehead, her arms were about his body. No two beings could be closer to each other, yet she guessed rather than understood the meaning of his last words that came out after a slight hesitation in a faint murmur, dying out imperceptibly into a profound and significant silence: 'The sea, O Nina, is like a woman's heart.'

She closed his lips with a sudden kiss, and answered in a steady voice –

'But to the men that have no fear, O master of my life, the sea is ever true.'

Over their heads a film of dark, thread-like clouds, looking like immense cobwebs drifting under the stars, darkened the sky with the presage of the coming thunderstorm. From the invisible hills the first distant rumble of thunder came in a prolonged roll which, after tossing about from hill to hill, lost itself in the forests of the Pantai. Dain and Nina stood up, and the former looked at the sky uneasily.

'It is time for Babalatchi to be here,' he said. 'The night is more than half gone. Our road is long, and a bullet travels quicker than the best canoe.'

'He will be here before the moon is hidden behind the clouds,' said Nina. 'I heard a splash in the water,' she added. 'Did you hear it too?'

'Alligator,' answered Dain shortly, with a careless glance towards the creek. 'The darker the night,' he continued, 'the shorter will be our road, for then we could keep in the current of the main stream, but if it is light – even no more than now – we must follow the small channels of sleeping water, with nothing to help our paddles.'

'Dain,' interposed Nina, earnestly, 'it was no alligator. I heard the bushes rustling near the landing-place.'

'Yes,' said Dain, after listening awhile. 'It cannot be Babalatchi, who would come in a big war canoe, and openly. Those that are coming, whoever they are, do not wish to make much noise. But you have heard, and now I can see,' he went on quickly. 'It is but one man. Stand behind me, Nina. If he is a friend he is welcome; if he is an enemy you shall see him die.'

He laid his hand on his kriss, and awaited the approach of his unexpected visitor. The fire was burning very low, and small clouds – precursors of the storm – crossed the face of the moon in rapid succession, and their flying shadows darkened the clearing. He could not make out who the man might be, but he felt uneasy at the steady advance of the tall figure walking on the path with a heavy tread, and hailed it with a command to stop. The man stopped at some little distance, and Dain expected him to speak, but all he could hear was his deep breathing. Through a break in the flying clouds a sudden and fleeting brightness descended upon the clearing. Before the darkness closed in again, Dain saw a hand holding some glittering object extended towards him, heard Nina's cry of 'Father!' and in an instant the girl was between him and Almayer's revolver. Nina's loud cry woke up the echoes of the sleeping woods, and the three stood still as if waiting for the return of silence before they would give expression to their various feelings. At the appearance of Nina, Almayer's arm fell by his side, and he made a step forward. Dain pushed the girl gently aside.

'Am I a wild beast that you should try to kill me suddenly and in the dark, Tuan Almayer?' said Dain, breaking the strained silence. 'Throw some brushwood on the fire,' he went on, speaking to Nina, 'while I watch my white friend, lest harm should come to you or to me, O delight of my heart!'

Almayer ground his teeth and raised his arm again. With a quick bound Dain was at his side: there was a short scuffle, during which one chamber of the revolver went off harmlessly, then the weapon, wrenched out of Almayer's hand, whirled through the air and fell in the bushes. The two men stood close together, breathing hard. The replenished fire threw out an unsteady circle of light and shone on the terrified face of Nina, who looked at them with outstretched hands.

'Dain!' she cried out warningly, 'Dain!'

He waved his hand towards her in a reassuring gesture, and, turning to Almayer, said with great courtesy –

'Now we may talk, Tuan. It is easy to send out death, but can your wisdom recall the life? She might have been harmed,' he continued, indicating Nina. 'Your hand shook much; for myself I was not afraid.'

'Nina!' exclaimed Almayer, 'come to me at once. What is this sudden madness? What bewitched you? Come to your father, and together we shall try to forget this horrible nightmare!'

He opened his arms with the certitude of clasping her to his breast in another second. She did not move. As it dawned upon him that she did not mean to obey he felt a deadly cold creep into his heart, and, pressing the palms of his hands to his temples, he looked down on the ground in mute despair. Dain took Nina by the arm and led her towards her father.

'Speak to him in the language of his people,' he said. 'He is grieving – as who would not grieve at losing thee, my pearl! Speak to him the last words he shall hear spoken by that voice, which must be very sweet to him, but is all my life to me.'

He released her, and, stepping back a few paces out of the circle of light, stood in the darkness looking at them with calm interest. The reflection of a distant flash of lightning lit up the clouds over their heads, and was followed after a short interval by the faint rumble of thunder, which mingled with Almayer's voice as he began to speak.

'Do you know what you are doing? Do you know what is waiting for you if you follow that man? Have you no pity for yourself? Do you know that you shall be at first his plaything and then a scorned slave, a drudge, and a servant of some new fancy of that man?'

She raised her hand to stop him, and turning her head slightly, asked –

'You hear this, Dain! Is it true?'

'By all the gods!' came the impassioned answer from the darkness – 'by heaven and earth, by my head and thine I swear: this is a white man's lie. I have delivered my soul into your hands for ever; I breathe with your breath, I see with your eyes, I think with your mind, and I take you into my heart for ever.'

'You thief!' shouted the exasperated Almayer.

A deep silence succeeded this outburst, then the voice of Dain was heard again.

'Nay, Tuan,' he said in a gentle tone, 'that is not true also. The girl came of her own will. I have done no more but to show her my love like a man; she heard the cry of my heart, and she came, and the dowry I have given to the woman you call your wife.'

Almayer groaned in his extremity of rage and shame. Nina laid her hand lightly on his shoulder, and the contact, light as the touch of a falling leaf, seemed to calm him. He spoke quickly, and in English this time.

'Tell me,' he said – 'tell me, what have they done to you, your mother and that man? What made you give yourself up to that savage? For he is a savage. Between him and you there is a barrier that nothing can remove. I can see in your eyes the look of those who commit suicide when they are mad. You are mad. Don't smile. It breaks my heart. If I were to see you drowning before my eyes, and I without the power to help you, I could not suffer a greater torment. Have you forgotten the teaching of so many years?'

'No,' she interrupted, 'I remember it well. I remember how it ended also. Scorn for scorn, contempt for contempt, hate for hate. I am not of your race. Between your people and me there is also a barrier that nothing can remove. You ask why I want to go, and I ask you why I should stay.'

He staggered as if struck in the face, but with a quick, unhesitating grasp she caught him by the arm and steadied him.

'Why you should stay!' he repeated slowly, in a dazed manner, and stopped short, astounded at the completeness of his misfortune.

'You told me yesterday,' she went on again, 'that I could not understand or see your love for me: it is so. How can I? No two human beings understand each other. They can understand but their own voices. You wanted me to dream your dreams, to see your own visions – the visions of life amongst the white faces of those who cast me out from their midst in angry contempt. But while you spoke I listened to the voice of my own self; then this man came, and all was still; there was only the murmur of his love. You call him a savage! What do you call my mother, your wife?'

'Nina!' cried Almayer, 'take your eyes off my face.'

She looked down directly, but continued speaking only a little above a whisper.

'In time,' she went on, 'both our voices, that man's and mine, spoke together in a sweetness that was intelligible to our ears only. You were speaking of gold then, but our ears were filled with the song of our love, and we did not hear you. Then I found that we could see through each other's eyes: that he saw things that nobody but myself and he could see. We entered a land where no one could follow us, and least of all you. Then I began to live.'

She paused. Almayer sighed deeply. With her eyes still fixed on the ground she began speaking again.

'And I mean to live. I mean to follow him. I have been rejected with scorn by the white people, and now I am a Malay! He took me in his arms, he laid his life at my feet. He is brave; he will be powerful, and I hold his bravery and his strength in my hand, and I shall make him great. His name shall be remembered long after both our bodies are laid in the dust. I love you no less than I did before, but I shall never leave him, for without him I cannot live.'

'If he understood what you have said,' answered Almayer, scornfully, 'he must be highly flattered. You want him as a tool for some incomprehensible ambition of yours.* Enough, Nina. If you do not go down at once to the creek, where Ali is waiting with my canoe, I shall tell him to return to the settlement and bring the Dutch officers here. You cannot escape from this clearing, for I have cast adrift your canoe. If the Dutch catch this hero of yours they will hang him as sure as I stand here. Now go.'

He made a step towards his daughter and laid hold of her by the shoulder, his other hand pointing down the path to the landing-place.

'Beware!' exclaimed Dain; 'this woman belongs to me!'

Nina wrenched herself free and looked straight at Almayer's angry face.

'No, I will not go,' she said with desperate energy. 'If he dies I shall die too!'

'You die!' said Almayer, contemptuously. 'Oh, no! You shall live a life of lies and deception till some other vagabond comes along to sing; how did you say that? The song of love to you! Make up your mind quickly.'

He waited for a while, and then added meaningly –

'Shall I call out to Ali?'

'Call out,' she answered in Malay, 'you that cannot be true to your own countrymen. Only a few days ago you were selling the powder for their destruction; now you want to give up to them the man that yesterday you called your friend. Oh, Dain,' she said, turning towards the motionless but attentive figure in the darkness, 'instead of bringing you life I bring you death, for he will betray unless I leave you for ever!'

Dain came into the circle of light, and, throwing his arm around Nina's neck, whispered in her ear –

'I can kill him where he stands, before a sound can pass his lips. For you it is to say yes or no. Babalatchi cannot be far now.'

He straightened himself up, taking his arm off her shoulder, and confronted Almayer, who looked at them both with an expression of concentrated fury.

'No!' she cried, clinging to Dain in wild alarm. 'No! Kill me! Then perhaps he will let you go. You do not know the mind of a white man. He would rather see me dead than standing where I am. Forgive me, your slave, but you must not.' She fell at his feet sobbing violently and repeating, 'Kill me! Kill me!'

'I want you alive,' said Almayer, speaking also in Malay, with sombre calmness. 'You go, or he hangs. Will you obey?'

Dain shook Nina off, and, making a sudden lunge, struck

Almayer full in the chest with the handle of his kriss, keeping the point towards himself.

'Hai, look! It was easy for me to turn the point the other way,' he said in his even voice. 'Go, Tuan Putih,' he added with dignity. 'I give you your life, my life, and her life. I am the slave of this woman's desire, and she wills it so.'

There was not a glimmer of light in the sky now, and the tops of the trees were as invisible as their trunks, being lost in the mass of clouds that hung low over the woods, the clearing, and the river. Every outline had disappeared in the intense blackness that seemed to have destroyed everything but space. Only the fire glimmered like a star forgotten in this annihilation of all visible things, and nothing was heard after Dain ceased speaking but the sobs of Nina, whom he held in his arms, kneeling beside the fire. Almayer stood looking down at them in gloomy thoughtfulness. As he was opening his lips to speak they were startled by a cry of warning by the riverside, followed by the splash of many paddles and the sound of voices.

'Babalatchi!' shouted Dain, lifting up Nina as he got upon his feet quickly.

'Ada! Ada!' came the answer from the panting statesman who ran up the path and stood amongst them. 'Run to my canoe,' he said to Dain excitedly, without taking any notice of Almayer. 'Run! we must go. That woman has told them all!'

'What woman?' asked Dain, looking at Nina. Just then there was only one woman in the whole world for him.

'The she-dog with white teeth; the seven times accursed slave of Bulangi. She yelled at Abdulla's gate till she woke up all Sambir. Now the white officers are coming, guided by her and Reshid. If you want to live, do not look at me, but go!'

'How do you know this?' asked Almayer.

'Oh, Tuan! what matters how I know! I have only one eye, but I saw lights in Abdulla's house and in his campong as we were paddling past. I have ears, and while we lay under the bank I have heard the messengers sent out to the white men's house.'

'Will you depart without that woman who is my daughter?' said Almayer, addressing Dain, while Babalatchi stamped with impatience, muttering, 'Run! Run at once!'

'No,' answered Dain, steadily, 'I will not go; to no man will I abandon this woman.'

'Then kill me and escape yourself,' sobbed out Nina.

He clasped her close, looking at her tenderly, and whispered, 'We will never part, O Nina!'

'I shall not stay here any longer,' broke in Babalatchi, angrily. 'This is great foolishness. No woman is worth a man's life. I am an old man, and I know.'

He picked up his staff, and, turning to go, looked at Dain as if offering him his last chance of escape. But Dain's face was hidden amongst Nina's black tresses, and he did not see this last appealing glance.

Babalatchi vanished in the darkness. Shortly after his disappearance they heard the war canoe leave the landing-place in the swish of the numerous paddles dipped in the water together. Almost at the same time Ali came up from the riverside, two paddles on his shoulder.

'Our canoe is hidden up the creek, Tuan Almayer,' he said, 'in the dense bush where the forest comes down to the water. I took it there because I heard from Babalatchi's paddlers that the white men are coming here.'

'Wait for me there,' said Almayer, 'but keep the canoe hidden.'

He remained silent, listening to Ali's footsteps, then turned to Nina.

'Nina,' he said sadly, 'will you have no pity for me?'

There was no answer. She did not even turn her head, which was pressed close to Dain's breast.

He made a movement as if to leave them and stopped. By the dim glow of the burning-out fire he saw their two motionless figures. The woman's back turned to him with the long black hair streaming down over the white dress, and Dain's calm face looking at him above her head.

'I cannot,' he muttered to himself. After a long pause he spoke again a little lower, but in an unsteady voice, 'It would be too great a disgrace. I am a white man.' He broke down completely there, and went on tearfully, 'I am a white man, and of good family. Very good family,' he repeated, weeping bitterly. 'It would be a disgrace . . . all over the islands, . . . the only white man on the east coast. No, it cannot be . . . white men finding my daughter with this Malay. My daughter!' he cried aloud, with a ring of despair in his voice.

He recovered his composure after a while and said distinctly –

'I will never forgive you, Nina – never! If you were to come back to me now, the memory of this night would poison all my life. I shall try to forget. I have no daughter. There used to be a half-caste woman in my house, but she is going even now. You, Dain, or whatever your name may be, I shall take you and that woman to the island at the mouth of the river myself. Come with me.'

He led the way, following the bank as far as the forest. Ali answered to his call, and, pushing their way through the dense bush, they stepped into the canoe hidden under the overhanging branches. Dain laid Nina in the bottom, and sat holding her head on his knees. Almayer and Ali each took up a paddle. As they were going to push out Ali hissed warningly. All listened.

In the great stillness before the bursting out of the thunderstorm they could hear the sound of oars working regularly in their row-locks.* The sound approached steadily, and Dain, looking through the branches, could see the faint shape of a big white boat. A woman's voice said in a cautious tone –

'There is the place where you may land, white men; a little higher – there!'

The boat was passing them so close in the narrow creek that the blades of the long oars nearly touched the canoe.

'Way enough!* Stand by to jump on shore! He is alone and unarmed,' was the quiet order in a man's voice, and in Dutch.

Somebody else whispered: 'I think I can see a glimmer of a fire through the bush.' And then the boat floated past them, disappearing instantly in the darkness.

'Now,' whispered Ali, eagerly, 'let us push out and paddle away.'

The little canoe swung into the stream, and as it sprung forward in response to the vigorous dig of the paddles they could hear an angry shout.

'He is not by the fire. Spread out, men, and search for him!'

Blue lights blazed out in different parts of the clearing, and the shrill voice of a woman cried in accents of rage and pain –

'Too late! O senseless white men! He has escaped!'

CHAPTER 12

'That is the place,' said Dain, indicating with the blade of his paddle a small islet about a mile ahead of the canoe – 'that is the place where Babalatchi promised that a boat from the prau would come for me when the sun is overhead. We will wait for that boat there.'

Almayer, who was steering, nodded without speaking, and by a slight sweep of his paddle laid the head of the canoe in the required direction.

They were just leaving the southern outlet of the Pantai, which lay behind them in a straight and long vista of water shining between two walls of thick verdure that ran downwards and towards each other, till at last they joined and sank together in the far-away distance. The sun, rising above the calm waters of the Straits,* marked its own path by a streak of light that glided upon the sea and darted up the wide reach of the river, a hurried messenger of light and life to the gloomy forests of the coast; and in this radiance of the sun's pathway floated the black canoe heading for the islet which lay bathed in sunshine, the yellow sands of its encircling beach shining like an inlaid golden disc on the polished steel of the unwrinkled sea. To the north and south of it rose other islets, joyous in their brilliant colouring of green and yellow, and on the main coast the sombre line of mangrove* bushes ended to the southward in the reddish cliffs of Tanjong Mirrah,* advancing into the sea, steep and shadowless under the clear light of the early morning.

The bottom of the canoe grated upon the sand as the little craft ran upon the beach. Ali leaped on shore and held on while Dain stepped out carrying Nina in his arms, exhausted by the events and the long travelling during the night. Almayer was the last to leave the boat, and together with Ali ran it higher up on the beach. Then Ali, tired out by the long paddling, laid down in the shade of the canoe, and incontinently fell asleep. Almayer sat sideways on the gunwale, and with his arms crossed on his breast, looked to the southward upon the sea.

After carefully laying Nina down in the shade of the bushes growing in the middle of the islet, Dain threw himself beside her and watched in silent concern the tears that ran down from under her closed eyelids, and lost themselves in that fine sand upon which they both were lying face to face. These tears and this sorrow were for him a profound and disquieting mystery. Now, when the danger was past, why should she grieve? He doubted her love no more than he would have doubted the fact of his own existence, but as he lay looking ardently in her face, watching her tears, her parted lips, her very breath, he was uneasily conscious of something in her he could not understand. Doubtless she had the wisdom of perfect beings. He sighed. He felt something invisible that stood between them, something that would let him approach her so far, but no farther. No desire, no longing, no effort of will or length of life could destroy this vague feeling of their difference. With awe but also with great pride he concluded that it was her own incomparable perfection. She was his, and yet she was like a woman from another world. His! His! He exulted in the glorious thought; nevertheless her tears pained him.

With a wisp of her own hair which he took in his hand with timid reverence he tried in an access of clumsy tenderness to dry the tears that trembled on her eyelashes. He had his reward in a fleeting smile that brightened her face for the short fraction of a second, but soon the tears fell faster than ever, and he could bear it no more. He rose and walked towards Almayer, who still sat absorbed in his contemplation of the sea. It was a very, very long time since he had seen the sea – that sea that leads everywhere, brings everything, and takes away so much. He had almost forgotten why he was there, and dreamily he could see all his past life on the smooth and boundless surface that glittered before his eyes.

Dain's hand laid on Almayer's shoulder recalled him with a start from some country very far away indeed. He turned round, but his eyes seemed to look rather at the place where Dain stood than at the man himself. Dain felt uneasy under the unconscious gaze.

'What?' said Almayer.

'She is crying,' murmured Dain, softly.

'She is crying! Why?' asked Almayer, indifferently.

'I came to ask you. My Ranee smiles when looking at the man she loves. It is the white woman that is crying now. You would know.'

Almayer shrugged his shoulders and turned away again towards the sea.

'Go, Tuan Putih,' urged Dain. 'Go to her; her tears are more terrible to me than the anger of gods.'

'Are they? You will see them more than once. She told me she could not live without you,' answered Almayer, speaking without the faintest spark of expression in his face, 'so it behoves you to go to her quick, for fear you may find her dead.'

He burst into a loud and unpleasant laugh which made Dain stare at him with some apprehension, but got off the gunwale of the boat and moved slowly towards Nina, glancing up at the sun as he walked.

'And you go when the sun is overhead?' he said.

'Yes, Tuan. Then we go,' answered Dain.

'I have not long to wait,' muttered Almayer. 'It is most important for me to see you go. Both of you. Most important,' he repeated, stopping short and looking at Dain fixedly.

He went on again towards Nina, and Dain remained behind. Almayer approached his daughter and stood for a time looking down on her. She did not open her eyes, but hearing footsteps near her, murmured in a low sob, 'Dain.'

Almayer hesitated for a minute and then sank on the sand by her side. She, not hearing a responsive word, not feeling a touch, opened her eyes – saw her father, and sat up suddenly with a movement of terror.

'Oh, father!' she murmured faintly, and in that word there was expressed regret and fear and dawning hope.

'I shall never forgive you, Nina,' said Almayer, in a dispassionate voice. 'You have torn my heart from me while I dreamt of your happiness. You have deceived me. Your eyes that for me were like truth itself lied to me in every glance – for how long? You know that best. When you were caressing my cheek you were counting the minutes to the sunset that was the signal for your meeting with that man – there!'

He ceased, and they both sat silent side by side, not looking at each other, but gazing at the vast expanse of the sea. Almayer's words had dried Nina's tears, and her look grew hard as she stared before her into the limitless sheet of blue that shone limpid, unwaving, and steady like heaven itself. He looked at it also, but his features had lost all expression, and life in his eyes seemed to have gone out. The face was a blank, without a sign of emotion, feeling, reason, or even knowledge of itself. All passion, regret, grief, hope, or anger – all were gone, erased by the hand of fate, as if after this last stroke everything was over and there was no need for any record. Those few who saw Almayer during the short period of his remaining days were always impressed by the sight of that face that seemed to know nothing of what went on within: like the blank wall of a prison enclosing sin, regrets, and pain, and wasted life, in the cold indifference of mortar and stones.

'What is there to forgive?' asked Nina, not addressing Almayer directly, but more as if arguing with herself. 'Can I not live my own life as you have lived yours? The path you would have wished me to follow has been closed to me by no fault of mine.'

'You never told me,' muttered Almayer.

'You never asked me,' she answered, 'and I thought you were like the others and did not care. I bore the memory of my humiliation alone, and why should I tell you that it came to me because I am your daughter? I knew you could not avenge me.'

'And yet I was thinking of that only,' interrupted Almayer, 'and I wanted to give you years of happiness for the short day of your suffering. I only knew of one way.'

'Ah! but it was not my way!' she replied. 'Could you give me happiness without life? Life!' she repeated with sudden energy that sent the word ringing over the sea. 'Life that means power and love,' she added in a low voice.

'That!' said Almayer, pointing his finger at Dain standing close by and looking at them in curious wonder.

'Yes, that!' she replied, looking her father full in the face and noticing for the first time with a slight gasp of fear the unnatural rigidity of his features.

'I would have rather strangled you with my own hands,' said Almayer, in an expressionless voice which was such a contrast to the desperate bitterness of his feelings that it surprised even himself. He asked himself who spoke, and, after looking slowly round as if expecting to see somebody, turned again his eyes towards the sea.

'You say that because you do not understand the meaning of my words,' she said sadly. 'Between you and my mother there never was any love. When I returned to Sambir I found the place which I thought would be a peaceful refuge for my heart, filled with weariness and hatred – and mutual contempt. I have listened to your voice and to her voice. Then I saw that you could not understand me; for was I not part of that woman? Of her who was the regret and shame of your life? I had to choose – I hesitated. Why were you so blind? Did you not see me struggling before your eyes? But, when he came, all doubt disappeared, and I saw only the light of the blue and cloudless heaven—'

'I will tell you the rest,' interrupted Almayer: 'when that man came I also saw the blue and the sunshine of the sky. A thunderbolt has fallen from that sky, and suddenly all is still and dark around me for ever. I will never forgive you, Nina; and tomorrow I shall forget you! I shall never forgive you,' he repeated with mechanical obstinacy while she sat, her head bowed down as if afraid to look at her father.

To him it seemed of the utmost importance that he should assure her of his intention of never forgiving. He was convinced that his faith in her had been the foundation of his hopes, the motive of his courage, of his determination to live and struggle, and to be victorious for her sake. And now his faith was gone, destroyed by her own hands; destroyed cruelly, treacherously, in the dark; in the very moment of success. In the utter wreck of his affections and of all his feelings, in the chaotic disorder of his thoughts, above the confused sensation of physical pain that wrapped him up in a sting as of a whiplash curling round him from his shoulders down to his feet, only one idea remained clear and definite – not to forgive her; only one vivid desire – to forget her. And this must be made clear to her – and to himself – by frequent repetition. That was his idea of his duty to himself – to his race – to his respectable connections; to the whole universe unsettled and shaken by this frightful catastrophe of his life. He saw it clearly and believed he was a strong man. He had always prided himself upon his unflinching firmness. And yet he was afraid. She had been all in all to him. What if he should let the memory of his love for her weaken the sense of his dignity? She was a remarkable woman; he could see that; all the latent greatness of his nature – in which he honestly believed – had been transfused into that slight, girlish figure. Great things could be done! What if he should suddenly take her to his heart, forget his shame, and pain, and anger, and – follow her! What if he changed his heart if not his skin and made her life easier between the two loves that would guard her from any mischance! His heart yearned for her. What if he should say that his love for her was greater than . . .*

'I will never forgive you, Nina!' he shouted, leaping up madly in the sudden fear of his dream.

This was the last time in his life that he was heard to raise his voice. Henceforth he spoke always in a monotonous whisper like an instrument of which all the strings but one are broken in a last ringing clamour under a heavy blow.

She rose to her feet and looked at him. The very violence of his cry soothed her in an intuitive conviction of his love, and she hugged to her breast the lamentable remnants of that affection with the unscrupulous greediness of women who cling desperately to the very scraps and rags of love, any kind of love, as a thing that of right belongs to them and is the very breath of their life. She put both her hands on Almayer's shoulders, and looking at him half tenderly, half playfully, she said –

'You speak so because you love me.'

Almayer shook his head.

'Yes, you do,' she insisted softly; then after a short pause she added, 'and you will never forget me.'

Almayer shivered slightly. She could not have said a more cruel thing.

'Here is the boat coming now,' said Dain, his arm outstretched towards a black speck on the water between the coast and the islet.

They all looked at it and remained standing in silence till the little canoe came gently on the beach and a man landed and walked towards them. He stopped some distance off and hesitated.

'What news?' asked Dain.

'We have had orders secretly and in the night to take off from this islet a man and a woman. I see the woman. Which of you is the man?'

'Come, delight of my eyes,' said Dain to Nina. 'Now we go, and your voice shall be for my ears only. You have spoken your last words to the Tuan Putih, your father. Come.'

She hesitated for a while, looking at Almayer, who kept his eyes steadily on the sea, then she touched his forehead in a lingering kiss, and a tear – one of her tears – fell on his cheek and ran down his immovable face.

'Goodbye,' she whispered, and remained irresolute till he pushed her suddenly into Dain's arms.

'If you have any pity for me,' murmured Almayer, as if repeating some sentence learned by heart, 'take that woman away.'

He stood very straight, his shoulders thrown back, his head held high, and looked at them as they went down the beach to the canoe, walking enlaced in each other's arms. He looked at the line of their footsteps marked in the sand. He followed their figures moving in the crude blaze of the vertical sun, in that light violent and vibrating, like a triumphal flourish of brazen trumpets. He looked at the man's brown shoulders, at the red sarong round his waist; at the tall, slender, dazzling white figure he supported. He looked at the white dress, at the falling masses of the long black hair. He looked at them embarking, and at the canoe growing smaller in the distance, with rage, despair, and regret in his heart, and on his face a peace as that of a carved image of oblivion. Inwardly he felt himself torn to pieces, but Ali – who now aroused – stood close to his master, saw on his features the blank expression of those who live in that hopeless calm which sightless eyes only can give.

The canoe disappeared, and Almayer stood motionless with his eyes fixed on its wake. Ali from under the shade of his hand examined the coast curiously. As the sun declined, the sea-breeze sprang up from the northward and shivered with its breath the glassy surface of the water.

'Dapat!'* exclaimed Ali, joyously. 'Got him, master! Got prau! Not there! Look more Tanah* Mirrah side. Aha! That way! Master, see? Now plain. See?'

Almayer followed Ali's forefinger with his eyes for a long time in vain. At last he sighted a triangular patch of yellow light on the red background of the cliffs of Tanjong Mirrah. It was the sail of the prau that had caught the sunlight and stood out, distinct with its gay tint, on the dark red of the cape. The yellow triangle crept slowly from cliff to cliff, till it cleared the last point of land and shone brilliantly for a fleeting minute on the blue of the open sea. Then the prau bore up to the southward: the light went out of the sail, and all at once the vessel itself disappeared, vanishing in the shadow of the steep headland that looked on, patient and lonely, watching over the empty sea.

Almayer never moved. Round the little islet the air was full of the talk of the rippling water. The crested wavelets ran up the beach audaciously, joyously, with the lightness of young life, and died quickly, unresistingly, and graciously, in the wide curves of transparent foam on the yellow sand. Above, the white clouds sailed rapidly southwards as if intent upon overtaking something. Ali seemed anxious.

'Master,' he said timidly, 'time to get house now. Long way off to pull. All ready, sir.'

'Wait,' whispered Almayer.

Now she was gone his business was to forget, and he had a strange notion that it should be done systematically and in order. To Ali's great dismay he fell on his hands and knees, and, creeping along the sand, erased carefully with his hand all traces of Nina's footsteps. He piled up small heaps of sand, leaving behind him a line of miniature graves right down to the water. After burying the last slight imprint of Nina's slipper he stood up, and, turning his face towards the headland where he had last seen the prau, he made an effort to shout out loud again his firm resolve to never forgive. Ali watching him uneasily saw only his lips move, but heard no sound. He brought his foot down with a stamp. He was a firm man – firm as a rock. Let her go. He never had a daughter. He would forget. He was forgetting already.

Ali approached him again, insisting on immediate departure, and this time he consented, and they went together towards their canoe, Almayer leading. For all his firmness he looked very dejected and feeble as he dragged his feet slowly through the sand on the beach; and by his side – invisible to Ali – stalked that particular fiend whose mission it is to jog the memories of men, lest they should forget the meaning of life. He whispered into Almayer's ear a childish prattle of many years ago. Almayer, his head bent on one side, seemed to listen to his invisible companion, but his face was like the face of a man that has died struck from behind – a face from which all feelings and all expression are suddenly wiped off by the hand of unexpected death.

They slept on the river that night, mooring their canoe under the bushes and lying down in the bottom side by side, in the absolute exhaustion that kills hunger, thirst, all feeling and all thought in the overpowering desire for that deep sleep which is like the temporary annihilation of the tired body. Next day they started again and fought doggedly with the current all the morning, till about midday they reached the settlement and made fast their little craft to the jetty of Lingard and Co. Almayer walked straight to the house, and Ali followed, paddles on shoulder, thinking that he would like to eat something. As they crossed the front courtyard they noticed the abandoned look of the place. Ali looked in at the different servants' houses: all were empty. In the back courtyard there was the same absence of sound and life. In the cooking-shed the fire was out and the black embers were cold. A tall, lean man came stealthily out of the banana plantation, and went away rapidly across the open space looking at them with big, frightened eyes over his shoulder. Some vagabond without a master; there were many such in the settlement, and they looked upon Almayer as their patron. They prowled about his premises and picked their living there, sure that nothing worse could befall them than a shower of curses when they got in the way of the white man, whom they trusted and liked, and called a fool amongst themselves. In the house, which Almayer entered through the back verandah, the only living thing that met his eyes was his small monkey which, hungry and unnoticed for the last two days, began to cry and complain in monkey language as soon as it caught sight of the familiar face. Almayer soothed it with a few words and ordered Ali to bring in some bananas, then while Ali was gone to get them he stood in the doorway of the front verandah looking at the chaos of overturned furniture. Finally he picked up the table and sat on it while the monkey let itself down from the roof-stick by its chain and perched on his shoulder. When the bananas came they had their breakfast together; both hungry, both eating greedily and showering the skins round them recklessly, in the trusting silence of perfect friendship. Ali went away, grumbling, to cook some rice himself, for all the women about the house had disappeared; he did not know where. Almayer did not seem to care, and, after he finished eating, he sat on the table swinging his legs and staring at the river as if lost in thought.

After some time he got up and went to the door of a room on the right of the verandah. That was the office. The office of Lingard and Co. He very seldom went in there. There was no business now, and he did not want an office. The door was locked, and he stood biting his lower lip, trying to think of the place where the key could be. Suddenly he remembered: in the women's room hung upon a nail. He went over to the doorway where the red curtain hung down in motionless folds, and hesitated for a moment before pushing it aside with his shoulder as if breaking down some solid obstacle. A great square of sunshine entering through the window lay on the floor. On the left he saw Mrs Almayer's big wooden chest, the lid thrown back, empty; near it the brass nails of Nina's European trunk shone in the large initials N. A. on the cover. A few of Nina's dresses hung on wooden pegs, stiffened in a look of offended dignity at their abandonment. He remembered making the pegs himself and noticed that they were very good pegs. Where was the key? He looked round and saw it near the door where he stood. It was red with rust. He felt very much annoyed at that, and directly afterwards wondered at his own feeling. What did it matter? There soon would be no key – no door – nothing! He paused, key in hand, and asked himself whether he knew well what he was about. He went out again on the verandah and stood by the table thinking. The monkey jumped down, and, snatching a banana skin, absorbed itself in picking it to shreds industriously.

'Forget!' muttered Almayer, and that word started before him a sequence of events, a detailed programme of things to do. He knew perfectly well what was to be done now. First this, then that, and then forgetfulness would come easy. Very easy. He had a fixed idea that if he should not forget before he died he would have to remember to all eternity. Certain things had to be taken out of his life, stamped out of sight, destroyed, forgotten. For a long time he stood in deep thought, lost in the alarming possibilities of unconquerable memory, with the fear of death and eternity before him. 'Eternity!' he said aloud, and the sound of that word recalled him out of his reverie. The monkey started, dropped the skin, and grinned up at him amicably.

He went towards the office door and with some difficulty managed to open it. He entered in a cloud of dust that rose under his feet. Books open with torn pages bestrewed the floor; other books lay about grimy and black, looking as if they had never been opened. Account books. In those books he had intended to keep day by day a record of his rising fortunes. Long time ago. A very long time. For many years there has been no record to keep on the blue and red ruled pages! In the middle of the room the big office desk, with one of its legs broken, careened* over like the hull of a stranded ship; most of the drawers had fallen out, disclosing heaps of paper yellow with age and dirt. The revolving office chair stood in its place, but he found the pivot set fast when he tried to turn it. No matter. He desisted, and his eyes wandered slowly from object to object. All those things had cost a lot of money at the time. The desk, the paper, the torn books, and the broken shelves, all under a thick coat of dust. The very dust and bones of a dead and gone business. He looked at all these things, all that was left after so many years of work, of strife, of weariness, of discouragement, conquered so many times. And all for what? He stood thinking mournfully of his past life till he heard distinctly the clear voice of a child speaking amongst all this wreck, ruin, and waste. He started with a great fear in his heart, and feverishly began to rake in the papers scattered on the floor, broke the chair into bits, splintered the drawers by banging them against the desk, and made a big heap of all that rubbish in one corner of the room.

He came out quickly, slammed the door after him, turned the key, and, taking it out, ran to the front rail of the verandah, and, with a great swing of his arm, sent the key whizzing into the river. This done, he went back slowly to the table, called the monkey down, unhooked its chain, and induced it to remain quiet in the breast of his jacket. Then he sat again on the table and looked fixedly at the door of the room he had just left. He listened also intently. He heard a dry sound of rustling; sharp cracks as of dry wood snapping; a whirr like of a bird's wings when it rises suddenly, and then he saw a thin stream of smoke come through the keyhole. The monkey struggled under his coat. Ali appeared with his eyes starting out of his head.

'Master! House burn!' he shouted.

Almayer stood up holding by the table. He could hear the yells of alarm and surprise in the settlement. Ali wrung his hands, lamenting aloud.

'Stop this noise, fool!' said Almayer, quietly. 'Pick up my hammock and blankets and take them to the other house. Quick, now!'

The smoke burst through the crevices of the door, and Ali, with the hammock in his arms, cleared in one bound the steps of the verandah.

'It has caught well,' muttered Almayer to himself. 'Be quiet, Jack,' he added, as the monkey made a frantic effort to escape from its confinement.

The door split from top to bottom, and a rush of flame and smoke drove Almayer away from the table to the front rail of the verandah. He held on there till a great roar overhead assured him that the roof was ablaze. Then he ran down the steps of the verandah, coughing, half choked with the smoke that pursued him in bluish wreaths curling about his head.

On the other side of the ditch, separating Almayer's courtyard from the settlement, a crowd of the inhabitants of Sambir looked at the burning house of the white man. In the calm air the flames rushed up on high, coloured pale brick-red, with violet gleams in the strong sunshine. The thin column of smoke ascended straight and unwavering till it lost itself in the clear blue of the sky, and in the great empty space between the two houses the interested spectators could see the tall figure of the Tuan Putih, with bowed head and dragging feet, walking slowly away from the fire towards the shelter of 'Almayer's Folly'.

In that manner did Almayer move into his new house. He took possession of the new ruin, and in the undying folly of his heart set himself to wait in anxiety and pain for that forgetfulness which was so slow to come. He had done all he could.

Every vestige of Nina's existence had been destroyed; and now with every sunrise he asked himself whether the longed-for oblivion would come before sunset, whether it would come before he died? He wanted to live only long enough to be able to forget, and the tenacity of his memory filled him with dread and horror of death; for should it come before he could accomplish the purpose of his life he would have to remember for ever! He also longed for loneliness. He wanted to be alone. But he was not. In the dim light of the rooms with their closed shutters, in the bright sunshine of the verandah, wherever he went, whichever way he turned, he saw the small figure of a little maiden with pretty olive face, with long black hair, her little pink robe slipping off her shoulders, her big eyes looking up at him in the tender trustfulness of a petted child. Ali did not see anything, but he also was aware of the presence of a child in the house. In his long talks by the evening fires of the settlement he used to tell his intimate friends of Almayer's strange doings. His master had turned sorcerer in his old age. Ali said that often when Tuan Putih had retired for the night he could hear him talking to something in his room. Ali thought that it was a spirit in the shape of a child. He knew his master spoke to a child from certain expressions and words his master used. His master spoke in Malay a little, but mostly in English, which he, Ali, could understand. Master spoke to the child at times tenderly, then he would weep over it, laugh at it, scold it, beg of it to go away; curse it. It was a bad and stubborn spirit. Ali thought his master had imprudently called it up, and now could not get rid of it. His master was very brave; he was not afraid to curse this spirit in the very Presence; and once he fought with it. Ali had heard a great noise as of running about inside the room and groans. His master groaned. Spirits do not groan. His master was brave, but foolish. You cannot hurt a spirit. Ali expected to find his master dead next morning, but he came out very early, looking much older than the day before, and had no food all day.

So far Ali to the settlement. To Captain Ford he was much more communicative, for the good reason that Captain Ford had the purse and gave orders. On each of Ford's monthly visits to Sambir Ali had to go on board with a report about the inhabitant of 'Almayer's Folly'. On his first visit to Sambir, after

Nina's departure, Ford had taken charge of Almayer's affairs. They were not cumbersome. The shed for the storage of goods was empty, the boats had disappeared, appropriated – generally in night-time – by various citizens of Sambir in need of means of transport. During a great flood the jetty of Lingard and Co. left the bank and floated down the river, probably in search of more cheerful surroundings; even the flock of geese – 'the only geese on the east coast' – departed somewhere, preferring the unknown dangers of the bush to the desolation of their old home. As time went on the grass grew over the black patch of ground where the old house used to stand, and nothing remained to mark the place of the dwelling that had sheltered Almayer's young hopes, his foolish dream of splendid future, his awakening, and his despair.

Ford did not often visit Almayer, for visiting Almayer was not a pleasant task. At first he used to respond listlessly to the old seaman's boisterous inquiries about his health; he even made efforts to talk, asking for news in a voice that made it perfectly clear that no news from this world had any interest for him. Then gradually he became more silent – not sulkily – but as if he was forgetting how to speak. He used also to hide in the darkest rooms of the house, where Ford had to seek him out guided by the patter of the monkey galloping before him. The monkey was always there to receive and introduce Ford. The little animal seemed to have taken complete charge of its master, and whenever it wished for his presence on the verandah it would tug perseveringly at his jacket, till Almayer obediently came out into the sunshine, which he seemed to dislike so much.

One morning Ford found him sitting on the floor of the verandah, his back against the wall, his legs stretched stiffly out, his arms hanging by his side. His expressionless face, his eyes open wide with immobile pupils, and the rigidity of his pose, made him look like an immense man-doll broken and flung there out of the way.* As Ford came up the steps he turned his head slowly.

'Ford,' he murmured from the floor, 'I cannot forget.'

'Can't you?' said Ford, innocently, with an attempt at joviality: 'I wish I was like you. I am losing my memory – age, I suppose; only the other day my mate—'

He stopped, for Almayer had got up, stumbled, and steadied himself on his friend's arm.

'Hallo! You are better today. Soon be all right,' said Ford, cheerfully, but feeling rather scared.

Almayer let go his arm and stood very straight with his head up and shoulders thrown back, looking stonily at the multitude of suns shining in ripples of the river. His jacket and his loose trousers flapped in the breeze on his thin limbs.

'Let her go!' he whispered in a grating voice. 'Let her go. Tomorrow I shall forget. I am a firm man, . . . firm as a . . . rock, . . . firm . . .'

Ford looked at his face – and fled. The skipper was a tolerably firm man himself – as those who had sailed with him could testify – but Almayer's firmness was altogether too much for his fortitude.

Next time the steamer called in Sambir Ali came on board early with a grievance. He complained to Ford that Jim-Eng the Chinaman had invaded Almayer's house, and actually had lived there for the last month.

'And they both smoke,' added Ali.

'Phew! Opium, you mean?'

Ali nodded, and Ford remained thoughtful; then he muttered to himself, 'Poor devil! The sooner the better now.' In the afternoon he walked up to the house.

'What are you doing here?' he asked of Jim-Eng, whom he found strolling about on the verandah.

Jim-Eng explained in bad Malay, and speaking in that monotonous, uninterested voice of an opium smoker pretty far gone, that his house was old, the roof leaked, and the floor was rotten. So, being an old friend for many, many years, he took his money, his opium, and two pipes, and came to live in this big house.

'There is plenty of room. He smokes, and I live here. He will not smoke long,' he concluded.

'Where is he now?' asked Ford.

'Inside. He sleeps,' answered Jim-Eng, wearily.

Ford glanced in through the doorway. In the dim light of the room he could see Almayer lying on his back on the floor, his head on a wooden pillow, the long white beard scattered over his breast, the yellow skin of the face, the half-closed eyelids showing the whites of the eye only. . . .

He shuddered and turned away. As he was leaving he noticed a long strip of faded red silk, with some Chinese letters on it, which Jim-Eng had just fastened to one of the pillars.

'What's that?' he asked.

'That,' said Jim-Eng, in his colourless voice, 'that is the name of the house. All the same like my house. Very good name.'

Ford looked at him for awhile and went away. He did not know what the crazy-looking maze of the Chinese inscription on the red silk meant. Had he asked Jim-Eng, that patient Chinaman would have informed him with proper pride that its meaning was: 'House of heavenly delight'.

In the evening of the same day Babalatchi called on Captain Ford. The captain's cabin opened on deck, and Babalatchi sat astride on the high step, while Ford smoked his pipe on the settee inside. The steamer was leaving next morning, and the old statesman came as usual for a last chat.

'We had news from Bali last moon,' remarked Babalatchi. 'A grandson is born to the old Rajah, and there is great rejoicing.'

Ford sat up interested.

'Yes,' went on Babalatchi, in answer to Ford's look. 'I told him. That was before he began to smoke.'

'Well, and what?' asked Ford.

'I escaped with my life,' said Babalatchi, with perfect gravity, 'because the white man is very weak and fell as he rushed upon me.' Then, after a pause, he added, 'She is mad with joy.'

'Mrs Almayer, you mean?'

'Yes, she lives in our Rajah's house. She will not die soon. Such women live a long time,' said Babalatchi, with a slight tinge of regret in his voice. 'She has dollars, and she has buried them, but we know where. We had much trouble with those people. We had to pay a fine and listen to threats from the white men, and now we have to be careful.' He sighed and remained silent for a long while. Then with energy:

'There will be fighting. There is a breath of war on the islands. Shall I live long enough to see? . . . Ah, Tuan!' he went on, more quietly, 'the old times were best. Even I have sailed with Lanun men,* and boarded in the night silent ships with white sails. That was before an English Rajah ruled in Kuching.* Then we fought amongst ourselves and were happy. Now when we fight with you we can only die!'

He rose to go. 'Tuan,' he said, 'you remember the girl that man Bulangi had? Her that caused all the trouble?'

'Yes,' said Ford. 'What of her?'

'She grew thin and could not work. Then Bulangi, who is a thief and a pig-eater, gave her to me for fifty dollars. I sent her amongst my women to grow fat. I wanted to hear the sound of her laughter, but she must have been bewitched, and . . . she died two days ago. Nay, Tuan. Why do you speak bad words? I am old – that is true – but why should I not like the sight of a young face and the sound of a young voice in my house?' He paused, and then added with a little mournful laugh, 'I am like a white man talking too much of what is not men's talk when they speak to one another.'

And he went off looking very sad.

* * *

The crowd massed in a semicircle before the steps of 'Almayer's Folly', swayed silently backwards and forwards, and opened out before the group of white-robed and turbaned men advancing through the grass towards the house. Abdulla walked first, supported by Reshid and followed by all the Arabs in Sambir. As they entered the lane made by the respectful throng there was a subdued murmur of voices, where the word 'Mati'* was the only one distinctly audible. Abdulla stopped and looked round slowly.

'Is he dead?' he asked.

'May you live!' answered the crowd in one shout, and then there succeeded a breathless silence.

Abdulla made a few paces forward and found himself for the last time face to face with his old enemy. Whatever he might have been once he was not dangerous now, lying stiff and lifeless in the tender light of the early day. The only white man on the east coast was dead, and his soul, delivered from the trammels* of his earthly folly, stood now in the presence of Infinite Wisdom. On the upturned face there was that serene look which follows the sudden relief from anguish and pain, and it testified silently before the cloudless heaven that the man lying there under the gaze of indifferent eyes had been permitted to forget before he died.

Abdulla looked down sadly at this Infidel he had fought so long and had bested so many times. Such was the reward of the Faithful! Yet in the Arab's old heart there was a feeling of regret for that thing gone out of his life. He was leaving fast behind him friendships, and enmities, successes, and disappointments – all that makes up a life; and before him was only the end. Prayer would fill up the remainder of the days allotted to the True Believer! He took in his hand the beads that hung at his waist.

'I found him here, like this, in the morning,' said Ali, in a low and awed voice.

Abdulla glanced coldly once more at the serene face.

'Let us go,' he said, addressing Reshid.

And as they passed through the crowd that fell back before them, the beads in Abdulla's hand clicked, while in a solemn whisper he breathed out piously the name of Allah! The Merciful! The Compassionate!*

NOTES

All page references to Conrad's works are to the Collected Edition published by J. M. Dent (London, 1946–54). Two other editions of Conrad's Malay novels have been especially useful in preparing the following explanatory notes: *Almayer's Folly*, ed. Jacques Berthoud, World's Classics (Oxford: O.U.P., 1992; referred to as Berthoud); and *An Outcast of the Islands*, ed. J. H. Stape and Hans van Marle, World's Classics (Oxford: O.U.P., 1992; referred to as Stape and van Marle).

p. 1 **Almayer's Folly:** Ian Watt points out that in addition to the primary meanings of the word 'Folly', referring to Almayer's foolish expectations and to the house as an eccentric monument to his conceit, Conrad may well have intended implications from the French word *folie*, whose primary sense is mania or madness. He adds: 'The stronger French connotation of *folie* would have included this theme of progressive psychotic breakdown, whereas the main English senses of "folly" tend to trivialize the import of the novel's title' (*Conrad in the Nineteenth Century* [London: Methuen, 1980], p. 66).

p. 1 **Epigraph:** taken from the 24 April 1852 diary-entry in the *Journal Intime* (published 1883–7) of Henri-Frédéric Amiel (1821–81), a Protestant Professor of Philosophy at the University of Geneva. Slightly misquoted by Conrad, the sentence occurs in a passage in which Amiel laments the evanescence of youthful dreams of immortality and the inevitability of disillusion in adult life, as exemplified in the fate of Moses: 'Thou too sawest undulating in the distance the ravishing hills of the Promised Land, and it was thy fate nevertheless to lay thy weary bones in a grave dug in the desert! – Which of us has not his promised land, his day of ecstasy and his death in exile? What a pale counterfeit is real life of the life we see in glimpses, and how these flaming lightnings of our prophetic youth make the twilight of our dull monotonous manhood more dark and dreary!' (*Amiel's Journal*, 2 vols., trans. Mrs Humphry Ward [London: Macmillan, 1885], I 41). Ian Watt has argued that the Amielian context makes the epigraph 'more appropriate to Conrad's youthful romantic reveries than to Almayer's more material aspirations' with the effect that 'in the novel this imputed universality of theme hardly stands up to examination' (*Conrad in the Nineteenth Century*, p. 66). This underestimates, however, the way in which Amielian resonances extend beyond Almayer and embrace, for example, Lingard's expectation of 'the promised land' (p. 9), Dain's sensation of entering through 'the gates of paradise' (p. 58), and Nina's flight to an anticipated paradise in Dain's Bali.

p. 2 T.B.: Tadeusz Bobrowski (1829–94), Conrad's maternal uncle, became self-appointed guardian to the eleven-year-old orphan in 1869. He was responsible for granting his nephew permission to leave Poland for Marseilles in 1874 and oversaw his sea-career and finances for the next twenty years. Bobrowski's death occurred the year before *Almayer's Folly* was published.

p. 3 Author's Note: this note constitutes Conrad's first critical essay, written after delivery of the manuscript of the novel to T. Fisher Unwin and completed by early January 1895. It remained unpublished until its appearance in the Doubleday, Page 'Sun-Dial' edition of 1921. For further details, see David Leon Higdon, 'The Text and Context of Conrad's First Critical Essay', *Polish Review*, 20 (1975), 97–105.

p. 3 a lady: Alice Meynell (1847–1922), poet, essayist and prominent literary reviewer, who was frequently mentioned during the 1890s as successor to the poet-laureateship. She knew most of the important literary figures of the late Victorian period, including Tennyson, Meredith and Coventry Patmore.

p. 3 decivilised: Alice Meynell published a short essay under this title in the *National Observer* (24 January 1891), reprinted in *The Rhythm of Life* (1893), where Conrad almost certainly first saw it. Meynell's article was also probably in Conrad's mind when, in early 1895, he suggested to his publisher that *Almayer's Folly* be advertised as a 'Civilised story in savage surroundings' (*The Collected Letters of Joseph Conrad: Volume 1, 1861–1897*, ed. Frederick R. Karl and Laurence Davies [Cambridge: C.U.P., 1983], p. 199). For the 1921 Heinemann Collected edition of the novel Conrad supplied the following additional paragraph to the Author's Note: 'I wrote the above in 1895 by way of a preface for my first novel. An essay by Mrs Meynell furnished the impulse for this artless outpouring. I let it now be printed for the first time, unaltered and uncorrected, as my first attempt at writing a preface and an early record of exaggerated but genuine feeling'. See Appendix for the full text of Meynell's essay.

p. 3 **assegai:** slender, iron-tipped spear.

p. 5 **Makan** (Malay): to eat. As is made clear later (p. 15), Almayer is being called by his wife to come to dinner. For critical commentary on the novel's opening, see the Introduction, pp. xxxiv–xxxv.

p. 5 **Almayer:** a character substantially modelled on a Java-born Dutch Eurasian, William Charles Olmeijer (1848–1900), whom Conrad had met on his four visits to Berau in eastern Borneo (see note to p. 14) in the *Vidar* between September and December 1887, and of whom he later wrote in *A Personal Record* (1911): 'if I had not got to know Almayer pretty well it is almost certain there would never have been a line of mine in print' (p. 87). Olmeijer was related by marriage to Captain William Lingard (see note to p. 8), went to Berau around 1869 to manage Lingard's trading agency, and, like Kaspar Almayer, built himself a large house which he neglected. For details of the significant ways in which Conrad changed Olmeijer's basic familial and racial situation, see the Introduction, p. xxix.

p. 5 **Pantai:** a river probably known as such at the time of Conrad's visit to the area, although, strictly speaking, the Muara Pantai is the southernmost passage of the Berau estuary. The region's two rivers, the Kelai and Segah, meet thirty-four miles from the sea and become the single river Berau.

p. 5 **Almayer's thoughts ..... with gold:** an obsession shared with the historical Olmeijer. Researches summarised by Jerry Allen (*The Sea Years of Joseph Conrad* [London: Methuen, 1967], p. 222) reveal that Olmeijer went inland from Berau in 1877 to prospect for gold and, still absorbed by gold-fever, applied for his last prospector's permit in 1890.

p. 5 **Dain:** although appearing to be used as a proper name throughout, it is a title of distinction among the Bugis people of south-west Celebes or their descendants. According to Allen, Conrad may have borrowed the name from a certain Dain Marola, a Buginese clerk working in Berau (*The Sea Years of Joseph Conrad*, p. 233). Whatever its origin, the name in Conrad's narrative is almost certainly a pseudonym adopted by the young Balinese prince who in Sambir 'passed ... under the name of Dain Maroola' (p. 96).

p. 5 **swollen by the rains:** as is indicated by the thunder and lightning later in this chapter, Sambir's monsoon season – from October to March – has already begun. This fact is itself a source of frustration to Almayer, since the rains will hinder Dain's expedition to find gold. Berthoud (p. 217) is incorrect in claiming that Conrad errs in his belief that East Borneo is subject to monsoon variations. In fact, the region has a recognisable monsoon climate: although rainfall is consistently high throughout the year, south-west winds from October to March bring considerably heavier rainfall and, hence, extensive flooding.

p. 6 **Macassar:** present-day Ujung Pandang, chief city and port of the Celebes (Sulawesi).

p. 6 **godowns** (Malay, *gudang*): storehouses, warehouses.

p. 6 **Hudig:** the name probably derives from a Dutch banker, who had spent some years working in the Dutch East Indies, whom Conrad met in early 1887 in Amsterdam and later described in *A Mirror of the Sea* (p. 51).

p. 6 **the Botanical Gardens of Buitenzorg:** detail possibly derived from Alfred Russel Wallace, an eminent nineteenth-century naturalist, who visited these celebrated botanical gardens (*The Malay Archipelago* [London: Macmillan, 1886], pp. 110–11). Buitenzorg, present-day Bogor, is thirty miles south of Jakarta in Java.

p. 6 **long easy-chair:** somewhat redundant translation of a French word already assimilated into English, a 'chaise-longue'. See also its usage on p. 53.

p. 7 **guilders:** the guilder is a silver Netherlands East Indies coin, since 1858 divided into 100 cents.

p. 7 **punkah:** large fan made of cloth or palm leaves, suspended from the ceiling and operated manually by cord and pulley.

p. 7 **rattan** (Malay, *rotan*): climbing palm with long thin stem, used for making matting, screens and ropes.

p. 7 **Bali:** an island due south of Borneo.

p. 7 **bonies:** *i.e.* ponies. According to *A Personal Record*, Conrad's first contact with the original Olmeijer involved the delivery of an imported 'Bali pony' (p. 76).

p. 7 **schooners:** two- or three-masted vessels with fore-and-aft rigging.

p. 8 **Malay Archipelago:** the world's largest group of islands including Java, Sumatra, the Celebes (Sulawesi) and the Philippines.

p. 8 **Tom Lingard:** largely based upon a British seaman-adventurer, Captain William Lingard (1829–88), who lived and worked on Archipelago waters from about 1850 until 1883 and enjoyed considerable renown as 'The King of the Sea'. Although Conrad probably did not meet Lingard, he could hardly have failed to hear of his exploits from a variety of sources – from general shore-talk and hearsay; from his meetings in Berau with Olmeijer, one of Lingard's protégés (see note to p. 5); and from his probable contacts with two of Lingard's nephews, Joshua and James. The fictional Tom Lingard plays a progressively important role in three of

Conrad's novels, the so-called 'Lingard trilogy'. These novels make up a trilogy-in-reverse in that they follow Lingard's life in a backwards chronological order, with *Almayer's Folly* (1895) set in the mid-1880s, *An Outcast* (1896) around 1872, and *The Rescue* (1920; begun 1896) in the 1850s. For further information on William Lingard, see later notes and Norman Sherry, *Conrad's Eastern World* (Cambridge: C.U.P., 1966), pp. 89–118.

p. 8 **'Rajah Laut':** 'King of the Sea', from the Malay *raja* (ruler) and *laut* (sea), a title conferred on the historical Lingard 'by the sultan of Gunung Tabur (in Berau) in 1862, perhaps as reward for assistance rendered in a fight with the praus of the neighbouring sultan of Bulungan' (Stape and van Marle, p. 373). Lingard also owned a boat that he renamed the *Rajah Laut*.

p. 8 **Sulu pirates:** people originally from the Sulu Islands, situated off the north-east coast of Borneo, and well known for their audacious piracy and slave-dealing. See also its usage on p. 15.

p. 8 **prau** (Malay, *perahu*): common kind of Malay boat, usually an undecked sailing-boat, with a small canoe rigged parallel to it.

p. 8 **discovered a river:** although Captain William Lingard was not the first European trader on the Berau River, he seems to have been the first European to survey the estuary's southernmost passage, the Muara Pantai, with a view to setting up a permanent trading agency in Berau. According to the *Eastern Archipelago Pilot* of 1949: 'Two beacons, equipped with reflectors one on each side of the river serve as crossing over marks for the bar in the channel westward of Sodang besar; this is known as the Lingard crossing. The western beacon was reported in 1946 to have disappeared' (quoted in Sherry, *Conrad's Eastern World*, p. 124).

p. 8 **Sunda Hotel:** hotel in Macassar also mentioned in *An Outcast of the Islands* (p. 5).

p. 8 **brig:** two-masted, square-rigged vessel.

p. 8 **roadstead:** sheltered expanse of water near a coast where ships may ride at anchor.

p. 9 **gutta-percha ..... and gum-dammar:** confirmed as the main forest produce of Berau by a report from the *Eastern Archipelago Pilot* in 1893: 'The principal articles of export are rattan, gutta-percha, and dammar (gum copal), in quantities of about 250 tons, 120 tons, and 300 tons respectively' (Sherry, *Conrad's Eastern World*, p. 128). **Gutta-percha** is a whitish leathery substance obtained from the latex or gum of various trees, used particularly for underground and underwater cables (see also its usage on p. 47); **rattans** are long, thin stems of the climbing palm, used in making matting, ropes and wickerwork products; **pearl** is 'mother of pearl'; **birds' nests** are those of the South East Asian swifts which use a gelatine-like secretion to attach their nests to cave-roofs and are much esteemed as an edible delicacy in the form of bird's-nest soup (see also its usage on p. 46); **wax** is beeswax for candles and polishes (see also p. 47); **dammar** is an inflammable resin obtained from various coniferous trees, used to make torches and as an ingredient in the production of varnishes and lacquers.

p. 9 **Titans ..... battle of the gods:** in Greek mythology, the sons and daughters of Uranus (sky) and Gaea (earth), originally twelve in number. The myth includes their rising against – and castrating – their father and, eventually, being overcome and hurled into a cavity below Tartarus.

p. 9 **supercargo:** an officer in a merchant ship who supervises commercial matters and is in charge of the cargo, though glossed here by Lingard, with Almayer in mind, as a sort of 'captain's clerk'.

p. 9 **quill-driving:** pen-pushing, doing routine paper-work.

p. 10 **Sourabaya:** present-day Surabaya, a major port on Java's north-east coast, used as an important setting in Conrad's *Victory* (1914).

p. 10 **bulwarks:** ship's sides above deck-level.

p. 12 **freshet:** the sudden overflowing of a river caused by heavy rains. See also its usage on p. 73.

p. 12 **Abdulla's:** the owner of the *Vidar*, in which Conrad sailed to Borneo, was a wealthy Arab trader, Syed Mohsin Bin Saleh Al Joffree. It was his eldest son, Syed Abdulla, who traded at Berau. See note to p. 21.

p. 12 **ya!** (Malay): yes!

p. 12 **Tuan** (Malay): 'sir' or 'master', regularly used when addressing European and Malay superiors. The problem of rendering Malay speech and idioms in English seems to have preoccupied Conrad from the very beginning of his first novel. The manuscript shows that he first tried to render Dain's speech in pidgin English. In response to Almayer's 'Where do you come from?' Dain replies: 'From down the river Tuan; men go to sleep often when the master is away' (MS, 18).

p. 12 **campong** (Malay, *kampung*): village or settlement, sometimes fortified by palisades. Conrad's transcription is an accurate phonetic rendering of the Malay.

p. 12 **Orang Blanda:** (Malay) Dutchman (*orang* = man; *belanda* = Holland).

p. 13 **bowman:** an oarsman nearest to the bow or forward part of a boat.

p. 14 **Sambir reach:** the fictional 'Sambir' is based upon the East Bornean coastal region or 'sultanate' of Berau. Conrad visited Berau four times while serving in the *Vidar* between September and December 1887. The sultanate was partitioned into the two sultanates of Sambaliung and Gunung Tabur, which the Dutch reunited into a single district. Its population was 20,500 in 1933 and 45,602 in 1980. In the novel, 'Sambir' is also the name given to the region's main settlement, which was and still is known as Tanjung Redeb. A 'reach' is an open expanse of water, here on the river.

p. 14 **bent-wood:** a wood bent in moulds after being heated by steaming, used mainly for furniture.

p. 15 **Great red stains ..... chewing:** excised by Conrad in his later revision of the text for the Collected Edition, so entailing the loss of a sharply etched characterising detail. Betel is a compound of areca-nut, the pungent betel-leaf and lime, chewed as a mild narcotic; its side-effect is to stain the lips red and the teeth black (see also note to p. 43 on 'siri').

p. 15 **genever:** a kind of Dutch gin or 'hollands', a spirit distilled from grain and flavoured with juniper berries.

p. 16 **you cannot imagine what is before you:** such is the pervasiveness of dramatic irony at Almayer's expense that almost all of his statements ironically recoil upon him. Here, for example, he is so imprisoned within his own fixed idea that *he* cannot 'imagine' that Nina has already conceived an alternative future with Dain.

p. 17 **merciless force:** the preceding description of the monsoon rains was subjected to considerable pruning in Conrad's later revision of the text for the Collected Edition.

p. 19 **fore-deck:** the deck between a ship's bridge and forecastle.

p. 19 **poop:** raised deck at a ship's stern, containing accommodation for the master and officers.

p. 19 **Being fourteen ..... appreciative admiration:** excised by Conrad in his later revision of the text for the Collected Edition.

p. 20 **Samarang:** present-day Semarang, in Java. Injured by a falling spar, Conrad left the *Highland Forest* here in 1887 before travelling on to a Singapore hospital.

p. 20 **fiat:** formal or solemn command.

p. 20 **the centre ..... society:** excised by Conrad in his later revision of the text for the Collected Edition. Batavia (present-day Jakarta) on the island of Java, is the capital of modern Indonesia.

p. 21 **Arabs had found out the river:** William Lingard's monopoly in Berau was broken in 1882 by the Arab-owned *Vidar*, the steamer in which Conrad later visited Berau. Syed Abdulla, the owner's son, built a large house on the point where Berau's two rivers meet, a site in the novel occupied by Almayer's 'Folly'. According to Sherry, William Lingard's loss of monopoly in Berau was rendered inevitable by the advent of steamers 'which were relentlessly chasing the sailing ships out of ..... archipelago trade' (*Conrad's Eastern World*, p. 110).

p. 22 **seven miles:** in *An Outcast of the Islands*, the distance is given as fourteen miles (p. 50).

p. 22 **salaams:** an Arabic salutation signifying peace, accompanied by a deep bow and the placing of the palm of the right hand on the forehead.

p. 22 **Syed:** strictly, a Muslim claiming descent from Muhammad's elder grandson Husain; but also a Muslim honorary title generally, meaning 'prince, lord or chief'.

p. 22 **small canoe ..... solitary occupant:** the suggestion of Mrs Almayer's sexual infidelity with Lakamba forms yet another strand in the web of deception and betrayal enmeshing Almayer.

p. 22 **aristocratic Malays ..... hated Dutchman:** excised by Conrad in his later revision of the text for the Collected Edition, leaving the word 'Malays' to stand.

p. 22 **banker ..... failed:** Sherry conjectures that the historical William Lingard may similarly have lost large amounts of money, in his case through the Singapore Oriental Bank collapse of 1884 (*Conrad's Eastern World*, p. 111).

p. 23 **quarter-deck:** upper deck, extending from a ship's stern to the main-mast, usually assigned for the use of officers.

p. 24 **whale-boat:** a long, narrow boat with a sharp prow and stern, like those formerly used in whaling.

p. 24 **Mrs Vinck:** as Berthoud points out (p. 212), this character seems quite unrelated to Mr Vinck, Hudig's cashier (p. 7).

p. 24 **Europe had swallowed up the Rajah Laut:** the historical William Lingard seems also to have been 'swallowed up' by Europe. According to Hans van Marle, he returned to Europe in 1883 and died in Macclesfield, Cheshire, in May 1888, leaving his assets in England to a nephew there, and his assets in South East Asia to another nephew, the James Lingard whom Conrad probably met ('Jumble of Facts and Fiction:

The First Singapore Reaction to *Almayer's Folly*', *Conradiana*, 10 [1978], 165).

p. 24 **Sumatrese:** from Sumatra, an island to the west of Borneo.

p. 24 **verdigris:** a green or bluish patina formed on copper, brass or bronze.

p. 25 **Straits Settlements:** formerly a British crown colony that included Singapore, Penang, Malacca, the Dindings and some smaller islands.

p. 26 **Captain Ford:** modelled on Captain James Craig (1846–1929) under whom Conrad sailed in the *Vidar*.

p. 27 **levées:** landing places on the river, quays or jetties.

p. 27 **Ubat** (Malay): medicine, including forms of 'medicine' such as a philtre or magical cure.

p. 27 **Mem Putih:** a polite form of address, the equivalent of 'white lady' (Malay *putih* = 'white'). This and other references by the Sambir community to Nina as a 'white' woman (see p. 93, for example) coincide with the official racial policy existing in the Dutch East Indies colony from 1856 onwards, which made no legal distinction between whites and Eurasians, all being classified as Europeans. Conrad, however, is clearly more interested in the ironic web created by *unofficial* attitudes harboured by Nina and others to the issue of her racial identity. These ironies emerge through the juxtaposition of Malay perceptions of Nina as 'white' with those of both Captain Ford ('You can't make her white' [p. 26]) and Nina herself, a disillusioned 'Mem Putih' in the process of severing her links with European attitudes and traditions.

p. 27 **Unbeliever:** non-Muslim, infidel.

p. 27 **Dyaks:** a collective name (from a Malay word originally meaning 'inland' or 'up-river') for numerous indigenous tribal peoples of Borneo who differ in language, customs, art-forms, and several other elements of culture and social organisation. Jan B. Avé and Victor T. King point out that all 'Dayak groups, however, have some fundamental features in common:

they live along rivers and practise rice agriculture. This common economic base combined with the broadly uniform ecosystem ..... go a long way to explain the similarities in religious conceptions and worldview of the Dayak peoples' (*Borneo: The People of the Weeping Forest* [Leiden, Netherlands: National Museum of Ethnology, 1986], p. 9). See also note to p. 33.

p. 28 **British Borneo Company:** as a way of extending British territorial claims in Borneo, a Royal Charter was granted to the British Borneo Company in 1881 to govern and administer an area of some 31,000 square miles in North Borneo, concessions for which had been obtained from the Sultans of Sulu and Brunei in consideration of stipulated annual payments. The references to the formation of the British Borneo Company in 1881 and to the consequent border disputes of 1882–3 (see note to p. 29) are consistent with the novel's developing temporal setting, whose main action takes place in the mid-1880s.

p. 28 sarongs (Malay, *sarung*): skirt-like garment made from a single piece of cloth worn by both men and women.

p. 29 **The claim ..... of Holland:** an allusion to the border disputes between the British and the Dutch in 1882–3 following upon the formation of the British North Borneo Company. These disputes led the Dutch to strengthen their territorial claims in eastern Borneo and culminated in 1884 with the setting up of a joint British–Dutch commission to look into the whole boundary question. These larger events represent an important turning point in the erosion of Almayer's hopes, since, as a partner in the English firm of Lingard and Co., he justifiably expects his commercial interests to prosper under British influence. Under the Dutch, on the other hand, Almayer can expect more hostile treatment since, as he hears from the chief of the Dutch Commission, 'the Arabs were better subjects than Hollanders who dealt illegally in gunpowder with the Malays' (p. 30).

p. 29 **The slaves were hurried out of sight:** *i.e.* out of sight of the Dutch, who were taking steps to eradicate slavery and made official moves to abolish the practice in 1892. See

Jérôme Rousseau, *Central Borneo: Ethnic Identity and Social Life in a Stratified Society* (Oxford: Clarendon Press, 1990), p. 178, who also notes: 'In Berau at the turn of the century, the Segai and Kenyah still enslaved the nomadic Basap, but the Malays had stopped doing so' (p. 174).

p. 29 **frigate:** a war-ship, next in size and strength to a line-of-battle ship, formerly carrying from 28 to 44 guns.

p. 29 **the great Rajah's:** the Governor-General of the Dutch East Indies, resident in Batavia.

p. 30 **lame armchairs:** probably a literal rendering of the French *fauteuils boiteux*, meaning 'rickety armchairs' (Yves Hervouet, 'Conrad and the French Language, Part Two', *Conradiana*, 14 [1982], 30–1). See also its usage on p. 37.

p. 30 **anent:** about, concerning, in respect of.

p. 31 **flotilla:** fleet of small vessels.

p. 32 **potentate:** possessing great power or authority, a ruler or monarch.

p. 32 **factotum:** someone employed to do all kinds of work for another. See also its usage on p. 33.

p. 33 **Dyaks or Head-hunters:** see note to p. 27. For a detailed explanation of the part played by headhunting in the social organisation, religion and world-view of the Dyak peoples, see Jérôme Rousseau, *Central Borneo*, pp. 264–81.

p. 33 **in his quality of:** a literal translation of the French *en sa qualité de* (Hervouet, 'Conrad and the French Language', 40).

p. 33 **Babalatchi:** this name and that of Lakamba derive from two Buginese traders who lived in Berau at the time of Conrad's visits (Allen, *The Sea Years of Joseph Conrad*, p. 233). One of these links is confirmed by a bill of lading (now among Conrad's papers at Yale) which refers to a trader called 'Babalatchie' having shipped a load of gum, via the *Vidar*, to the Celebes.

p. 33 **Datu Besar!** (Malay): a title equivalent to 'great chief' or 'most revered elder', deleted by Conrad in his later revision of the text for the Collected Edition, perhaps because it could be mistaken for a proper name.

p. 33 **surat** (Malay): letter, epistle.

p. 34 **Djinns:** a class of supernatural spirits in Muslim mythology, formed of fire and assuming various and sometimes grotesque shapes.

p. 35 **Brow:** a variant of 'Berau' or 'Berow', which probably survives in the text by accident, since elsewhere the actual Bornean region is consistently designated as the fictional 'Sambir'. See note to p. 14.

p. 35 **She had tasted ..... impending change:** the longest of the passages excised by Conrad in his later revision of the text for the Collected Edition. John Dozier Gordan (*Joseph Conrad: The Making of a Novelist* [New York: Cambridge, Mass.: Harvard U.P., 1940], pp. 119–20) suggests that Conrad wished to avoid repetition of Captain Ford's explanation in the preceding chapter as to why he has brought Nina back to Sambir. In fact, the passage might be seen as a marvellously sardonic amplification of that earlier explanation, engaging the reader in Nina's bitter inward sense of her ostracism from white society and expanding upon the motives that underlie her rejection of European traditions.

p. 36 **the cathedral ..... Singapore promenade:** St Andrew's Cathedral (built in 1861) and very close to the Sailors' Home where Conrad stayed after leaving the *Vidar*.

p. 37 **Hadji:** title given to a Muslim who has undertaken, always on the eighth to the tenth days of the twelfth month, the greater pilgrimage to Mecca, the birthplace of Muhammad. Such a pilgrim would at this time normally be identified by a green turban (though it should be noted that green is also the general colour of Islam). In his discussion of Conrad's use of the colour as a mark of distinction among pilgrims, Berthoud (p. 226) refers to *The Shadow-Line*: 'an Arab owned her, and a Syed at that. Hence the green border on the flag' (p. 4). See also its usage on p. 38.

p. 37 **greybeards:** old (and wise) men.

p. 37 **'Commissie'** (Dutch): Commission.

p. 38 **Allah the All-merciful:** for Muslims, one of Allah's ninety-nine names and attributes, others of which are later mentioned in the text.

p. 38 **Bombay:** main port and commercial centre on the west coast of India. Conrad had stayed there for some six weeks in 1884.

p. 38 **impassible:** unmoved, unresponsive.

p. 39 **kidnapped:** an echo of an earlier usage, when Nina is described as being 'kidnapped' by Lingard and taken to Singapore (p. 34) and perhaps also linking with her mother's sense of being Lingard's kidnapped 'captive' (p. 20). These echoes throw a double ironic perspective on the developing narrative – backwards upon Lingard's predisposition towards acts of 'piracy' and forwards upon what will later be seen by Almayer as an act of 'kidnapping' – that is, Dain's elopement with Nina. It is perhaps also worth adding that in Dain's Bali at this time the practice of kidnapping brides was still a common one.

p. 40 **south-west monsoon:** see note to p. 5.

p. 40 ***Straits Times*:** one of Singapore's main newspapers, founded in 1845 as a weekly publication, becoming a daily paper in 1858.

p. 40 **Acheen war:** in March 1873, the Dutch colonial government declared war on the powerful north Sumatran Sultanate of Achin. The Dutch force that landed there was defeated with heavy losses in April 1873. Achin eventually fell to the Dutch in January 1874. Since, however, the Achin disputes lingered on for many years (despite an official peace), one of the later 'unsuccessful' Dutch expeditions, such as that of 1881, may be in Conrad's mind here. The Achin unrest contributed to a tighter official Dutch policy on piracy and the sale of gunpowder in eastern Borneo from the mid-1870s onwards, a policy felt in Conrad's 'Sambir', where the community laments Dutch 'exaction, severity, and general tyranny, as exemplified in the total stoppage of gunpowder trade' (p. 40).

p. 40 **Nakhodas** (Malay): ships' captains, leading traders.

p. 41 **Nipa palms:** a coastal palm with long, feathery leaves, used for thatching and basket-weaving.

p. 41 **foresail:** the lowest sail on a ship's foremast.

p. 41 **yards squared:** sail-spars set at right-angles to a vessel's fore-and-aft line.

p. 42 **Soldat:** soldier; cf. Dutch *soldaat*.

p. 43 **a Son of Heaven:** see note to p. 65.

p. 43 **siri-vessels:** siri is a compound made up of areca-nut, pungent betel-leaf, gambier and lime, chewed as a mild narcotic. The 'vessels' are the spitoons accompanying the habit of siri-chewing. See also note to p. 15.

p. 43 **Chelakka!** (Malay, *celaka*): bad luck; though possibly referring to bringers of bad luck, and hence the equivalent of 'scoundrels' or 'rogues'. Conrad's transcription is an accurate phonetic rendering of the Malay.

p. 44 **Inchi** (Malay): mister.

p. 45 **hair in disorder:** a literal rendering of the French *cheveux en désordre* (Hervouet, 'Conrad and the French Language', 38).

p. 45 **kriss:** dagger with scalloped or wavy edges, a weapon formerly much prized in the Malay world and generally believed to have magical properties: 'The Malays are exceedingly punctilious in the shape, size, and general formation of their kris, and look upon its due perfection with superstitious awe' (Major Fred. McNair, *Perak and the Malays* [London, 1878], p. 243).

p. 45 **open-mouthed admiration:** in the preceding description of this first meeting between Dain and Nina, Yves Hervouet finds several echoes from Gustave Flaubert's *L'Education sentimentale* (1869) (*The French Face of Joseph Conrad* [Cambridge: C.U.P., 1990], pp. 21–2).

p. 46 **stern sheets:** area of a boat between the stern and the nearest rowing bench.

p. 46 **trepang:** also called *bêche-de-mer*, a dried sea-cucumber (a worm-like sea-slug) much esteemed as a delicacy in the Malay world and China.

p. 46 **birds' nests:** see note to p. 9.

p. 47 **Bugis:** people of south-west Celebes (Sulawesi) or their descendants. 'The men of that race are intelligent, enterprising, revengeful, but with a more frank courage than the other Malays, and restless under oppression' (*Lord Jim*, p. 256).

p. 47 **Bali . . . . . refusing all food:** Bali, to the south of Borneo, has from the earliest periods of its history been strongly influenced by Hinduism. Dain Maroola, a Brahmin, belongs to the highest caste in the Hindu caste system. Berthoud (p. 229) explains that 'Brahminism forbade the eating of food that had not been duly consecrated by offering of a portion of it to the god, the "beings" (prophets) and the "manes" (ancestors)'.

p. 49 **expectorate:** cough up and spit out.

p. 50 **skiff:** a small, light boat.

p. 50 **sheered:** swerved towards.

p. 53 **Mexican dollars:** 'from the Flemish *daler* and the German *thaler*, the familiar terms for the Spanish "pieces of eight". These were withdrawn in 1821, surviving only in the Mexican dollar . . . . . [which] circulated throughout the Archipelago until well into the present century' (Berthoud, p. 230).

p. 54 **a Son of Heaven:** see note to p. 43.

p. 54 **Ranee:** the wife of a rajah, therefore a queen or princess.

p. 54 **the time of start:** an awkward gallicism (cf. *l'heure du départ*) for 'the time of departure' (Hervouet, 'Conrad and the French Language', 46).

p. 55 **canted:** tilted, slanted.

p. 55 **broadside to:** *i.e.* with a vessel's side facing the river's prevailing current.

p. 56 **gunwales:** the upper rails or edges of a boat's sides.

p. 57 **nipas:** see note to p. 41.

p. 57 **sleeping water:** an evocative gallicism (*eau dormante*) for 'still water' (Hervouet, 'Conrad and the French Language', 42).

p. 58 **long and burning kiss:** as Berthoud points out (p. 231), what surprises and delights Dain is not only Nina's sexual boldness, but the form it takes. In many parts of the world, including the Malay Archipelago, kissing on the lips has not been generally practised; hence Dain's surprise at the 'strange and to him unknown contact'.

p. 59 **Kajang-mats:** waterproof matting made from leaves of the screw-pine and used on boats and carts.

p. 60 **Nina watched the angry river:** so repeating the picture given of Nina at the end of Chapter 1 and signalling a return to the novel's setting in the 'present' (with the re-appearance of Dain Maroola) after its extensive retrospective movement.

p. 61 **arm-rack:** a rack standing at the entrance of a building in which to deposit swords and rifles.

p. 62 **bitcharra** (Malay, *bicarra*): formal discussion or deliberation. Conrad's transcription is an accurate phonetic rendering of the Malay.

p. 63 **fire-ship:** *i.e.* gun-boat, and a literal translation from Malay (cf. *kereta-api* [fire-car] = train).

p. 63 **the great Rajah in Batavia:** see note to p. 29.

p. 65 **Anak Agong:** specific title of distinction for the ruling princes of Bali, from the Malay *anak* (child) and *agung* (exalted, supreme). Conrad's translation of the title as 'Son of Heaven' probably derives from Wallace, *The Malay Archipelago*, p. 166.

p. 65 **tranquillised:** here meaning 'satisfied' or 'reassured'.

p. 65 **siri-box:** container for the ingredients of the siri-chew (see note to p. 43). Conrad refers here to the common practice of storing the siri-box in a loose waist-cloth.

p. 66 **independent Rajah of Bali:** northern Bali was forced to recognise Dutch suzerainty in 1849 and was placed under the direct administration of the Dutch East Indies government in 1882. The southern Balinese principalities remained 'independent' until the early years of the twentieth century.

p. 66 **no Dutch resident:** *i.e.* no Dutch diplomatic representative. After the border disputes between the British and the Dutch in 1882–3, the Dutch established 'residents' or 'controllers' to oversee their coastal territories in eastern Borneo.

p. 67 **Gunong Mas:** from the Malay *gunung* (mountain) and *mas* (gold), and so 'the mountain of gold' as the text translates.

p. 69 **Ada** (Malay): to be present, often having the sense of 'at your service'. See also its usage on p. 143.

p. 69 **from Poulo Laut to Tanjong Batu:** Lakamba's reputation extends over approximately 400 miles of coastline, from Pulo Laut, an island off the south-east tip of Borneo, to a coastal settlement north of the Berau River. Pulo Laut, a port of call on the *Vidar*'s round trip from Singapore to Berau, was one of the places where Conrad first heard about the original Olmeijer (*A Personal Record*, p. 75).

p. 69 **at the pit of his stomach:** the unusual preposition here echoes French usage – *au creux de l'estomac* (Hervouet, 'Conrad and the French Language', 43).

p. 70 **Sheitan** (Arabic): Satan, devil, evil spirit.

p. 71 **hand-organ:** another name for a barrel organ, a mechanical instrument for playing tunes by means of a revolving drum set with pins.

p. 71 **Verdi's music:** a reference to the first scene of the final act of *Il Trovatore* (1853) by the Italian composer Giuseppe Verdi (1813–1901). Manrico, the troubadour, captured in battle and about to be beheaded, sings his farewell to life and his beloved Leonora (or, in the French version, 'Leonore', as in the text). Ian Watt valuably draws attention to similarities in method and function between this episode and the blind man's song in Part III, Ch. 5 of Flaubert's *Madame Bovary*. He concludes: 'Both Conrad and Flaubert present a brief but memorable *tableau* not to make a direct contribution to the plot, but to prefigure later events without recourse to authorial commentary, and to set the action in a larger choric perspective' (*Conrad in the Nineteenth Century*, p. 54).

p. 73 **bourrouh:** one of the more obscure Malay words used by Conrad. Of the possible cognates reviewed by David Leon Higdon and Floyd Eugene Eddleman, two in particular seem most appropriate to the context: '*Bora* and *bura* describe the act and sound of releasing air from the mouth such as when deliberately releasing warm breath in cold weather with lips and tongue vibrating' ('A Glossary of Malay Words in Conrads's *Almayer's Folly*', *Conradiana*, 10 [1978], 75).

p. 78 **Hai!** (Malay): an exclamation registering surprise, dismay and even, occasionally, anger. See also its usage on p. 117.

p. 78 **eater of pig's flesh:** an obvious insult to a Muslim, who is forbidden by the Koran to eat pork. See also p. 162.

p. 79 **hold of the idea:** in the preceding description, Hervouet has identified numerous verbal borrowings from an account of the hero's solitary dejection in Flaubert's *L'Education sentimentale* (1869) (*The French Face of Joseph Conrad*, pp. 22–3).

p. 81 **The sense ..... shudder:** this echoes Guy de Maupassant's description of a woman abandoned by her lover in *Mont-Oriol* (1887) (Hervouet, *The French Face of Joseph Conrad*, p. 21).

p. 82 **Kaffir:** an offensive term used by Muslims to signify a non-Muslim or infidel.

p. 82 **strong water:** *i.e.* Almayer's gin. The Koran's prohibition on the abuse of alcoholic drink lies behind Babalatchi's response here.

p. 83 **lips and forehead:** see note to p. 22.

p. 84 **painter:** rope attached to a boat's bow for tying it up.

p. 84 **report from the gun:** a motif that contributes to a pattern of narrative synchrony, since Reshid and Taminah hear this same report in the next chapter (p. 87) as does Dain in Chapter 11 (p. 131). For later variations of this technique, see notes to pp. 114, 122.

p. 86 **Allah . . . . . the Compassionate:** see note to p. 38.

p. 86 **lintel:** one of several instances in Conrad's fiction where he mistakenly uses the term 'lintel' (the horizontal beam over a door) to refer to its vertical post or jamb. For other examples, see *An Outcast of the Islands*, pp. 256, 339.

p. 89 **blocks:** pulleys and their casings.

p. 94 **leeward:** towards the sheltered side.

p. 95 **the only white man on the east coast:** *i.e.* of Borneo. This was not true of the original Olmeijer, since there were at least three other white men in Berau at the time of Conrad's visits. The novel emphasises Almayer's sense of racial isolation and makes his claim a recurring motif – see also pp. 144, 162.

p. 96 **scientific explorer:** according to Allen (*The Sea Years of Joseph Conrad*, p. 218), this character may partially derive from a heavy-drinking Russian wanderer, part-naturalist and part-orchid hunter, who was living in Berau at the time of Conrad's visits. A variant of this figure – a Roumanian naturalist engaged in 'writing a scientific book about tropical countries' – also appears in *An Outcast of the Islands* (pp. 360–1).

p. 96 **the only geese on the east coast:** *i.e.* of Borneo. In *A Personal Record*, this tag is attributed to the original Olmeijer who is described as uttering it 'without a spark of faith, hope or pride' (p. 85). See also its usage on p. 159.

p. 96 **An Arab trader . . . . . information:** Cedric Watts has suggested that this cryptic piece of information identifying Abdulla as central instigator of Almayer's downfall forms a crucial pivot in what may be seen as the novel's 'covert plot': 'One of the major ironies is that though white men are in the foreground, dominating the overt plots, they are often the dupes of the Malays and Arabs in the background who are instigating the covert plots' (*The Deceptive Text: An Introduction to Covert Plots* [Brighton: Harvester, 1984], p. 136).

p. 98 **sub:** i.e. sub-lieutenant.

p. 98 **coxswain:** senior petty officer in a small vessel, in charge of the boat and its crew.

p. 100 **advise:** used here in the sense of 'confer'.

p. 102 **Ampanam:** a port on the west coast of the island of Lombok, to the east of Bali. As Berthoud points out (pp. 234–5), this place-name is probably an uncorrected anachronism surviving from the manuscript, where Dain was originally conceived as coming from Lombok.

p. 104 **amok:** the Malay word *āmoq*, meaning 'furious or frenzied attack', was the original source for the English 'to run amok', it being thought by European observers that Malays had a special propensity for indulging in 'amoks'. As Berthoud points out (p. 235), Conrad represents the phenomenon in his later description of Dain (pp. 132–3).

p. 104 **Madura:** a small island, near Surabaya, off the north-east coast of Java.

p. 105 **nothing pressed:** a literal translation of the French *rien ne pressait*, meaning 'there is no hurry' (Hervouet, 'Conrad and the French Language', 46).

p. 105 **objurgations:** rebukes, insults.

p. 106 **Canton dialect:** strictly a language, not a dialect, spoken in the Canton, Kwangtung and Kwangsi provinces of China, and in Hong Kong.

p. 108 **white ruler in Batavia:** see note to p. 29.

p. 108 **tse!:** tut!

p. 109 **A hand on the windpipe:** cf. 'a frog in the throat'. This conventional figure of speech links with more powerfully metaphoric usages of strangulation in connection with Almayer (pp. 99, 112).

p. 110 **freak:** whim, caprice.

p. 114 **woman's voice:** another teasing example of narrative synchrony not clarified until the next chapter when the reader learns that the 'woman's voice' is that of Mrs Almayer as she tries to prevent her daughter from saying goodbye to her father. See also notes to pp. 84, 122.

p. 116 **It has set ..... had sunk:** as Adam Gillon shows, a significant Polish echo, recalling a passage in Adam Mickiewicz's epic poem of 1827, *Konrad Wallenrod* (*Conrad and Shakespeare, and Other Essays* [New York: Astra Books, 1976], p. 202).

p. 122 **strange sounds:** yet another example of artful narrative synchrony for the reader to decode: the 'strange sounds' heard throughout the chapter are those of the slave-girl Taminah who has decided to betray Nina and Dain. See also notes to pp. 84, 114.

p. 122 **burnt the paper ..... buried:** for a full explanation of the magical functions of fire (and the burning of paper, hair and fish) among Bornean peoples in order to lay malignant ghosts and propitiate wandering spirits, see the chapter on 'The Disposal of the Dead', in Henry Ling Roth's *The Natives of Sarawak and British North Borneo*, 2 vols. (Kuala Lumpur: University of Malaya Press, 1968), I 135–63.

p. 123 **cocoanut lamp:** described earlier as made up of half 'a shell of cocoanut filled with oil, where a cotton rag floated for a wick' (p. 53).

p. 125 **under the spell of his dream:** the imagery of the later part of this paragraph is Sisyphean, recalling the punishment meted out to Sisyphus in Hades for his misdeeds, whereby he was eternally condemned to roll a heavy boulder up a hill: every time he approached the top, the boulder escaped his grasp and rolled to the bottom.

p. 128 **O God! how much longer?:** the pervasive tone of metaphysical anguish here evokes the extremity of Joban complaint. Cf. Job xix:2, 19: 'How long will ye vex my soul, and break me in pieces with words? ..... All my inward friends abhorred me; and they whom I loved are turned against me.'

p. 130 **and at every deep breath ..... Bulangi's clearing:**

excised by Conrad in his later revision of the text for the Collected Edition.

p. 132 **sounder:** collective noun for wild swine.

p. 133 **paddy-field:** a field or clearing where rice is grown.

p. 135 **long looks ..... recesses of the being:** this passage echoes a similar scene of searching eye-contact in Guy de Maupassant's *Une vie* (1893) (Hervouet, *The French Face of Joseph Conrad*, p. 21).

p. 137 **the mountain peak:** an allusion to the volano Gunung Agung ('the mountain of the gods'), the highest and most sacred mountain in Bali.

p. 141 **You want him ..... ambition of yours:** which, ironically, is just as applicable to Almayer as it is to Nina.

p. 145 **row-locks:** swivelling devices attached to both sides of a boat and serving as fulcrums for the oars.

p. 145 **Way enough!:** a nautical command to stop a boat's 'way' or progress.

p. 146 **the Straits:** the Strait of Macassar, separating Borneo from the Celebes.

p. 146 **mangrove:** evergreen trees and shrubs forming dense thickets on tropical coasts and swampy ground.

p. 146 **southward ..... Tanjong Mirrah:** Tanjong Mirrah (or more accurately 'Tanah merah', meaning 'red earth') is the name of a cape that lies not 'southward' of the Berau estuary but some hundred miles to the north. See also note to p. 152.

p. 151 **What if he should say ..... greater than . . . :** greater than 'racial prejudice' suggests Watts, who sees this as a moment that fleetingly offers Almayer a chance to transcend his racial prejudices, avert his own tragedy and start a new life (*The Deceptive Text*, p. 53).

p. 152 **Dapat!** (Malay): found, got (in view).

p. 152 **Tanah** (Malay): earth, land, country. See also note to p. 146.

p. 156 **careened:** tilted or swayed dangerously to one side.

p. 159 **his legs . . . . . the way:** cf. Conrad's memory, recalled in a letter of 16 October 1891 to Marguerite Poradowska, of the 'Punch of my childhood . . . . . his spine broken in two, his nose on the floor between his feet; his legs and arms flung out stiffly in that attitude of profound despair, so pathetically droll, of dolls tossed in a corner' (*The Collected Letters of Joseph Conrad: Volume 1, 1861–1897*, ed. Frederick R. Karl and Laurence Davies [Cambridge: C.U.P., 1983], pp. 98–9).

p. 161 **Lanun men:** originally from Mindanao, the southernmost island of the Philippines, the Lanuns established various settlements in northern Borneo as convenient piratical stations. As Babalatchi implies, they were the most audacious and feared of the sea-robbers.

p. 161 **English Rajah . . . . . Kuching:** a reference to Sir James Brooke (1803–68), who in 1839 undertook a scientific expedition to Borneo and, in return for helping the Sultan of Brunei to quell a Dyak rebellion, was made first Rajah of Sarawak in 1841, with his seat of government in its capital of Kuching. Situated on the north-west coast of Borneo, Sarawak became a British Protectorate in 1878. Brooke's life and career provided Conrad with important source material for the Patusan chapters of *Lord Jim*.

p. 162 **Mati** (Malay): dead.

p. 162 **trammels:** hindrances, obstructions.

p. 163 **Allah! . . . . . The Compassionate!:** see note to p. 38. As Watts points out, Abdulla's seemingly quiet philosophical epitaph proves to be the novel's crowning irony, since his treacherous plotting has been a prime cause of Almayer's downfall (*The Deceptive Text*, p. 52).

APPENDIX:
ALICE MEYNELL, 'DECIVILISED' (1891)

The difficulty of dealing – in the course of any critical duty – with decivilised man lies in this: when you accuse him of vulgarity – sparing him no doubt the word – he defends himself against the charge of barbarism. Especially from new soil – transatlantic, colonial – he faces you, bronzed, with a half conviction of savagery, partly persuaded of his own youthfulness of race. He writes, and recites, poems about ranches and canyons; they are designed to betray the recklessness of his nature and to reveal the good that lurks in the lawless ways of a young society. He is there to explain himself, voluble, with a glossary for his own artless slang. But his colonialism is only provincialism very articulate. The new air does but make old decadences seem more stale; the young soil does but set into fresh conditions the ready-made, the uncostly, the refuse feeling of a race decivilising. American fancy played long this pattering part of youth. The New-Englander hastened to assure you with so self-denying a face he did not wear war-paint and feathers, that it became doubly difficult to communicate to him that you had suspected him of nothing wilder than a second-hand dress coat. And when it was a question not of rebuke, but of praise, the American was ill-content with the word of the judicious who lauded him for some delicate successes in continuing something of the literature of England, something of the art of France; he was more eager for the applause that stimulated him to write romances and to paint panoramic landscape, after brief training in academies of native inspiration. Even now English voices, with violent commonplace, are constantly calling upon America to begin – to begin, for the world is expectant. Whereas there is no beginning for her, but instead a continuity which only a constant care can guide into sustained refinement and can save from decivilisation.

But decivilised man is not peculiar to new soil. The English town, too knows him in all his dailiness. In England, too, he has a literature, an art, a music, all his own – derived from many and various things of price. Trash, in the fulness of its insimplicity and cheapness, is impossible without a beautiful past. Its chief characteristic – which is futility, not failure – could not be achieved but by the long abuse, the rotatory reproduction, the quotidian disgrace, of the utterances of Art, especially the utterance by words. Gaiety, vigour, vitality, the organic quality, purity, simplicity, precision – all these are among the antecedents of trash. It is after them; it is also, alas, because of them. And nothing can be much sadder than such a proof of what may possibly be the failure of derivation.

Evidently we cannot choose our posterity. Reversing the steps of time, we may, indeed, choose backwards. We may give our thoughts noble forefathers. Well begotten, well born our fancies must be; they shall be also well derived. We have a voice in decreeing our inheritance, and not our inheritance only, but our heredity. Our minds may trace upwards and follow their ways to the best well-heads of the arts. The very habit of our thoughts may be persuaded one way unawares by their antenatal history. Their companions must be lovely, but need be no lovelier than their ancestors; and being so fathered and so husbanded, our thoughts may be intrusted to keep the counsels of literature.

Such is our confidence in a descent we know. But, of a sequel which of us is sure? Which of us is secured against the dangers of subsequent depreciation? And, moreover, which of us shall trace the contemporary tendencies, the one towards honour, the other towards dishonour? Or who shall discover why derivation becomes degeneration, and where and when and how the bastardy befalls? The decivilised have every grace as the antecedent of their vulgarities, every distinction as the precedent of their mediocrities. No ballad-concert song, feign it sigh, frolic, or laugh, but has the excuse that the feint was suggested, was made easy, by some living sweetness once. Nor are the decivilised to blame as having in their own persons possessed civilisation and marred it. They did not possess it; they were born into some tendency to derogation, into an inclination for things mentally inexpensive. And the tendency can hardly do other than continue. Nothing can look duller than the future of this second-hand and multiplying world. Men need not be common merely because they are many; but the infection of commonness once begun in the many, what dulness in their future! To the eye that has reluctantly discovered this truth – that the vulgarised are not *un*civilised, and that there is no growth for them – it does not look like a future at all. More ballad-concerts, more quaint English, more robustious barytone songs, more piecemeal pictures, more anxious decoration, more colonial poetry, more young nations with withered traditions. Yet it is before this prospect that the provincial overseas lifts up his voice in a boast or a promise common enough among the incapable young, but pardonable only in senility. He promises the world a literature, an art, that shall be new because his forest is untracked and his town just built. But what the newness is to be he cannot tell. Certain words were dreadful once in the mouth of desperate old age. Dreadful and pitiable as the threat of an impotent king, what shall we name them when they are the promise of an impotent people? 'I will do such things: what they are yet I know not.'

CONRAD AND HIS CRITICS

The following selection of extracts from criticism of *Almayer's Folly* combines a variety of historical readings, evaluations and approaches with access to some of the important discussion points raised by the novel.

Unsigned review, *World*, 15 May 1895, p. 31.

This is one of the few entirely negative first reviews of the novel.

Almayer's Folly, by Joseph Conrad, is a dreary record of the still more dreary existence of a solitary Dutchman doomed to vegetate in a small village in Borneo. The only European in the place, he pits his wits against those of the astute Arab dealers, much to the advantage of the latter. His is a life of bitter disappointment; the half-caste wife he marries turns out to be a bad bargain, his only daughter leaves him, not unwillingly, for a native lover, and he sinks into the depths of opium degradation. The life is monotonous and sordid, and the recital thereof is almost wearisome, unrelieved by one touch of pathos or gleam of humour. Altogether the book is as dull as it well could be.

H. G. Wells, unsigned review, *Saturday Review*, 15 June 1895, p. 797.

An early champion of Conrad's fiction, Wells also reviewed Conrad's second novel, *An Outcast of the Islands*.

Almayer's Folly is a very powerful story indeed with effects that will certainly capture the imagination and haunt the memory of the reader. Almayer is a Dutchman who marries a Malay woman, and the central conception is the relapse of their daughter from the colonial version of civilization to a barbaric life. It is a gloomy tale, but its gloom is relieved by the rare love-story between Nina and Dain, and by such flashes of humour as Babalatchi's grinding at the hand-organ when the Rajah, his master, could not sleep. It is exceedingly well imagined and well written, and it will certainly secure Mr Conrad a high place among contemporary story-tellers.

Unsigned review, *Bookman*, September 1895, p. 176.

A bald summary is the most unsuitable way of presenting any idea of the book, which is vague, subtle, and mysterious, and whose story is rather told by suggestion than in asserted fact ..... What is wrong with *Almayer's Folly*? In bits it is excellent and earns instant admiration. As a whole it is a little wearisome. The author is immensely interested in his subject, pities profoundly the weak, luckless Almayer; but he gives you the idea of muttering the story to himself. It is indeed hard to follow, and the minor characters are very hard to distinguish till the story is well advanced. The action drags. He stops to describe in what should be breathless dramatic moments. The style has beauty, but it lacks swiftness. The slow, vague, mysterious East has cast its spell over Mr Conrad, with results not conducive to the interest of volatile European readers. But he has written pages of singular fascination.

Unsigned review, *Straits Times* [Singapore], 16 January 1896.

This is the first Singapore reaction to *Almayer's Folly* and applies a distinctively 'Eastern' perspective.

It is a sad story. The author has drawn with great power and fidelity the miserable results of a mixed marriage under existing social conditions. He does not allow us to feel that the end might have been different in the case of an abler man than the weak and foolish Almayer: No man, however able, can force his will upon Society. The social prejudice, against mixed blood, unjust in itself, has been aroused by the narrowing influence of local education and limited interests, and serves to save many foolish lives from mental shipwrecks. Its general utility does not, however, prevent its operating with very cruel harshness against individuals ..... [Some] blemishes do not detract from the general truthfulness of the book. The power of the European has substituted a sullen peace for the open war of the past. It has done so in the interests of trade, not of civilisation, however much we may disguise the fact. Civilisation makes no proselytes; it indeed rejects them with its barrier of racial prejudice. Left to themselves the natives are forced to judge civilisation and Christianity by the Europeans with whom they are brought most in contact, by the ethics of the trader and the manners of the beachcomber. The result is deplorable but it has none the less to be faced.

Extract from a letter signed 'G', *Straits Times*, 17 January 1896. A spirited rejoinder to the previous review.

I have no interest in referring to any minor errors, in what is, undoubtedly, a powerful and interesting work, but surely the author and the reviewer must know very little of Dutch Indian Society when they dwell so deeply on the social disabilities of the results of mixed marriages, 'the half-caste girl' as it is put. Had the scene been laid in British India, no doubt the social bar is strong and deep as the author makes it. It has been shown admirably in some of Kipling's sketches. But to imply that it exists to anything like the same extent in Dutch Indian Society, is ludicrous. Society in these colonies is so thoroughly permeated with the tinge of colour that it would be considered a most extraordinary thing to hint at any such disability being recognised. More especially is it so in the class of society in which Almayer, a mercantile clerk in Macassar, would be likely to move in. The writer is evidently drawing upon his British Indian experience, if he has had any, and foolishly applying it to a very different set of circumstances.

Vernon Young, 'Lingard's Folly: The Lost Subject', *Kenyon Review*, 15 (1953), 528–9.
From a general appraisal of the Lingard 'trilogy'.

Whatever imperfections this extraordinary first novel suffers from, it does bring into play hints, at least, of the ruling gifts and obsessions of the novelist. With it, Conrad stepped into his magnetic field – life as the steadfast maintenance of a necessary illusion – spun that webbed prose so essentially the medium of the romantic vision, which was to undergo modulations of the exotic up to the controlled illumination of *The Shadow-Line* and then return, in *The Rescue*, and accompanying terminations, to a strained encore of its earlier floridity. All of Conrad's ruling motifs are adumbrated in *Almayer's Folly*: the terror of isolation, the idiocy of trust in ownership, the uncalculated effects of altruism, the irrepealable alienation of racial opposition, and the destructive elusiveness of Woman.

Jocelyn Baines, *Joseph Conrad: A Critical Biography* (London: Weidenfeld & Nicolson, 1960), p. 164.
On the limited symbolic appeal of Almayer.

> Although Almayer is a type and the situation which confronts him is typical there is no question of his transcending his particularity as do, for instance, Charles and Emma Bovary, who, without losing their individuality, come to symbolise aspects of human nature and the human predicament.

Thomas Moser: *Joseph Conrad: Achievement and Decline* (Cambridge, Mass.: Harvard University Press, 1957; repr. Hamden, CT: Archon Books, 1966), pp. 52, 53.
A key work in Conrad criticism, powerfully arguing the case for Conrad's artistic decline after *Under Western Eyes*. For Moser, the root-problem lies in Conrad's direct involvement with the 'uncongenial subject' of love and sexually charged relationships, a problem already present in the early fiction.

> Whatever the conscious reason for their creation, the two lovers are, artistically speaking, the weakest part of *Almayer's Folly*. They lack the moral and psychological interest of Almayer, the vitality of Babalatchi. Their conventional good looks and their wooden dialogue, consisting primarily of high-flown sentiments, mark them as stereotyped noble savages. Yet their failure is more complex than one simply of dullness. The inconsistency of the lovers' attitudes toward each other, the curious relationship between Nina and her father, the inappropriate imagery used in connection with the lovers – all these suggest that their creator is so seriously confused that he cannot carry out his artistic intentions ..... Although only one critic has noticed it, there is another love story in *Almayer's Folly*, one that tends to obscure the meaning of the novel. This is Almayer's unrequited, incestuous love for Nina. Miserable in his henpecked existence, Almayer gives all the love he possesses to his daughter. Therefore, when Nina finally leaves him for Dain, he rages like a betrayed lover rather than a disappointed father ..... Nina, on the other hand, rather enjoys this scene in which she rejects her father; her farewell to him has all the characteristics of a coquette being sweet to one of her suitors. The scene becomes a sympathetic defense of Almayer, the betrayed lover. But this is to sentimentalize him and

> negate the central meaning of the book which is that the foolish Almayer has destroyed himself through egotistic longings for wealth and power.

Juliet McLauchlan, 'Almayer and Willems: "How Not To Be"', *Conradiana*, 11 (1979), 121–2.

A response to Baines (see above), asserting the universality of theme in *Almayer's Folly*.

> The 'folly' of this particular father is only an extreme presentation of the foolishness, even madness, of erecting a structure for someone else's life, particularly for a beloved child's life, with no understanding of its personality and real needs. Besides the universality of this situation, there is the folly of living in a dream, an illusion, as does Almayer ..... The fact that Almayer's dreams for Nina are so clearly grounded in illusion, and the close connection of his dreams for her with death, show how vital it is for her to escape, and the escape thus takes on value from its association with life. This is coupled with Nina's positive rejection of what her father considers to be 'civilized' life. In line with this, the commercial success which lies at the heart of Almayer's dream, the 'treasure' and vast 'fortune' which will make dream reality, are shown in the novel to be valueless by contrast to life, love, freedom of choice. Thus we see here the announcement of a major and recurring Conradian theme: it is folly and death to trust to 'material interests'.

John A. McClure, *Kipling and Conrad: The Colonial Fiction* (Cambridge, Mass. and London: Harvard University Press, 1981), pp. 105, 107.

Argues that Conrad's Polish background and 'principled despair' allow him sceptical insights into the Imperial adventure unavailable to Kipling.

> Conrad traces Almayer's weaknesses to his membership in the very element of European society that Kipling considers the great source of heroes: the country-born-and-bred colonials. While Kipling concentrates on the invigorating influences of a colonial childhood, Conrad gives a convincing picture of its debilitating effects ..... In *Almayer's Folly*, then, the European colonists are not the modern knights of a new feudalism, but the wanton destroyers of living feudal communities. They are identified, and rightly, not with the forces opposed to commercialism and bour-

geois values, but as forces spreading these values throughout the world ..... *Almayer's Folly* initiates, in a manner that is sometimes confusing, sometimes, perhaps, confused, a task of demystification that continues through Conrad's finest colonial novels. It is a remarkable beginning.

Cedric Watts, *Joseph Conrad: A Literary Life* (London: Macmillan, 1989), p. 57.

Follows the evolution of Conrad's literary life generally, emphasising how his first novel makes sophisticated use of features found in commercial fiction of the time.

A remarkable aspect of many of Conrad's novels and tales is that, in brief and superficial summary, they seem to belong to the realm of popular commercial fiction. *Almayer's Folly* does indeed tell of piracy, smuggling, shipwreck, exotic races, strife in the jungle, and the elopement of a beautiful Eurasian with a Balinese prince. But Conrad made adventure introspective, heroism ambiguous, the exotic subversive; he liked to undermine stereotypical contrasts between the 'civilised' and the 'primitive'; and dominant themes in *Almayer's Folly* include the isolation of individuals and the littleness of humanity beside the inhuman vastness of nature. He transmuted the elements of romantic melodrama into the ambiguities of philosophical tragedy.

Ruth Nadelhaft, *Joseph Conrad* (Hemel Hempstead: Harvester Wheatsheaf, 1991), pp. 13–14.

Offers a sympathetic feminist approach.

Conrad's early novels and tales examine the practice of colonialism, the tensions and subterfuges which preoccupy both the white colonisers and the native populations. As readers, we may be so drawn to the analysis of colonialism that we ignore the deeper investigation which Conrad makes into the system of which colonialism is only one manifestation: patriarchy, especially patriarchal religion, which sanctions and even outlines the forms of colonialism which the early novels explore and expose. In this analysis of patriarchy, the attentive reader understands the significance of the women characters in a new light, for it is they who grope to envision and articulate another sort of reality which would transcend or at least deny the struggle between white and native which absorbs energies needed (and lost) for resistance to

> the patriarchal system firmly in place in white cultures and to some degree binding in the native world as well.

Jacques Berthoud, 'Introduction: Conrad's Realism', *Joseph Conrad, Almayer's Folly*, World's Classics (Oxford: Oxford University Press, 1992), pp. xxxvii–xxxviii.

On Conrad's sense of the absurd as the basis of his vision of human solidarity in the novel.

> Thwarted hopes are, as we know, an ineradicable part of a state of affairs that offers us life only in order to deprive us of it. In the way in which *Almayer's Folly* presents this it makes . . . . . an egalitarian gesture. Both Conrad's eloquent epigraph and his sardonic 'Author's Note' announce this gesture, the first in its implication that the loss of a promised land is an experience known to all, the second in its rejection of the view that the 'decivilized' inhabitants of far-off lands have nothing in common with the refined citizens of Europe. In Conrad's first novel, this common denominator, to which he gives the name of 'solidarity', is more precise than participation in a generalized human predicament. Almayer's sense of the absurd may be remote indeed from the philosophical afflictions of a Nietzsche or a Dostoevsky, but it retains the mark of a historical moment. For all his uneducated isolation he remains a product of the late nineteenth century. He is also the product of the mind of a man who shared that century's anxieties in full measure.

SUGGESTIONS FOR FURTHER READING

Readers who wish to know more about Conrad's life, work and times in general should consult Zdzisław Najder's *Joseph Conrad: A Chronicle* (Cambridge: Cambridge University Press, 1983); Cedric Watts, *A Preface to Conrad* (London: Longman, 1982; second edn., 1993); and John Batchelor's *The Life of Joseph Conrad: A Critical Biography* (Oxford: Blackwell, 1994). Other relevant reading might include (a) Conrad's own autobiographical account in *A Personal Record* (1912) of his voyages to Berau and meetings with the original Almayer; and (b) the two other novels of the 'Lingard trilogy', *An Outcast of the Islands* (1896) and *The Rescue* (1920). Graham Irwin's *Nineteenth-Century Borneo: A Study in Diplomatic Rivalry* (Singapore: Donald Moore Books, 1955) offers clear and helpful background reading, while Gavin Young's *In Search of Conrad* (London: Hutchinson, 1991) provides an absorbing account of his re-tracing of Conrad's footsteps in Borneo.

The following books contain valuable material on *Almayer's Folly* and its place within the larger body of Conrad's Malay fiction:

John Dozier Gordan, *Joseph Conrad: The Making of a Novelist* (Cambridge, Mass.: Harvard University Press, 1940; repr. New York: Russell & Russell, 1963). A scholarly study of Conrad's emergence from amateur to professional writer, examining sources, genesis of texts, chronology of composition and the growth of Conrad's early literary reputation.

Elmer A. Ordoñez, *The Early Joseph Conrad: Revisions and Style* (Quezon City: University of the Philippines, 1969). Offers a close and patient analysis of developing stylistic practices in Conrad's early novels.

Ian Watt, *Conrad in the Nineteenth Century* (London: Chatto & Windus, 1980). Contains an extremely valuable critical and contextual introduction to the novel.

John A. McClure, *Kipling and Conrad: The Colonial Fiction* (Cambridge, Mass.: Harvard University Press, 1981). Includes a useful and readable chapter on 'The Malay Novels: Imperial Romance and Reality' (pp. 98–130).

Lloyd Fernando, *Cultures in Conflict: Essays on Literature and the English Language in South East Asia* (Singapore: Graham Brash, 1986). See Fernando's chapter on 'Conrad's South East Asian Expatriates' (pp. 33–60).

John Lester, *Conrad's Religion* (London: Macmillan, 1988). See in particular Chapter 4, 'The Mirror of Islam', for useful insights into Conrad's knowledge and treatment of Eastern religions.

Heliéna Krenn, *Conrad's Lingard Trilogy: Empire, Race, and Women in the Malay Novels* (New York: Garland, 1990). Considers the place of women in Conrad's treatment of empire and race.

Jacques Berthoud, 'Introduction: Conrad's Realism', *Joseph Conrad: Almayer's Folly*, World's Classics (Oxford: Oxford University Press, 1992). A lucid and wide-ranging introduction to the novel's form, themes and techniques.

Robert Hampson, *Joseph Conrad: Betrayal and Identity* (London: Macmillan, 1992). Considers forms of betrayal in *Almayer's Folly*, with an interesting comparison between Conrad's novel and Flaubert's *Madame Bovary*.

Andrea White, *Joseph Conrad and the Fiction of Adventure: Constructing and Deconstructing the Imperial Subject* (Cambridge: Cambridge University Press, 1993). Sets Conrad within the context of nineteenth-century adventure fiction in order to show how, even while inheriting some of its traditions, he modified and subverted the imperial subject constructed in earlier writing.

Joseph Conrad, *Almayer's Folly*, ed. Floyd Eugene Eddleman and David Leon Higdon with an introduction by Ian Watt. The Cambridge Edition of the Works of Joseph Conrad (Cambridge: Cambridge University Press, 1994). A handsome, scholarly edition of the novel, with full textual apparatus.

Three scholarly journals are devoted exclusively to Conrad studies: *Conradiana: A Journal of Joseph Conrad Studies* (Texas Tech University, Lubbock, Texas); *The Conradian: Journal of the Joseph Conrad Society (UK)*, (published by Editions Rodopi at Amsterdam and Atlanta); and *L'Epoque Conradienne* (published by the Société Conradienne Française, Faculté des Lettres et des Sciences Humaines de Limoges).

TEXT SUMMARY

Chapter 1
Standing at sunset on the verandah of his half built but already decaying house ('Almayer's Folly') in Bornean Sambir, Almayer dreams of large amounts of gold that will bring escape to Europe for himself and his Eurasian daughter Nina. He awaits the arrival of Dain Maroola, who is to be employed in a plan to find it. Almayer retrospectively reviews 'twenty-five years of heart-breaking struggle' in Sambir, where, as the protégé of Tom Lingard, a seaman-adventurer, he has managed Lingard's trading company. The racially proud, white Almayer is especially offended by his long-standing marriage to Lingard's 'adopted daughter', a woman of Sulu origin, whom he would now like to abandon. Reverting from reverie to the present, Almayer is overjoyed by the sudden return of Dain who, however, disappoints him by first visiting Lakamba, the Rajah of Sambir. Almayer returns to his 'old' home, where Nina reacts with unusual expectancy to news of Dain's arrival.

Chapter 2
Mrs Almayer's early life and the mutual racial bitterness underlying the Almayers' marriage are recounted. There follows a review of Almayer's failed hopes over a number of years, failures brought about by Lingard's bankruptcy and disappearance to Europe, inter-tribal rivalry in Sambir and the steady deterioration of Almayer's commercial powers. Two years after the Almayers marry, a daughter, Nina, is born. At about the age of six, she is sent by Almayer to Singapore for ten years to receive a 'white' education. On her unexpected return to Sambir, the grown-up Nina adds prestige to Almayer's position, although she remains bitterly silent about her life in Singapore and now seems closer to her Malay mother than her white father. On the formation of the British North Borneo Company on the island, Almayer builds his 'new' house.

Chapter 3
Retrospective narration continues, with an account of the border disputes between the British and the Dutch. These have led to the Dutch

securing possession of Sambir, much to Almayer's disappointment, since his commercial activities will now be even more severely hampered. While Almayer sometimes rouses himself to take river-trips in search of gold, his wife begins to work on behalf of Lakamba against Almayer, while Nina – whose unhappy stay in Singapore is detailed – has, after three years back in Sambir, become increasingly responsive to her Malay heritage.

Chapter 4
Events in Almayer's more recent past are outlined, notably the first appearance in Sambir of Dain, a Balinese prince, and his early contacts with the Almayers. Dain's mysterious reasons for being in Sambir arouse much general speculation, centred upon the fact that he has effected a new alliance between Almayer and Lakamba.

Chapter 5
Unwillingly entering into partnership with Lakamba, Almayer agrees to supply Dain with gunpowder that can be taken to Bali on condition that Dain will then help him find gold. Ironically, while Almayer dreams of a future in Europe for himself and Nina, she – with her mother's encouragement – is falling in love with Dain. Dain departs with the dynamite on a brig supplied by Almayer, leaving Nina disconsolate and Almayer waiting impatiently for his return so that the expedition for gold can begin. The conclusion sees a return to Almayer's 'present' of Chapter 1 and to Dain's sudden reappearance in Sambir.

Chapter 6
From this point to the first part of Chapter 12, the action covers twenty-four eventful hours. In his nocturnal interview with Lakamba, Dain reveals that the dynamite-brig has been run aground and exploded, a catastrophe forcing him back to Sambir to seek refuge from the pursuing Dutch. Lakamba and his 'prime minister', Babalatchi, agree that he should be hidden away at a clearing belonging to Bulangi, a local rice-farmer. Dain departs on a turbulent river, swollen by the monsoon rains.

Chapter 7
The next morning Almayer awaits Dain's return from his nocturnal interview with Lakamba. Sambir is suddenly thrown into confusion by the appearance of a headless body fished from the river but wearing Dain's jewellery. The shock of Dain's supposed death leaves Almayer in 'the utter abandonment of despair' at the loss of his dream of wealth.

Nina, on the other hand, pretends an indifference to her father's reactions, while secretly maintaining a 'watchful anxiety'. By late morning the Dutch authorities arrive in pursuit of Dain.

Chapter 8

Taminah, a slave-girl who is jealous that Dain loves Nina, knows the true facts behind Dain's supposed death – in reality, a simulation devised in order to hide him from the Dutch authorities. Still unaware of the meaning of all recent events, Almayer confronts the Dutch authorities, who inform him of the fate of Dain's brig and reveal that they were forewarned of events by information passed on to them two months earlier by Abdulla, the Arab trader in Sambir. Charging Almayer with trading in gunpowder, they demand the fugitive Dain.

Chapter 9

At an early afternoon conference, Lakamba hears from Babalatchi further details of the plot behind Dain's alleged death. Devised during the night by Mrs Almayer, with Nina's help, the plot has involved disguising one of Dain's dead boatmen in order to mislead the Dutch into believing that Dain has drowned. Babalatchi persuades Lakamba that they should actively work to ensure Dain's escape that same night. He then returns to Almayer's compound to watch Almayer, now drunk, entertaining the Dutch authorities. In response to their command that the fugitive be handed over, Almayer takes them to what he believes to be Dain's body. That night, the Dutch hold an inquiry into the day's events.

Chapter 10

At sunset, Nina goes to Bulangi's clearing to meet Dain and, with him, to flee Sambir. Mrs Almayer, taking refuge with Lakamba, also deserts Almayer. The isolated and drunken Almayer awakens to find himself confronted by Taminah who, telling him of the women's desertion, opens his eyes to the full measure of his blindness.

Chapter 11

At Bulangi's clearing, an agitated Dain awaits Nina, who finally arrives at nightfall. Almayer, armed with a revolver, interrupts their mutual absorption. He threatens, pleads and finally tries to blackmail Nina into deserting Dain. Babalatchi arrives with news that Taminah has informed the Dutch authorities of recent events and that they are now in pursuit of Dain. The distracted Almayer insists upon helping Nina and Dain escape, claiming that it would be a disgrace if the island's community were to know of his daughter's attraction for a native.

Chapter 12

After further strenuous appeals to his daughter, a despairing Almayer watches Nina and Dain's departure. Next day, he returns to his wrecked home and, in an effort to erase all evidence of the past, burns down the remains of Lingard's trading company. Retiring to 'Almayer's Folly', he vainly seeks oblivion and escape. On periodic visits to Sambir over the next few months, Captain Ford is shocked by evidence of Almayer's steadily worsening plight: Almayer's possessions are stolen, he is locked away in the darkest rooms of the house and has become an opium addict. Babalatchi tells Captain Ford the news that Nina has given birth to a son. Almayer dies alone and in squalor, his epitaph delivered by his greatest enemy, the Arab Abdulla.

ACKNOWLEDGEMENTS

I am grateful to the following for their help in preparing this edition: Mario Curreli; Cedric Watts; J. H. Stape; and the staff of the Brynmor Jones Library, University of Hull.